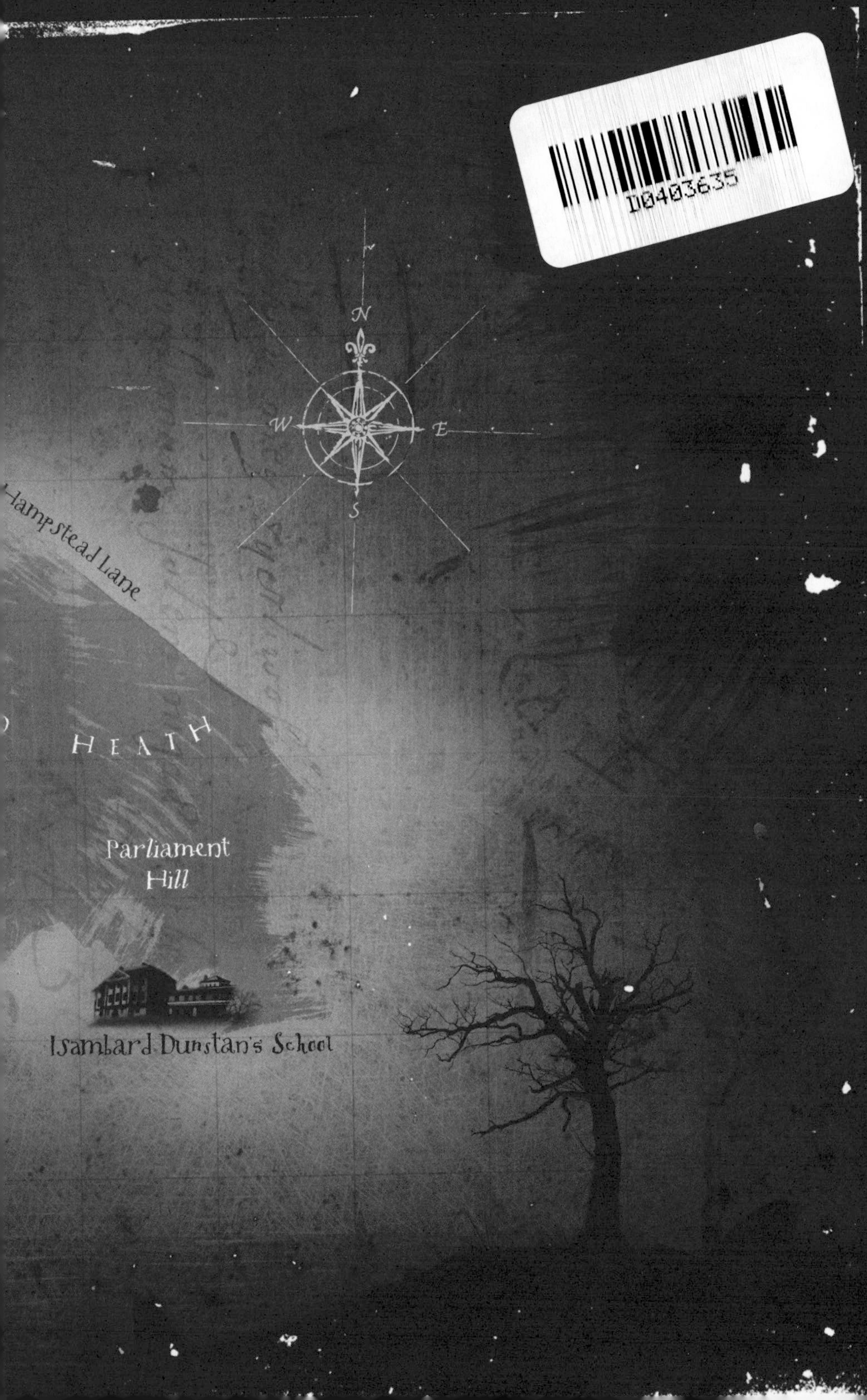
N
W
E
S
Hampstead Lane
HEATH
Parliament Hill
Isambard Dunstan's School

G. P. Taylor

THE
DOPPLE GANGER
C H R O N I C L E S

THE FIRST ESCAPE

SALT**RIVER**®

AN IMPRINT OF
TYNDALE HOUSE PUBLISHERS, INC.
CAROL STREAM, ILLINOIS

Visit Tyndale's exciting Web site at www.tyndale.com

Visit Markosia's Web site at www.markosia.com

Visit the Dopple Ganger Chronicles Web site at www.dopplegangerchronicles.com

TYNDALE, Tyndale's quill logo, SALTRIVER, and the SaltRiver logo are registered trademarks of Tyndale House Publishers, Inc.

THE FIRST ESCAPE

Previously published in 2006 as THE TIZZLE SISTERS AND ERIK by Markosia Enterprises, Ltd. under ISBN 978-1-905692-22-4.

Cover designed by Stephen Vosloo

Art directed by Joseph Sapulich

Edited by Elizabeth R. Kletzing

G. P. Taylor is represented by the Caroline Sheldon Literary Agency.

THE FIRST ESCAPE first published in 2008.

Library of Congress Cataloging-in-Publication Data

Taylor, G. P.
[Tizzle sisters and Erik]
The first escape / G. P. Taylor.
p. cm. — (The Dopple Ganger chronicles ; #1)
Summary: At Isambard Dunstan's School for Wayward Children, life is trouble for fourteen-year-old identical twins Sadie and Saskia Dopple and their friend Erik Morrissey Ganger, but when a mysterious woman adopts Saskia and takes her to a mansion filled with secrets and threats, Sadie and Erik escape the orphanage to save her.
ISBN-13: 978-1-4143-1947-6 (hc)
ISBN-10: 1-4143-1947-9 (hc)
[1. Orphans—Fiction. 2. Adoption—Fiction. 3. Schools—Fiction. 4. Twins—Fiction. 5. Schools--Fiction. 6. Supernatural—Fiction. 7. Mystery and detective stories.] I. Title.
PZ7.T2134Tiz 2008
[Fic]--dc22 2008012511

Printed in China

14 13 12 11 10 09 08

7 6 5 4 3 2 1

FOR

GRACE AND RACHAEL,

JOHN AND PAUL,

AND EVERY TWIN I HAVE EVER MET

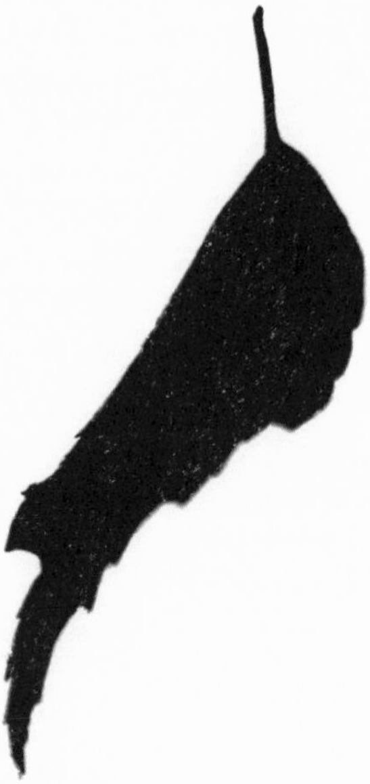

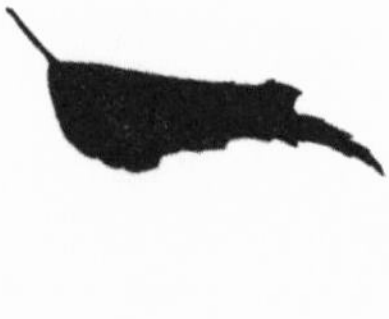

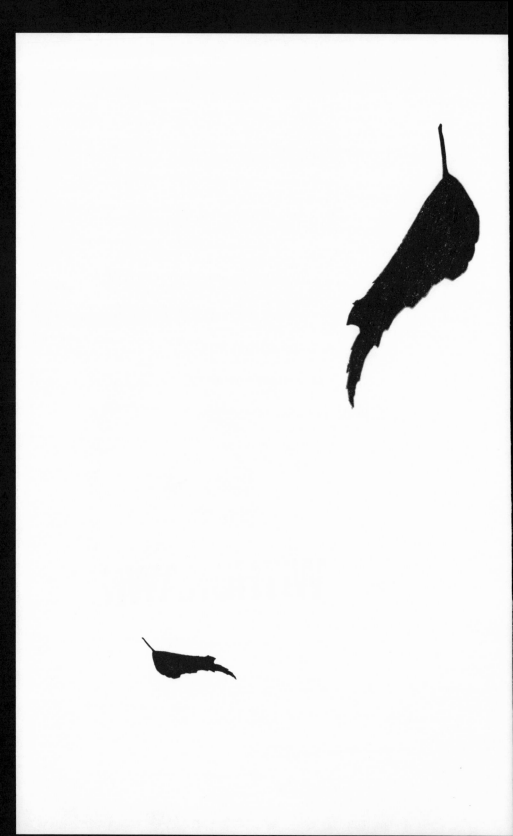

Contents

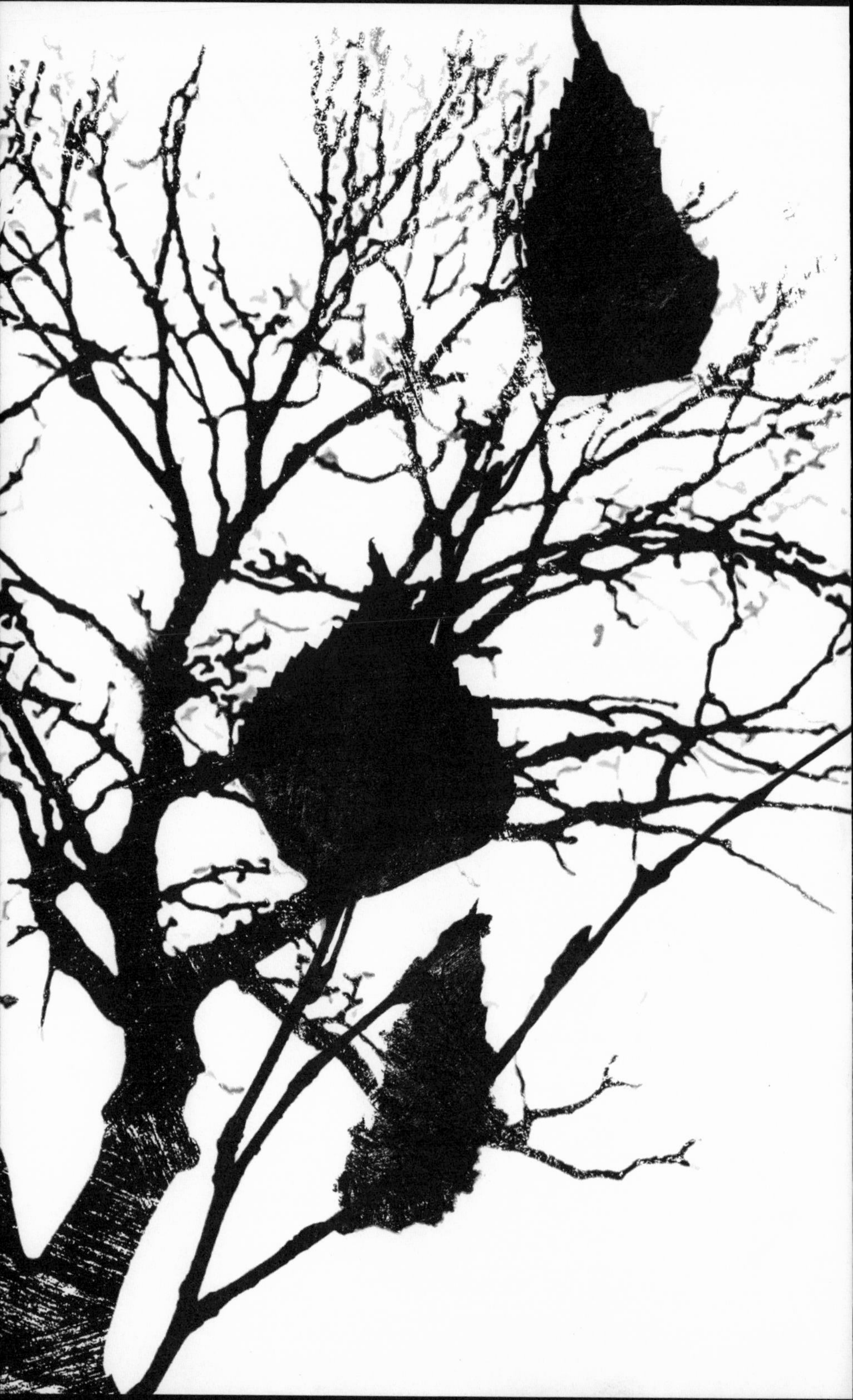

Chapter One
Porridge

IN THE DINING ROOM of Isambard Dunstan's
School for Wayward Children, all was not well. Shards
of lightning blasted from a black morning sky and burst
upon the heath outside. Rain beat and battered against the
leaded windows that reached upward in vast stone arches.

Staring down upon a sheltered gathering of
children was the pointed face of Isambard
Dunstan himself. The noted explorer's
likeness had been captured in stained glass
for two hundred years, a look of dread
upon his face and a scowl upon his lips.
He had left the house to be a home for children
abandoned by their parents, but no one who had
the misfortune to live there was sure whether his
action was a blessing or a curse.

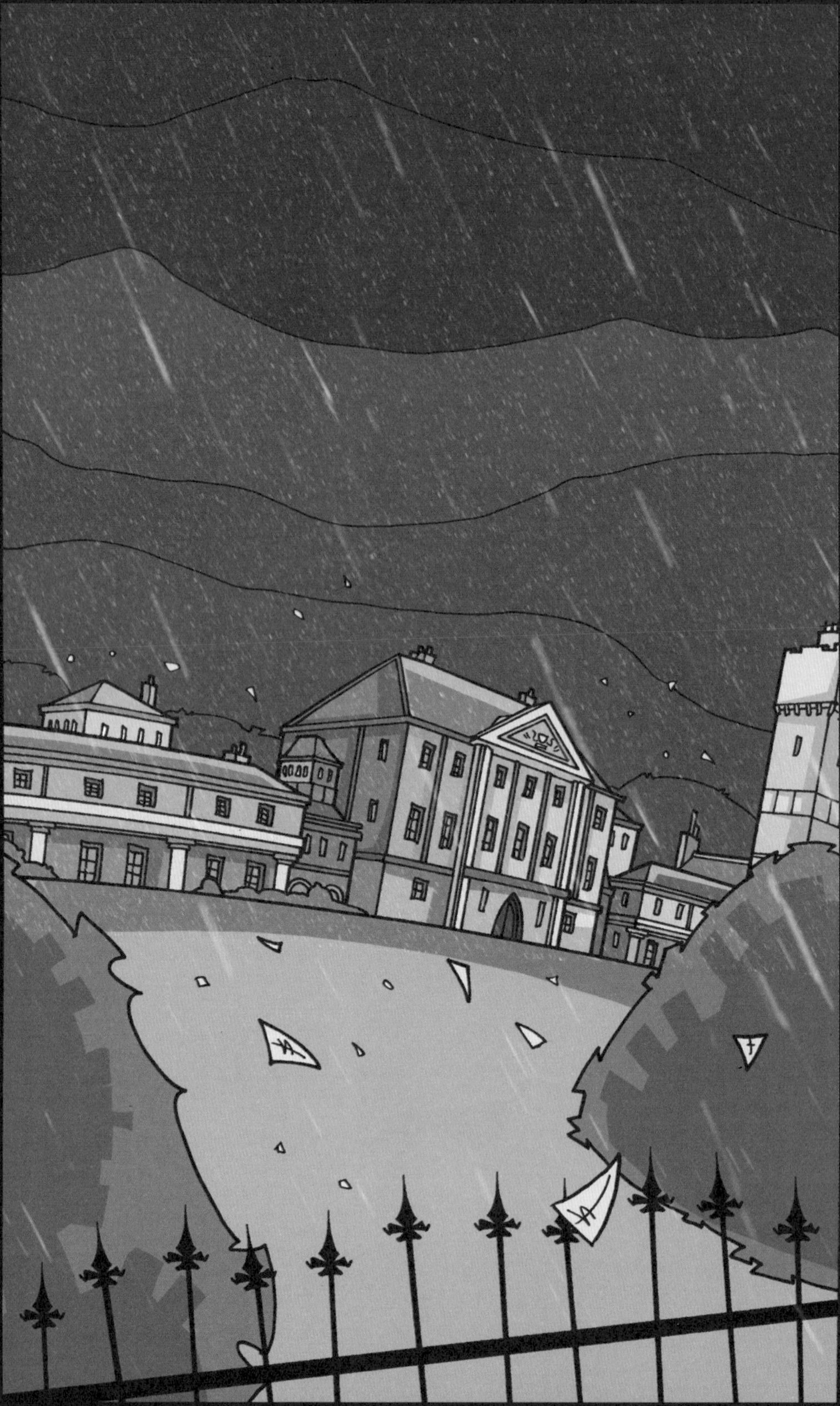

A large wooden door swung open and a fat cook barged through.

In her stubby fingers she carried a massive pot of brown gruel that steamed and gurgled like the rumblings of a cow's belly. She glanced up at the image of Isambard Dunstan, who scowled at her as she began ladling the food from the dirty tureen into 166 bowls.

Every eye gazed hungrily. Sniveling noses sniffed each bowl as it was passed from one hand to the next. Fingers dipped quickly into the gruel and then popped into mouths as each child waited to begin breakfast.

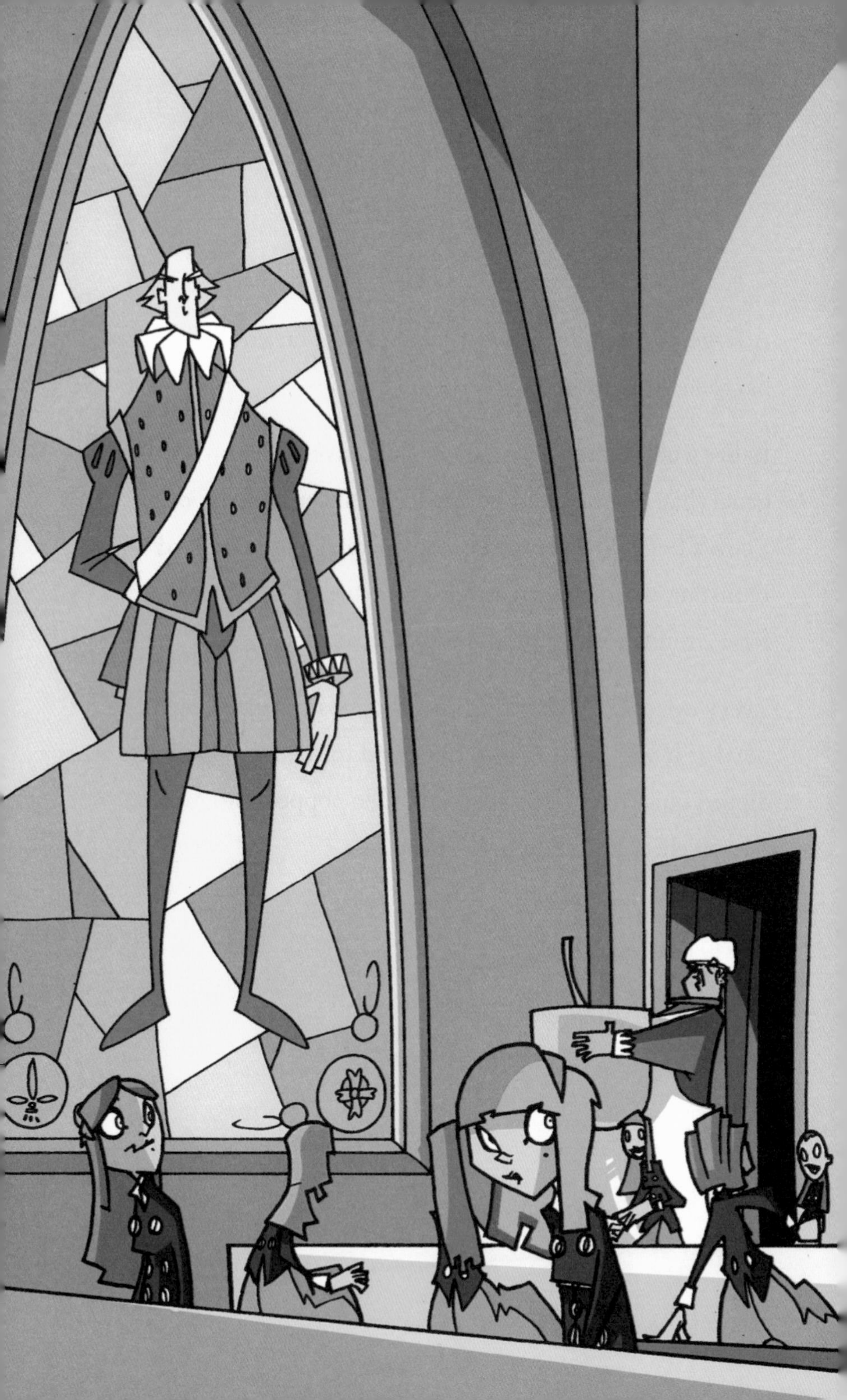

"No one eats!"

screamed the cook, spitting the words from her toothless mouth. "You eat when I eat and not a moment before." The fierce look on her face dared anyone to take one morsel without her permission. If there was one thing Mrs. Omeron hated more than children, it was children who ate before she did.

On the far side of the room, nearest to the fire, were two girls. Each was a mirror image of the other. Each stared about the room as she waited to eat. Around them, row upon row of neatly dressed girls sat silently in starched

collars, gray jackets, and tall boots. The twins fidgeted, unable to keep still even for a moment. They moved in concert like two puppets connected by invisible strands.

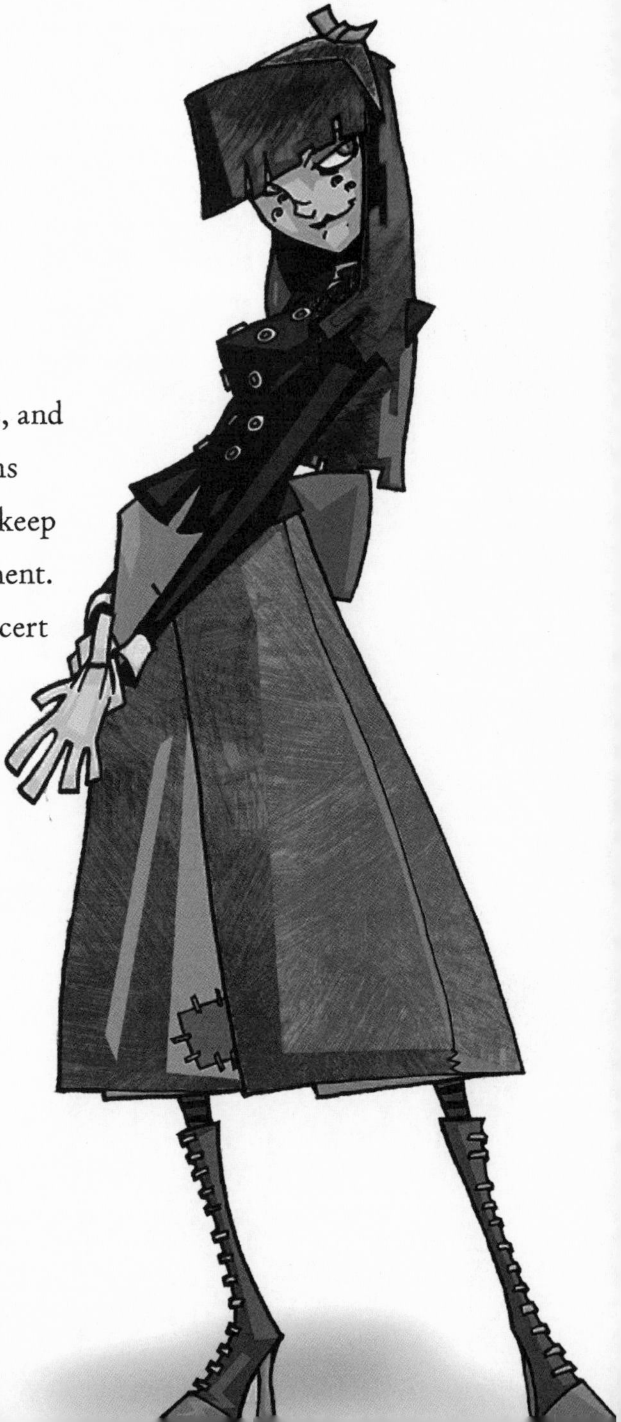

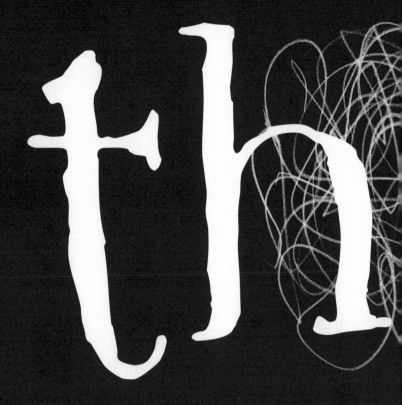

Known to everyone who worked at Isambard Dunstan's School for Wayward Children as them, they were known to each other as Sadie and Saskia Dopple. Each was the likeness of the other in almost every way. They had identical ears, identical noses, identical lips, and even identical moles upon their chins. The only thing that set them apart was that Sadie had a yellow right eye and

a blue left and Saskia a blue right eye and a yellow left. Apart from their eyes, the only difference between them was that Sadie thought before she acted or spoke. She was the quieter of the two—and in many ways the most dangerous. Together, they were like two wild cats that had taken human form, sent by an avenging angel to wreak havoc on humanity.

The children had been sitting at the table since six-thirty. Seven o'clock had come and gone, and still they waited. The porridge they were fed every morning had chilled to a congealed mush. In desperation, Sadie nudged Saskia and scoffed under her breath, "Old wart face, who does she think she is?"

"I think I'm the cook!" shouted Mrs. Omeron, whose ancient ears had become attuned to the sarcastic mutterings of children. With that, she picked up a spoon from the table and threw it at Sadie, hitting her upon the head with it before she could say another word.

Sadie looked stunned but quickly recovered. As she turned to look in the cook's direction, another smug face caught her eye. There, smiling at Sadie from across the table, sat the loathsome Charlotte Grimdyke.

"Something wrong?" Grimdyke asked with the lopsided grin of a baboon. "Get hit by a spoon?"

"You'll pay for that . . ." Sadie said through her teeth, staring first at Grimdyke and then at the cook.

"Whatever," Grimdyke muttered again, holding the palm of her hand toward Sadie as if to stop her from speaking.

"Speak to the hand, Miss Dopple, speak to the hand."

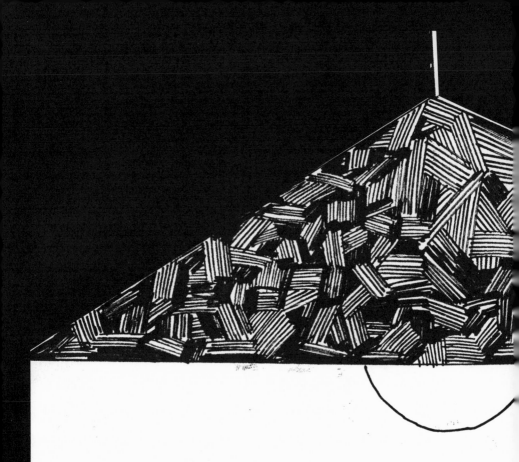

Sadie knew this was not the time or place to bring about her vengeance. But when the moment came, she would bring torment to Grimdyke's life. In the meantime, there was no harm in having a little fun. Quietly and carefully Sadie put a hand on the bowl before her and set her spoon to the side as she gazed innocently at the ceiling of the refectory. Hanging from the thick oak beams was the swinging pendant of the only electric light in the whole room. It dangled like a gallows as it swayed from side to side, casting cold shadows across an even colder room.

All eyes were turned toward the large mahogany clock that clucked and crowed as it ticked the seconds. The children waited eagerly as the long hand swung slowly toward the half of the hour. No one spoke; no one moved. Every hand was poised, clutching a long spoon. Above their heads, the clock began to whir. Suddenly, there was the tightening of a spring and then the first strike of the hammer. But before the clock could chime again, the silence of the room had gone.

In one quick motion, Sadie scooped a large dollop of sticky brown porridge with her hand and plastered it on her forehead.

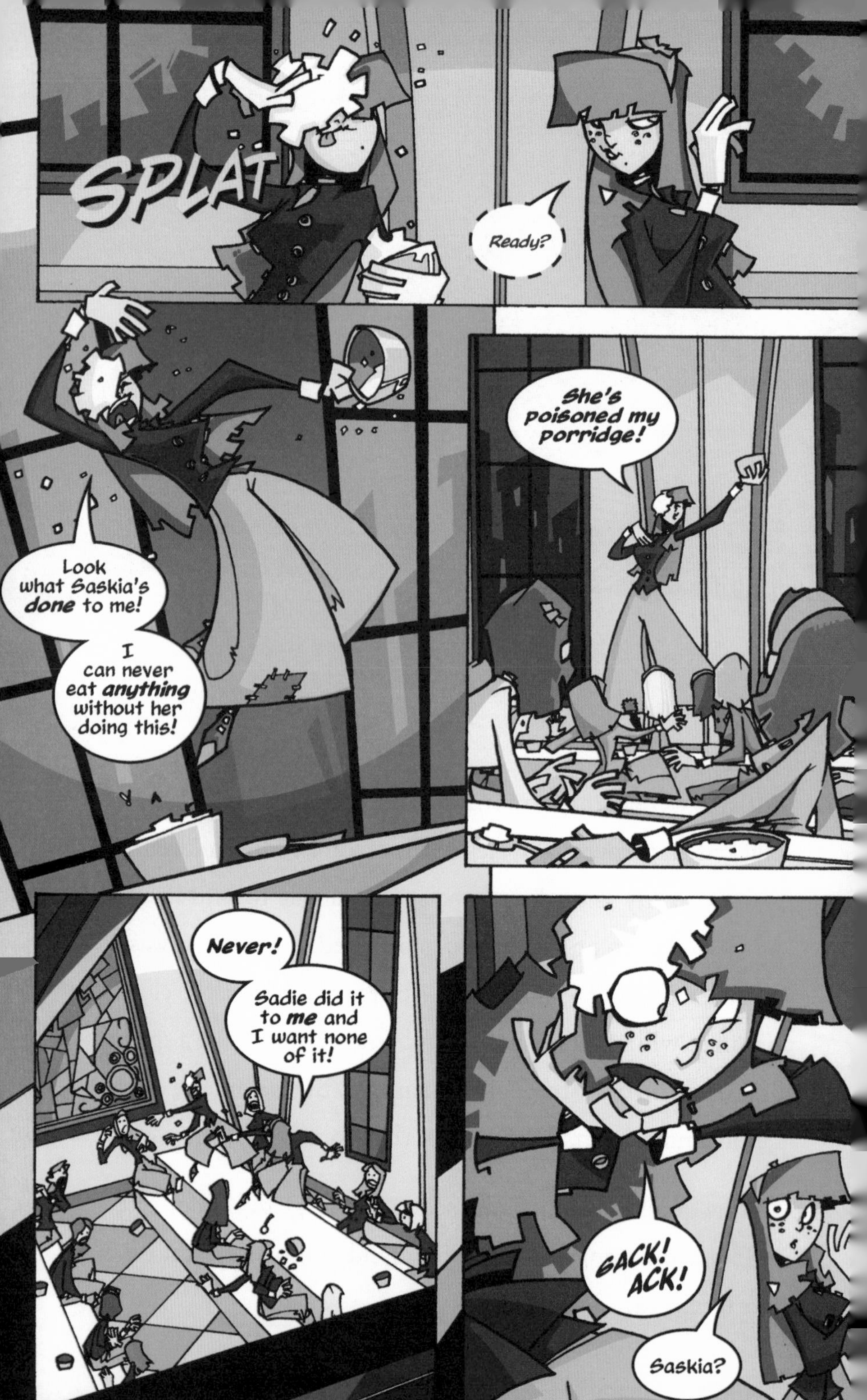
SPLAT
Ready?
Look what Saskia's *done* to me!
I can never eat *anything* without her doing this!
She's poisoned my porridge!
Never!
Sadie did it to *me* and I want none of it!
GACK! ACK!
Saskia?

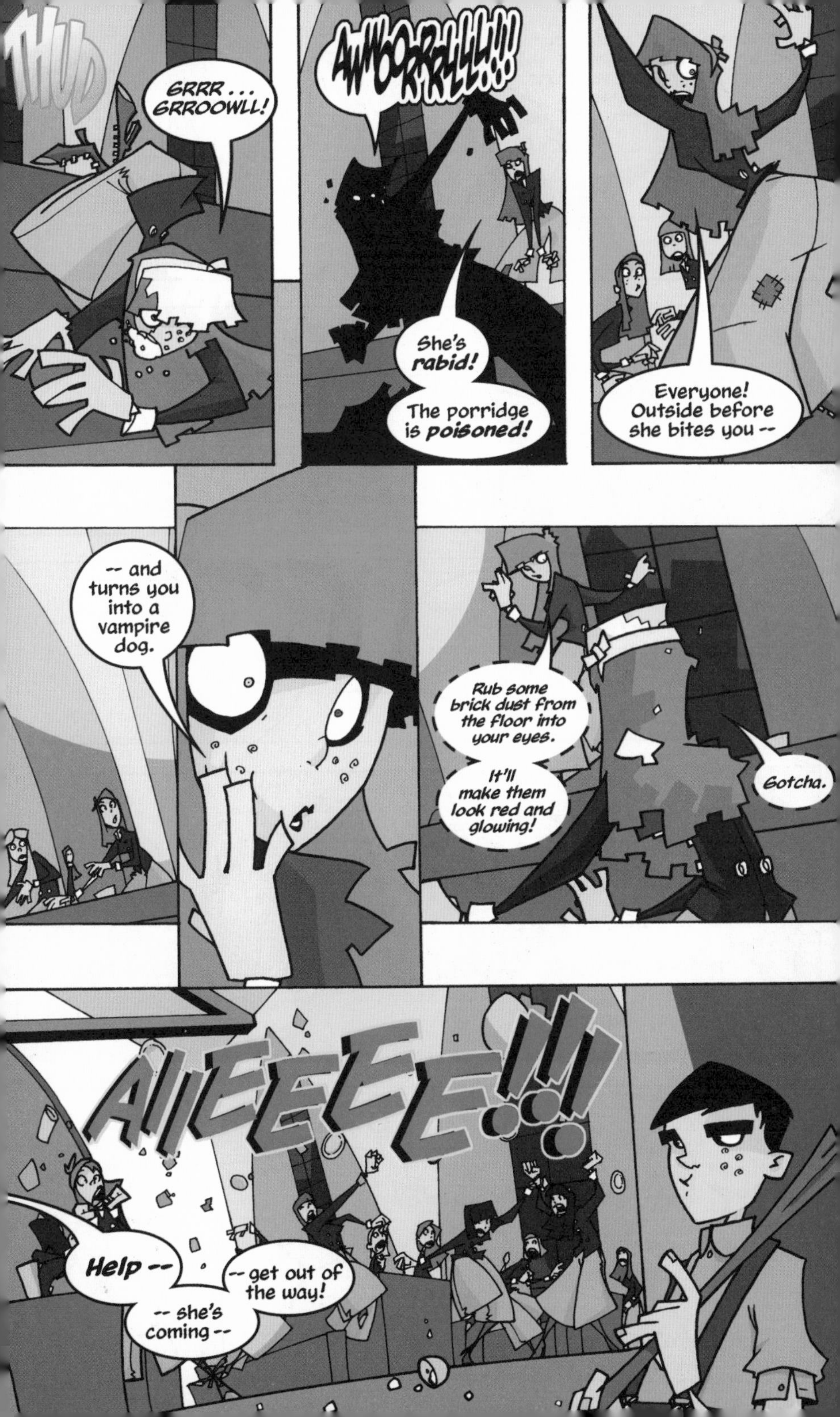
THUD
GRRR . . . GRROOWLL!
AWWOORRLLL!!!
She's rabid!
The porridge is poisoned!
Everyone! Outside before she bites you --
-- and turns you into a vampire dog.
Rub some brick dust from the floor into your eyes.
It'll make them look red and glowing!
Gotcha.
AIIEEEE!!!
Help --
-- she's coming --
-- get out of the way!

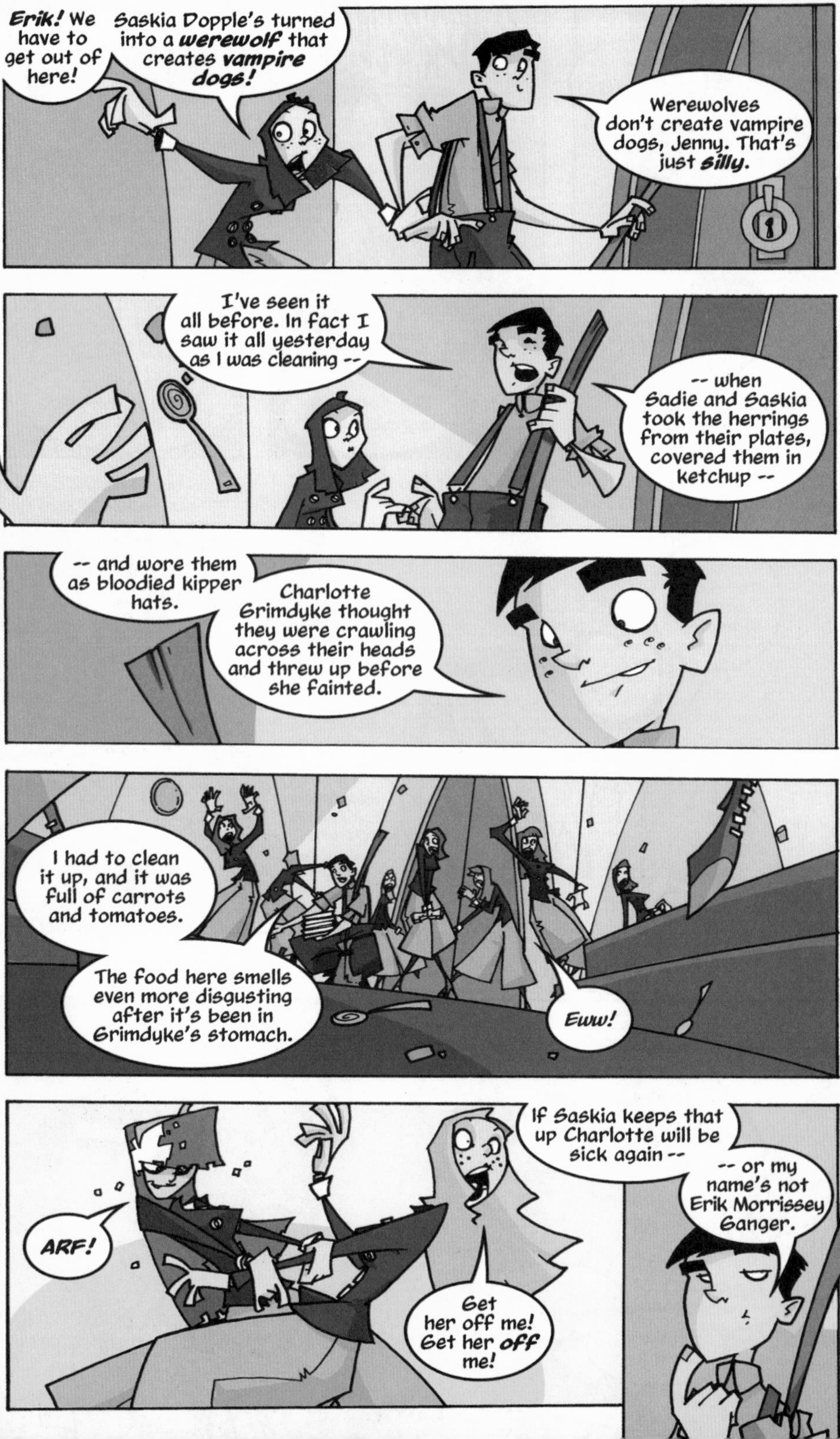

Erik! We have to get out of here!
Saskia Dopple's turned into a werewolf that creates vampire dogs!
Werewolves don't create vampire dogs, Jenny. That's just silly.
I've seen it all before. In fact I saw it all yesterday as I was cleaning --
-- when Sadie and Saskia took the herrings from their plates, covered them in ketchup --
-- and wore them as bloodied kipper hats.
Charlotte Grimdyke thought they were crawling across their heads and threw up before she fainted.
I had to clean it up, and it was full of carrots and tomatoes.
The food here smells even more disgusting after it's been in Grimdyke's stomach.
Eww!
ARF!
Get her off me! Get her off me!
If Saskia keeps that up Charlotte will be sick again --
-- or my name's not Erik Morrissey Ganger.

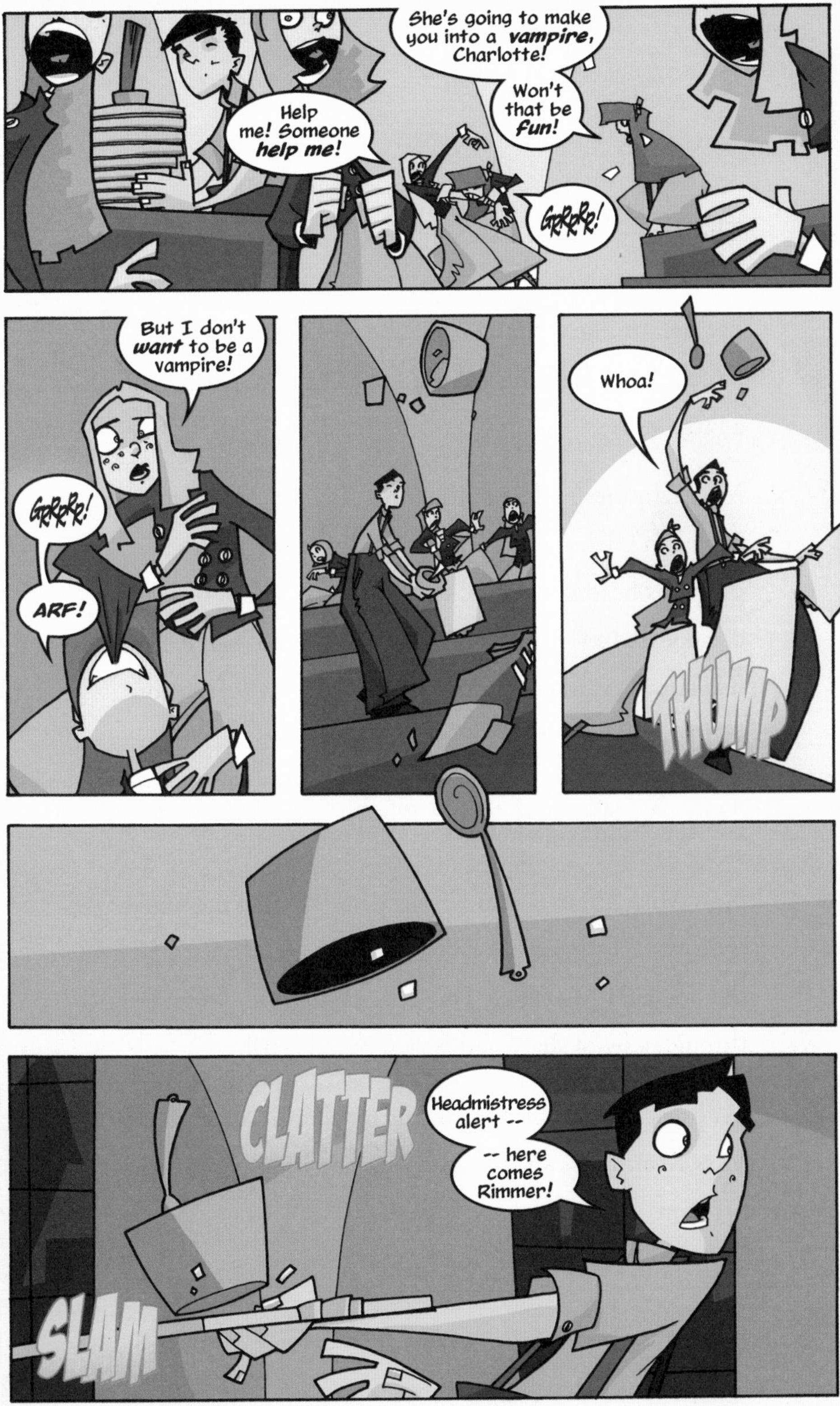
She's going to make you into a vampire, Charlotte!
Won't that be fun!
Help me! Someone help me!
GRRRRR!
But I don't want to be a vampire!
GRRRR!
ARF!
Whoa!
THUMP
CLATTER
Headmistress alert --
-- here comes Rimmer!
SLAM

The door of the refectory crashed open to reveal the headmistress, Miss Rimmer, scowling and grunting under her breath like a raging bull. She was dressed in thick tweed, and a tight bun clung to the back of her head like a large wart.

Miss Rimmer had been the merciless ruler of Isambard Dunstan's School for Wayward Children since the previous headmistress, Olivia Dart-Winston, had disappeared a year before. Miss Olivia, as she was called, had simply vanished without warning or explanation, and Miss Rimmer had been quick to take over, turning the once-pleasant home into a place where discontent and rebellion reigned.

Now Miss Rimmer stood in the doorway shaking with anger. By her side grunted her only friend—Darcy, a short, fat dog that looked like a stunted pig covered with fur and drooling through a set of sharp and very serrated teeth.

"Who is responsible for all this mayhem?" demanded Miss Rimmer as she charged into the room, brandishing her cane.

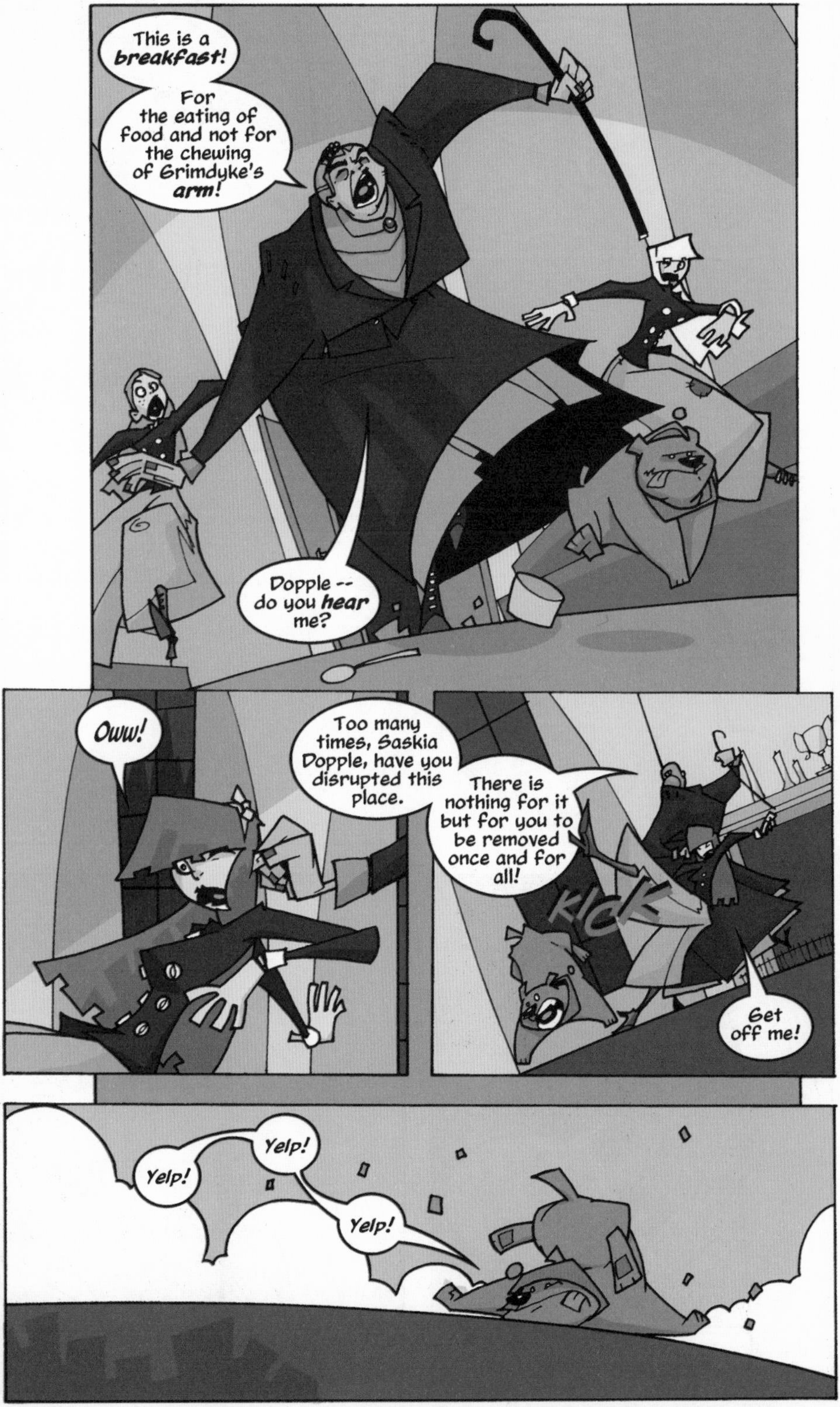
This is a breakfast!
For the eating of food and not for the chewing of Grimdyke's arm!
Dopple -- do you hear me?
Oww!
Too many times, Saskia Dopple, have you disrupted this place.
There is nothing for it but for you to be removed once and for all!
KICK
Get off me!
Yelp!
Yelp!
Yelp!

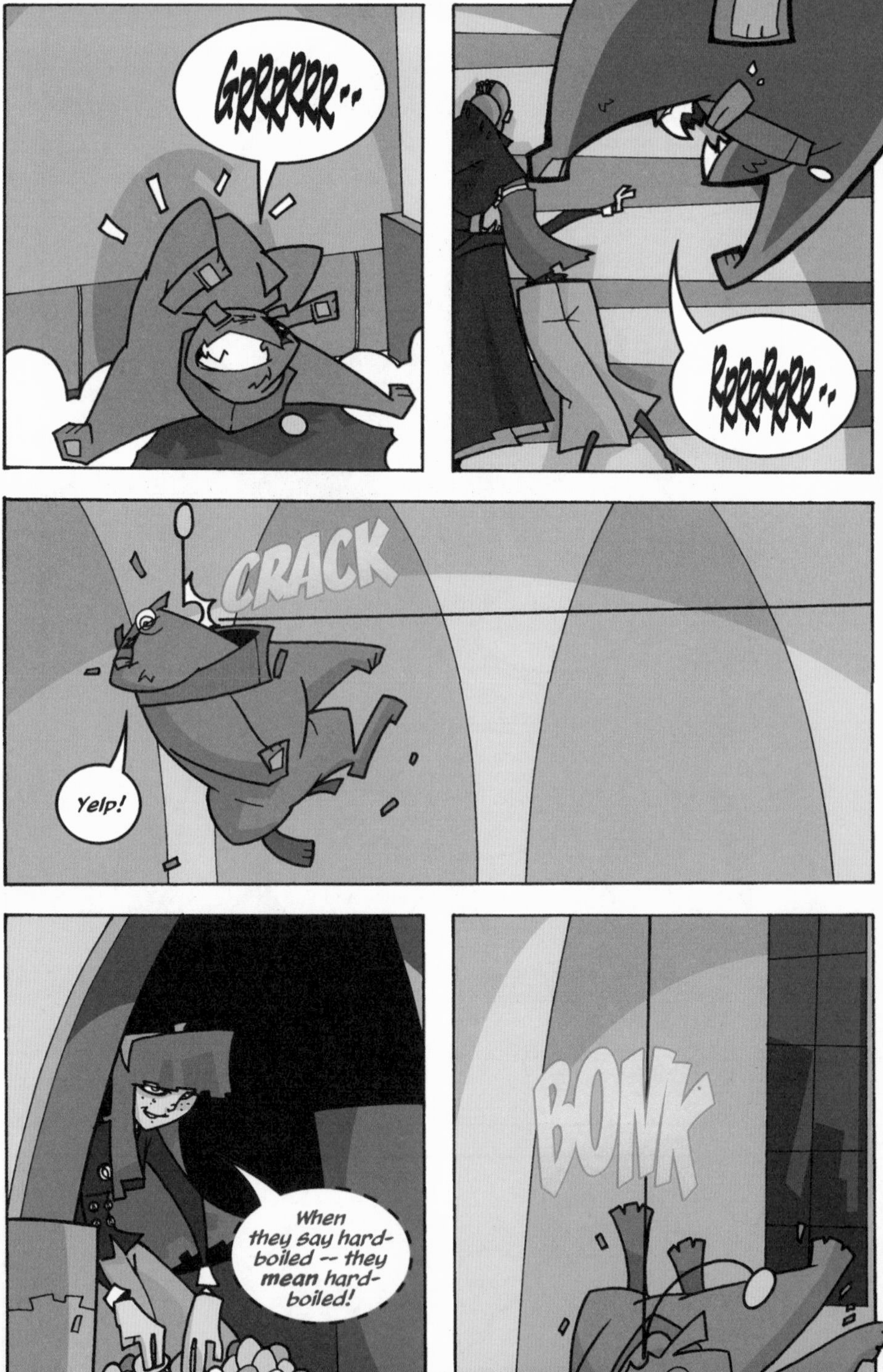
GRRRRRR..
RRRRRRR..
CRACK
Yelp!
When they say hard-boiled -- they mean hard-boiled!
BONK

Darcy lay sprawled upon the polished floor. Miss Rimmer, seeing that her precious pet was dazed and drooling, dropped Saskia to the ground and turned her attention to the animal.

"Darcy, darling, what has happened to you?" she asked in a voice that made the Dopple sisters want to be sick. "Is my Darcy hurt?"

"It was . . . Sa . . . Sa . . . Sa . . ." began Grimdyke, but she was mysteriously struck dumb as a hard-boiled egg bounced off the back of her head. Rimmer spun on the soles of her thick leather boots and looked at Grimdyke, who held her head and spluttered into tears.

NOne of You deserve to be hEre, nOne of You!

Like a hungry lion, Rimmer eyed the room, searching every face for a sign of weakness and some clue as to the culprit.

"Don't think I don't know who would do such a thing," she bawled as she looked at Sadie. "Some people here have forgotten what it is like to be grateful. Think, my dear, frail children. Where would you be without Isambard Dunstan's? On the street in a cardboard box, living under the arches of Charing Cross? Picking through the trash bins in St James's Park? Think of it, children. Without me that would be your life.

"None of you deserve to be here—none of you." Rimmer paused as she lifted her disoriented pet from the floor and looked into the dog's dazed eyes. "Some of you . . . some of you have outstayed your welcome, and if I could rid myself of you I would. Wait until the day you are sixteen and I see you slide down the banister and into the street for the last time.

"Then—then—will you rue the day you treated me and this poor, unfortunate animal so badly."

Miss Rimmer sniffed and held out Darcy for all to see as she nodded her head like a great actor at the end of some fine speech.

Charlotte Grimdyke began to quietly applaud, cooing like a pigeon. Miss Rimmer gave her an approving smile. Behind her, Saskia folded her arms, raised a thin black eyebrow, and rolled her eyes.

"Don't think I have finished with you," Rimmer said as she spun again, almost casting Darcy across the room and only just managing to hold on to her by the tail. "I will see both you and your troublesome sister in my office at eight o'clock. Be not a minute late—or else!"

Saskia looked at the floor and swallowed the laughter in her throat like a gulping frog. Tears began to slowly roll across her white cheeks, and her lips began to quiver as she fought to keep the laughter in. Thinking Saskia was about to cry, Miss Rimmer threw her a look of disgust as she rushed from the room, muttering under her breath.

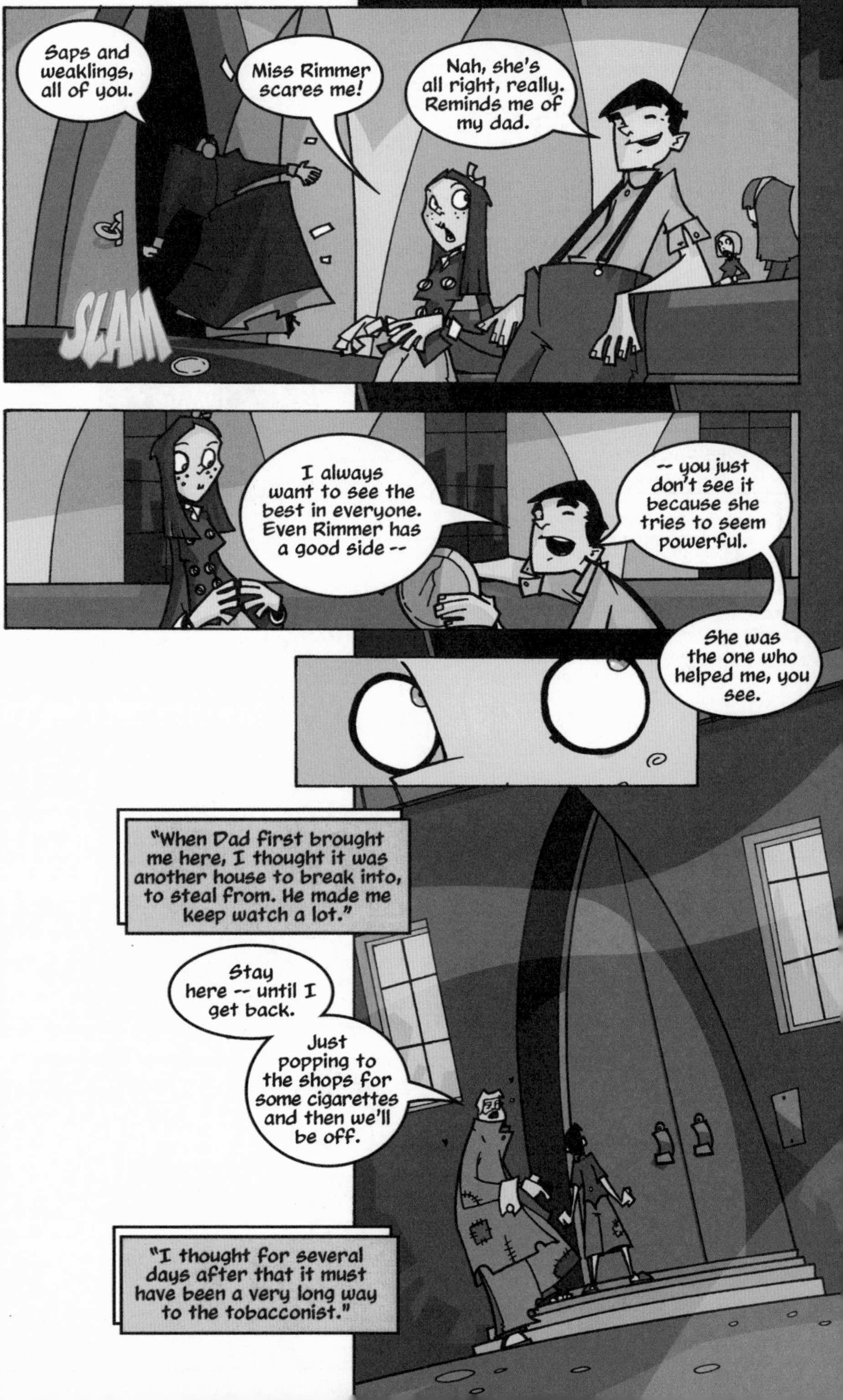
Saps and weaklings, all of you.
Miss Rimmer scares me!
Nah, she's all right, really. Reminds me of my dad.
SLAM
I always want to see the best in everyone. Even Rimmer has a good side --
-- you just don't see it because she tries to seem powerful.
She was the one who helped me, you see.
"When Dad first brought me here, I thought it was another house to break into, to steal from. He made me keep watch a lot."
Stay here -- until I get back.
Just popping to the shops for some cigarettes and then we'll be off.
"I thought for several days after that it must have been a very long way to the tobacconist."

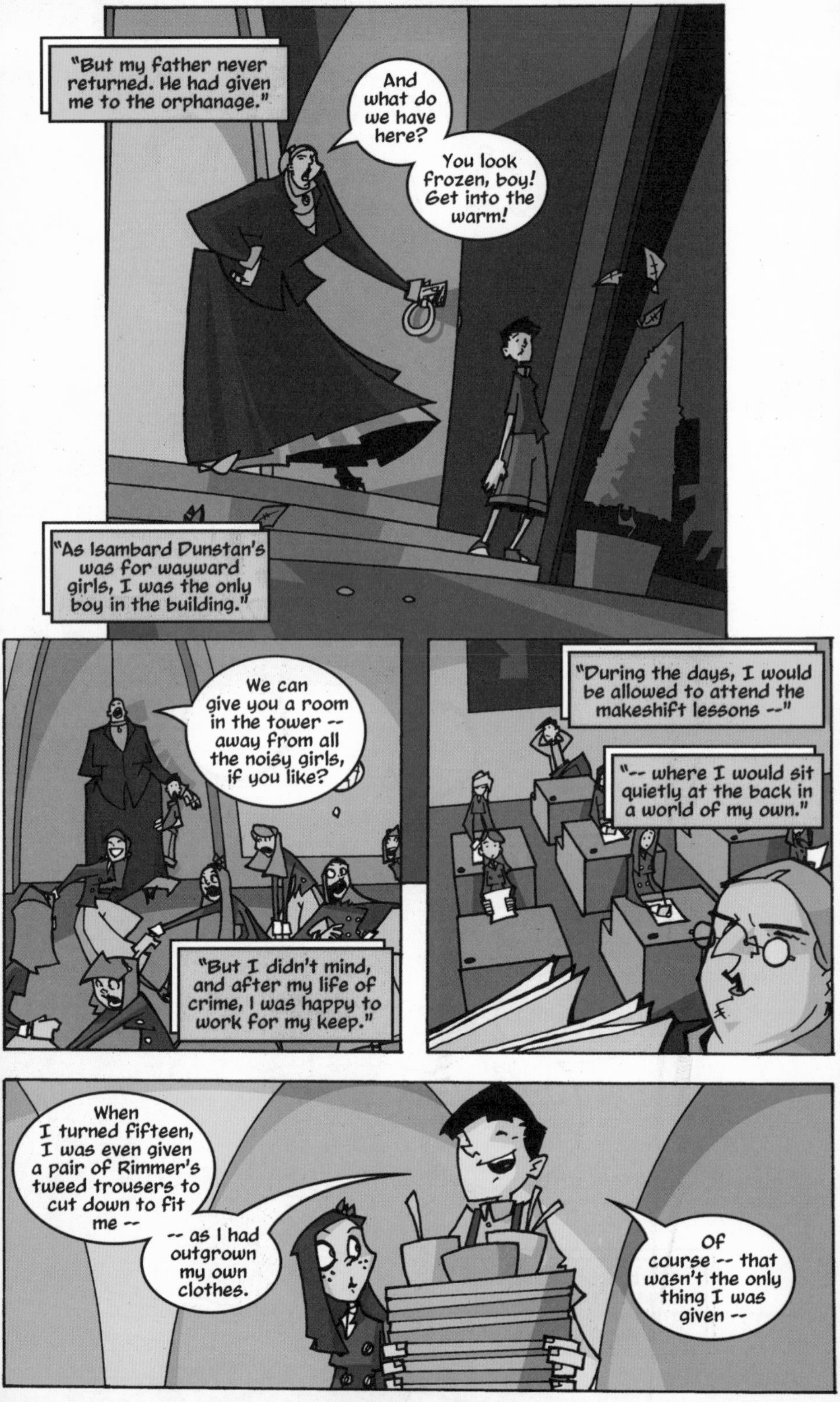
"But my father never returned. He had given me to the orphanage."
And what do we have here?
You look frozen, boy! Get into the warm!
"As Isambard Dunstan's was for wayward girls, I was the only boy in the building."
We can give you a room in the tower -- away from all the noisy girls, if you like?
"But I didn't mind, and after my life of crime, I was happy to work for my keep."
"During the days, I would be allowed to attend the makeshift lessons --"
"-- where I would sit quietly at the back in a world of my own."
When I turned fifteen, I was even given a pair of Rimmer's tweed trousers to cut down to fit me --
-- as I had outgrown my own clothes.
Of course -- that wasn't the only thing I was given --

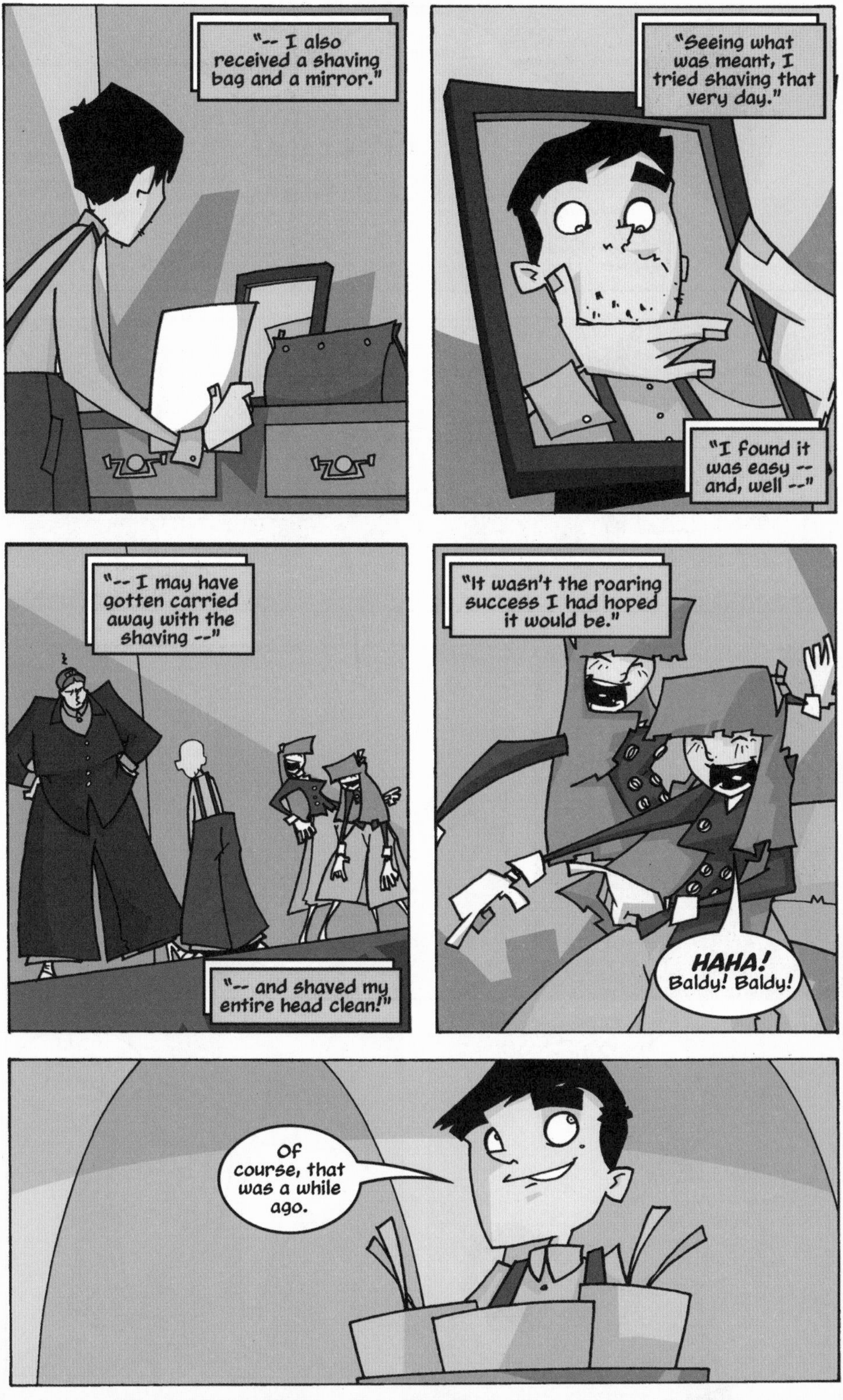
"-- I also received a shaving bag and a mirror."
"Seeing what was meant, I tried shaving that very day."
"I found it was easy -- and, well --"
"-- I may have gotten carried away with the shaving --"
"-- and shaved my entire head clean!"
"It wasn't the roaring success I had hoped it would be."
HAHA! Baldy! Baldy!
Of course, that was a while ago.

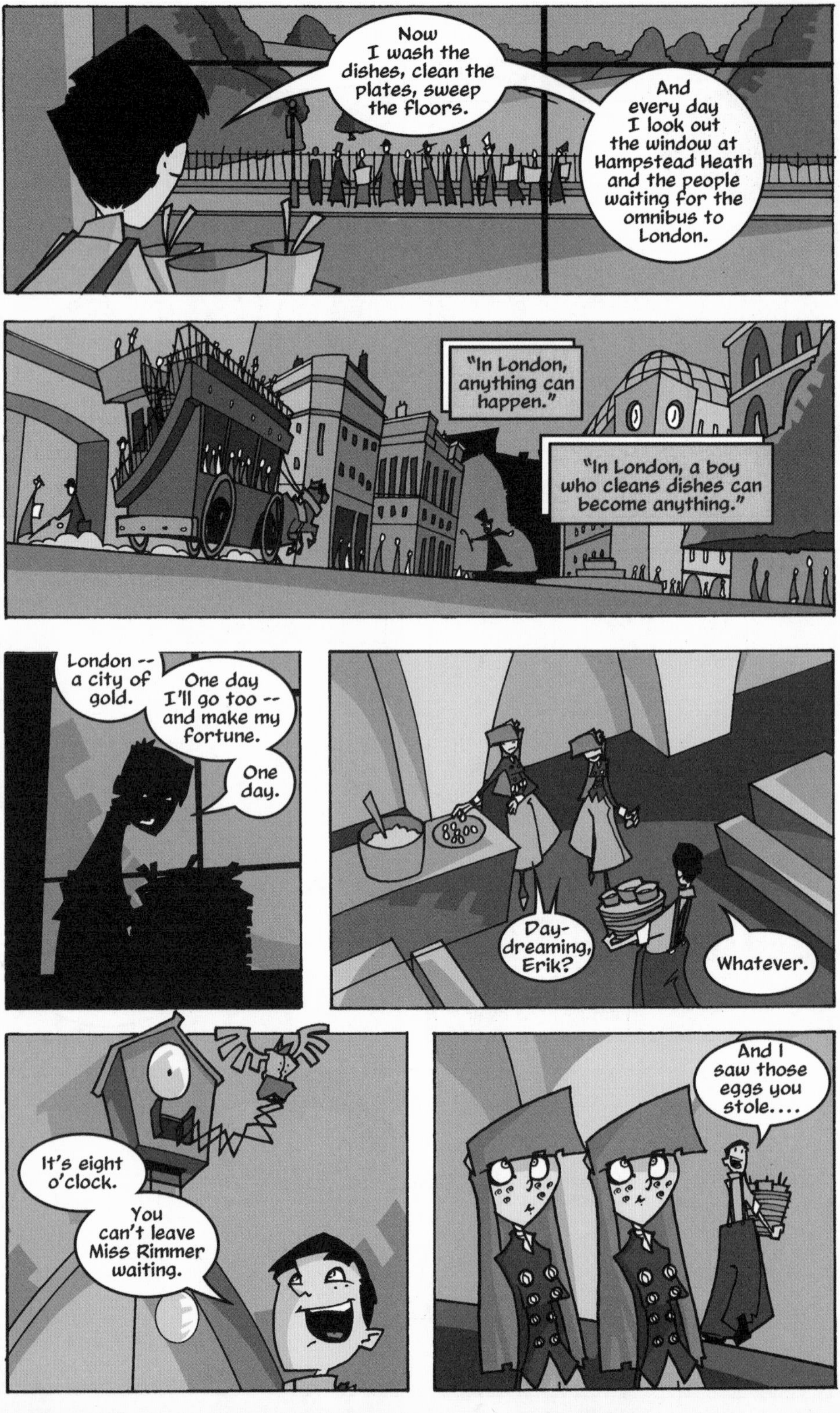
Now I wash the dishes, clean the plates, sweep the floors.
And every day I look out the window at Hampstead Heath and the people waiting for the omnibus to London.
"In London, anything can happen."
"In London, a boy who cleans dishes can become anything."
London -- a city of gold.
One day I'll go too -- and make my fortune.
One day.
Day-dreaming, Erik?
Whatever.
It's eight o'clock.
You can't leave Miss Rimmer waiting.
And I saw those eggs you stole....

Chapter Two

Muzz Elliott

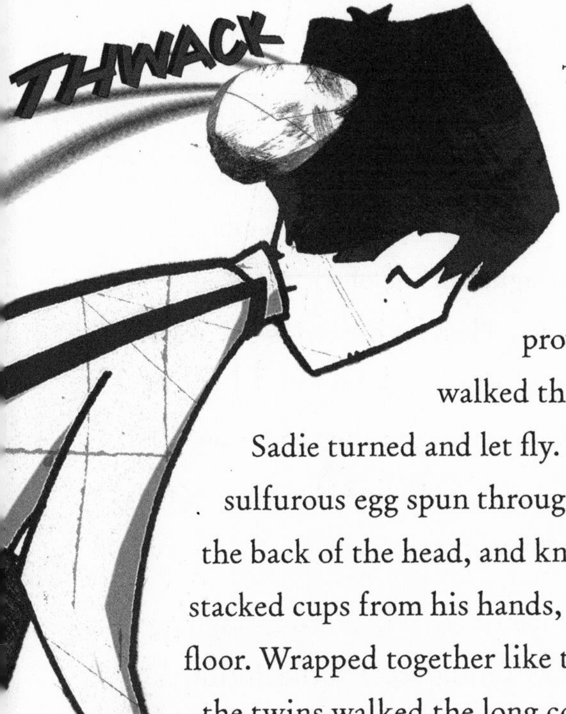
THWACK

THEY WERE TWO minutes late. The urge to throw one last egg as they left the refectory proved too much. As she walked through the great door, Sadie turned and let fly. The triple hard-boiled, sulfurous egg spun through the air, hit Erik on the back of the head, and knocked a tray of neatly stacked cups from his hands, crashing them to the floor. Wrapped together like two writhing snakes, the twins walked the long corridor with its ugly brown floor and stink of bleach until they reached the office of Miss Rimmer.

Darcy, the obnoxious lap dog, sat as usual on the chair outside the office door. Saskia was sure the dog bared her teeth at the girl in a shallow grin. As the twins approached, Darcy squirmed on the blue velvet cushion and pricked her ears, listening intently to the hollow echo of their footsteps. She seemed to count their steps, waiting for the moment to strike.

Sadly for Darcy, the dog was still only semiconscious. All she could see was the vague outline of what looked like six people walking toward her. As the twins got nearer, Darcy was suddenly and terrifyingly aware it was them To her complete horror, Darcy thought they had been magically multiplied into six egg-wielding Dopples who now came to do more mischief upon her.

In an instant she had vanished from the chair, dragging the cushion with her and running toward the dormitory,

whimpering and howling as she went. Saskia gave a bemused smile, unsure that this was not some kind of elaborate trap.

"I thought dogs could only remember a few seconds at a time—she should have forgotten the egg by now," Saskia said and untwined herself from her sister's arms.

"That's goldfish, not dogs," corrected Sadie as she looked through the blurred glass at the outline of Miss Rimmer at her desk, telephone to her ear and a rather mysterious shape to her right. "She has a guest," she whispered.

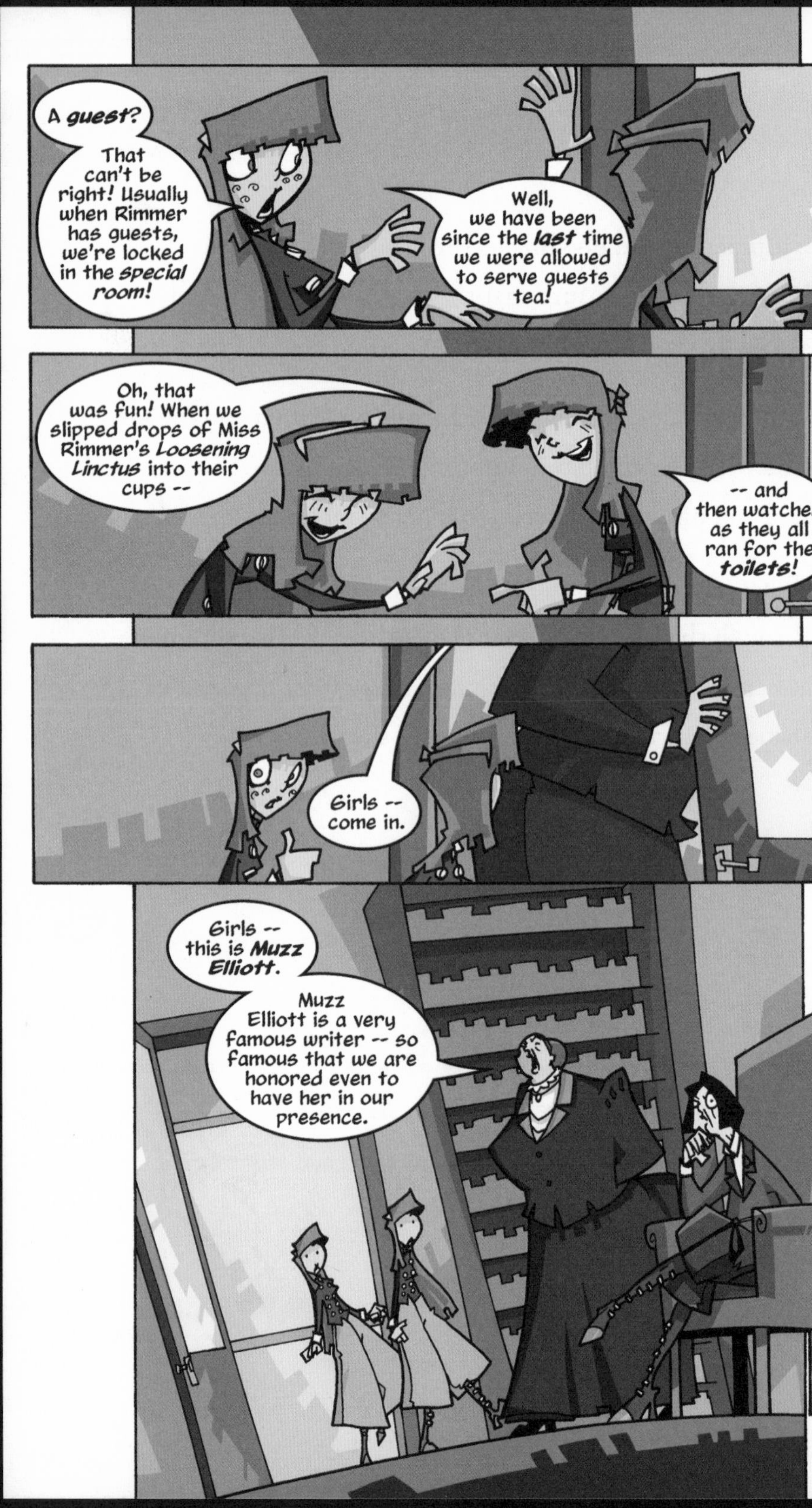
A *guest*?
That can't be right! Usually when Rimmer has guests, we're locked in the *special room*!
Well, we have been since the *last* time we were allowed to serve guests tea!
Oh, that was fun! When we slipped drops of Miss Rimmer's *Loosening Linctus* into their cups --
-- and then watched as they all ran for the ***toilets***!
Girls -- come in.
Girls -- this is ***Muzz Elliott***.
Muzz Elliott is a very famous writer -- so famous that we are honored even to have her in our presence.

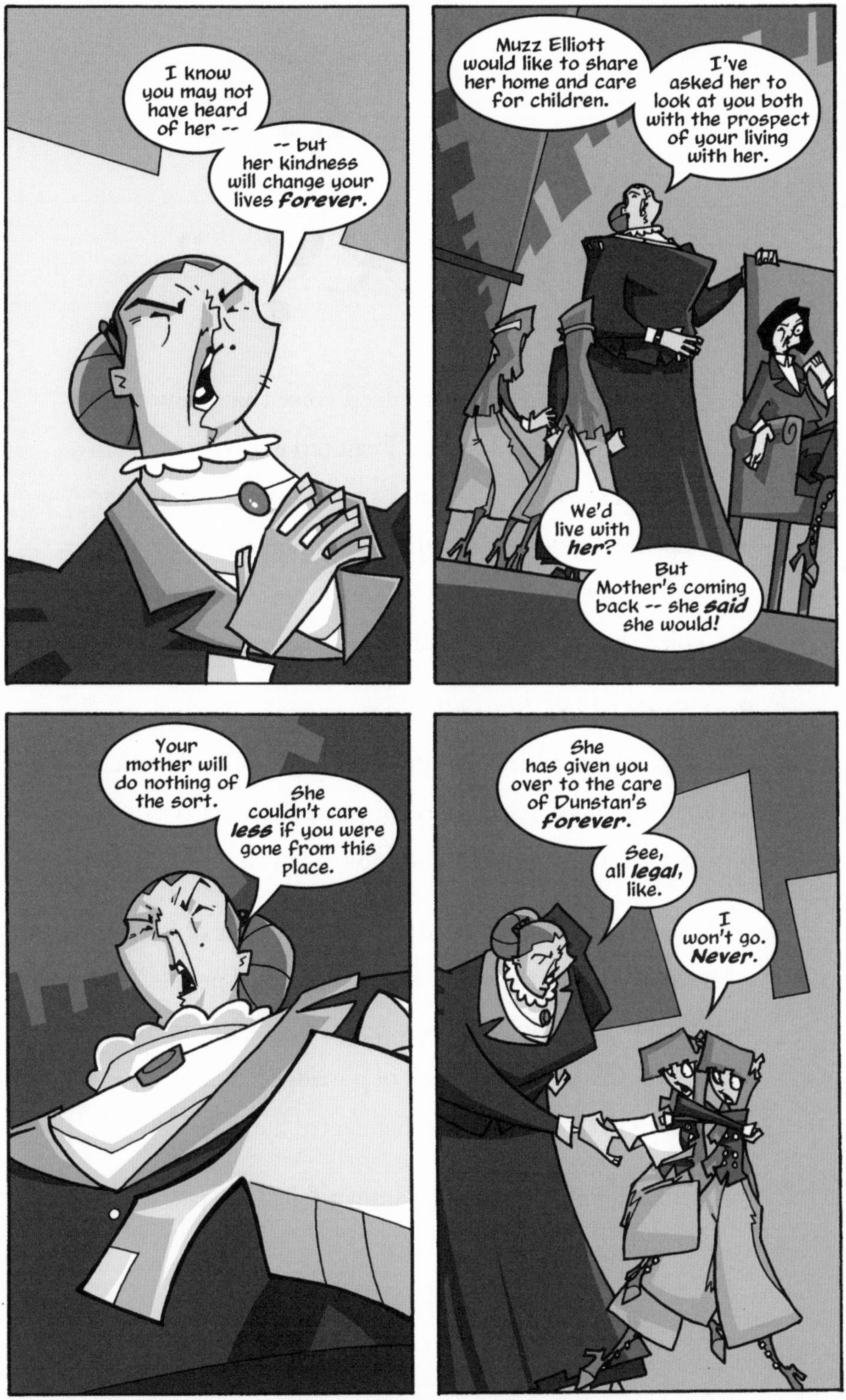
I know you may not have heard of her --
-- but her kindness will change your lives *forever*.
Muzz Elliott would like to share her home and care for children.
I've asked her to look at you both with the prospect of your living with her.
We'd live with *her*?
But Mother's coming back -- she *said* she would!
Your mother will do nothing of the sort.
She couldn't care *less* if you were gone from this place.
She has given you over to the care of Dunstan's *forever*.
See, all *legal*, like.
I won't go. *Never*.

"Will you smile?"

. . . asked Muzz Elliott in a deep voice that drew the girls' attention immediately. "I can tell everything from a smile." Sadie looked at her and saw that her eyes glinted with flecks of gold set in swirls of brown, as if a sandstorm raged through her head. "Will you smile?" she asked again in a voice that made the request into a command.

Both Sadie and Saskia smiled immediately. Their teeth sparkled. Muzz Elliott got up from her seat, and Sadie noticed she was carrying a riding crop. Muzz Elliott pulled open their mouths and looked inside.

"Horses and people," she said as she hit the side of her boot with the crop. "All the same: good teeth, good people." And then with a single turn she flopped back in the chair. Muzz Elliott sniffed; the smell of porridge had become even stronger than the odor of the disinfected hallway.

"So, Muzz Elliott," asked Miss Rimmer, "shall you take them?"

Muzz Elliott thought for a while as she tapped her boot menacingly. Sadie and Saskia held their breath as her gaze shifted between them. They feared the worst—and then it came.

“That one,” Muzz Elliott said, pointing the crop at Saskia. “I’ll take her. The other one had a weak smile; she can stay.”

“Stay?” gasped Miss Rimmer, her voice sharp and alarmed. “Only one? They come together—they’re sisters.”

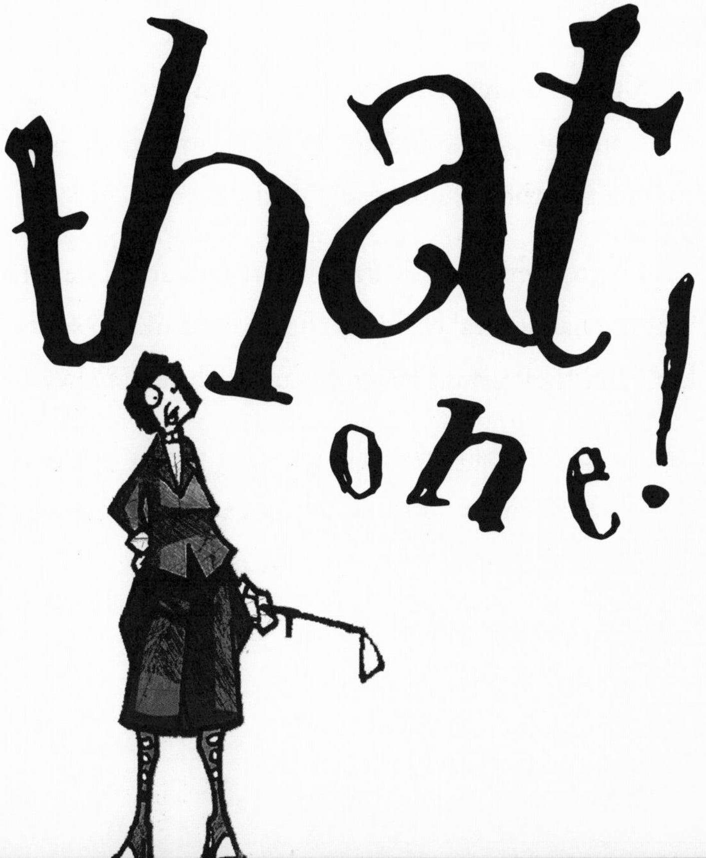
that one!

"One or none," Muzz Elliott said calmly. "Two mouths and two minds are more than I can cope with. I want a child, a foster daughter, someone I can share my life with. I do not want a tribe with which I shall be engaged in warfare, and your eagerness to be rid of them both leads me to suspect that they are not what they seem. One or none, Miss Rimmer, one or none . . ."

It was as if a whirlpool had washed over them. Sadie looked at Saskia and gripped her hand as she frantically tried to think of what to do. She was the eldest; she would decide. She had beaten Saskia into the world by three minutes, and now she would not let her go to anyone else. "We come together or not at all," Sadie demanded.

"Then I'll go elsewhere," Muzz Elliott replied. "I hear the workhouse has several children they would like to see the back of, and they would never put up with such behavior."

"Muzz Elliot," Miss Rimmer said as the patron got to her feet to leave the room. "Please, give me a moment alone with them, and let us see what can be done."

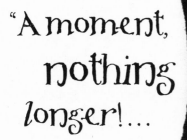

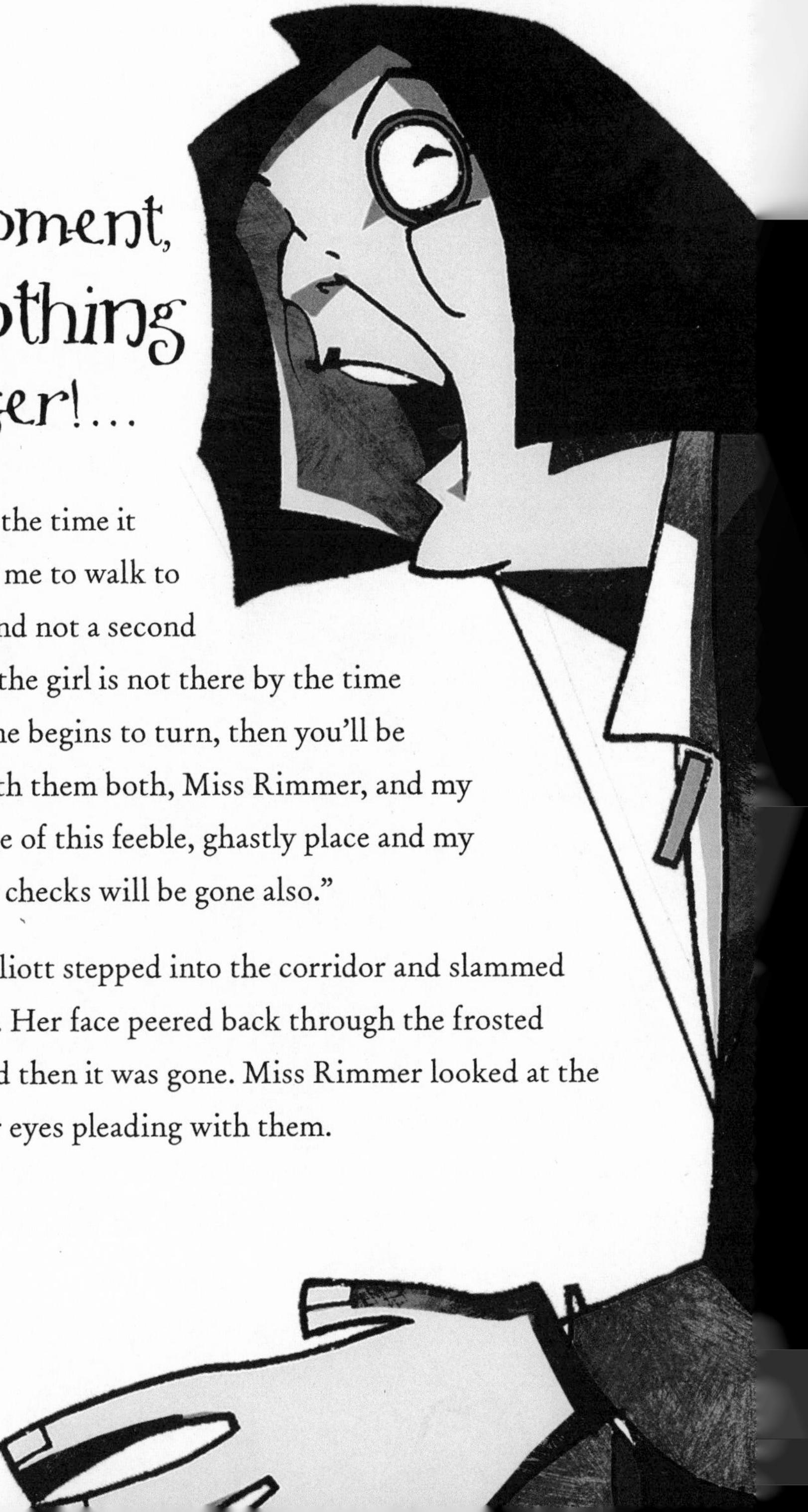

"A moment, nothing longer!...

Let it be the time it
takes for me to walk to
my car and not a second
more. If the girl is not there by the time
the engine begins to turn, then you'll be
stuck with them both, Miss Rimmer, and my
patronage of this feeble, ghastly place and my
monthly checks will be gone also."

Muzz Elliott stepped into the corridor and slammed
the door. Her face peered back through the frosted
glass, and then it was gone. Miss Rimmer looked at the
girls, her eyes pleading with them.

"Sadie,"

she said softly. . . .

"This is no place for your sister. Give her a chance to better herself. She'll be brought up a lady and have a good life. If you love her, you'll let her go."

"We said we'd always be together,"

Saskia snapped.

"flesh and blood are thicker than water."

"You have a minute to decide, and then the chance is gone. Muzz Elliott pays for this place to stay open, the bread on your plates, and the food in your bellies. If she doesn't get her way, then it's all gone, everything. Saskia will have to go so that you'll have a place to stay. Understand?"

They had never heard her talk like this before. It was like the voice of someone else was speaking through her. They looked at each other as if it were the last look they would ever give. Sadie opened her eyes as wide as she could so that she could see more and more of her sister.

"Will I see her again?"

she asked Miss Rimmer, who by now had come to them and taken their hands.

"I don't know, but she'll always know where you are, and I will ask Muzz Elliott if she can write."

"What about her things?"

Sadie asked, ever the older sister.

"Both your bags were packed during breakfast; they are at the door waiting for you. I thought she was coming for you both. That was my plan."

"So you're stuck with Sadie, and I'm gone?"

Saskia asked as a tear ran across her cheek and dripped to the floor.

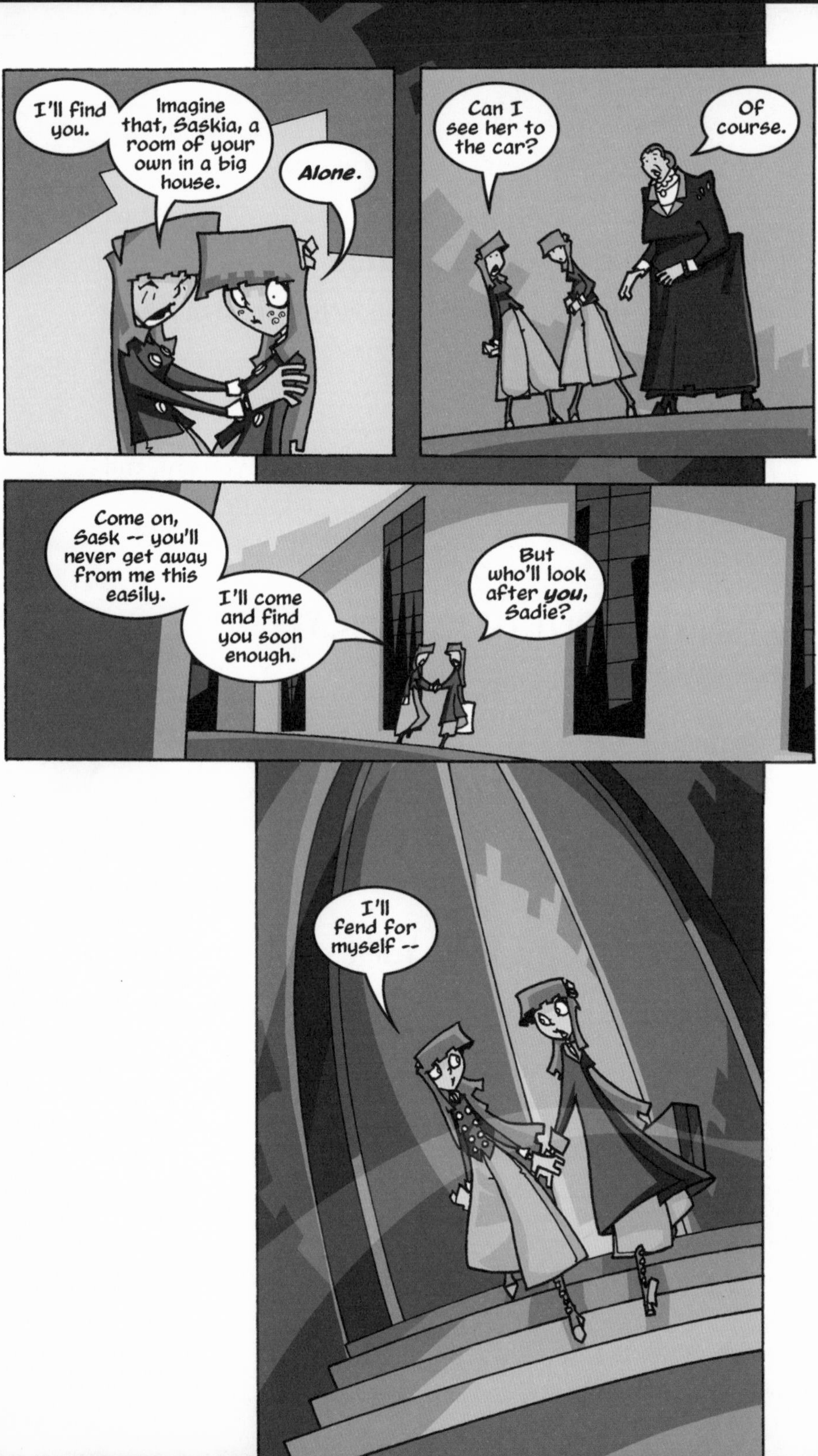

I'll find you.
Imagine that, Saskia, a room of your own in a big house.
Alone.
Can I see her to the car?
Of course.
Come on, Sask -- you'll never get away from me this easily.
I'll come and find you soon enough.
But who'll look after you, Sadie?
I'll fend for myself --

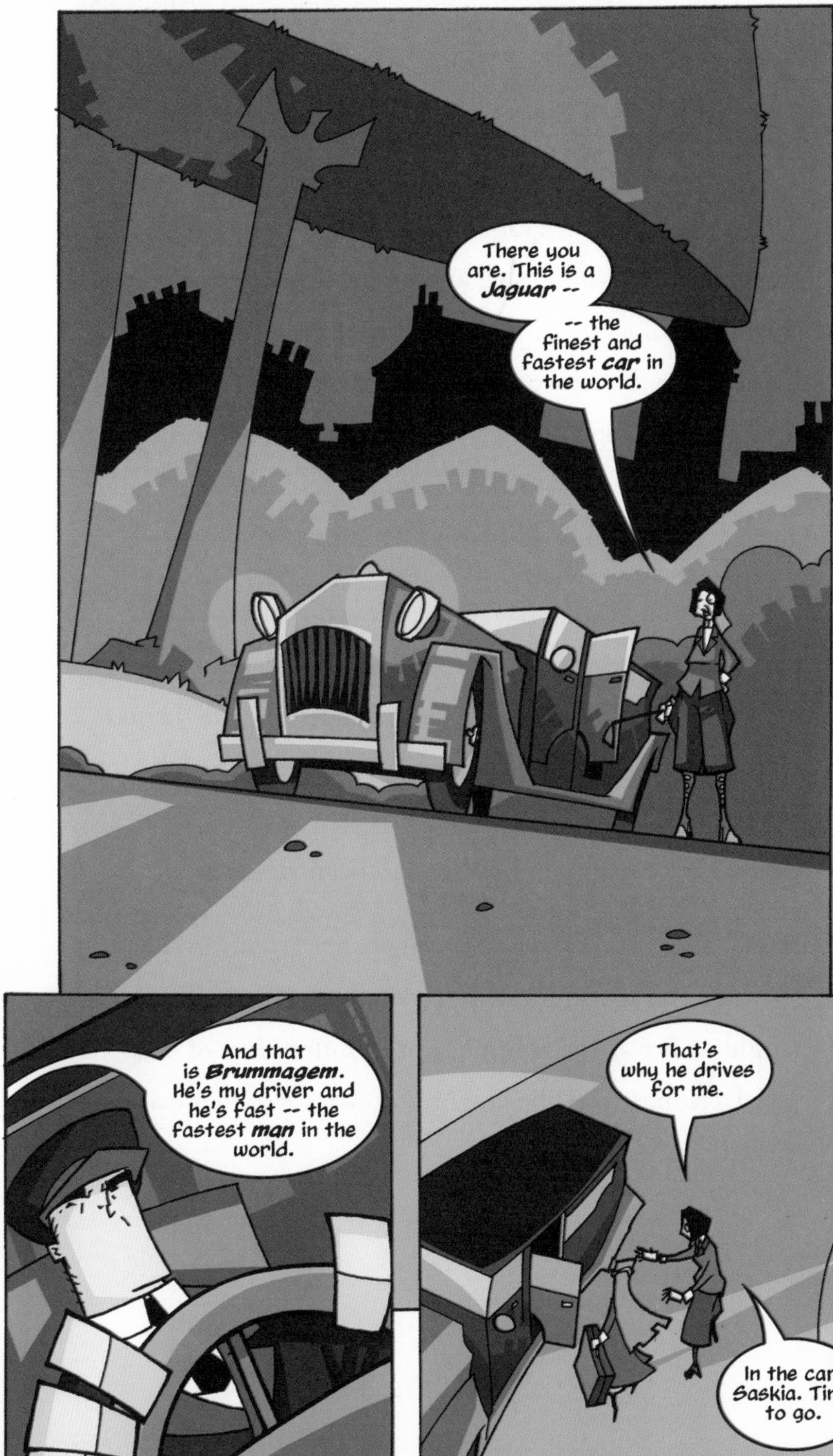
There you are. This is a *Jaguar* --
-- the finest and fastest *car* in the world.
And that is *Brummagem*. He's my driver and he's fast -- the fastest *man* in the world.
That's why he drives for me.
In the car, Saskia. Time to go.

There was no chance for Sadie to say good-bye. The engine started with a loud growl, and as the other door slammed, the car clunked into gear and sped off. Gravel sprayed from under the tires as the Jaguar dashed to speed and disappeared along the driveway. In three seconds it was gone. All that was left was a faint wisp of smoke dancing along the path that led from the house to the road.

Sadie looked at the gates. She heard the car brake and speed off again across the heath. She wondered if she would ever see Saskia again. She wondered if the Jaguar would return and take her as well. Suddenly she felt alone for the first time in her life. It was as if she had been cleaved in two and half of her had been stolen away.

Something inside the house caught her attention. Echoing through the corridors and hallways was the sound of laughter. It was the laughter not of humor but of deep satisfaction. It was the laughter of Miss Rimmer cackling merrily in her office.

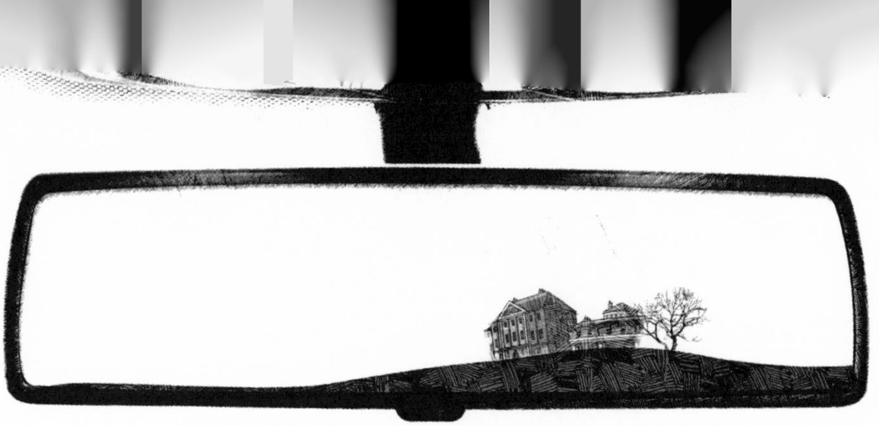

Chapter Three

Spaniards House

MUZZ ELLIOTT SAT in the back of the Jaguar in a state of annoyance. She bristled anxiously as the car lurched from side to side, progressing quickly along High Street and out along the heath. Pedestrians leaped from its path as it roared along. Even the old policeman who stood on the corner of Park Road stepped back into a doorway and averted his eyes as it thrust along in a whirl of dust and winter leaves. Brummagem sat rigidly in the high-backed leather seat. His foot was wedged against the accelerator, and his right hand hit the horn whenever anyone came near. All Saskia could see of his face were his deep brown eyes framed in the rearview mirror.

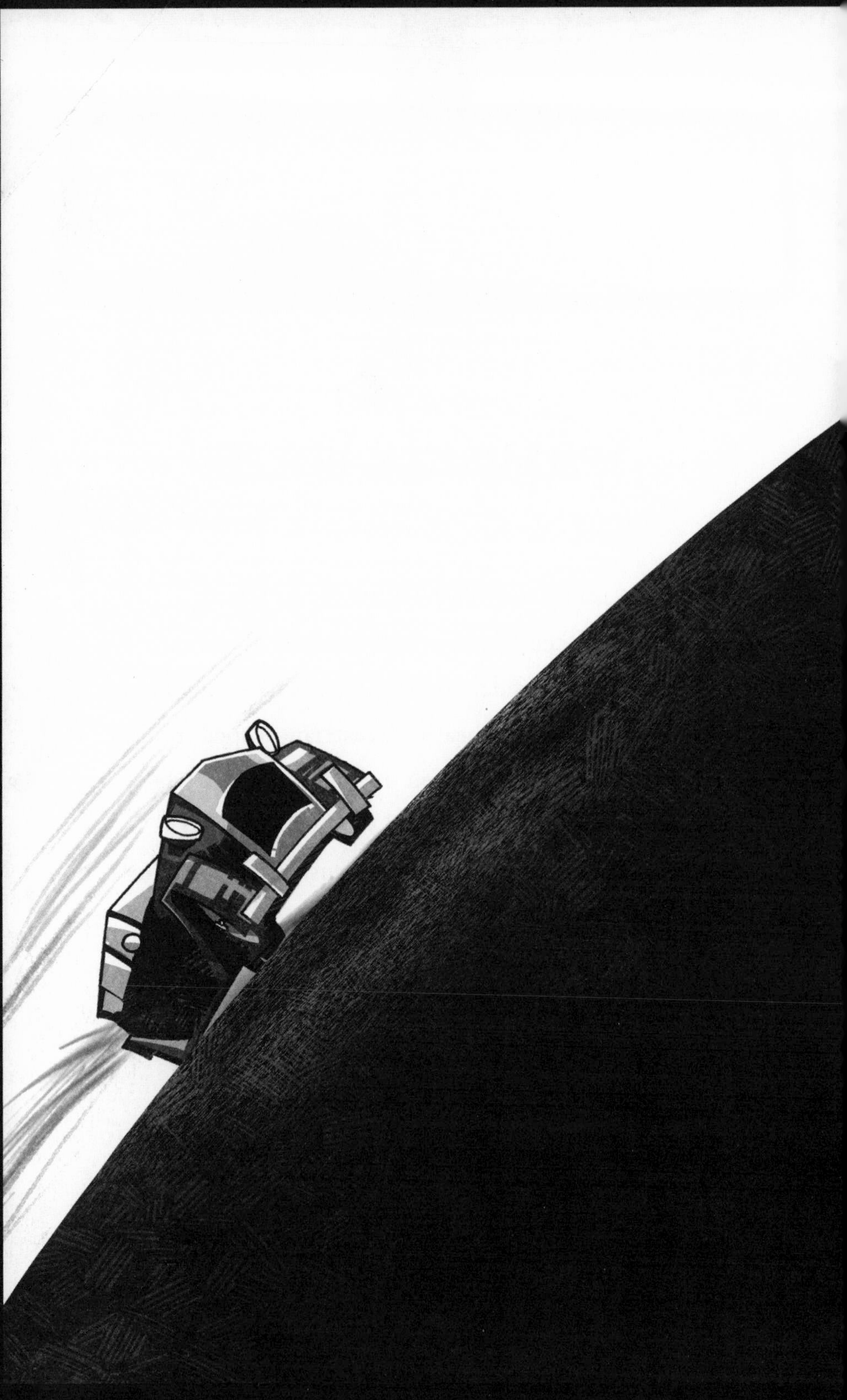

Brummagem's leather-gloved hands occasionally gripped the steering wheel, but more often than not they were used to gesticulate wildly at passersby. It was obvious that he was a man who hated dogs, pigeons, and most of all people, for whenever any of these creatures dared to come into the path of the Jaguar, he would shout loudly in his thick Irish accent, uttering curses and dire threats of what he would do to them if he had the chance.

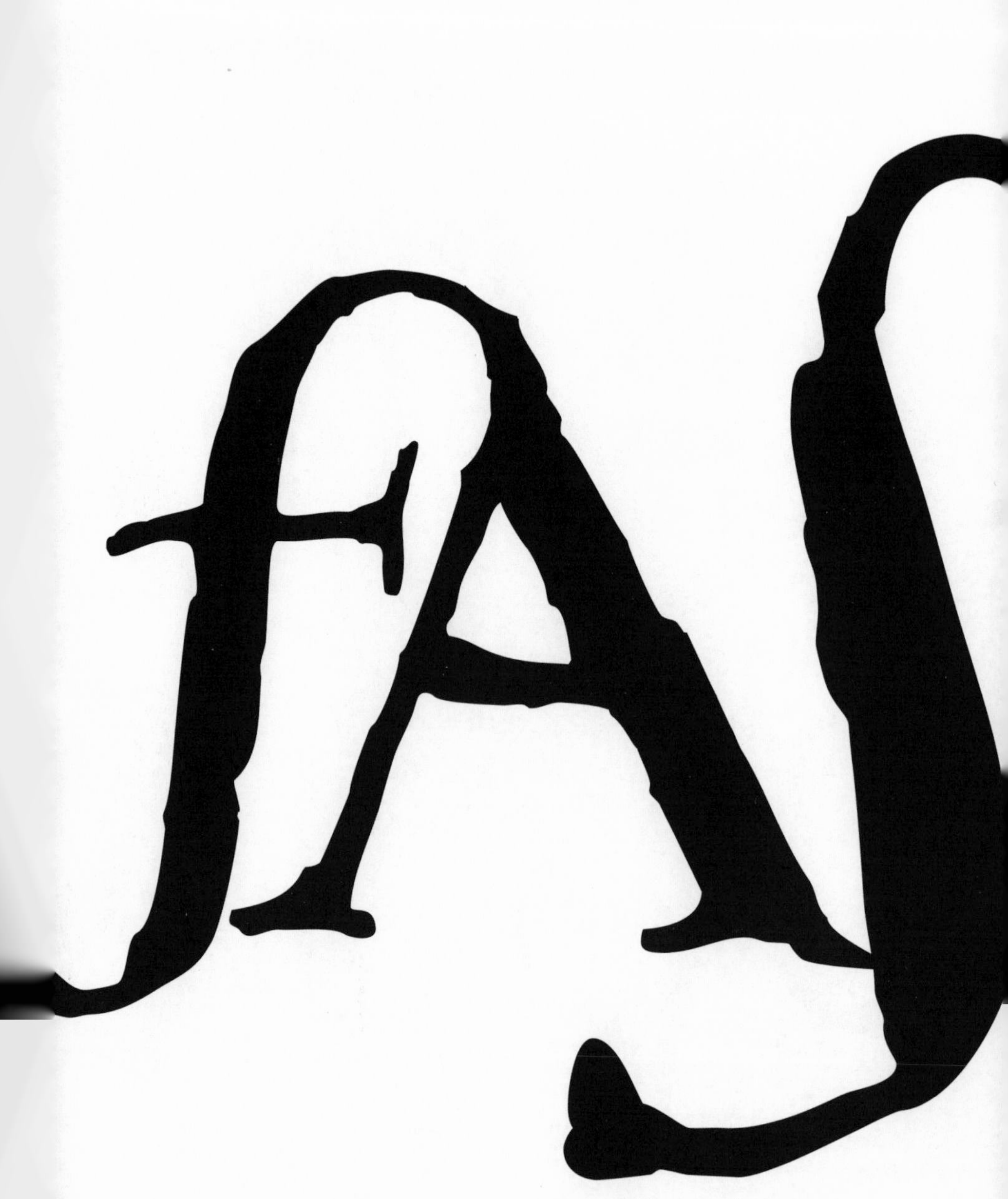

tER

This is a Jaguar!

Saskia's companion sat stiffly in the car and said nothing, except for occasionally screaming, "*FASTER!* " and "THIS IS A JAGUAR!" She shouted these words as if she were a demented parrot whenever Brummagem dropped the speed to below fifty miles per hour. It was like they came from the depths of her subconscious and she could do nothing to stop them from being blurted from her lips. Muzz Elliott would scream each word as loudly as she possibly could—her favorite, from the ferocity with which she screamed it, was "*FASTER!* "

Going slowly was something that Brummagem appeared to be incapable of doing. As they left the village of Hampstead, the car got even quicker. Something in the engine began to roar. The soft purring that had accompanied them was now replaced by a ferocious growling, and even at such high speeds the wheels would spin when Brummagem changed gear and would send shards of gravel like a hail of bullets at anything that followed.

As they turned onto the heath, Saskia noticed a solitary onion seller in the distance, pedaling sedately on his black bicycle. When he heard the approaching ferocious Jaguar, he turned momentarily and then began to cycle faster. It looked like he had encountered the beast before, for even at a distance, Saskia could see the look of horror on his face as they approached with the closing speed of a charging rhinoceros.

In vain, he cycled as fast as he could along the side of the road, garlands of garlic and onions bobbing around his neck. His spider legs sped faster and faster, pushing hard against the pedals and the approaching hill. In the basket on the front of his bicycle he carried a large jug. Brummagem winked at Saskia, muttering curses upon the man as he hit the accelerator even harder. The car lurched forward. Saskia screamed as she was flung from side to side.

"Stop!" she shouted, gripping the back of the leather seat. "You'll kill him!"

Saskia looked at Muzz Elliott, who smiled and sniggered wildly. Brummagem laughed as they sped on at break-neck speed. Then as he passed the wobbling, fearful peddler, he dropped the gear, spun the wheels, and sent a shower of grit from the tires. Saskia turned to see the poor vendor machine-gunned from his bicycle. The jar from the basket exploded with a direct hit. The man fell to the ground and was pinned to the fence that ran along the road by a particularly strong bandanna of garlic.

Brummagem swerved back into the road as he laughed. Saskia slid across the highly polished red leather seat and fell to the floor. Muzz Elliott said nothing but clutched the ivory handle above the door and somehow managed to sit perfectly still while Saskia was pitched from side to side by Brummagem's demented driving.

"Shall I go back and get him again?" he asked Muzz Elliott.

"No, Brummagem," she replied as she contemplated the man's fate. "I think that is a good enough lesson for selling me unripe tomatoes and saying they were love apples. How can any man mistake an apple for a tomato?"

"Swindling loony, Muzz Elliott. If he calls again I'll crush his bicycle so he cannot ride it again," Brummagem scoffed as he pressed the Jaguar to go even faster.

Still on the floor, Saskia curled herself into a ball and held on as hard as she could. All she could see from the windows were the flashing of the sky and the whizzing of branches as the car barreled along the road. The Jaguar bounced and rolled, screeching as it turned, and wound its way across the heath. There was a sudden and unexpected thud as they passed the long pond. The car was enveloped in a shroud of feathers, and the windows were splattered with tiny droplets of blood.

"Swan!" screamed Brummagem with glee. "Stuck to the radiator, Muzz Elliott, big enough to eat."

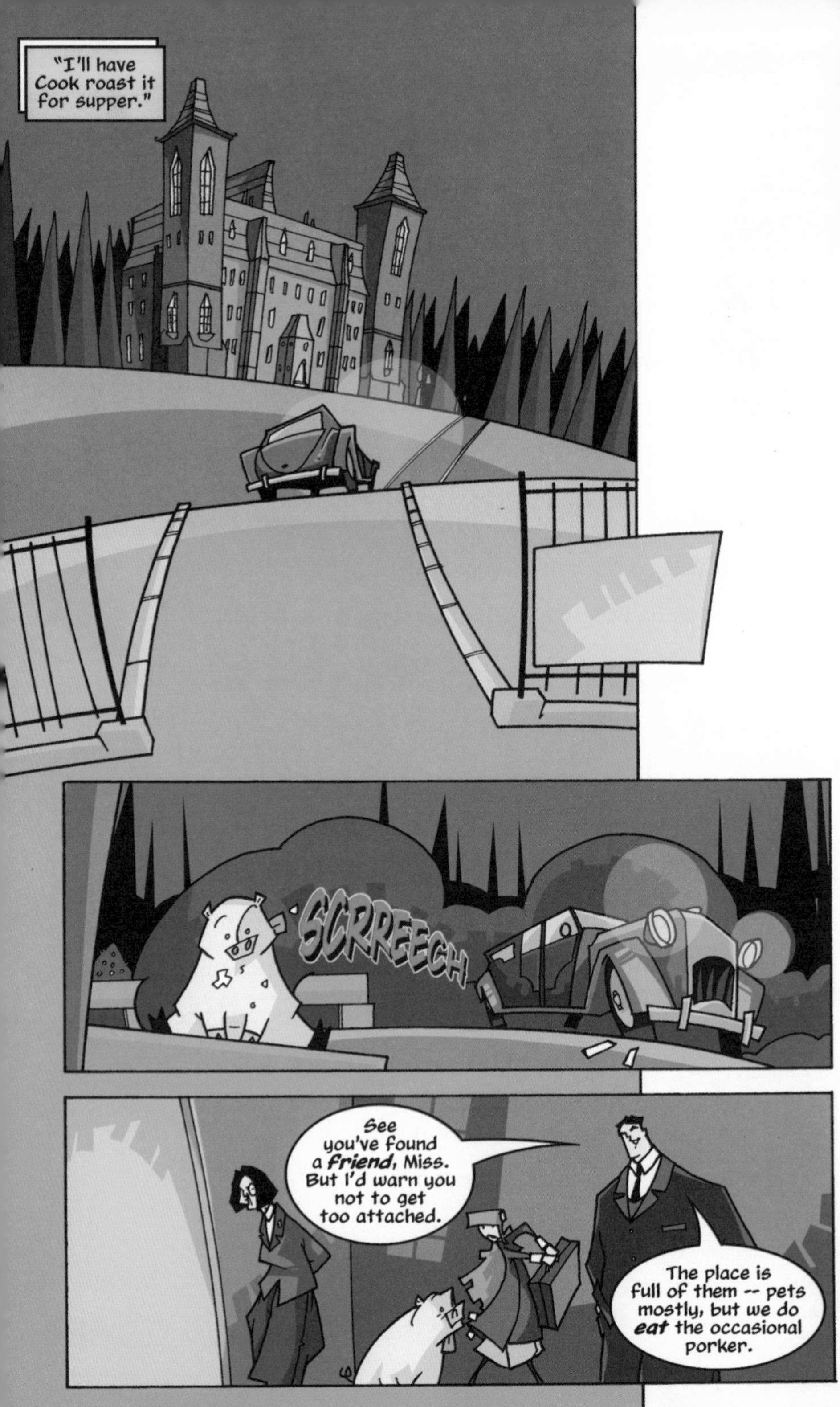
"I'll have Cook roast it for supper."
SCRREECH
See you've found a *friend*, Miss. But I'd warn you not to get too attached.
The place is full of them -- pets mostly, but we do *eat* the occasional porker.

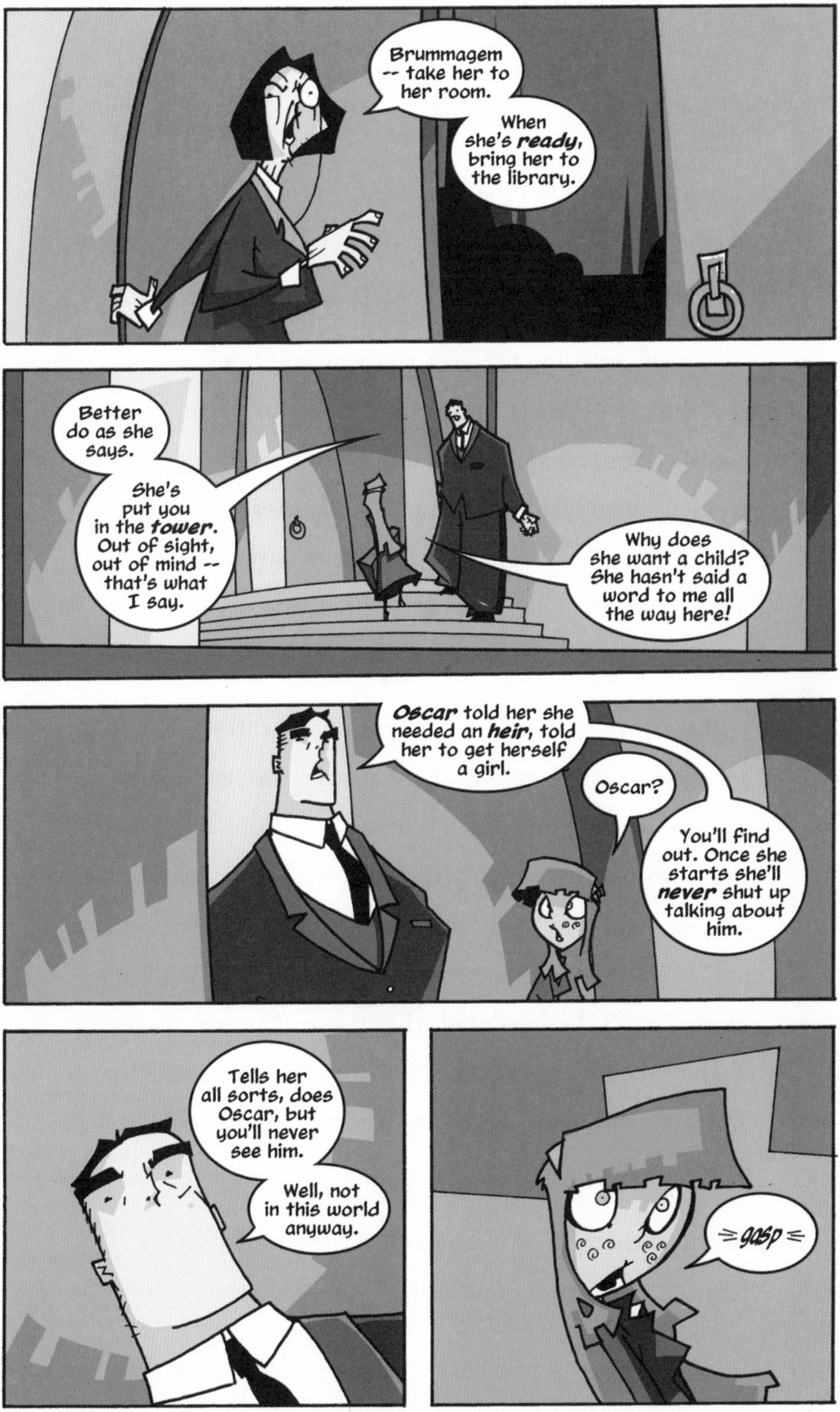
Brummagem -- take her to her room.
When she's *ready*, bring her to the library.
Better do as she says.
She's put you in the *tower*. Out of sight, out of mind -- that's what I say.
Why does she want a child? She hasn't said a word to me all the way here!
Oscar told her she needed an *heir*, told her to get herself a girl.
Oscar?
You'll find out. Once she starts she'll *never* shut up talking about him.
Tells her all sorts, does Oscar, but you'll never see him.
Well, not in this world anyway.
gasp

Brummagem ended the conversation with a nod of the head, motioning Saskia to follow behind. Suddenly aware of her surroundings, Saskia looked up and gasped.

They were walking through the grandest house she had ever seen. A gigantic wooden stairway burst from the marble floor and spiraled to an upper level. Hanging from every paneled wall were countless pictures, all framed in gilt. Each portrait appeared to stare at Saskia and follow her movements with its eyes. She felt like she was in a vast room filled with people, each one looking at her.

One portrait in particular caught her attention. Just above a doorway was a peculiar painting of a thin gentleman in gold braid. He looked just like Muzz Elliott. He shared her short stumpy nose, wide eyes, and high forehead. It looked as if he wanted to smile but something within the painting forbade him from doing so. Saskia thought for a moment and then realized what it was. Painted discreetly in the background was the faint image of someone else. The man was being watched—and watched by someone he didn't like.

"Who is that?" Saskia pointed to the painting as Brummagem trudged ahead.

He turned slowly and rubbed his chin. "That is Muzz Elliott's grandfather. The less said about him the better," Brummagem scoffed.

"Looks worried," Saskia chirped.

"Wouldn't you if you had lost all your money and couldn't find it?"

"Lost it . . . how?" she asked.

"You ask a lot of questions for an orphan girl," Brummagem said sharply.

"I'm not an orphan," snapped Saskia. "My mother has just forgotten about us."

"Can't be much of a mother to forget all about you. Muzz Elliott will do a better job."

"So what did he lose?" Saskia pressed him again.

"Every penny he had to his name. Lord Trevellyn buried it but forgot where. Thought the Irish famine would come here, but it never did, and he was left without." Brummagem stopped for a moment and turned to look Saskia in the eyes. "You'll hear stories of him. Don't believe them."

Saskia wondered what he meant.

Brummagem took to the stairs and nodded for her to follow. Quickly they went up one flight, turned, then went up another and onto a landing. Through a door he led on along a narrow corridor with no windows. Turning sharply, he took her up a narrower flight of stone steps that had no carpet and no handrail. The ceiling arched above her head. Saskia was sure that the roof was getting closer and closer and that with every step the staircase grew narrower and narrower.

"Is it far?" she asked Brummagem, who trotted on ahead as if he were a mountain goat.

"Far?" he replied. "Of course it's far. Didn't you hear me say you're in the tower?"

After several more twists and two more staircases, they arrived at a set of fine wooden steps that spiraled around a stone column. On the outside of the staircase were windows that went upward and around the tower.

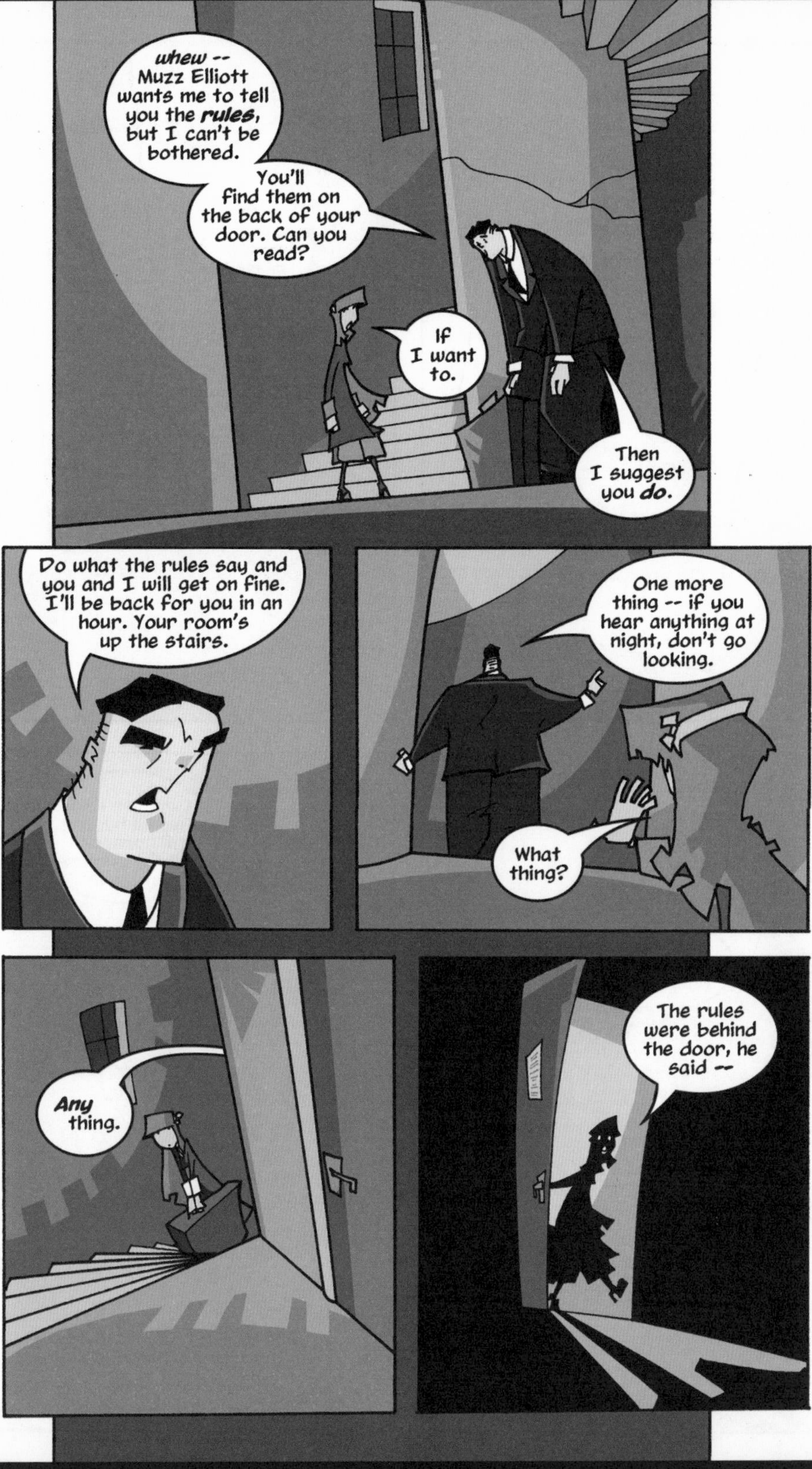

whew -- Muzz Elliott wants me to tell you the ***rules***, but I can't be bothered.
You'll find them on the back of your door. Can you read?
If I want to.
Then I suggest you ***do***.
Do what the rules say and you and I will get on fine. I'll be back for you in an hour. Your room's up the stairs.
One more thing -- if you hear anything at night, don't go looking.
What thing?
Any thing.
The rules were behind the door, he said --

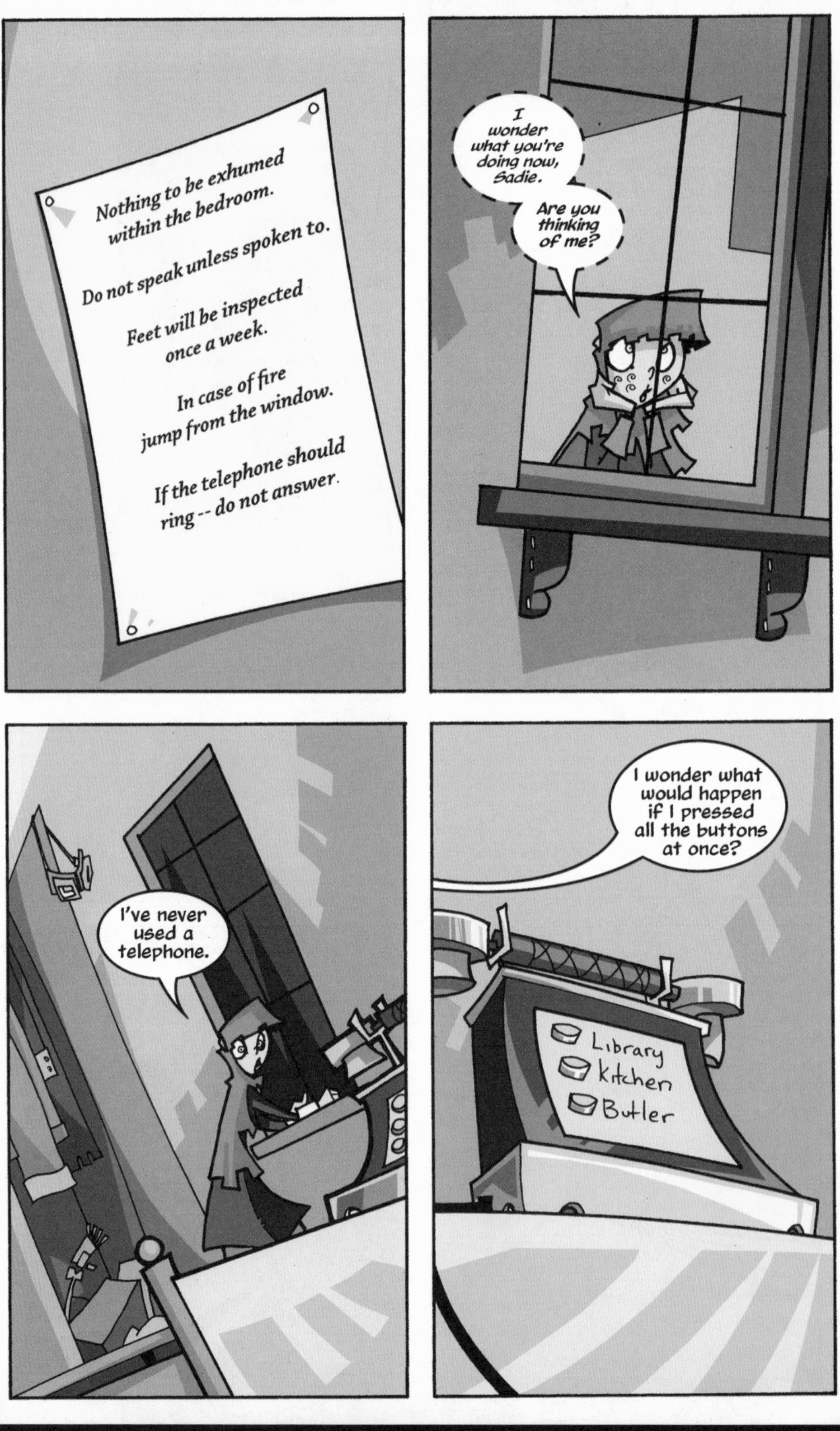
Nothing to be exhumed within the bedroom.
Do not speak unless spoken to.
Feet will be inspected once a week.
In case of fire jump from the window.
If the telephone should ring -- do not answer.
I wonder what you're doing now, Sadie.
Are you thinking of me?
I've never used a telephone.
I wonder what would happen if I pressed all the buttons at once?
Library
Kitchen
Butler

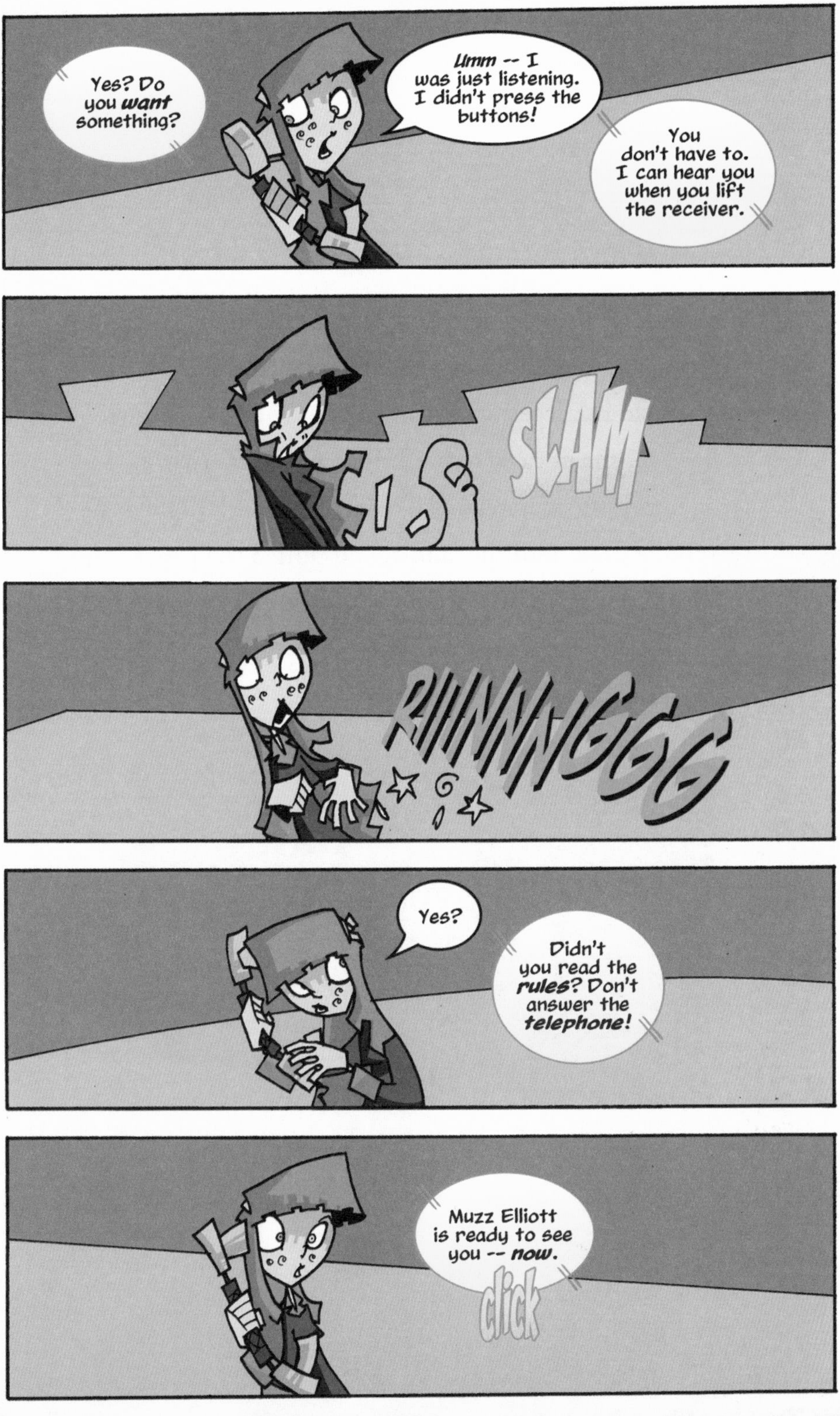
Yes? Do you *want* something?
Umm -- I was just listening. I didn't press the buttons!
You don't have to. I can hear you when you lift the receiver.
SLAM
RIINNGGG
Yes?
Didn't you read the *rules*? Don't answer the *telephone*!
Muzz Elliott is ready to see you -- *now*.
click

In the room, the large window frame rattled in the wind, and the carpet lifted from the boards with every draft. Saskia held the receiver and shivered. Out of the corner of her eye, she noticed a small sheet of paper sticking out from under the mattress. She reached down, dropped the telephone back onto the cradle, and pulled the paper from its hiding place. With both hands, she quickly opened the note and read the words.

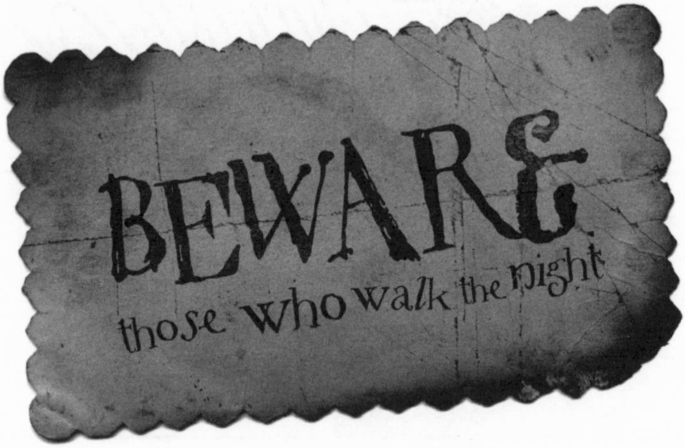
BEWARE
those who walk the night

Chapter Four
foul fiends

IT WAS NEARLY NOON when Erik finished in the kitchen, hung up his apron, and sneaked into the classroom. "Of course it's important to know what city is the capital of France!" Miss Rimmer screamed, answering a question that had not been asked. "You may want to go there one day and will need to know the way."

The class was silent. Erik could see Sadie at the front of the room, three feet from Miss Rimmer's tall desk. He could see that she was dreaming: Her eyes were glazed, and her mouth hung open. Miss Rimmer could see this too and prowled toward her.

"Dopple! What world do you live in?" Rimmer's whole body quivered as the rest of the class cowered with her words.

Sadie didn't reply—because Sadie didn't hear. Since Muzz Elliott had kidnapped Saskia, Sadie had decided she no longer wished to live in the world and had filled her ears with candle wax to keep out the noise. This dangerous activity had singed the hair on the side of her head and burned her ears, but Sadie didn't care. She sat in her own world listening to her own thoughts, oblivious to anything else.

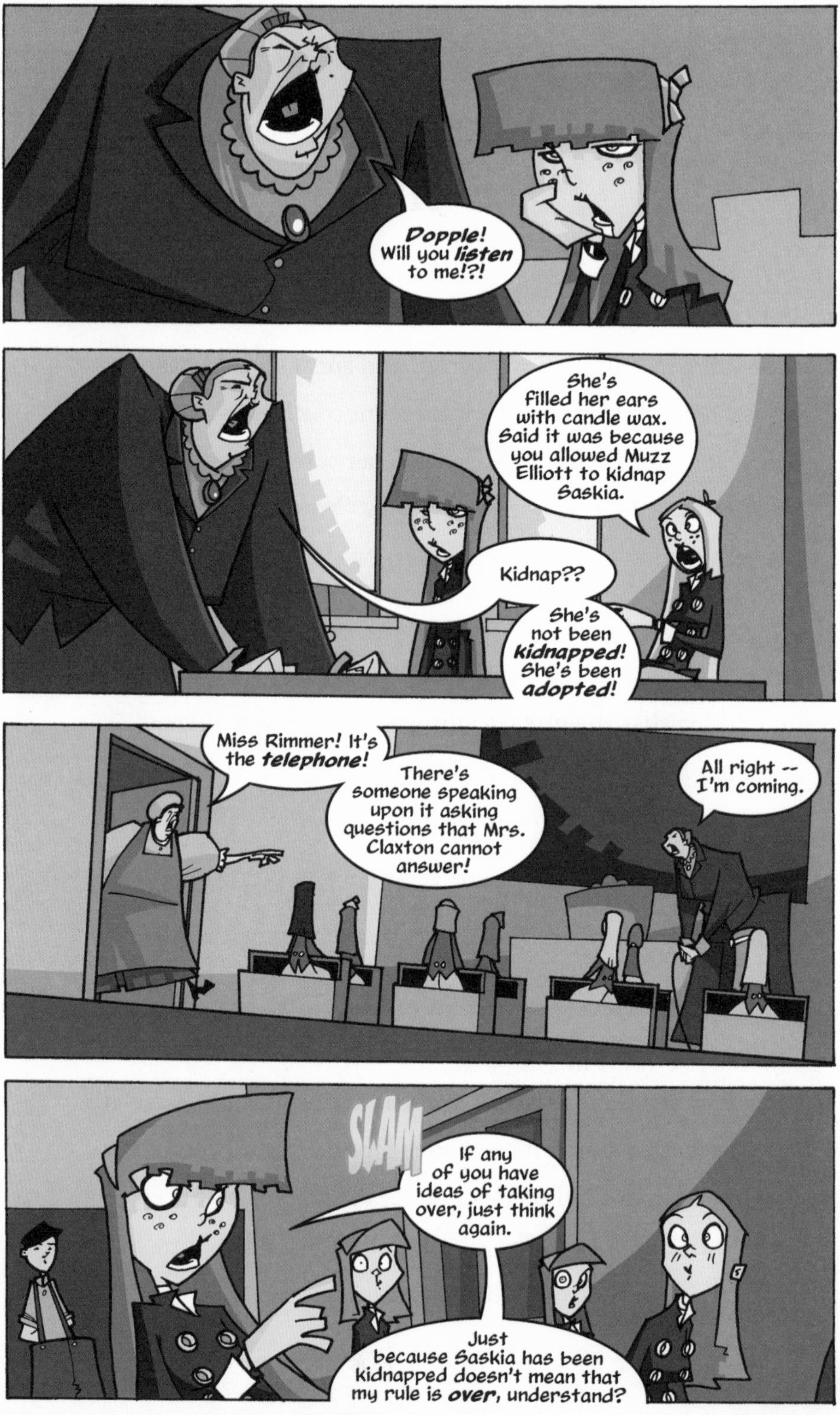
Dopple! Will you listen to me!?!
She's filled her ears with candle wax. Said it was because you allowed Muzz Elliott to kidnap Saskia.
Kidnap??
She's not been kidnapped! She's been adopted!
Miss Rimmer! It's the telephone!
There's someone speaking upon it asking questions that Mrs. Claxton cannot answer!
All right -- I'm coming.
SLAM
If any of you have ideas of taking over, just think again.
Just because Saskia has been kidnapped doesn't mean that my rule is over, understand?

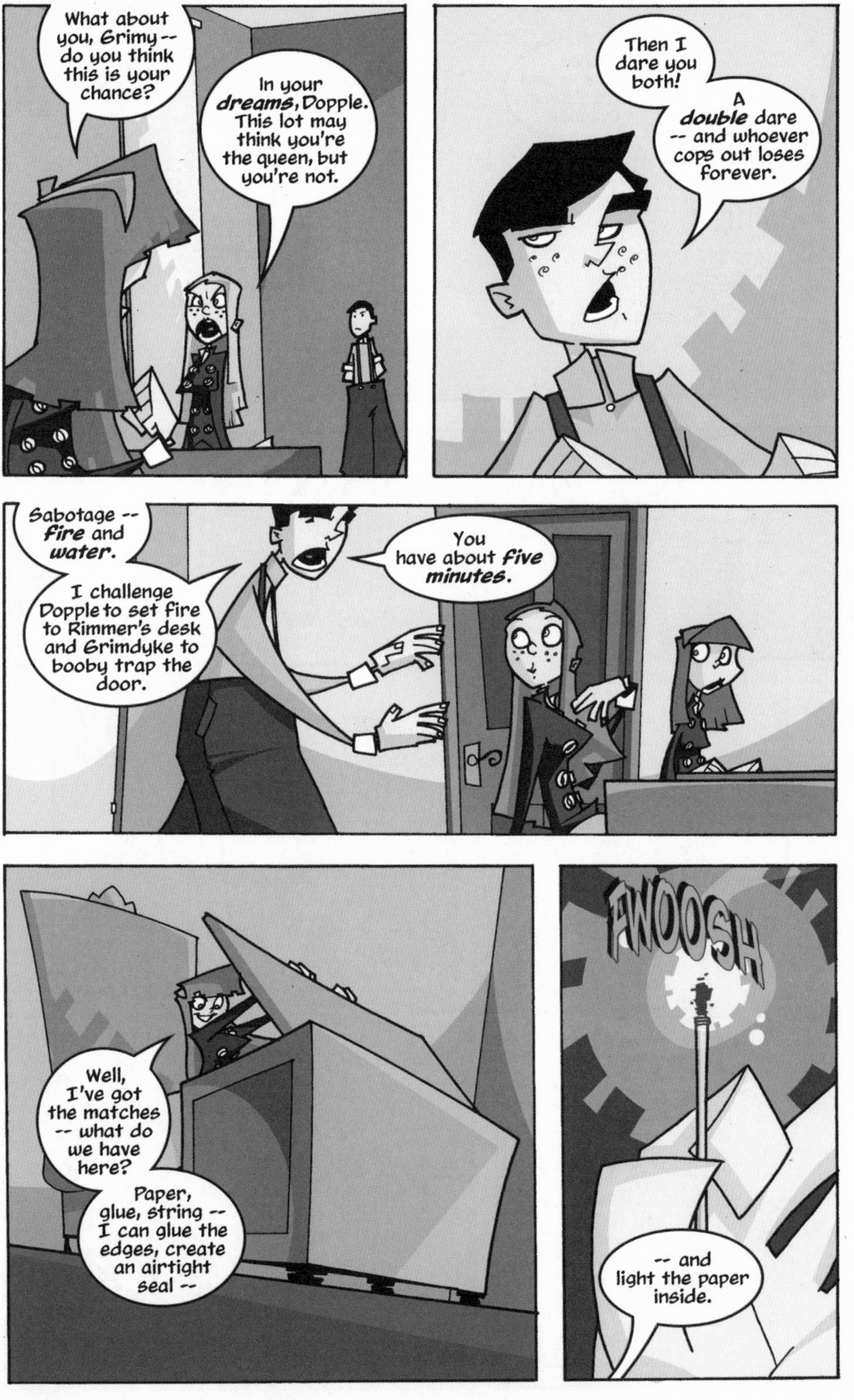
What about you, Grimy -- do you think this is your chance?
In your dreams, Dopple. This lot may think you're the queen, but you're not.
Then I dare you both!
A double dare -- and whoever cops out loses forever.
Sabotage -- fire and water.
I challenge Dopple to set fire to Rimmer's desk and Grimdyke to booby trap the door.
You have about five minutes.
Well, I've got the matches -- what do we have here?
Paper, glue, string -- I can glue the edges, create an airtight seal --
FWOOSH
-- and light the paper inside.

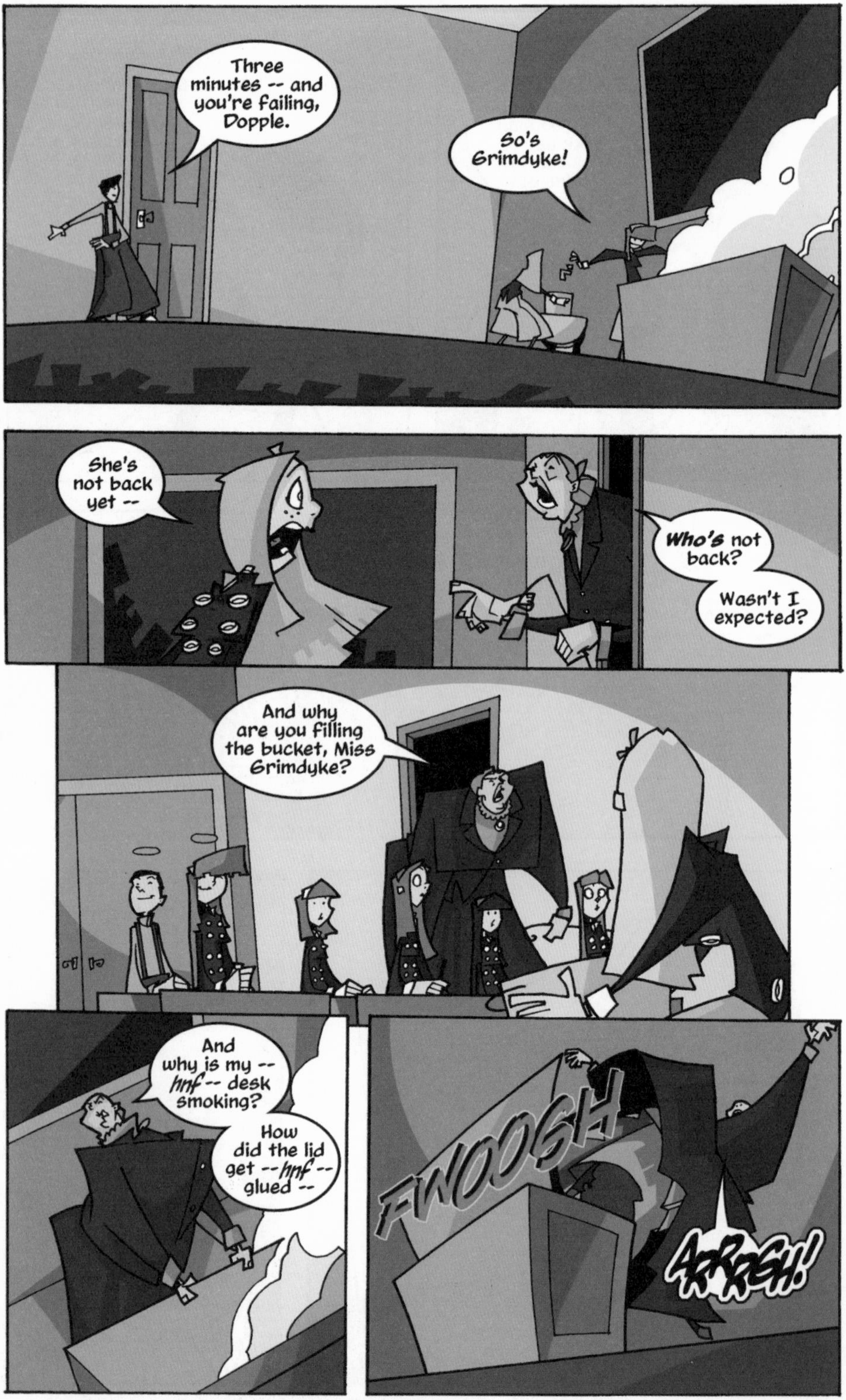
Three minutes -- and you're failing, Dopple.
So's Grimdyke!
She's not back yet --
Who's not back?
Wasn't I expected?
And why are you filling the bucket, Miss Grimdyke?
And why is my -- *hnf* -- desk smoking?
How did the lid get -- *hnf* -- glued --
FWOOSH
ARRRGH!

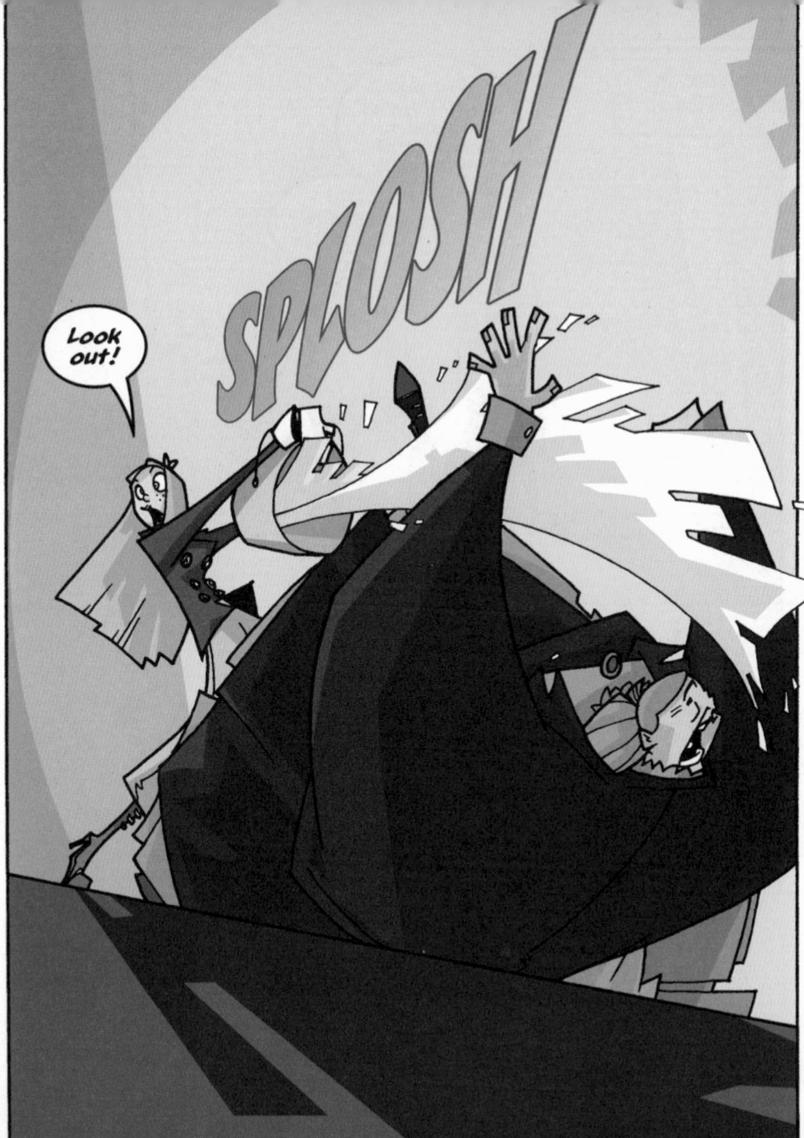
Look out!
SPLOSH

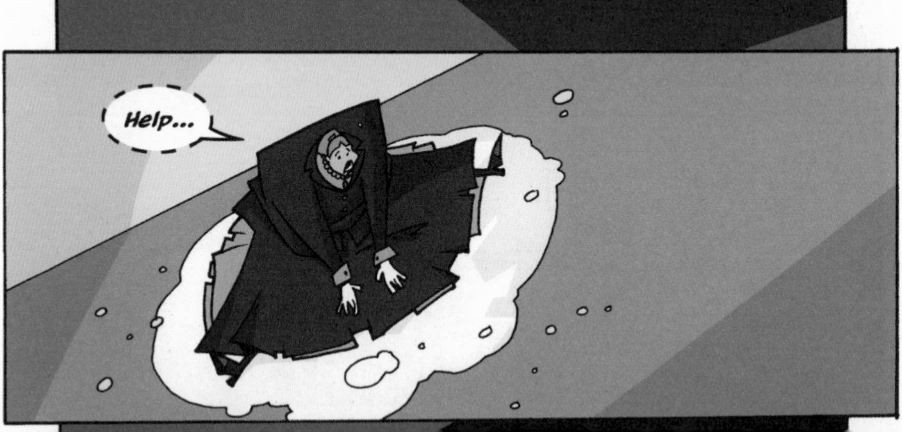
Help...

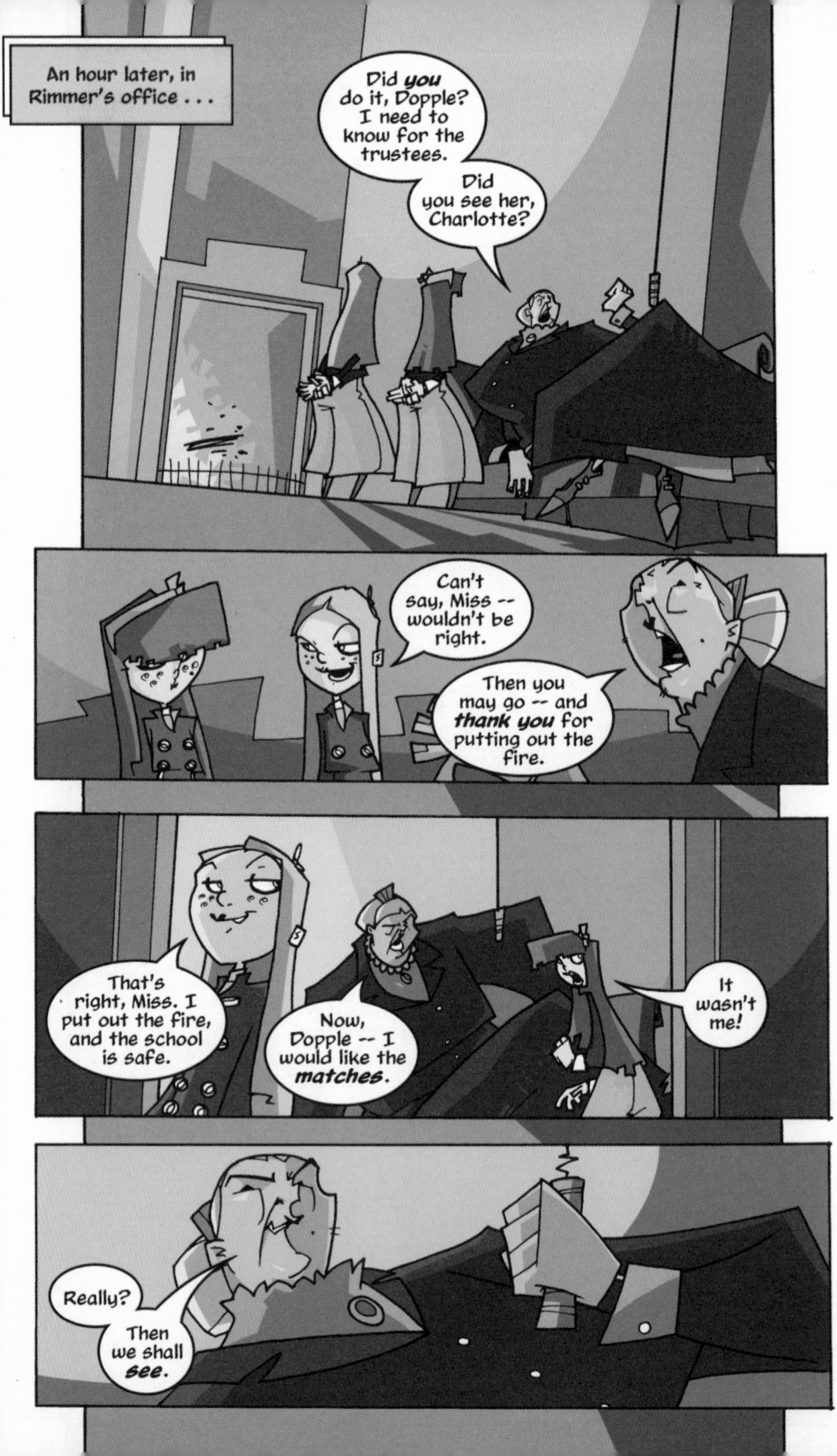
An hour later, in Rimmer's office . . .
Did *you* do it, Dopple? I need to know for the trustees.
Did you see her, Charlotte?
Can't say, Miss -- wouldn't be right.
Then you may go -- and ***thank you*** for putting out the fire.
That's right, Miss. I put out the fire, and the school is safe.
Now, Dopple -- I would like the ***matches***.
It wasn't me!
Really?
Then we shall ***see***.

Miss Rimmer pulled a long cord that dangled above the couch. In two seconds an old drying rack had descended from the ceiling. Its rough wooden bars were held in place by two iron molds at each end. In the middle of the rack was a set of leather straps. Miss Rimmer smiled, curling up the sides of her face and wrinkling the skin around her eyes until pieces of cracked makeup fell off.

"Don't make me do this, Dopple. Just give me the matches," Rimmer said quietly as she stalked toward Sadie.

Darcy appeared from under the velvet chaise longue and began to growl. The dog snarled her teeth and frothed at the mouth. Miss Rimmer grabbed Sadie and before she could utter a sound strapped her to the drying rack and once again pulled the cord. Sadie rose from the ground and dangled in the air as Darcy snapped at her heels.

Miss Rimmer began to search the pockets of Sadie's pants as she hung helplessly.

"Would be easier if you told the truth," Rimmer said, fumbling in the pockets.

"Would be easier if you let me go!" Sadie shouted back. Darcy leaped into the air, caught the heel of Sadie's boot, and hung on.

"You know that I have to keep you until you're sixteen and not a day longer. I would love to throw you out on the street, but I can't, not now," Miss Rimmer said. She rummaged further and deeper into Sadie's pockets. "Just tell me. . . . Did you start the fire?"

The matches rustled in the secret pocket where they had for so long avoided detection in all Miss Rimmer's searches.

"Aha!" Miss Rimmer shouted as if she had struck gold. "A secret pocket. I should have known. All the time you kept them in a secret pocket. Very clever. Now you'll have to admit it." Miss Rimmer strode to the door and called out, "Mrs. Claxton!" In a moment, the teacher appeared. She had a pointed face and was, as usual, covered from head to foot in cat hair—though the Dopples had never understood why, as Mrs. Claxton didn't own a cat.

"Mrs. Claxton, get Mr. Martinet so he can be a witness."

These were words that Sadie did not want
to hear. Miss Rimmer was vile, but Mr. Martinet
was a monster. In the room next door she heard
Mrs. Claxton frantically dialing the telephone and
waiting for a reply. Sadie hung from the drying rack four
feet from the floor, the leather straps digging into her wrists
and Darcy swinging from her heel as if the dog would never
let go. Darcy twisted and turned and snarled. Sadie kicked her
heels, but the dog was stuck fast, her teeth embedded in the
heel of Sadie's boot so she couldn't escape.

Mrs. Claxton began to shout into the telephone in her
shrill voice. It was not a device she fully understood, and
she always made calls standing up, holding the telephone at
arm's length, and shouting as loudly as she could. This was
in the belief that she had to throw her voice the distance
of the person she was calling. She had once made a call to
Edinburgh by placing the telephone inside the megaphone
used by Miss Rimmer for sports day and screaming as
loudly as her shrill voice would allow.

"Mr. Martinet! Miss Rimmer needs you . . . in the office . . . NOW!"

. . . she screeched, her voice rattling the windows. This in itself was an incredible feat, as Mrs. Claxton was a tiny woman.

Mr. Martinet appeared before Mrs. Claxton had time to put down the telephone. He barged into Miss Rimmer's office without even a single knock. He was tall and exceedingly thin and wore clothes that looked as if they belonged to a shorter and fatter man. His pants were severely belted around the waist and only just touched the tops of boots that were as pointed as his nose.

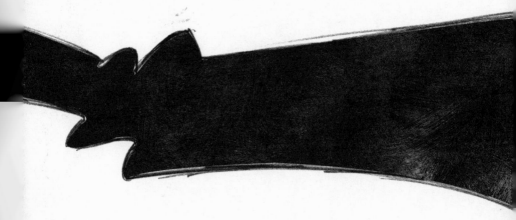

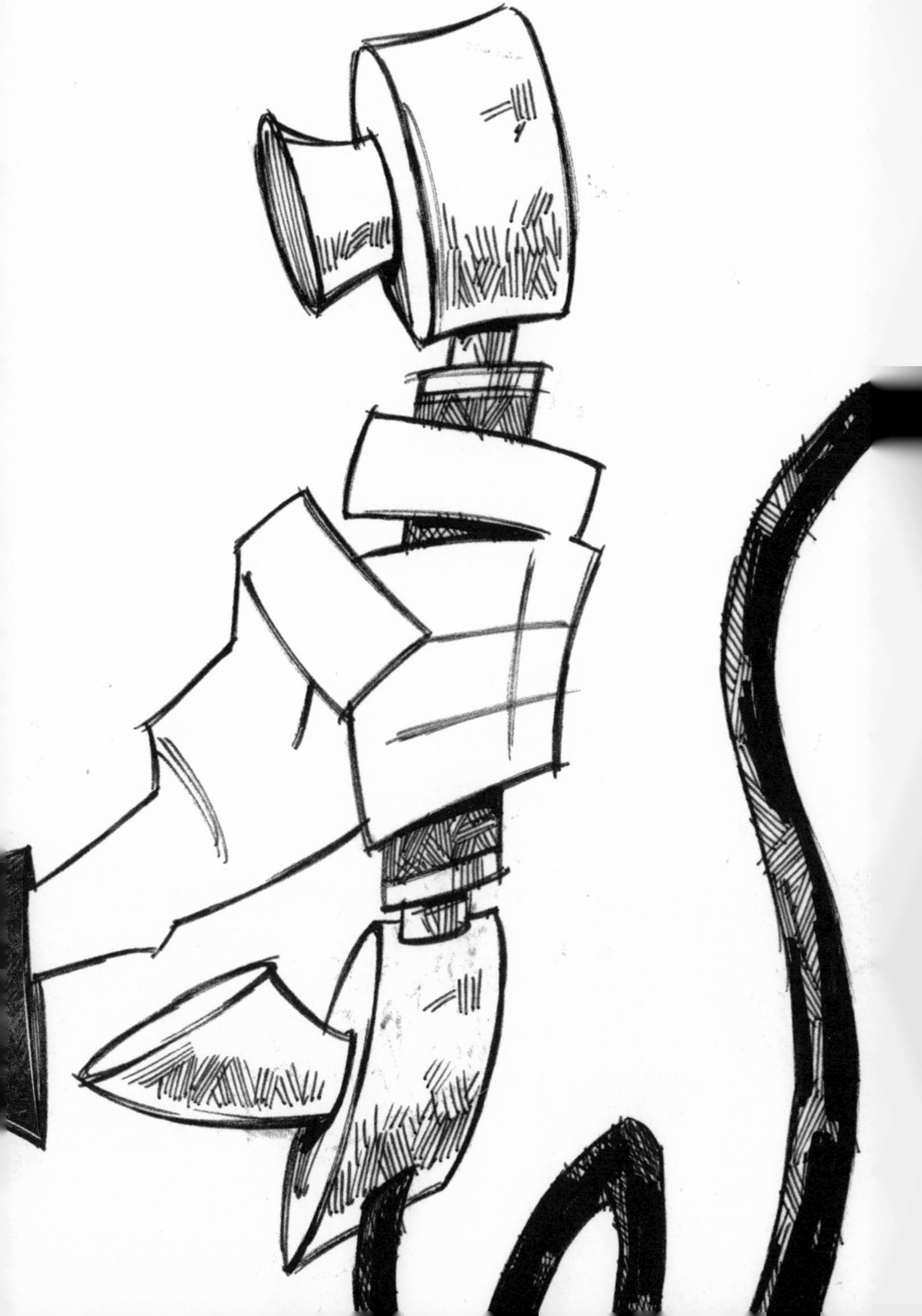

He looked at Miss Rimmer with one eye and Sadie with the other, something only Mr. Martinet was able to do. His peculiar birdlike impediment gave him the ability to gaze at two people at the same time, even if they were several feet apart. It also gave him the appearance of a large vulture in checked pants.

"Dwopple," he said with a look of joy on his thin face and a glint in his beady eye, "what have you been doing?"

"Arson, explosions, murder," Miss Rimmer replied before Sadie could speak. "She set fire to my desk, and now I have the evidence, Mr. Martinet."

Miss Rimmer rooted in the secret pocket and pulled out the matches as if she were performing a conjuring trick.

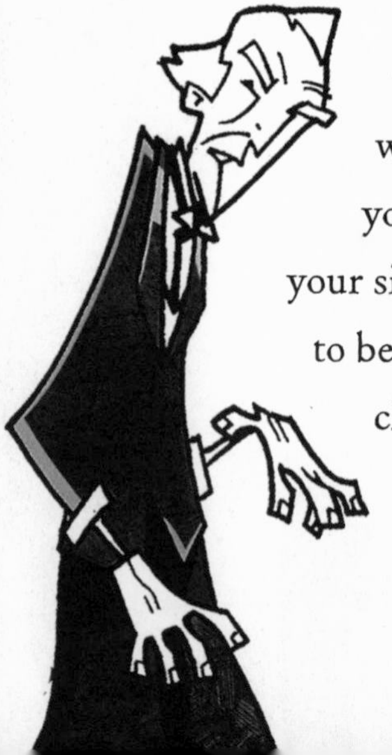

"Matches!" Martinet gasped in a triumphant voice as he picked his nose with one hand. "How I will enjoy seeing you disciplined, Miss Dwopple. Now that your sister is no longer with us, I expect you to be bwoken within the week and of new chawacter by next Fwiday." Martinet paused momentarily as he sucked in a gallon of breath.

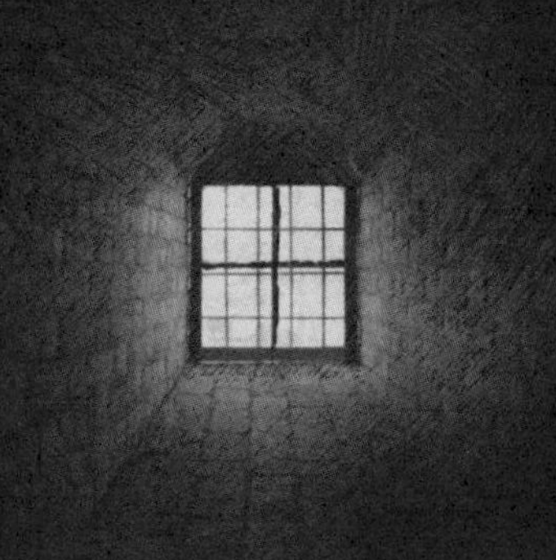

"for this
there is only
one
punishment:

my special woom. . . ."

Chapter Five

The Forbidden Portrait

THE DOOR TO THE LIBRARY was firmly shut. Brummagem, dressed in a starched high collar and an evening suit with long tails, stood to one side. He tried to smile, his eyes creasing into folds of skin. Saskia looked up. The doorway touched the high ceiling, and staring down at her from the four corners of the hallway were the plaster faces of small children. It was as if they were embedded in the chalk and behind each white mask was a real face, stuffed under the floorboards above and imprisoned forever. They all smiled plaster smiles and looked back at her through milky white eyes.

RIIINNNGGG RIIINNNGGG

The sudden, sharp ring of a bell echoed down the long, dark corridor and up the equally dark stairs. Without a word, Brummagem reached out a white-gloved hand, turned the brass handle, and opened the door. Then with a sudden jolt, he pushed Saskia in the back so sharply that she shot forward, tripped over the carpet, and twisted her ankle.

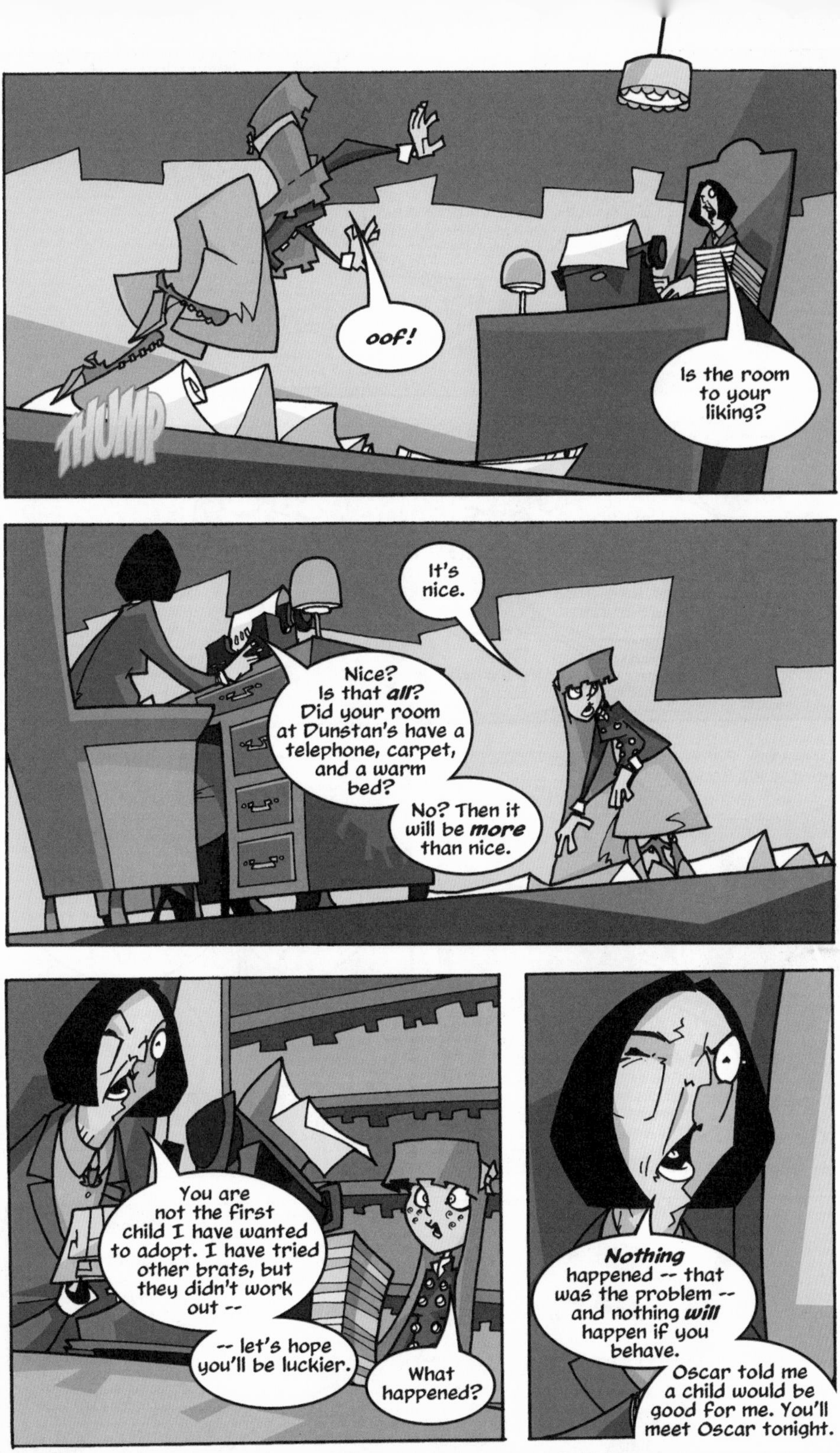
oof!
THUMP
Is the room to your liking?
It's nice.
Nice? Is that all? Did your room at Dunstan's have a telephone, carpet, and a warm bed?
No? Then it will be more than nice.
You are not the first child I have wanted to adopt. I have tried other brats, but they didn't work out --
-- let's hope you'll be luckier.
What happened?
Nothing happened -- that was the problem -- and nothing will happen if you behave.
Oscar told me a child would be good for me. You'll meet Oscar tonight.

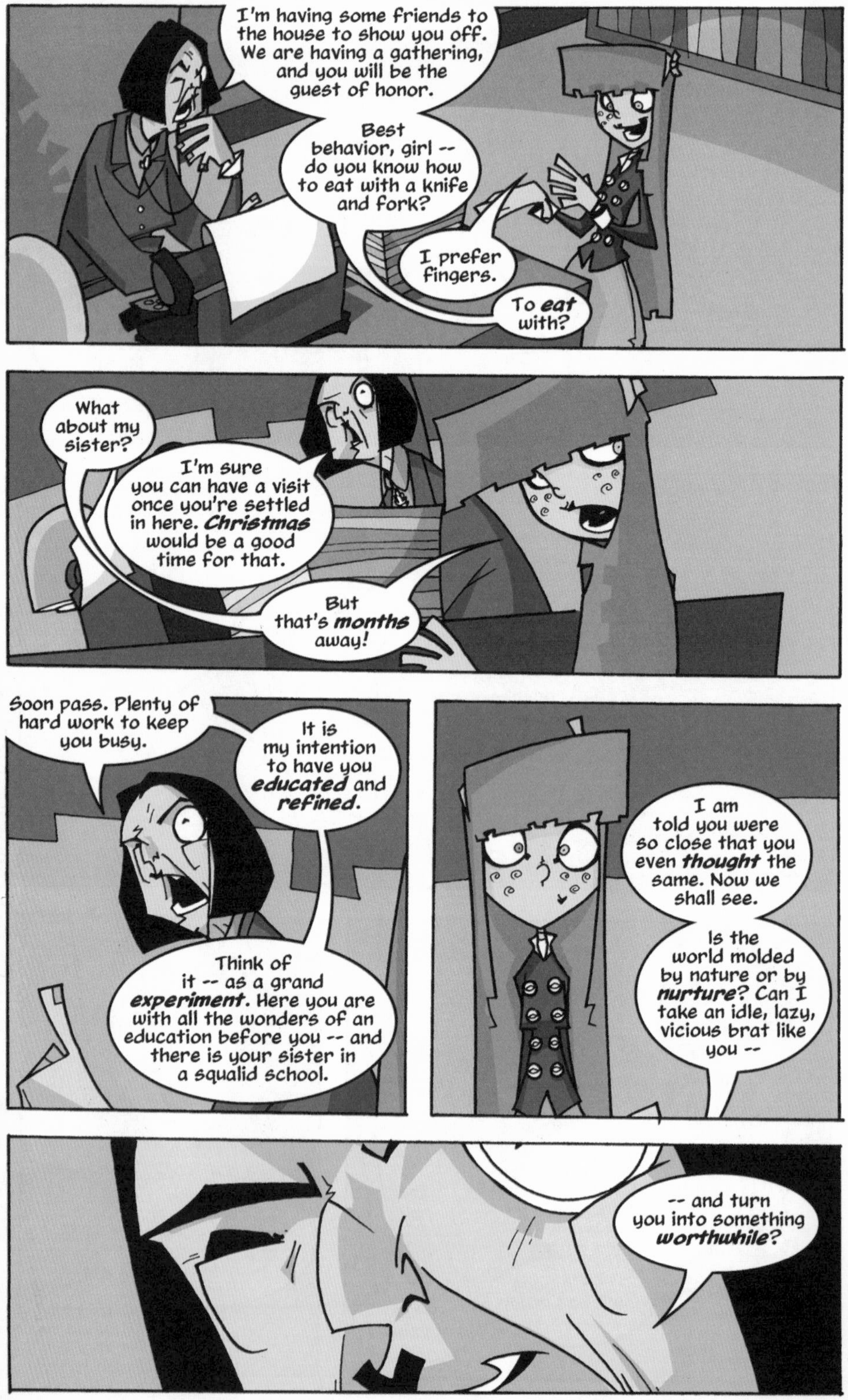
I'm having some friends to the house to show you off. We are having a gathering, and you will be the guest of honor.
Best behavior, girl -- do you know how to eat with a knife and fork?
I prefer fingers.
To *eat* with?
What about my sister?
I'm sure you can have a visit once you're settled in here. *Christmas* would be a good time for that.
But that's *months* away!
Soon pass. Plenty of hard work to keep you busy.
It is my intention to have you *educated* and *refined*.
Think of it -- as a grand *experiment*. Here you are with all the wonders of an education before you -- and there is your sister in a squalid school.
I am told you were so close that you even *thought* the same. Now we shall see.
Is the world molded by nature or by *nurture*? Can I take an idle, lazy, vicious brat like you --
-- and turn you into something *worthwhile*?

Muzz Elliott peered at Saskia, her left eye magnified to twice its normal size by the monocle, her right eye reduced to a narrow slit. "Believe me," she continued, "you will thank me for what I have done. In ten years' time, when your sister is begging on Southampton Row, you will be driving past in the most sumptuous Jaguar motorcar and will think nothing of throwing a coin to the poor beggar in the gutter. Then, my child, I will know that I was right. That is why you are here."

"I thought you wanted a daughter," Saskia said, puzzled.

"I do," Muzz Elliott replied.

"Well, I already have a mother," Saskia retorted. "She is kind . . . if a little forgetful."

"Your mother left you at the school so she could pursue her own ends. She thought nothing of you. If that is kindness, then the whole world is a happy place."

"She smiled and sang to us," Saskia said.

"You have a maid who will sing whatever you want and a tutor who will mop your fevered brow when you are sick."

"But when will *you* smile?"

"When I am taken by a happy notion, and thankfully that does not occur too often. Love, kindness, and joy are like flowers of the field, here today and gone tomorrow. I am thankful that I am in control of my emotions and am not controlled by them. If you want me to smile, then do what I say when I say it, and be assured that though you may not often see my face crack, in my heart I will be pleased."

Muzz Elliott looked down and resumed tapping the keys on her typewriter, beating out a senseless tune and snorting occasionally through her nose. Saskia sensed that the conversation was over. She stood uncertainly in front of the desk and looked about the room. Clinging to every wall from floor to ceiling were shelves containing hundreds of books. Every book was bound in crusty green leather, inlaid with gold writing. The volumes were squeezed together and, from the dust that covered each one, looked as if they had never been read.

Saskia glanced back at Muzz Elliott, who was now typing faster and faster. Every now and then she would talk to herself; her fingers would stop and then, as her mind found a wisp of inspiration, would charge on again, dancing upon the keys. Saskia continued to wait, eyeing everything about her. Set upon the desk before her was a stone pot in the shape of a human skull. The top of the head was gone, and the eye socket was being used as a resting place for various chewed pencils, a gold ink pen, and a dangerously sharp letter opener.

To one side of the desk was a fireplace that looked like the doorway of a fine building. Above the fireplace was the only piece of wall that was not covered in books. A large brass shield and two crossed swords hung on the wall. Above them was the stuffed rear of a donkey, mounted on a wooden shield. Its tail dangled limply down between two brown, dusty legs. Underneath, Saskia could see a large brass plaque, and upon it were written the words AFRICAN WILD DONKEY—SHOT WITH A HOWITZER BY LORD TREVELLYN, 1886.

To one side of the stuffed donkey was a portrait of the scene. There, painted in oil, was the regal lord standing with his foot upon what was left of the cannon-blasted beast. Saskia pictured the mad colonialist shooting the calm, grazing animal and blowing it to pieces. All that was left was the posterior, which was now stuffed and mounted as a memento of his expedition.

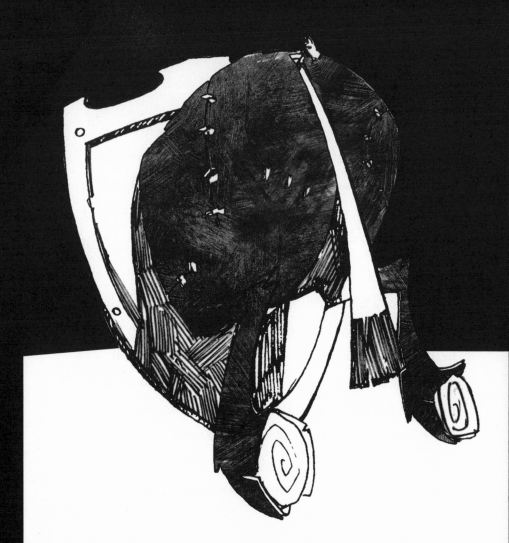

Beneath the donkey, by the side of the fireplace, was a tall picture stand covered by a thick cloth. Poking from underneath the cloth was the side of a frame. Its ornate edges were coated in gilt that had flaked away in several places.

Muzz Elliott glanced up from her typing and saw Saskia staring at the cloth-covered picture.

"Never look at the picture. Not if you want to remain in this house or see your sister again. Look beneath that cover, and I will have you sent to the workhouse in Dublin, and from such a place you will never escape."

"What is the painting of?" Saskia asked without thinking.

"Never you mind," Muzz Elliott replied as she pulled a sheet of paper from the typewriter, scrunched it into a ball, and threw it into the fire. "Brummagem, take my girl back to her room. She needs to be told how to dress and eat. Can't have her chewing her fingers in front of Mr. Crowley. And make sure she knows the customs. I don't want her squawking and crying when Oscar makes his presence known."

Brummagem didn't speak. He nodded to Saskia to follow him from the room. Once outside, he closed the great doors and gave them a final push with his backside.

"Go straight to your room," Brummagem said softly, as if he wanted no one else to hear.

Saskia turned to reply, but he was gone. There were no footsteps in the corridor or slamming of doors. All was deathly still. Brummagem had vanished. He was clearly not going to give her any sort of instructions. Saskia felt that she was completely alone. She took seven steps up the long flight toward the third landing and then stopped.

Suddenly and uncontrollably, in her mind she could see Sadie being dragged through the corridors of the school. It was as if she were there, as if it were happening to Saskia herself. She could feel the hands of Mr. Martinet gripping her arms and pulling her along. Saskia could hear Sadie calling her name and could see the villainous grin on Mr. Martinet's face. As soon as the vision had started it was gone.

A disembodied voice came from somewhere behind Saskia.

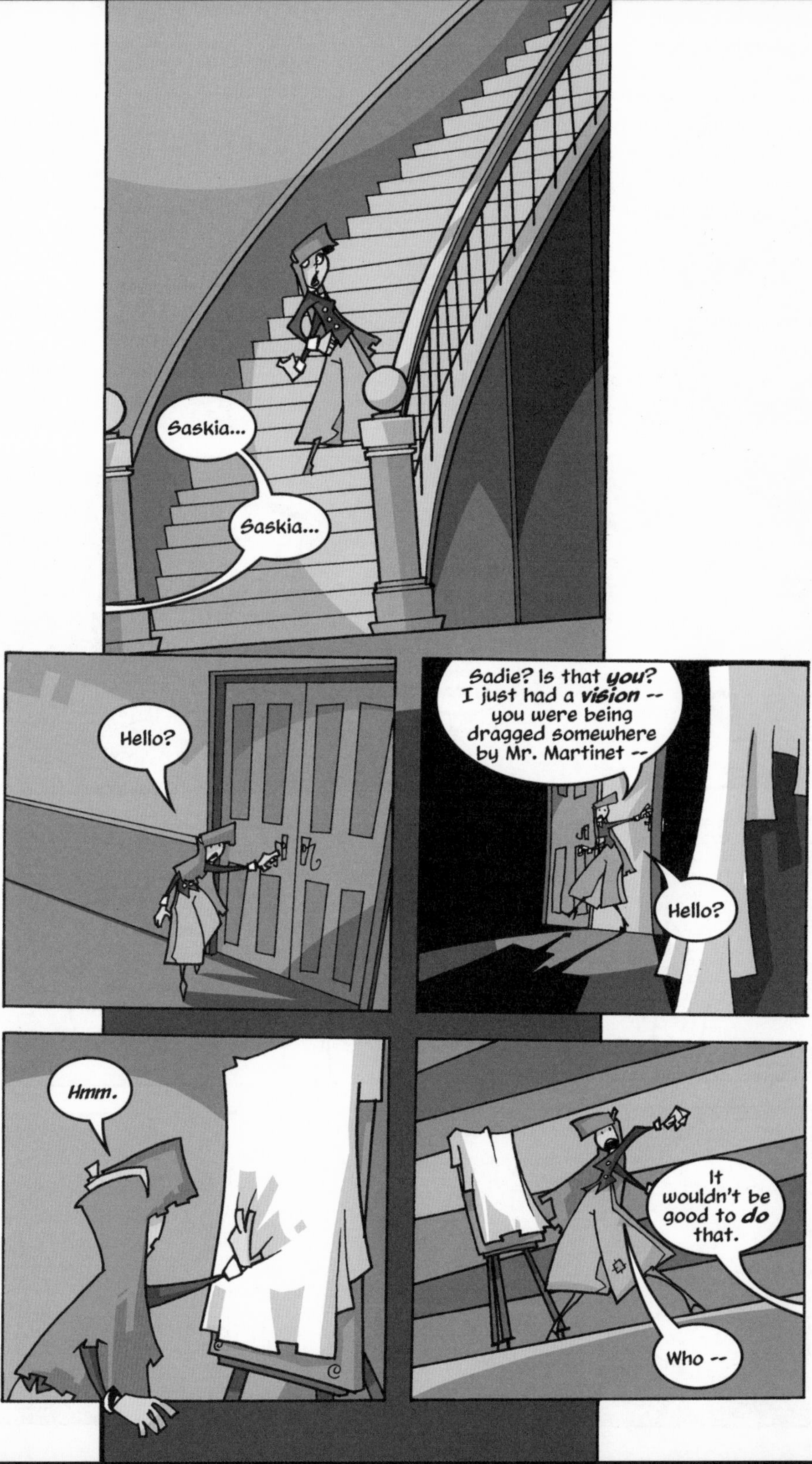
Saskia...
Saskia...
Hello?
Sadie? Is that *you*? I just had a *vision* -- you were being dragged somewhere by Mr. Martinet --
Hello?
Hmm.
It wouldn't be good to *do* that.
Who --

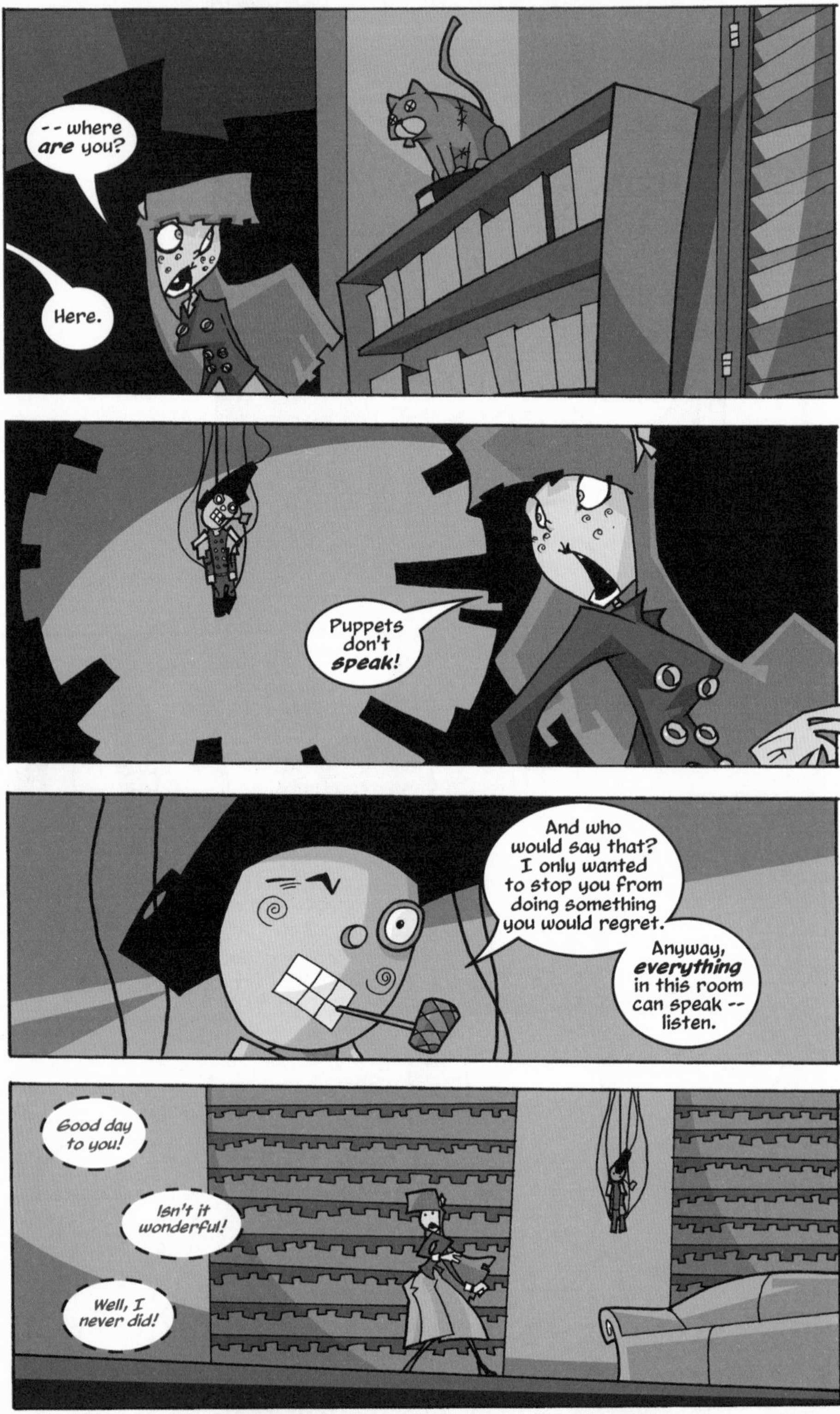
-- where *are* you?
Here.
Puppets don't *speak*!
And who would say that? I only wanted to stop you from doing something you would regret.
Anyway, *everything* in this room can speak -- listen.
Good day to you!
Isn't it wonderful!
Well, I never did!

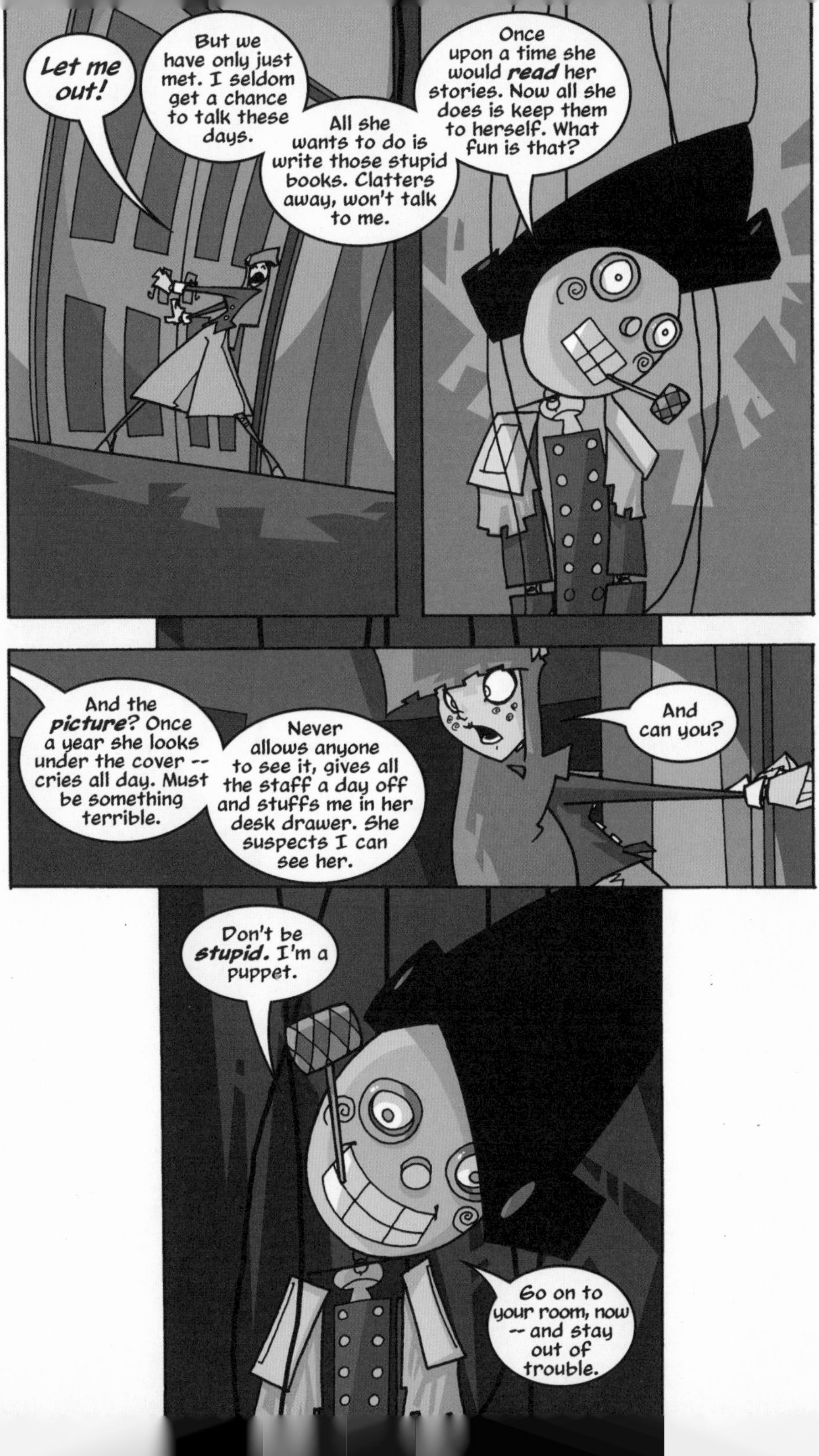

Let me out!
But we have only just met. I seldom get a chance to talk these days.
All she wants to do is write those stupid books. Clatters away, won't talk to me.
Once upon a time she would *read* her stories. Now all she does is keep them to herself. What fun is that?
And the *picture*? Once a year she looks under the cover -- cries all day. Must be something terrible.
Never allows anyone to see it, gives all the staff a day off and stuffs me in her desk drawer. She suspects I can see her.
And can you?
Don't be *stupid*. I'm a puppet.
Go on to your room, now -- and stay out of trouble.

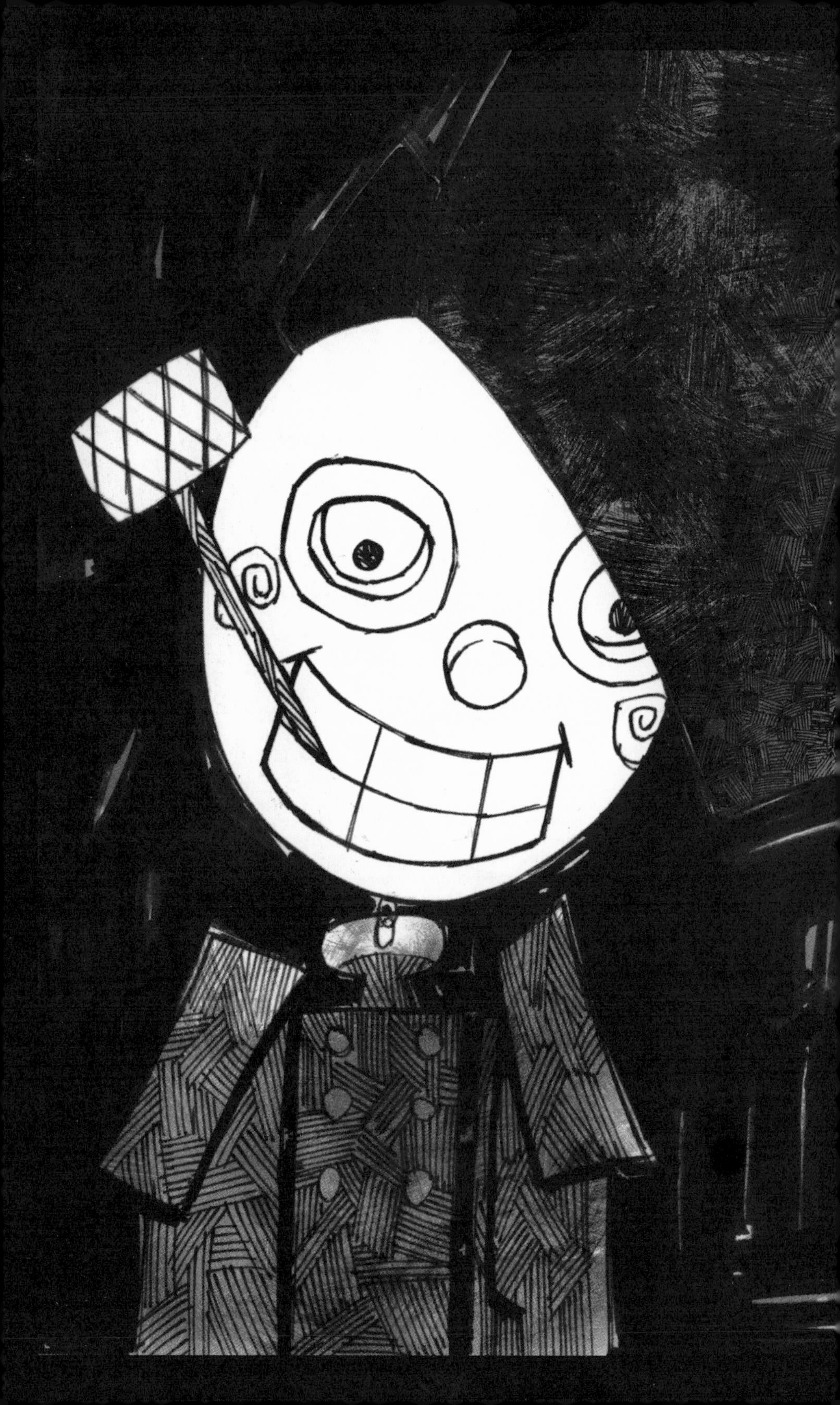

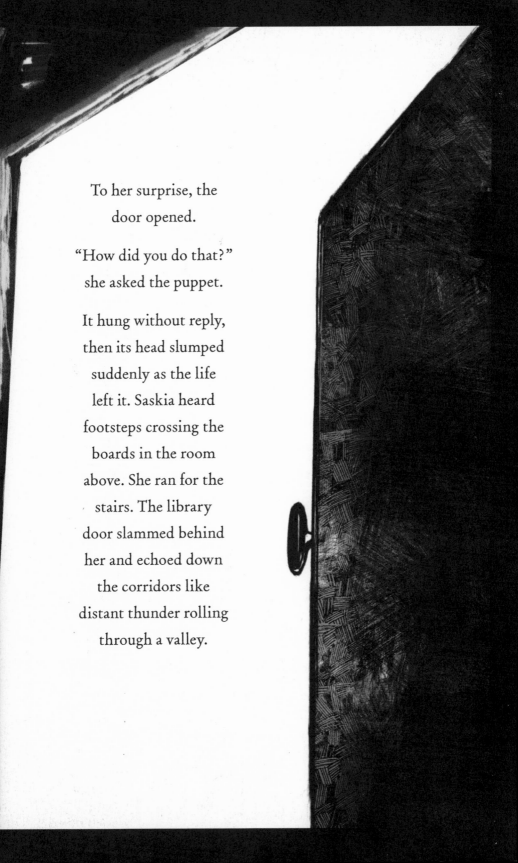

To her surprise, the
door opened.

"How did you do that?"
she asked the puppet.

It hung without reply,
then its head slumped
suddenly as the life
left it. Saskia heard
footsteps crossing the
boards in the room
above. She ran for the
stairs. The library
door slammed behind
her and echoed down
the corridors like
distant thunder rolling
through a valley.

She leaped the steps two at a time and bolted along the corridors. Across the landing, down the passageway, and up the spiral stairs, faster and faster as the footsteps pounded closer. Saskia looked behind but could see no one.

She raced on, sure she was being chased by something very noisy but completely invisible. Eventually, out of breath, she reached the door of her room and bounded inside. Saskia dived onto the bed in a crumpled, panting heap and sighed.

"What took you so long?" said a voice. Saskia looked up. In the large leather chair by the fireplace was a neat middle-aged woman. Her hair was tied back, and her mouth was tinted with a hint of pink lipstick. She was exceedingly thin, with large eyes and a pointed chin, and to Saskia she looked incredibly important.

"Who are you?" Saskia asked, sitting up.

"Madame Raphael," the woman replied. "I have lived here a long time and seen other girls like you."

"A long time?" Saskia asked as she noticed a strange glow that seemed to come from the woman's skin.

"Precisely," Madame Raphael replied with a grin.

Chapter Six

The Tower Room

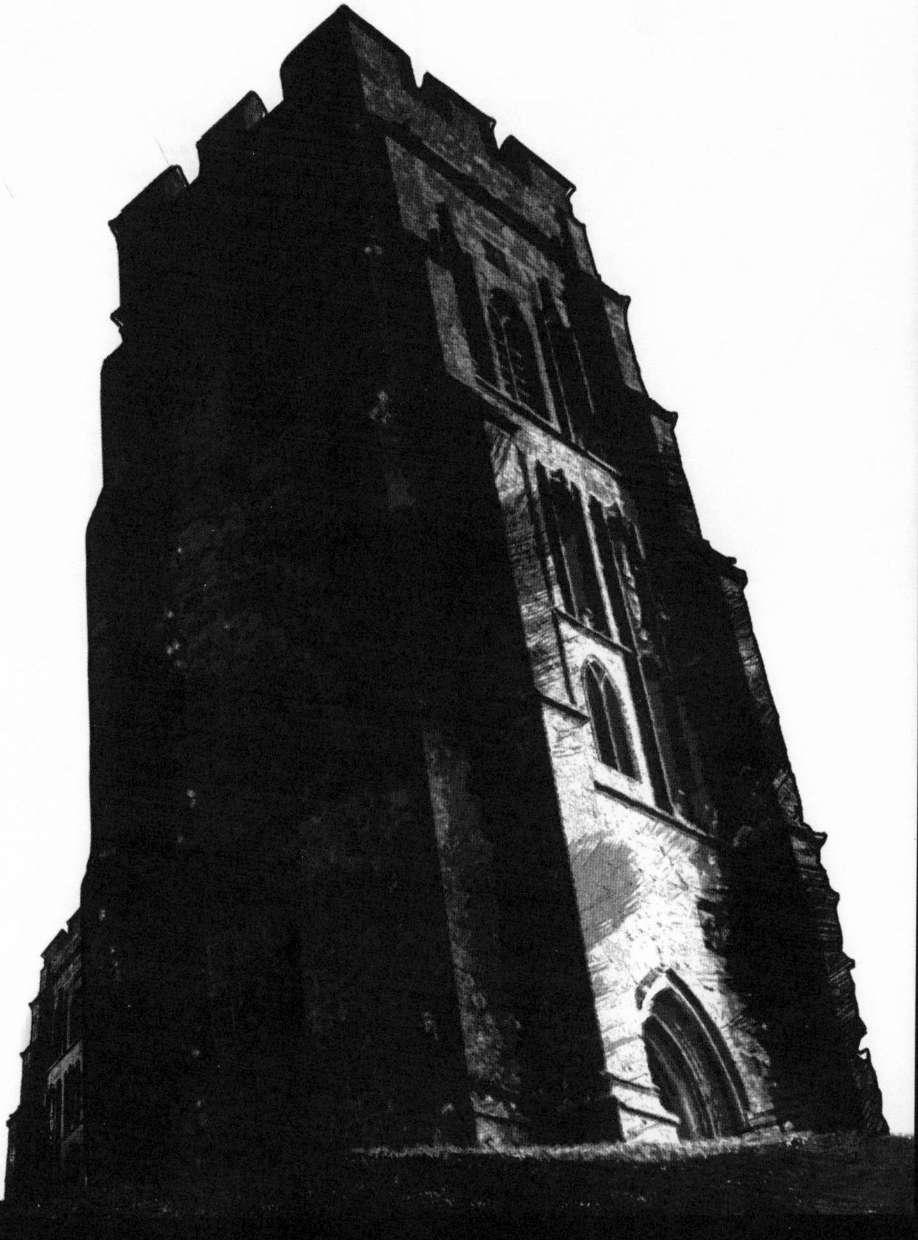

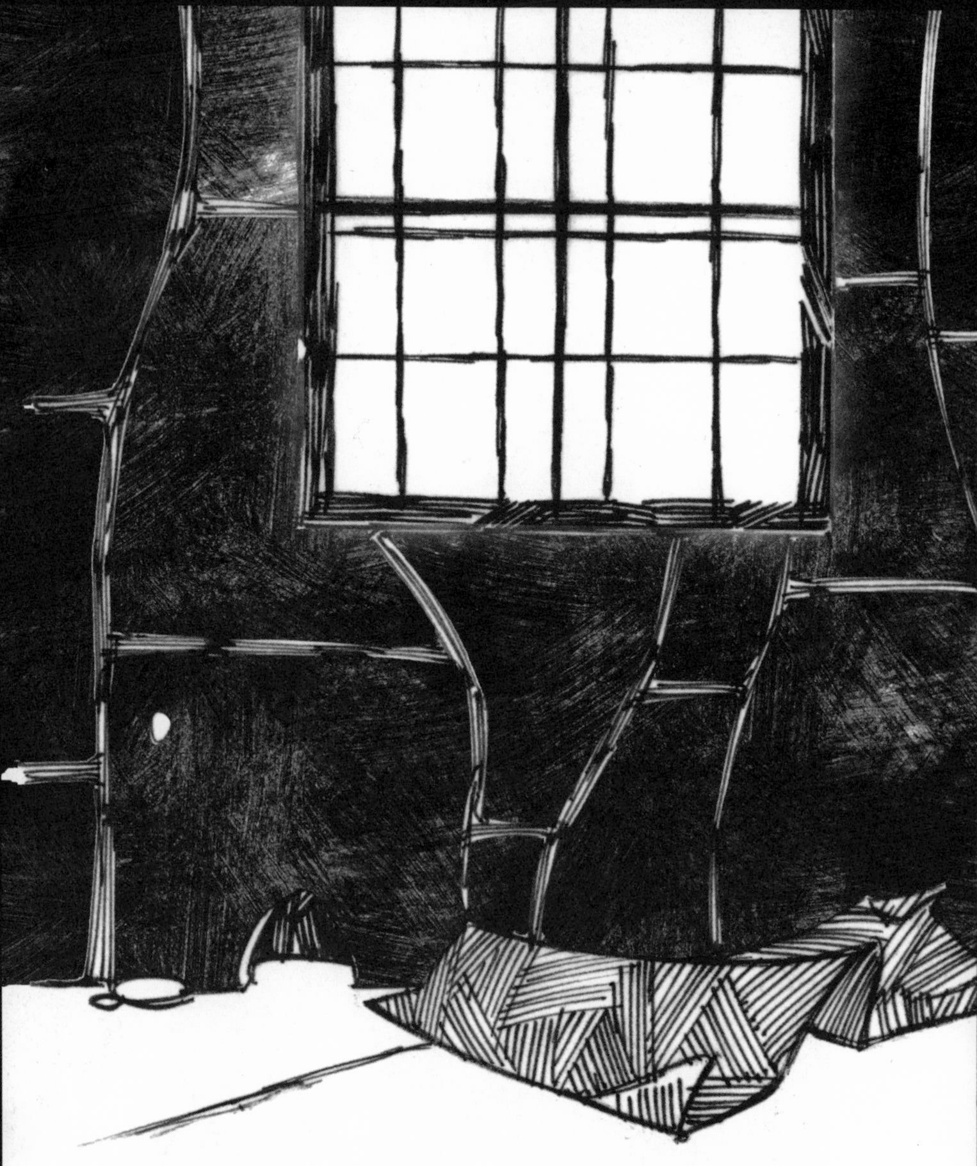

MR. MARTINET LAUGHED as he dragged Sadie along the corridors and up the dark stairs of the school. He stood at the door of the high tower room that overlooked the heath and pushed her inside.

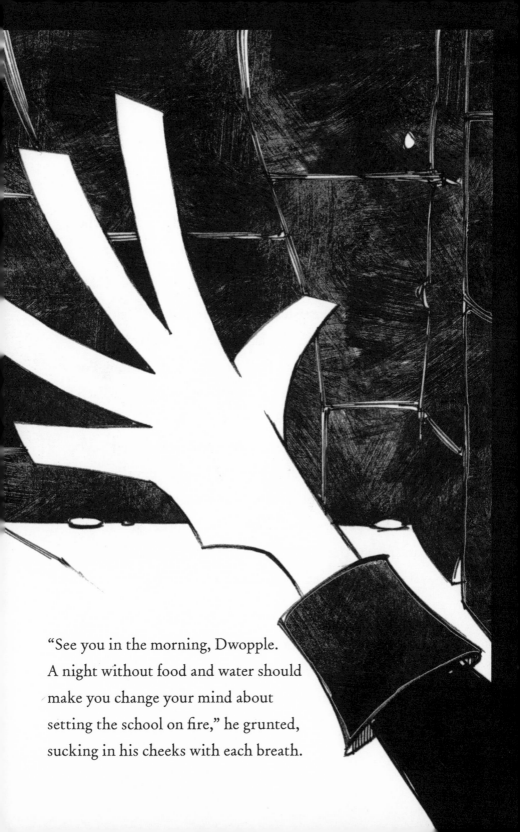

"See you in the morning, Dwopple. A night without food and water should make you change your mind about setting the school on fire," he grunted, sucking in his cheeks with each breath.

Sadie was left alone, the door locked and bolted. The wind whistled through the gaps of the windows and rattled each pane of glass, sounding ready to smash them into a million pieces. Far below she heard the bell ring for lunch.

She thought of her sister and tried to picture Saskia in her mind. All was blank. She scrunched up her eyes, wanting to envision Saskia's face, but she could see nothing. For all of their lives they had shared thoughts, known each other's emotions, and even felt each other's pains. Once Sadie had swallowed a large wasp, and it had been Saskia who had exploded in bumps and blisters from the sting. There had been another time just weeks before when Saskia had cut her hand. Observers considered it more than strange that Sadie had bled from the same place, as if the girls shared the wound.

But now, in the high tower, Sadie felt like an only child, and what was more, she feared that far below, Charlotte Grimdyke would be taking over her kingdom with Erik Morrissey Ganger at her side. . . .

From the darkening sky, Sadie knew that the afternoon would soon be at an end. A cold sun hid behind the faraway trees and cast long shadows across the heath. Sadie watched the lights gradually turn on in the distant town to the south.

Dark clouds rolled over a darker sky, and the chill of night crept up the windowpanes and into the room. There was no lamp, no fire, and the warmth of only a single, furry blanket that smelled like a dead horse.

Sadie sat by the door, shivering beneath the blanket. It was then that she heard footsteps coming up the stairs.

She listened intently. Step by step they came closer. Deliberate and slow, nearer and nearer. One by one they thudded upon the stone steps and then across the metal grate that led to the spiral staircase.

Sadie could see the glow of a flashlight beam that glinted from under the door and onto the whitewashed walls. She crouched down and looked through the gap between the floor and the door.

A shadow danced across the wall. It was tall and thin, with a long, sharp chin. Already the size of a giant, the shadow got taller and thinner with every step until it towered to the height of the hallway and covered the ceiling.

Sadie slid to the far side of the doorway and waited.

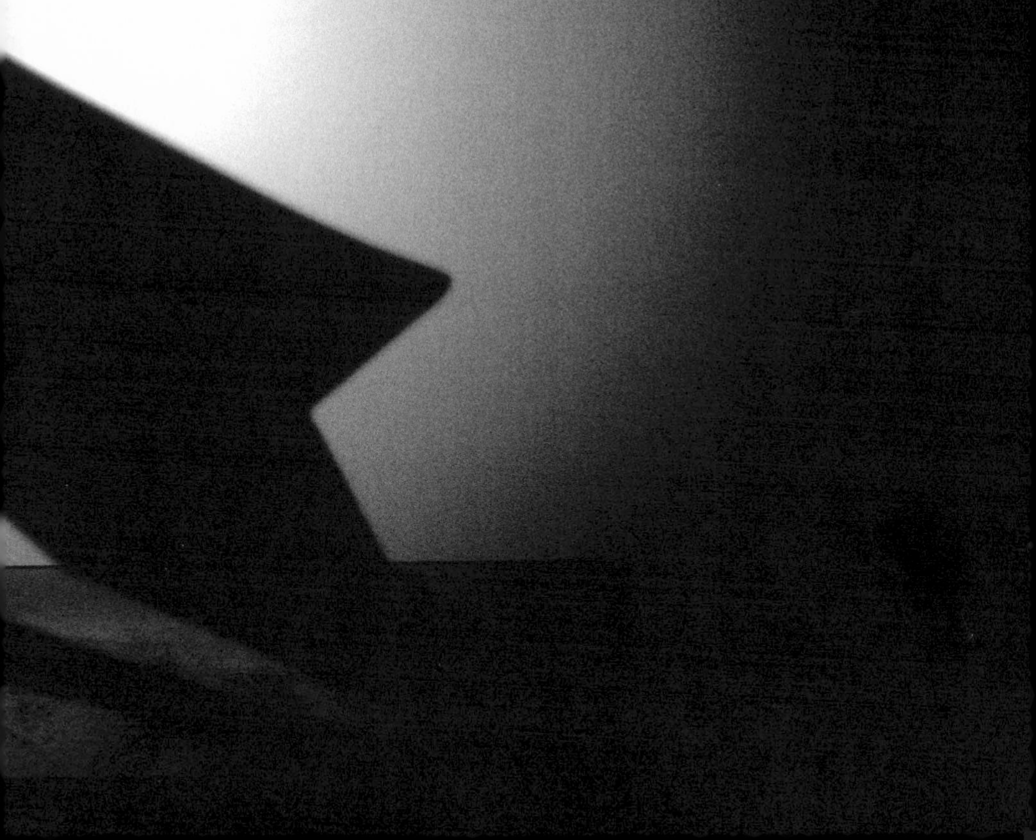

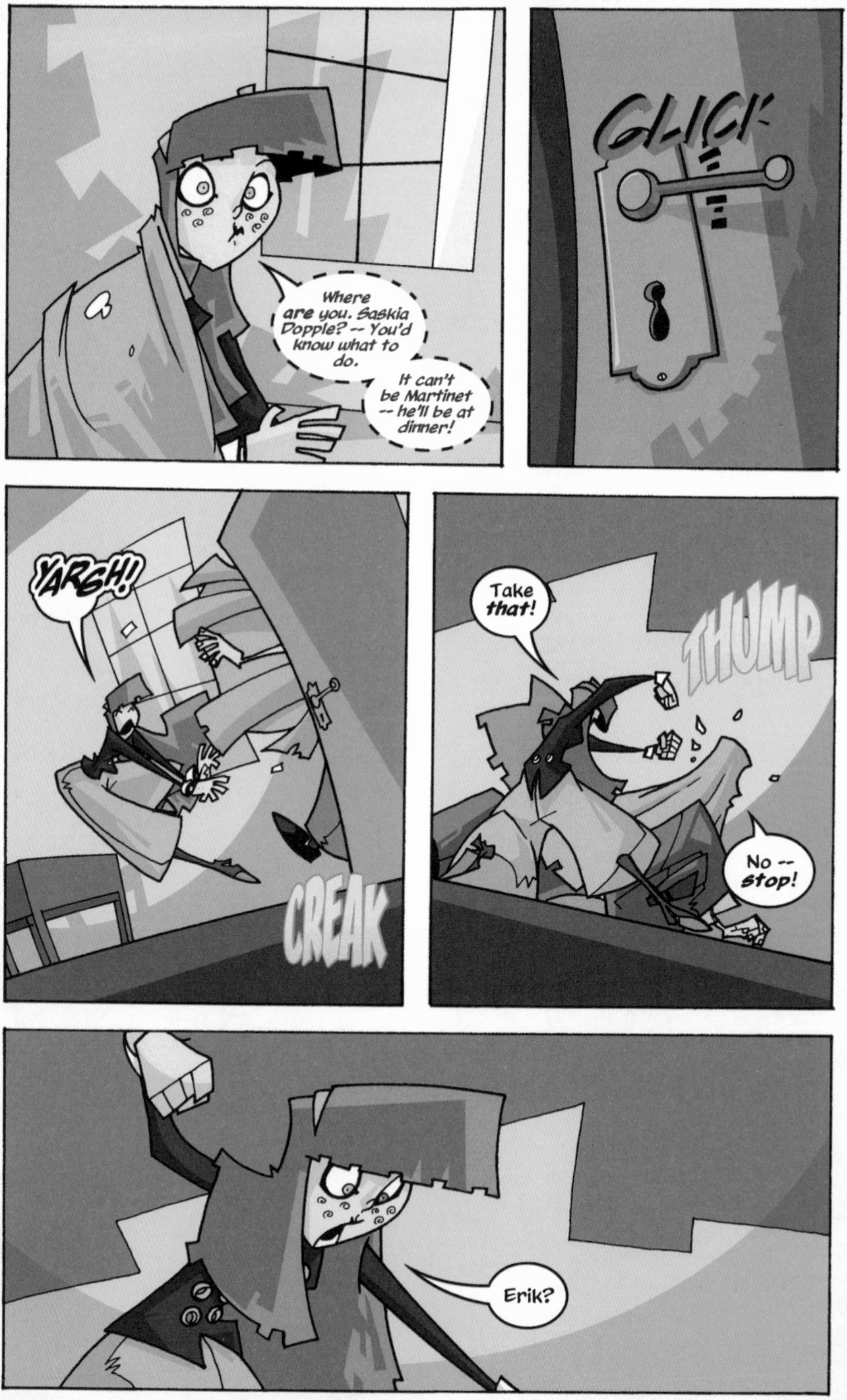
Where are you. Saskia Dopple? -- You'd know what to do.
It can't be Martinet -- he'll be at dinner!
CLICK
YARGH!
CREAK
Take *that*!
THUMP
No -- *stop*!
Erik?

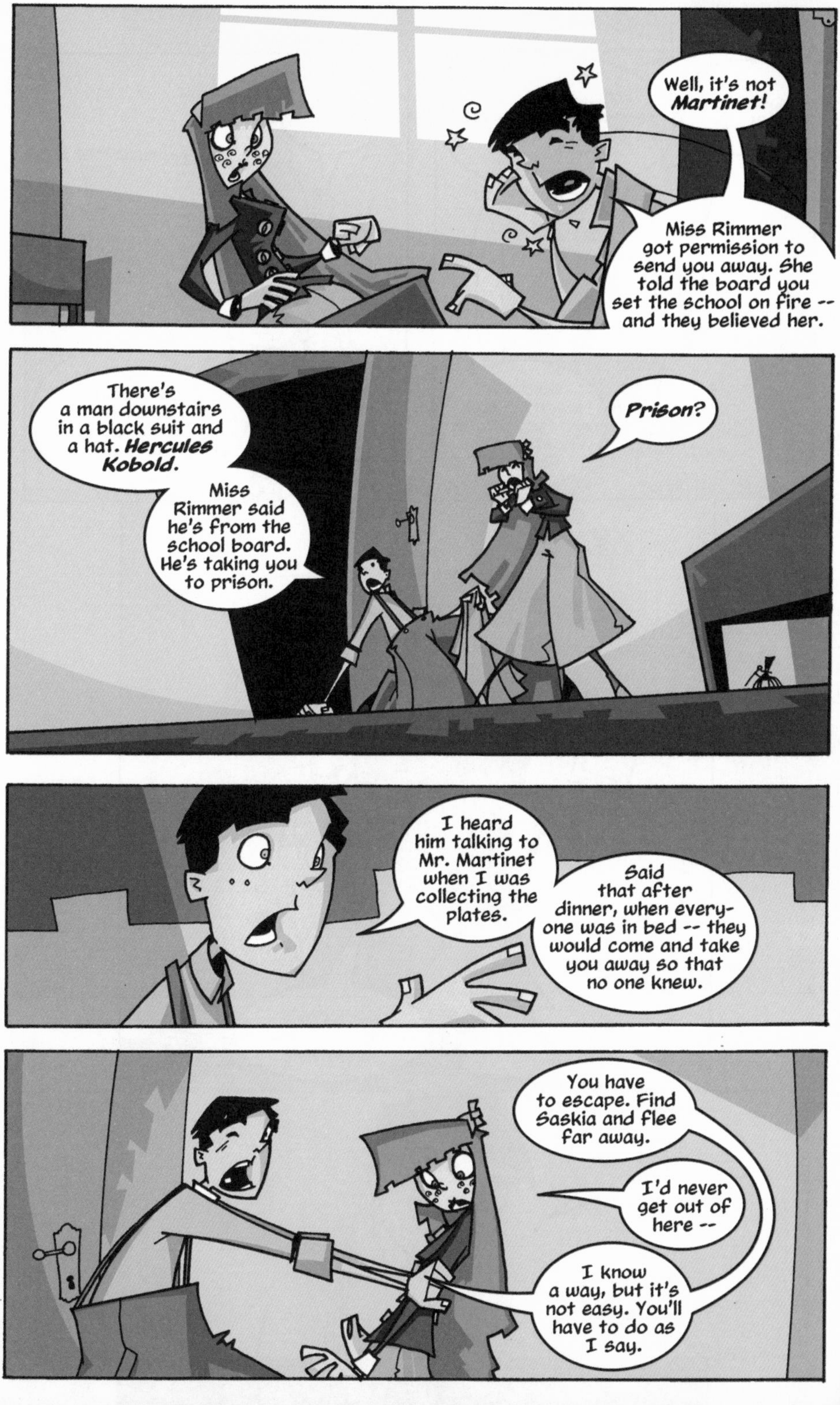

Well, it's not *Martinet!*
Miss Rimmer got permission to send you away. She told the board you set the school on fire -- and they believed her.
There's a man downstairs in a black suit and a hat. ***Hercules Kobold.***
Miss Rimmer said he's from the school board. He's taking you to prison.
Prison?
I heard him talking to Mr. Martinet when I was collecting the plates.
Said that after dinner, when every-one was in bed -- they would come and take you away so that no one knew.
You have to escape. Find Saskia and flee far away.
I'd never get out of here --
I know a way, but it's not easy. You'll have to do as I say.

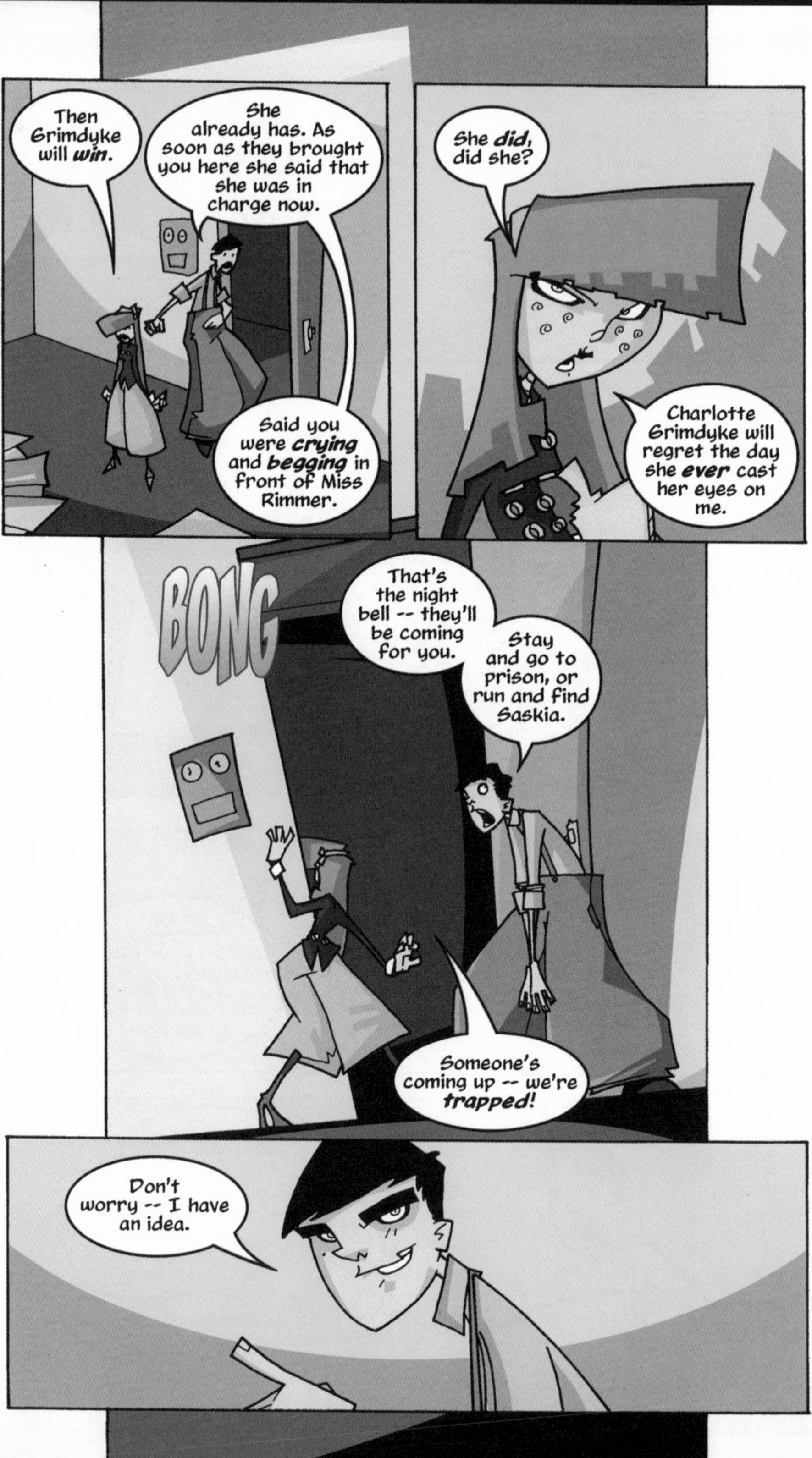
Then Grimdyke will *win*.
She already has. As soon as they brought you here she said that she was in charge now.
Said you were *crying* and *begging* in front of Miss Rimmer.
She *did*, did she?
Charlotte Grimdyke will regret the day she *ever* cast her eyes on me.
BONG
That's the night bell -- they'll be coming for you.
Stay and go to prison, or run and find Saskia.
Someone's coming up -- we're *trapped*!
Don't worry -- I have an idea.

Sadie quickly closed the door.

Outside on the staircase, Mr. Martinet led upward, his heels keeping time on the stone steps. He stopped in his tracks and turned to look at the man beside him, who wore a tattered checked suit that was pulled across his large frame. His hat was perched on a shaved head and held in place by a pus-filled lump that appeared to rest on a continuous brow stretching across the man's forehead.

"Do you have the handcuffs?" Martinet asked.

"She'll not fight me," came the gruff reply. "I've been locking up children all my life, and regardless of what Miss Rimmer says, this one ain't no different."

"Believe you me, Mr. Kobold, Sadie Dwopple is not to be taken for gwanted. She is a slippewy fish and one that should be caught and then have her entwails fed to the seagulls. That child has made my life misewable, and I intend to make her last moments in this school as unpleasant as I possibly can."

Hercules Kobold stepped back in surprise at what Mr. Martinet had just said. The words echoed high into the tower and bounced back and forth between the walls.

"Then we shall do it together," he said gleefully as he rubbed his boil with the back of his hand and pulled a pair of black handcuffs from his pocket.

Martinet continued walking, his breath turning to steam in the cold night air. Soon both men stood outside the door to the tower room. Martinet fished a key from his pocket and slipped it into the latch. He quickly discovered that the door was already unlocked.

Looking at Kobold, he twisted the handle and pushed open the door very slowly. Kobold peered over his shoulder, trying to see a sign of the girl. There on the floor was the shape of the child, wrapped in a blanket. It moved slightly as though in a fitful sleep, snuffling and snoring in discontent.

"Sleeping like a baby," Martinet said as he bent down to grab the blanket.

"Cuff her while she sleeps and we'll have no trouble," Kobold muttered sternly, passing the handcuffs to Martinet.

Before either man could move another muscle, a sudden, blinding flash of brilliant blue light sparked across the room.

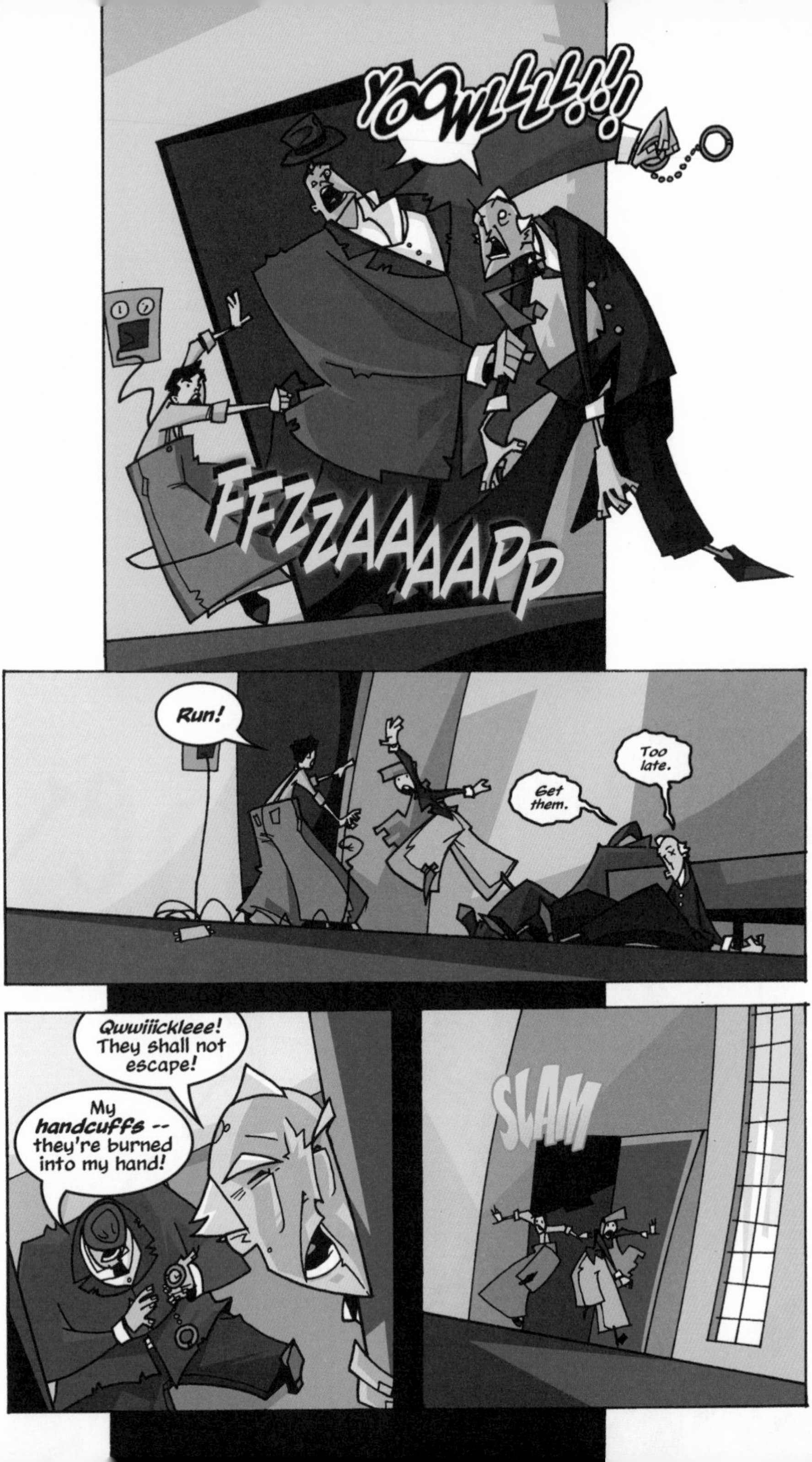
YOOWLLL!!!
FFZZAAAAAPP
Run!
Get them.
Too late.
Qwwiiickleee! They shall not escape!
My handcuffs -- they're burned into my hand!
SLAM

Martinet and Kobold heard a door slam shut as Erik and Sadie escaped from the tower and into the school.

"They mustn't get away! I'll bet you a silver dwollar that they'll be out the window on the first floor and onto the heath," Martinet shouted as he stumbled down the steps.

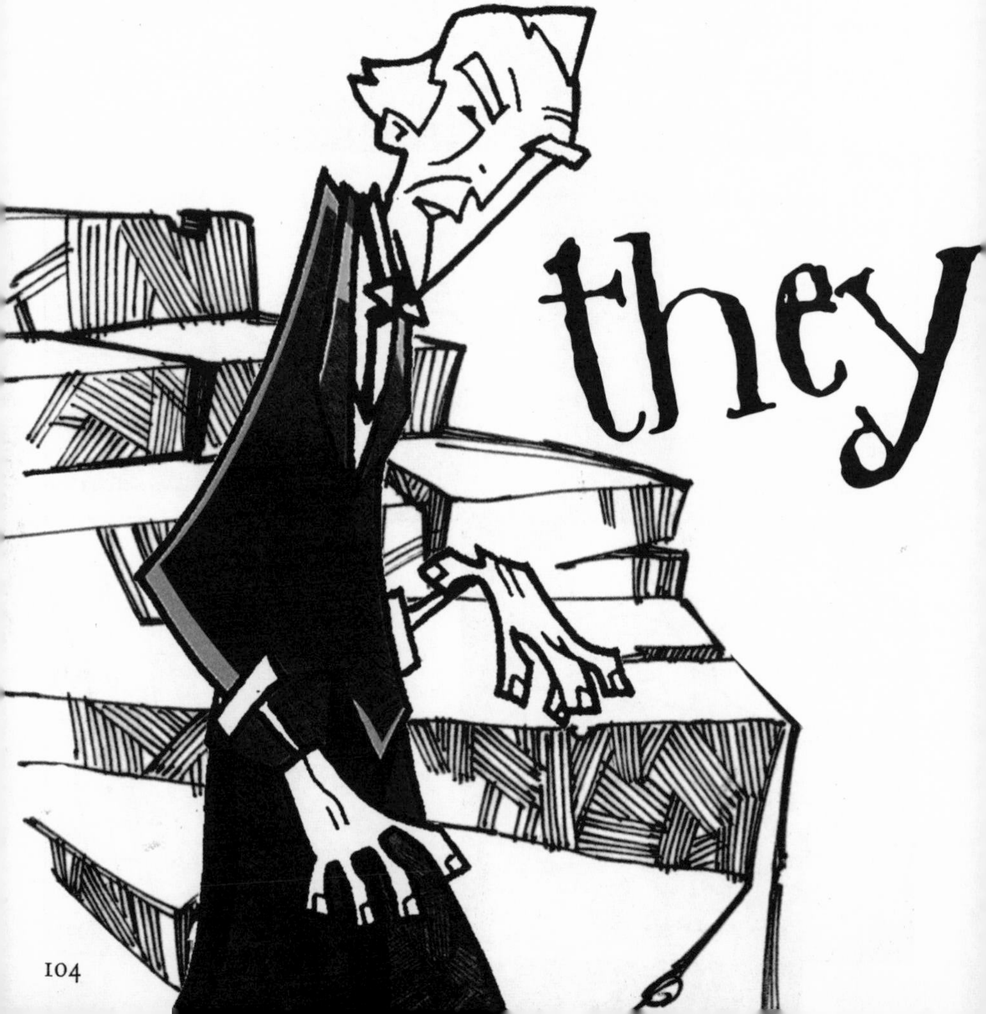
they

"They won't get far," said Kobold, staggering behind. "I come prepared for every eventuality."

"Don't tell me," blustered Martinet, "you can see in the dark and twack them acwoss the heath?"

"Not I, but a creature that can do even more than that."

mustn't get
away

GRo

Chapter Seven
Visitors

MADAME RAPHAEL DIDN'T waste any time before beginning to inspect Saskia. She sat in the leather chair and stared for several long and looming minutes without speaking. Saskia waited on the footstool in front of the woman, growing suspicious. Then, just as the clock began to chime the hour, Madame Raphael spoke.

"How do you think I will turn you into a girl acceptable in polite society?" she asked in an accent that had changed considerably from when she had first spoken.

"Why should I want to change?" Saskia asked, feeling that no matter what she said life could not get worse. The prospect of being sent to the workhouse was becoming quite appealing. "I didn't want to come here— I've been kidnapped."

"Kidnapped? Perhaps you have been brought here for your own good. There is a power at work in your life greater than either of us."

On the last few words, her voice changed again, and for a moment she sounded exactly like the puppet that had spoken to Saskia when she'd sneaked in to look at Muzz Elliott's painting.

"Was it you who warned me to stay out of trouble?"

"I'm glad to hear you talking sense. Even the bookshelves and typewriters in this house can do that . . . as you have already learned." Madame Raphael laughed. It was an odd, shrill sound that seemed to get stuck halfway up her throat, yet somehow it didn't frighten Saskia.

When the woman continued, her voice was quiet and had taken on yet another accent.

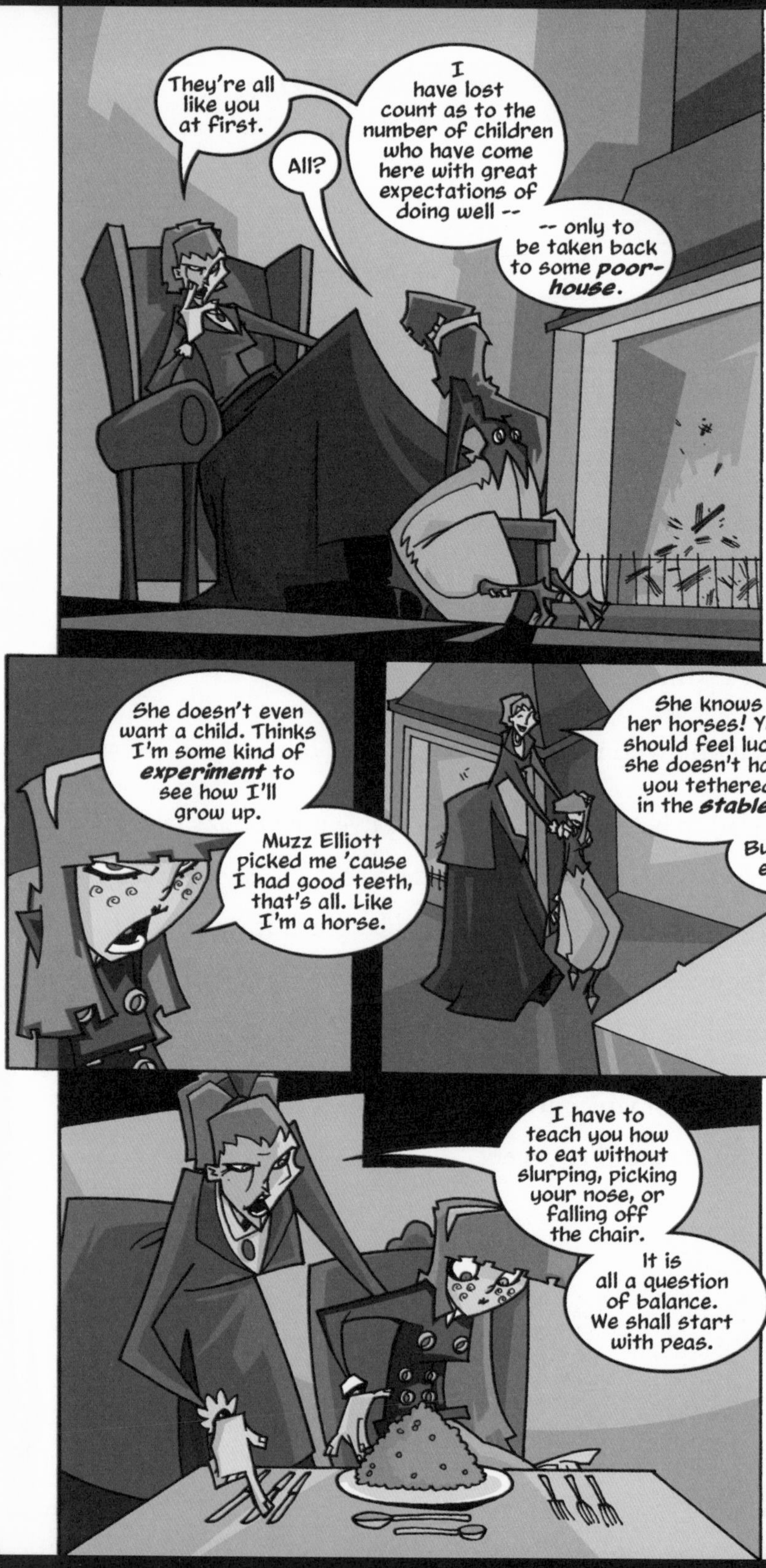
They're all like you at first.
All?
I have lost count as to the number of children who have come here with great expectations of doing well --
-- only to be taken back to some *poor-house*.
She doesn't even want a child. Thinks I'm some kind of *experiment* to see how I'll grow up.
Muzz Elliott picked me 'cause I had good teeth, that's all. Like I'm a horse.
She knows her horses! You should feel lucky she doesn't have you tethered in the *stable*!
But that's enough.
I have to teach you how to eat without slurping, picking your nose, or falling off the chair.
It is all a question of balance. We shall start with peas.

Within half an hour, Saskia had mastered peas, diced carrots, tomato slivers, and duck liver. Throughout the lesson, Madame Raphael prodded Saskia with her long fingers, moving Saskia's elbows to the right height and, when necessary, wiping the juice from her chin with a white handkerchief. All the while Saskia couldn't help but notice her tutor's unearthly glow.

By the time the clock chimed the next hour, Saskia was sitting on the bed pleasantly full, and Madame Raphael looked content that her charge was now skilled at table manners. Saskia felt there was something endearing and warm about her teacher. It was as if Saskia were in the presence of a kind aunt and for the first time since she could remember was willing just to enjoy the company, whatever she was asked to do.

She felt comfortable enough to ask a question that had been puzzling her:

"do you knOW who Oscar is?"

Madame Raphael got to her feet and began to tidy away everything from the table back into her bag. "Not all in this house is as it should be, Saskia. Don't believe everything you see and hear."

"Is Oscar real?" Saskia persisted. "There was something strange about the way Brummagem and Muzz Elliott talked about him."

The woman paused and came back over to Saskia. "The gathering you will attend this evening is not just a dinner party. There will be a séance, a ceremony where they will talk to the dead—or think they will. It is a foolish practice and more dangerous than they know. But in this house they mostly just talk to themselves."

"Why do they do it?" Saskia asked.

Madame Raphael looked around to make sure the room was completely empty and she could not be overheard. She stepped to the window and peered into the garden before she pulled the drapes closed. The fire had dulled in the grate, and there was a chill to the room.

"There is a secret in this house that Muzz Elliott seeks to discover, but she is traveling a dark and risky path to find it. She is trying to contact her dead grandfather to see if he can remember where he hid the—"

"Money?" interrupted Saskia. "Lord Trevellyn hid the money to escape the potato famine and forgot where he put it. Brummagem told me."

"Then you know more than you should," Madame Raphael said, her voice severe. "If she finds out you know, you'll be gone."

"I don't want to be gone," Saskia said tearfully. Her thoughts turned to Sadie yet again. "I couldn't stand the poorhouse—being all alone."

"Does it frighten you?" Madame Raphael asked softly, her eyes wide in the fading glow of the fire.

"Sometimes," Saskia admitted. "I hate being alone, especially since my mother left us."

"We are never alone, Saskia," Madame Raphael said, putting her arm around the girl. "Even when we think we are. I know the name of someone you can call out to at any time. The Companion is never far away. We don't need words to speak to him, just the thoughts of our hearts."

"Is he a ghost?" Saskia asked suspiciously.

"Not in the slightest," Madame Raphael replied, her voice quaking with laughter. "He is very wonderful and can hear all we say—even now. He listens to us and knows our hearts. I speak with him often."

"Even though you can't see him?" Saskia asked.

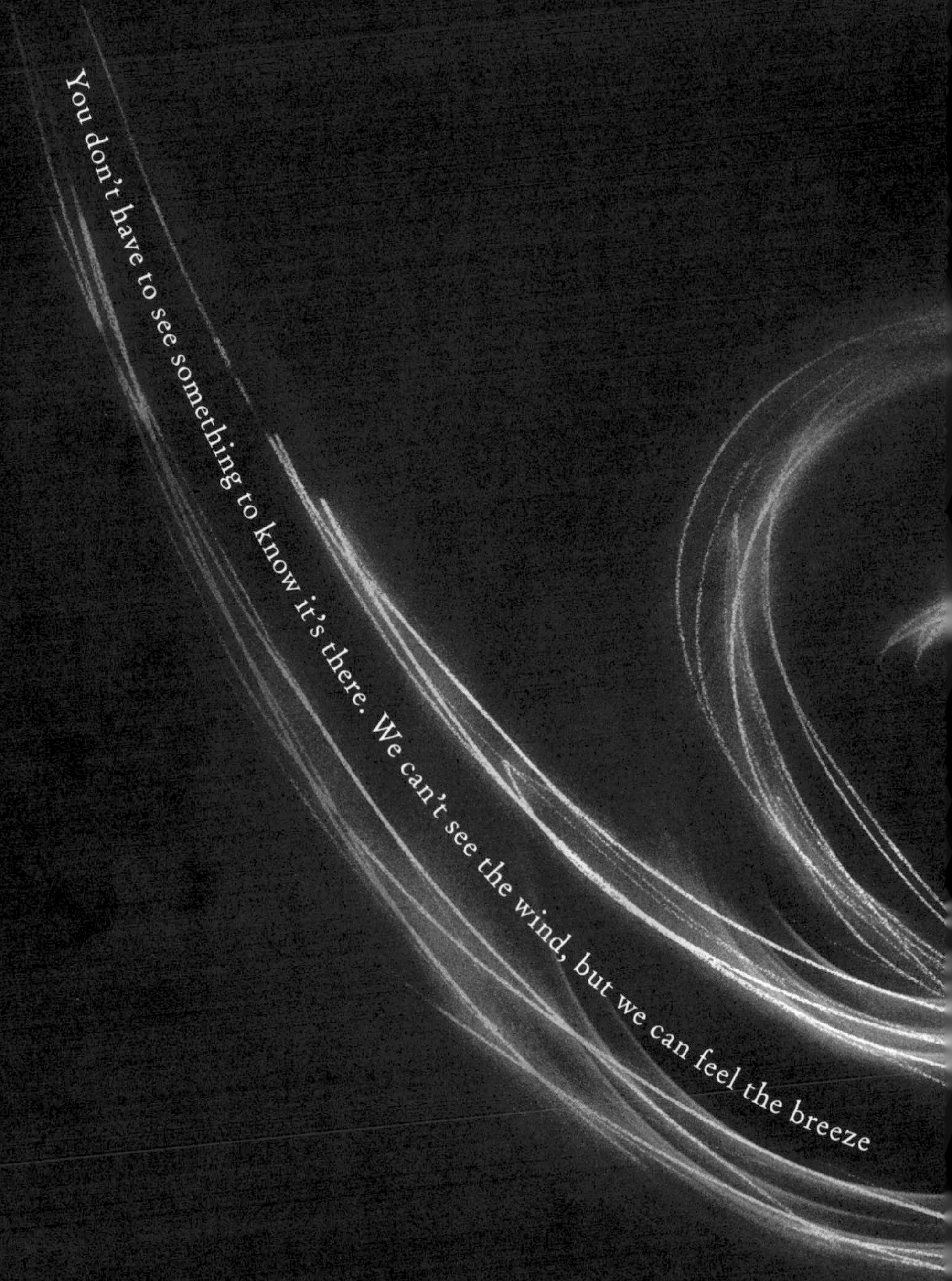

You don't have to see something to know it's there. We can't see the wind, but we can feel the breeze

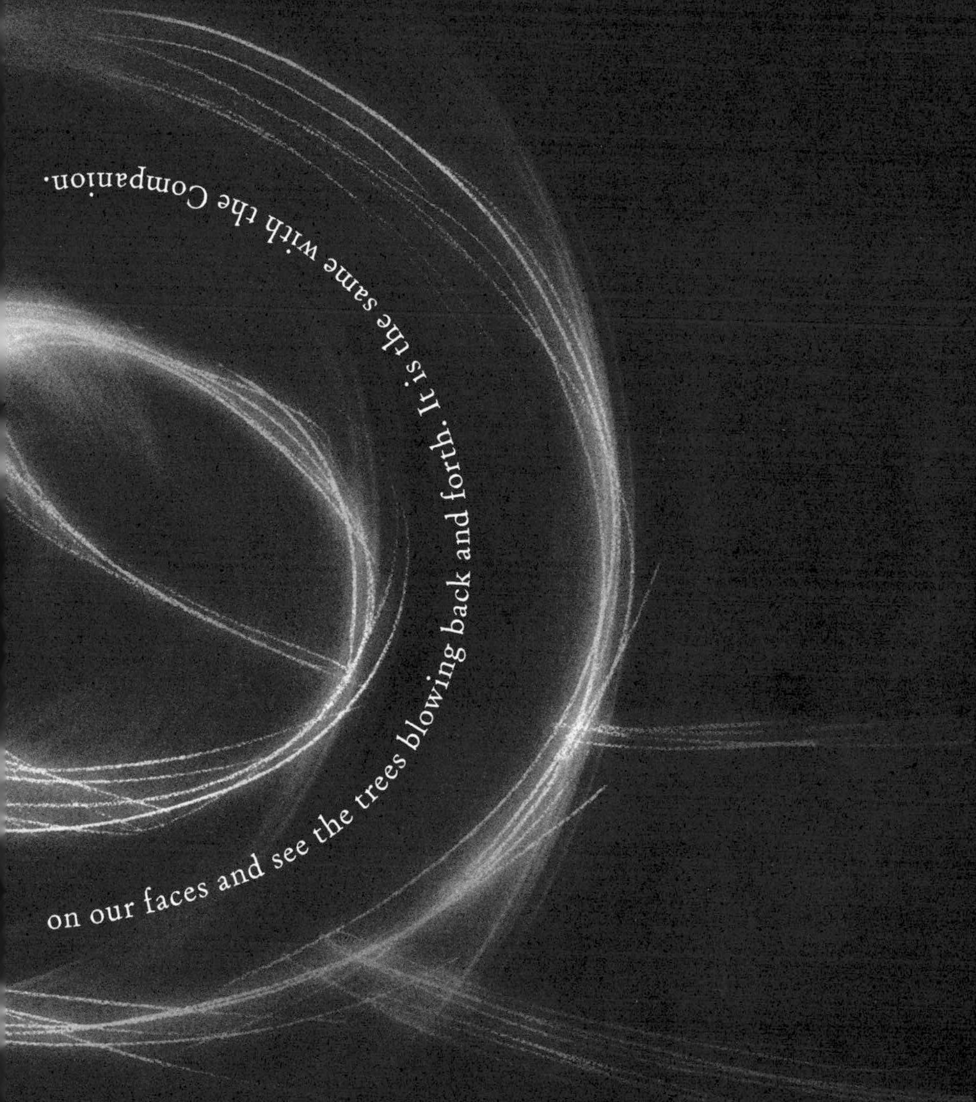

on our faces and see the trees blowing back and forth. It is the same with the Companion.

"We can't see him, but his works are many in this world. Everything was made by him—even you, Saskia Dopple."

"Then I want to speak with him," Saskia said adamantly.

"One day I will tell you how," Madame Raphael replied. "For now, know that he is watching over you—and so am I." With that, she picked up her bag and said nothing more. The door slammed behind her.

Saskia listened as Madame Raphael's footsteps echoed through the long halls. She got up and peeked through the chink in the drapes. The night was bleak with storm clouds. Far away the glow of the city lit the southern sky. It edged the clouds blood red and set the heath silver against the night.

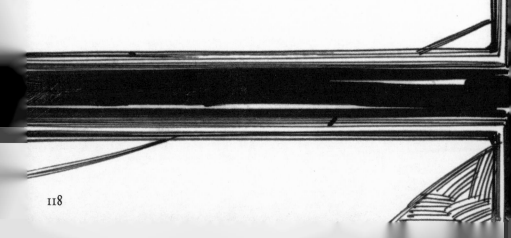

In the cluster of trees that formed a small wood by the road, a faint light caught Saskia's eye. It moved back and forth, sometimes hidden as it got closer. The light edged near the drive, making slow progress toward Spaniards House.

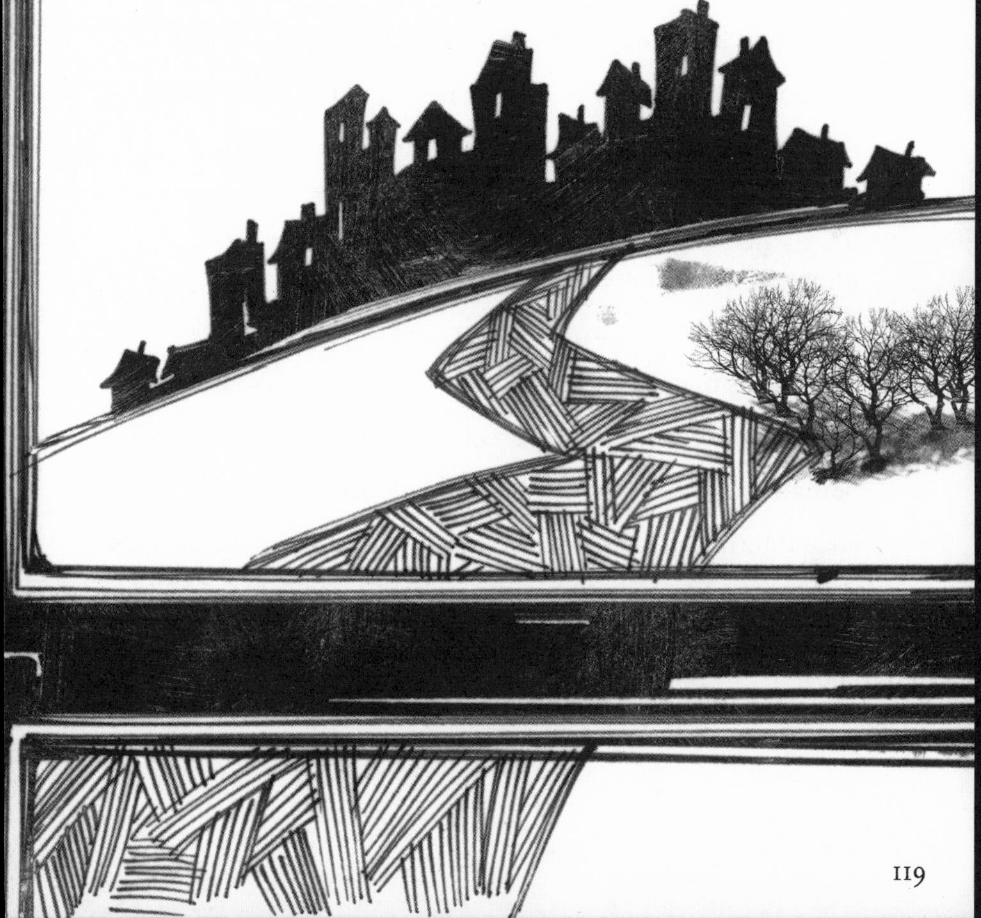

Saskia soon realized that whoever was carrying the lamp didn't want to be seen. A car turned from the Hampstead road toward the house. Its large headlights lit the night as it sped along the drive toward her. As the car turned, the light in the wood vanished, only to quickly reappear after the vehicle had roared by.

From her tower room Saskia kept watch, wondering who would use a path through the wood instead of the road. For a moment she thought it could be Sadie coming to find her. Then with a sudden rush she remembered the vision and realized her sister was locked away from the world.

All of their lives, both girls had had an uncanny way of knowing each other's thoughts. It was as if they shared the same subconscious, that their minds remained locked together as one, even though they inhabited two separate bodies. But what Saskia had seen that evening was something new and powerful. She felt like she had been with Sadie, encountering all that Sadie was going through. It wasn't like the gentle whispers and impressions she had felt before. This time it was real, urgent, and foreboding.

As she looked out the window, Saskia tried to bring the image of Sadie back to her mind. All was blank; all was black. She wanted to see her sister's face, but there was nothing. Whatever vision she had seen had been for that one moment. It had been like a scream uttered once, never to be heard again.

In the wood, the fragmented shadows thrown by the lamp got closer to the house. Saskia watched the glow as it meandered in and out of the trees and then stopped by a small gazebo opposite the front door. Now she could see the shape of the figure who carried the lamp. She wondered why someone who was prepared to come to the house by the wood should be so concerned about the darkness as to carry a light. What she knew of robbers was that they loved the night. To them it was a velvet glove that concealed their wickedness. But the person Saskia now observed appeared to hesitate before extinguishing the flames and hiding the lamp in a large rhododendron bush.

Saskia kept watch as the figure stealthily crossed the gravel to the side of the house before slipping from view.

With a sudden trill, the telephone on the bedside table rattled to life, and Saskia nearly jumped from her skin. She lifted the receiver without thinking, and before she could even speak, Brummagem's voice shouted down the wire. "What did I tell you about the rules? Don't answer the telephone!"

"I—er—" Saskia stammered.

"Fortunately for me, your being a disobedient brat will save me a trip up the stairs. Dinner at half the hour— dining room. Get changed. AND DON'T be late!"

The voice stopped abruptly, and Brummagem got off the line before Saskia could tell him about the person prowling outside. But she kept the phone to her ear. She was sure she could hear breathing and the faint sound of talking far away. It was as if someone was listening to her.

"Hello?" she asked after a while.

"Hello?" her own voice repeated back to her.

"Who's that?" she asked.

"Who's that?" said the voice again, a semitone higher.

She was about to speak a third time when there was a sudden click and the line began to purr like an old wheezing cat.

Saskia hurriedly put the phone back on the cradle and looked out the window. She could see no one, but she knew that the prowler was somewhere in the garden. Saskia turned and looked at herself in the long mirror. She took a scarf from the wardrobe and wrapped it around her waist as a sash. Then she quickly tied up her hair and pierced the bun with two peacock feathers.

Saskia set off down the stairs and as she did so wondered again why someone would be prowling around the garden. From the spiral staircase of the tower, she could hear voices far below. Brummagem was welcoming someone at the door—someone obviously very important by the way he tried to soften his Dublin accent.

"Come in, Mr. Yeats," he said politely. "Nice journey from town?"

There was a muffled answer. Saskia listened carefully as she tiptoed down each stair and across the landings. She stopped at a window that overlooked the front door.

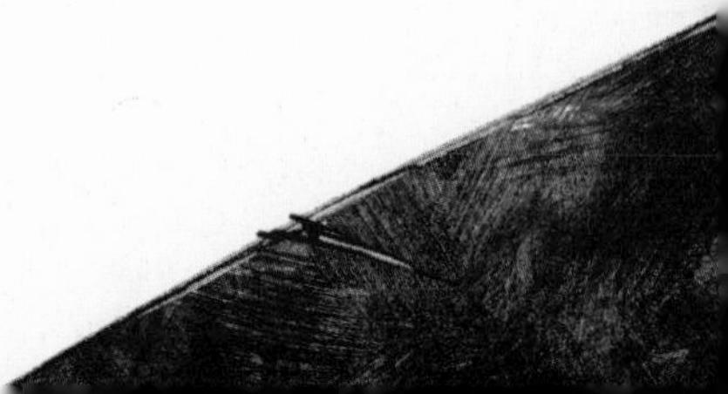

Another car zoomed along the driveway toward the house. The headlights beamed through the night like two bright eyes and lit up her face. Saskia ducked from sight.

Two flights down, she found herself in front of a wooden door she had not seen before. Where a door handle ought to have been, a rough hole was gouged into the wood, and a broken bolt lay on the carpet below.

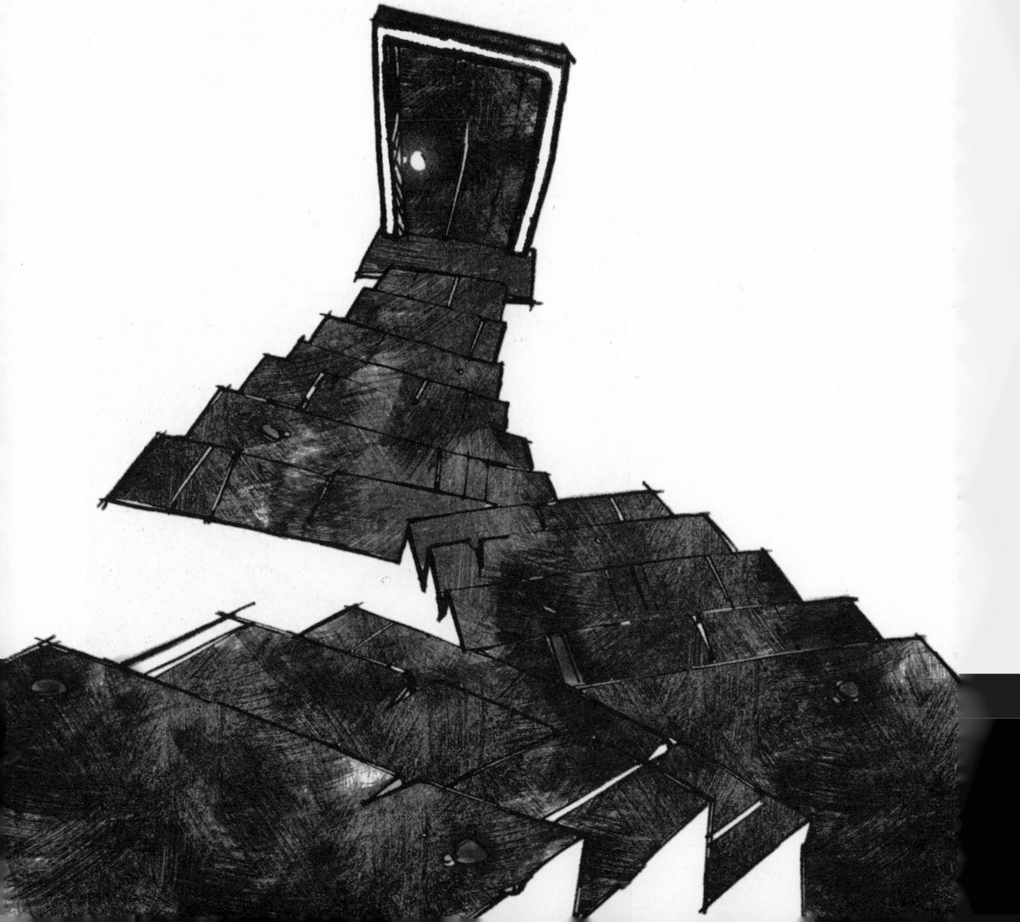

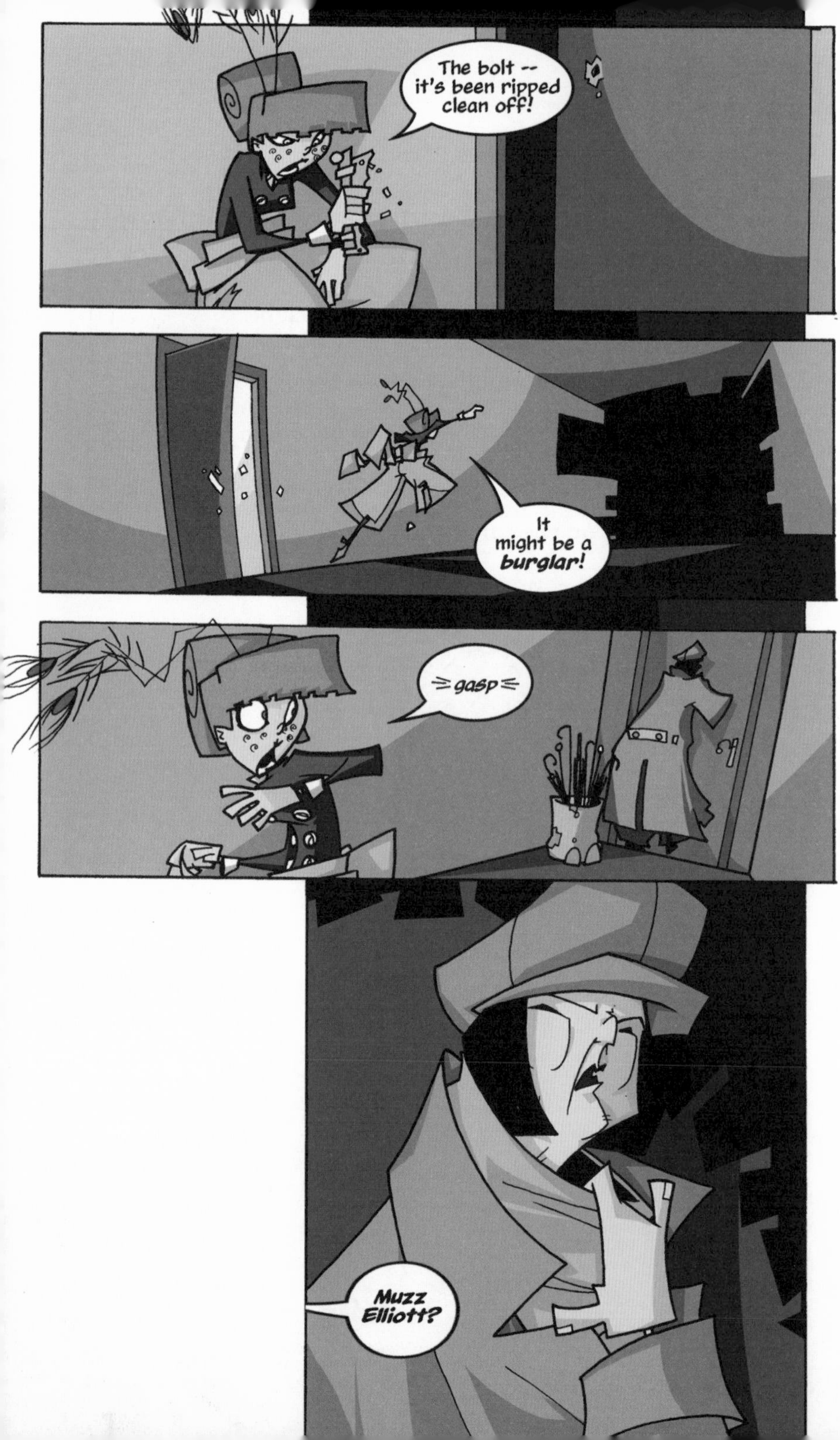
The bolt -- it's been ripped clean off!
It might be a *burglar!*
gasp
Muzz Elliott?

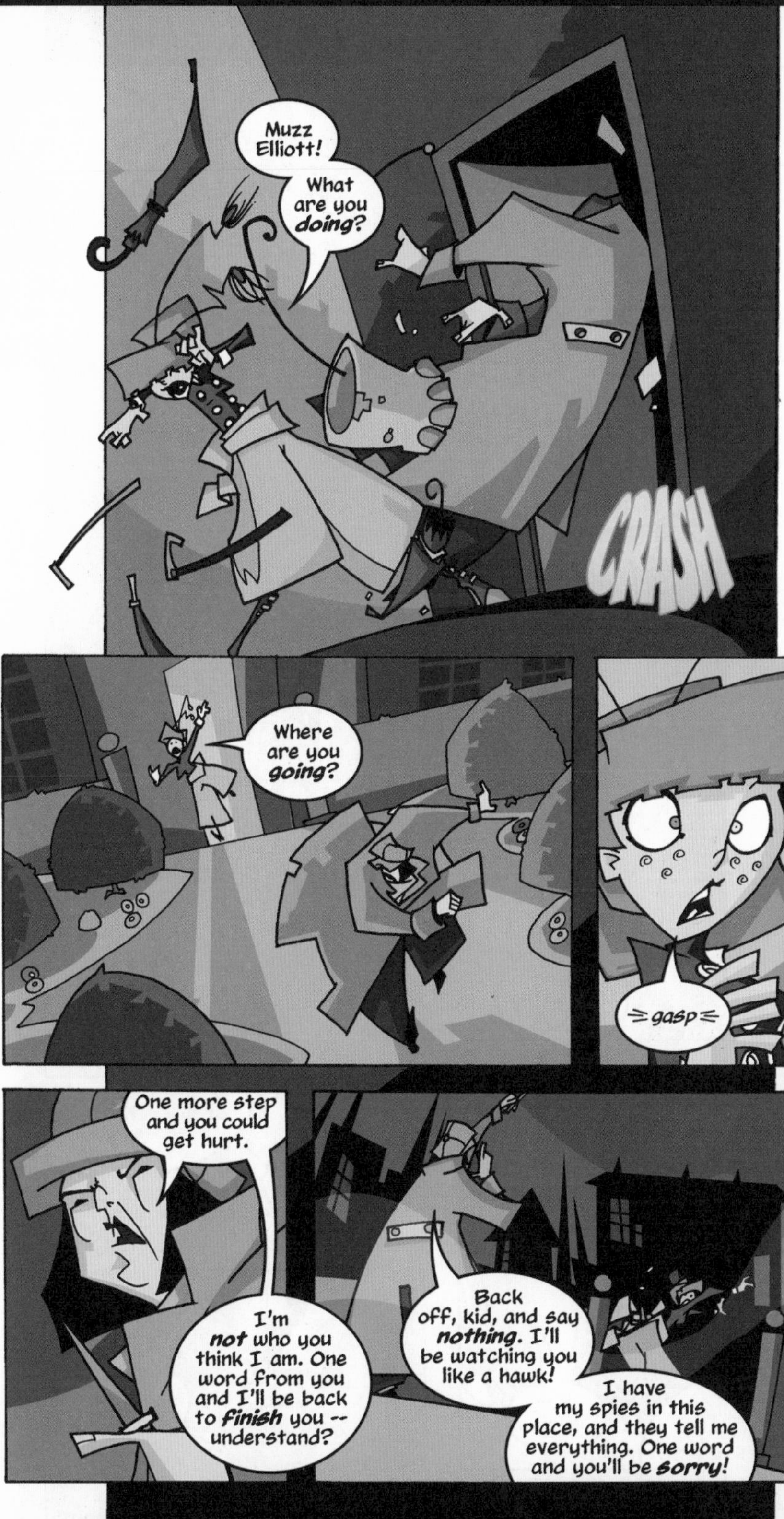
Muzz Elliott!
What are you *doing*?
CRASH
Where are you *going*?
≥gasp≤
One more step and you could get hurt.
I'm *not* who you think I am. One word from you and I'll be back to *finish* you -- understand?
Back off, kid, and say *nothing*. I'll be watching you like a hawk!
I have my spies in this place, and they tell me everything. One word and you'll be *sorry*!

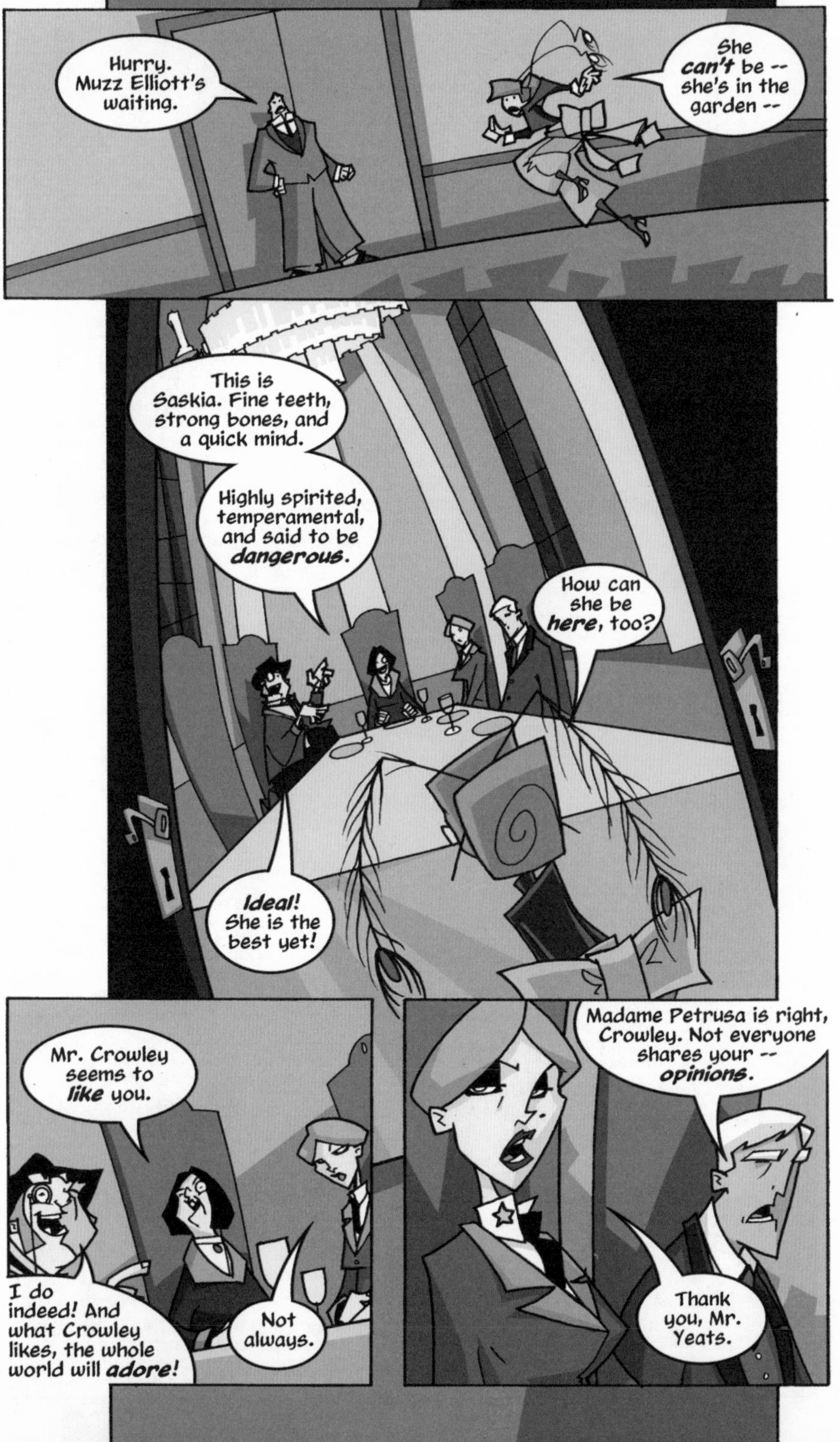
Hurry. Muzz Elliott's waiting.
She *can't* be -- she's in the garden --
This is Saskia. Fine teeth, strong bones, and a quick mind.
Highly spirited, temperamental, and said to be *dangerous*.
How can she be *here*, too?
Ideal! She is the best yet!
Mr. Crowley seems to *like* you.
I do indeed! And what Crowley likes, the whole world will *adore*!
Not always.
Madame Petrusa is right, Crowley. Not everyone shares your -- *opinions*.
Thank you, Mr. Yeats.

"Does she eat?" asked Crowley, holding his knife and fork like a hungry child. "If she eats, then so can we, and I am starved beyond death. If I sit here a moment longer I shall be thinner than ever. I know that before we get to the business of the night, Mr. Yeats will insist on reciting poetry. As the paint in this room appears to have dried already, I shall be better contented with my boredom on a full stomach."

From out of nowhere, a single crystal crashed from the chandelier onto the table. It broke into dozens of tiny pieces, just missing Crowley and shattering the goblet he held in his hand.

Instantly the lights flashed on and off, and the dinner guests could hear crashing sounds all around as an unexpected breeze slammed doors all over the house. At that same moment, Madame Petrusa rolled her head and then suddenly crashed forward. She moaned as a harsh voice seemed to cry out from within her.

Chapter Eight
The Hounds of Hampstead Heath

IN THE FAR DORMITORY of Isambard Dunstan's School for Wayward Children, everyone was sound asleep. Everyone except Sadie Dopple and Erik Morrissey Ganger. With frightening precision, Erik had managed to open the dormitory door without being heard and sneak between the rows of sleeping girls to the small kitchen at the end of the room. Every bed had a blanket and a starched white pillow, a side table, and a regulation glass of water filled to the top. Beneath every bed was a bright white chamber pot for use only in the case of extreme emergency. Children at Isambard Dunstan's were expected to go only once a day and never at night.

Sadie followed Erik, annoyed at him for bringing them this way instead of escaping through the first open window they found and out over the heath.

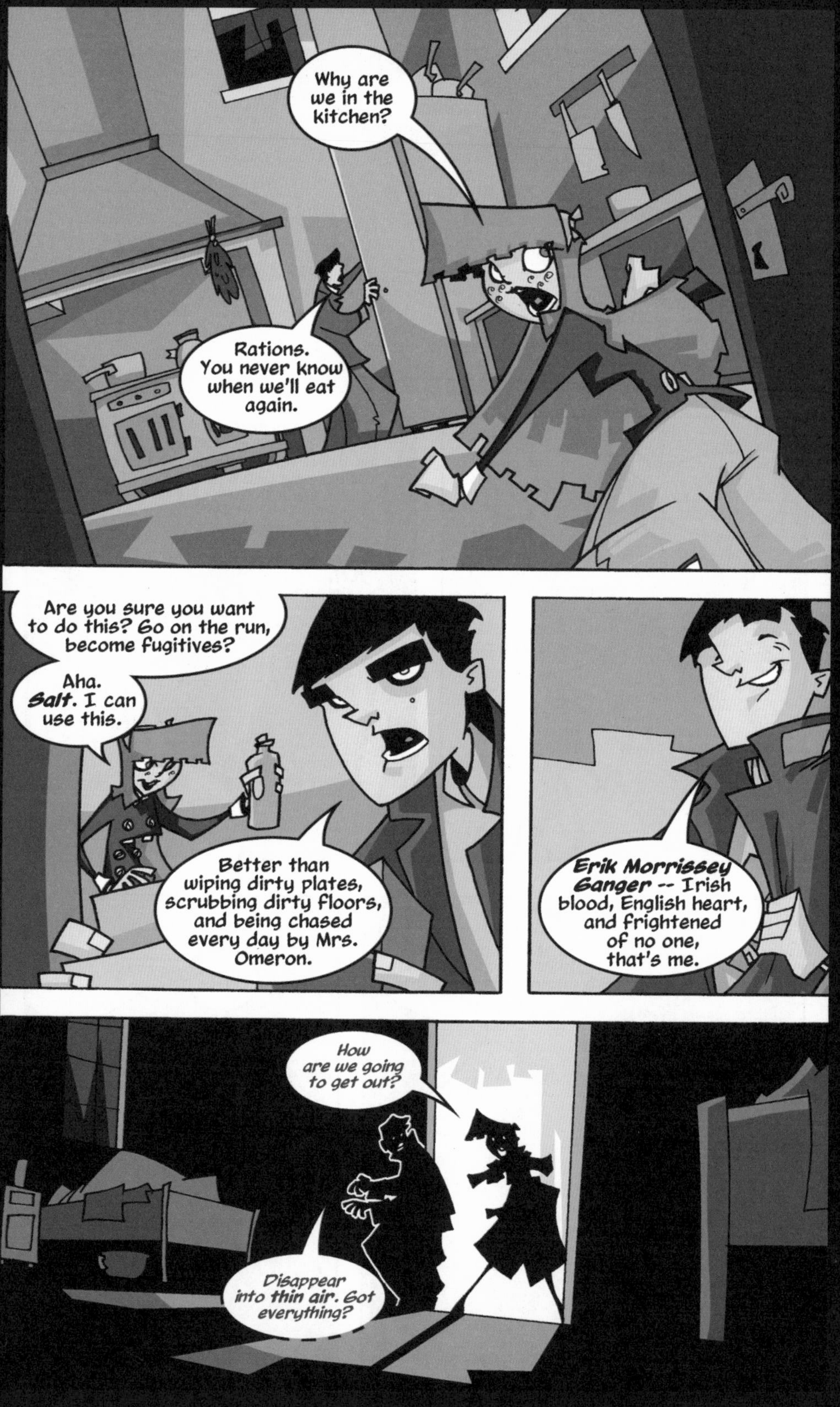
Why are we in the kitchen?
Rations. You never know when we'll eat again.
Are you sure you want to do this? Go on the run, become fugitives?
Aha. *Salt*. I can use this.
Better than wiping dirty plates, scrubbing dirty floors, and being chased every day by Mrs. Omeron.
Erik Morrissey Ganger -- Irish blood, English heart, and frightened of no one, that's me.
How are we going to get out?
*Disappear into **thin air**. Got everything?*

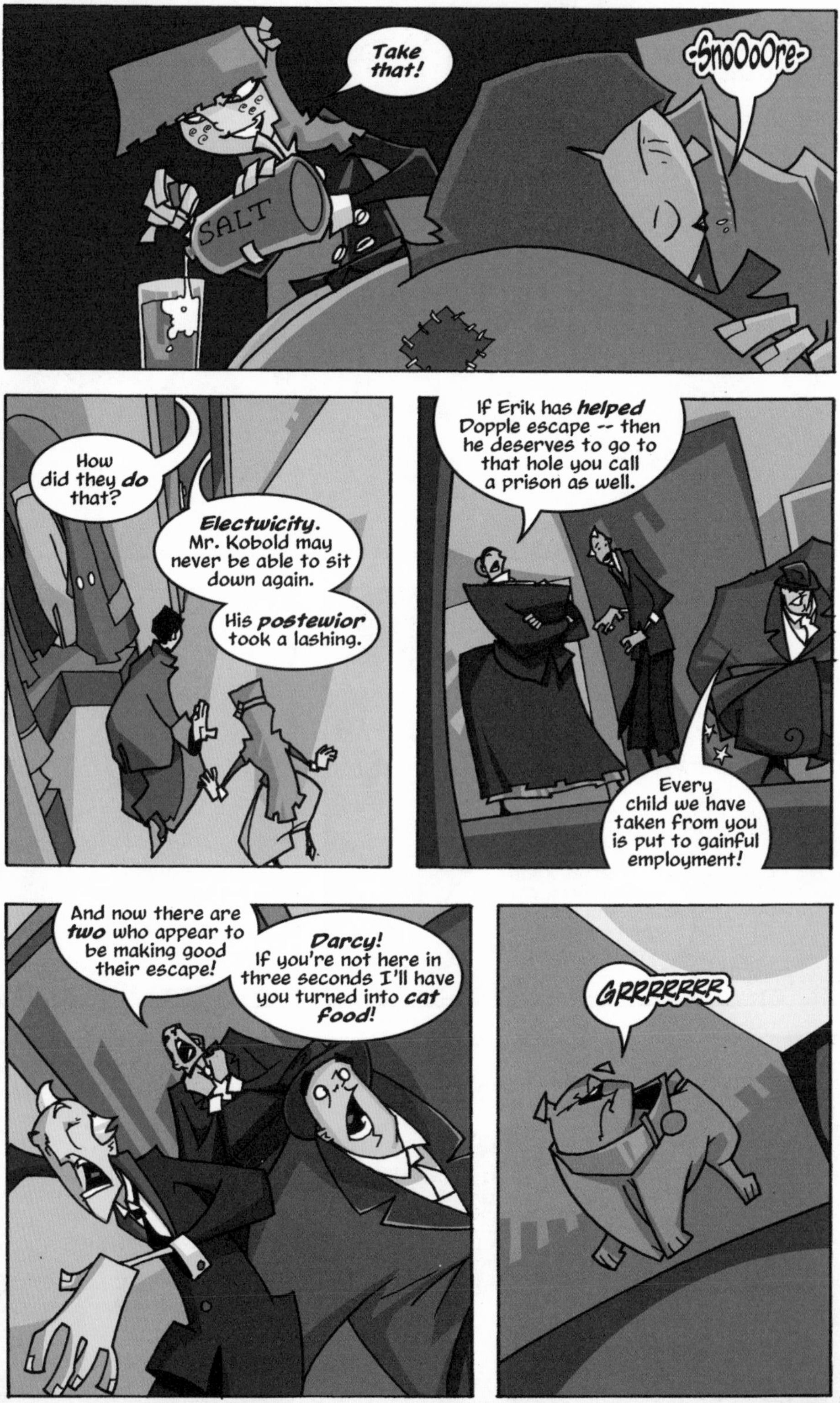
Take that!
-SnoOoOre-
How did they do that?
Electwicity. Mr. Kobold may never be able to sit down again.
His postewior took a lashing.
If Erik has helped Dopple escape -- then he deserves to go to that hole you call a prison as well.
Every child we have taken from you is put to gainful employment!
And now there are two who appear to be making good their escape!
Darcy! If you're not here in three seconds I'll have you turned into cat food!
GRRRRRRR
SALT

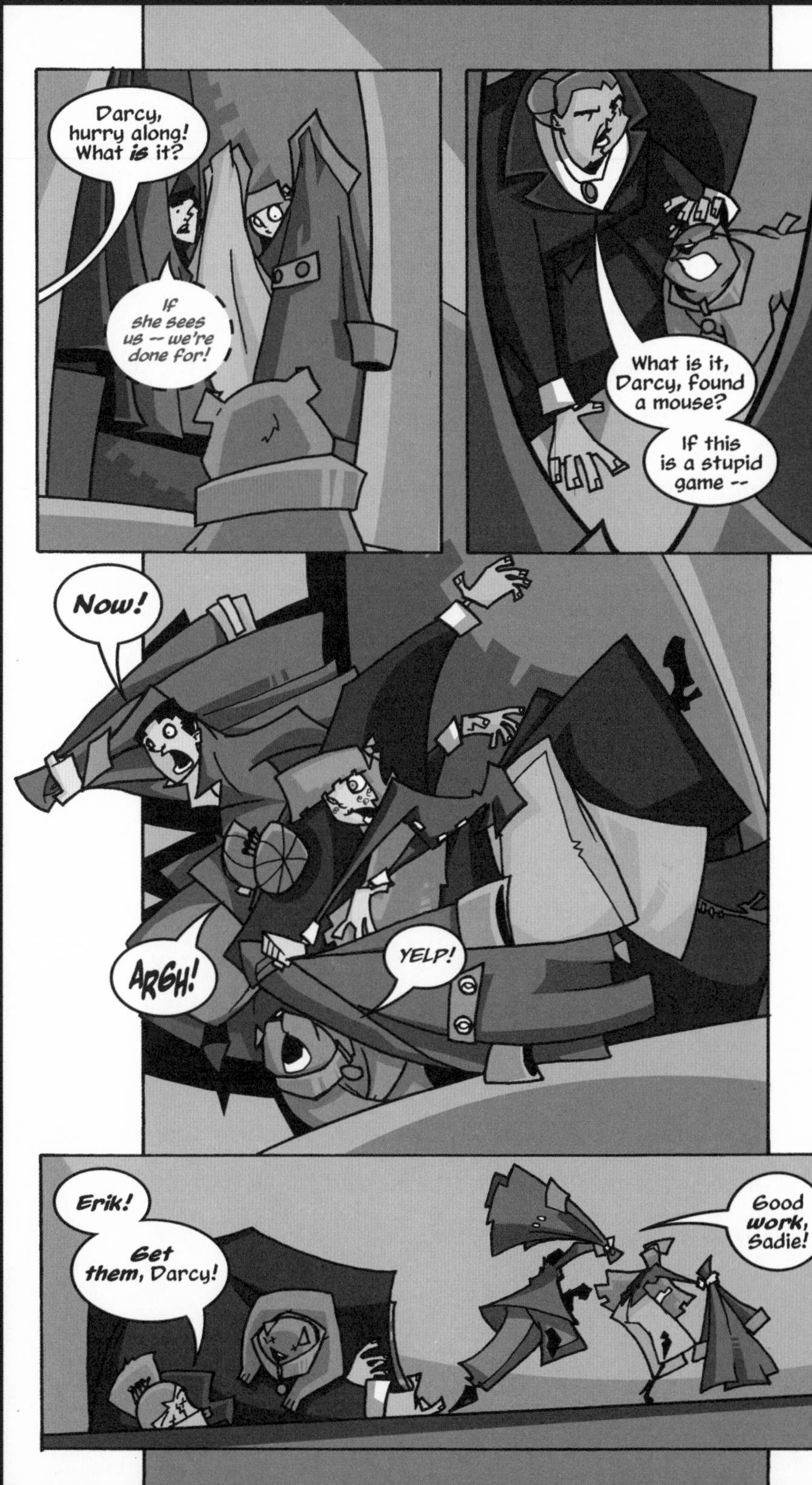

Darcy, hurry along! What *is* it?
If she sees us -- we're done for!
What is it, Darcy, found a mouse?
If this is a stupid game --
Now!
ARGH!
YELP!
Erik!
Get them, Darcy!
Good work, Sadie!

Miss Rimmer rolled off the dog onto all fours and struggled to get to her feet. She immediately tripped on her large skirt, slipping on the tile floor. "Get them, Darcy," she panted again. "It's Dopple."

Dopple was a word Darcy knew well. Dopple meant disaster and eggs at breakfast. Dopple meant she would be allowed to bite. In an instant, Darcy was revived and was running as fast as her fat legs would allow her to go. She believed she was a match for any troublemaker; after all, she was the mistress's dog, and Isambard Dunstan's School belonged to her.

Far ahead she could see Erik and Sadie. They were at the open front door and running hard. Darcy chased on, Miss Rimmer hobbling behind. Erik and Sadie ran; Darcy followed. They were out into the night, cold and black.

"This way!" shouted Erik as he skidded on the gravel and turned to run toward the heath. A blinding light was suddenly cast upon them as the headlights of Kobold's prison van were switched on.

"Thought you'd get away, did you?" Kobold asked from somewhere in the blinding haze.

Sadie thought she could see the vague outline of two men and a small horse on a long leash. She shielded her eyes from the light, made even brighter by the darkness surrounding it.

"It's no use, Dwopple. You and Ganger are coming with us. Pointless wunning fwom Mr. Kobold's bloodhound," said Martinet with great joy.

Sadie realized that what she had taken for a small horse was in fact a large—a very large—dog. Kobold stepped from the glare of the headlights. His hand was wrapped in a thick leather strap that was tethered securely to the monstrous hound. From far behind, Darcy still gave chase, running toward them and barking furiously—until she, too, saw the bloodhound.

All fell silent. Martinet clicked open the handcuffs and stepped toward Sadie and Erik. The bloodhound saw Darcy, and Darcy saw the bloodhound.

All seemed to fade into slow motion. Erik grabbed Sadie and pulled her toward the wood. The bloodhound stood upon his hind legs and snarled at Darcy, who by now had decided that her home was being invaded by a prehistoric animal.

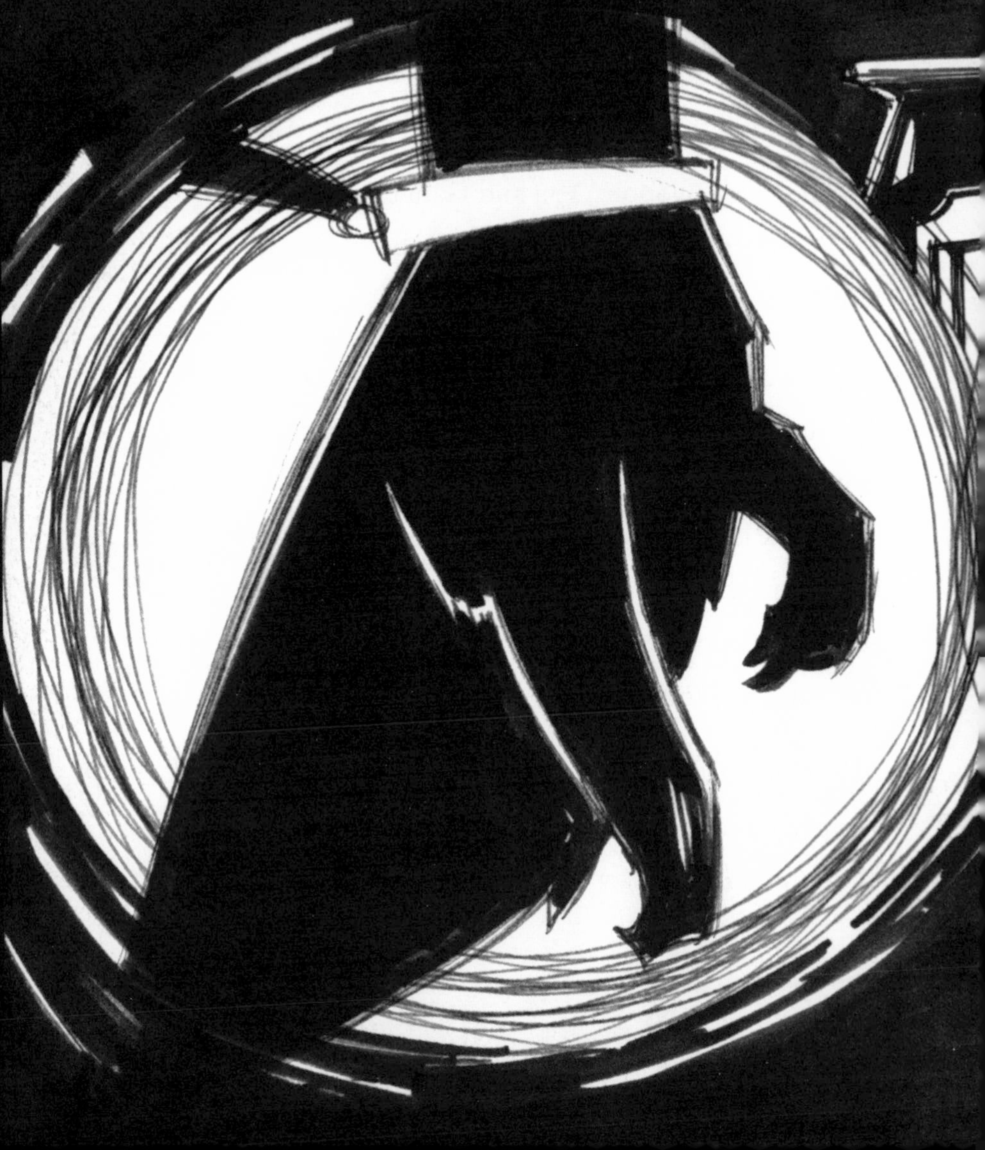

Martinet snatched at Sadie as she ran by. Kobold was pulled through the air as the bloodhound shot forward, knocking Martinet from his feet. Darcy jumped at the dog and grabbed the nearest piece of flesh.

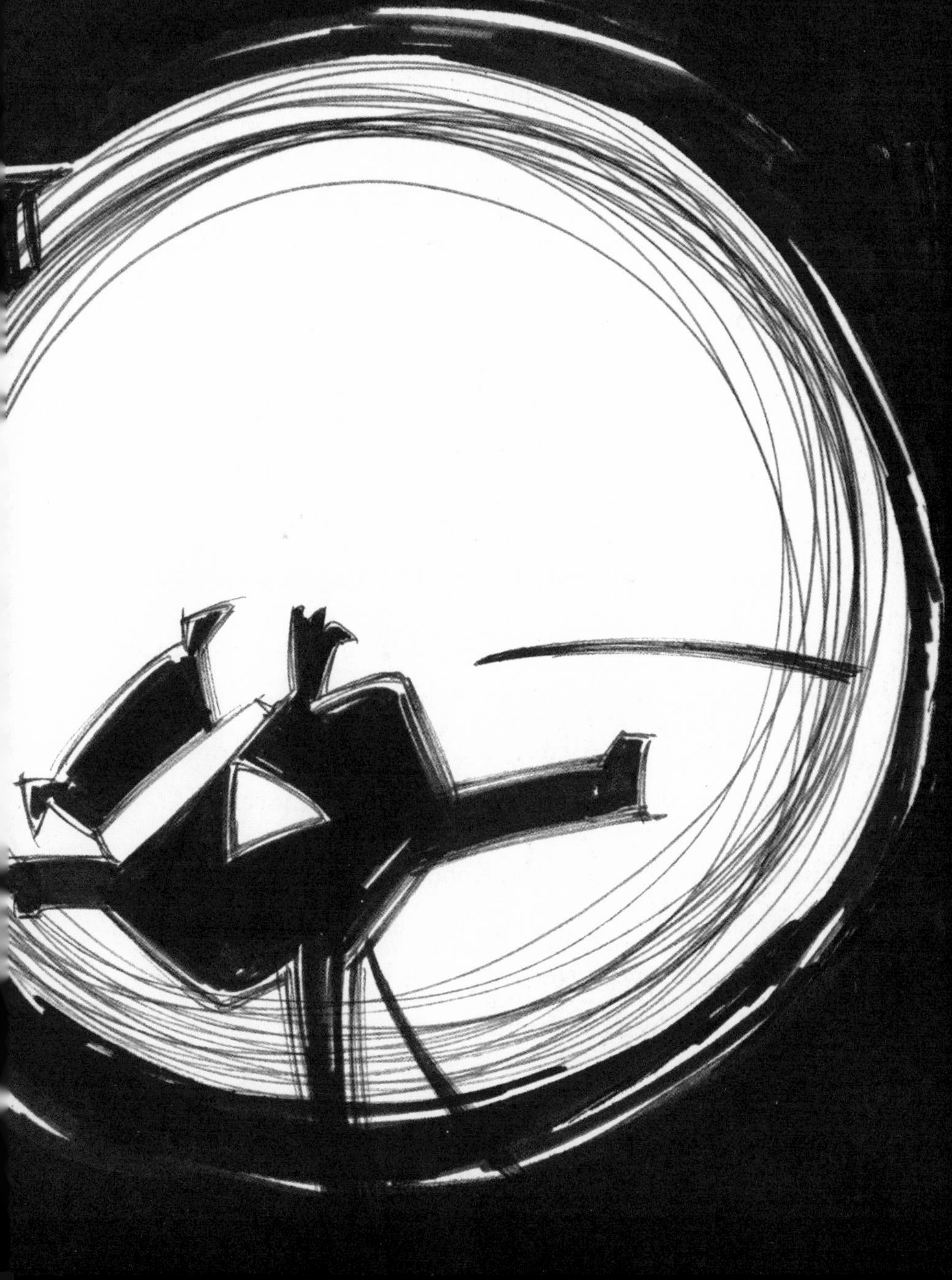

HOWWWWLLLLLL!!!

Bloodcurdling howls went up into the night as Darcy clung for dear life to the bloodhound's hindquarters. He shook and shook to rid himself of the menacing little dog, but Darcy bit even harder, and Kobold was pulled from his feet as his bloodhound attempted to free himself from the intense pain by running. The bloodhound set pace like a racehorse. Darcy dangled from the animal's hind legs, now unwilling to let go for fear of being trampled underfoot and later eaten as a morsel by the hound.

"Gilbert—stop!" shouted Kobold to his precious hound.

Seizing their chance, Erik and Sadie ran into the wood that circled the heath. Martinet got to his feet, unsure which way they had gone. All he could see was the hound dragging Kobold across the gravel toward the door of the school.

Then the leash snapped, and Kobold thudded to a halt. The hound leaped forward, yelping with each stride as Darcy held fast. He made toward the door in the hope that Darcy, who had now increased her deathlike grip, would let go.

Squinting from one eye, Darcy saw the open door of Isambard Dunstan's and feared the invasion of her home. She bit even harder—which only prompted the hound to run faster. He leaped the steps just as Miss Rimmer came to the open door. Darcy saw her mistress knocked from her feet as the two dogs flew through the doorway.

Within seconds, every child in the school had been shocked from her slumber by the cries of the hound that now raced the corridors howling and yelping, unable to free himself from Darcy's jaws. The door to the dormitory burst open, and girls were jolted from sleep by the sight of a beast racing frantically around the room with Darcy firmly attached to his rear.

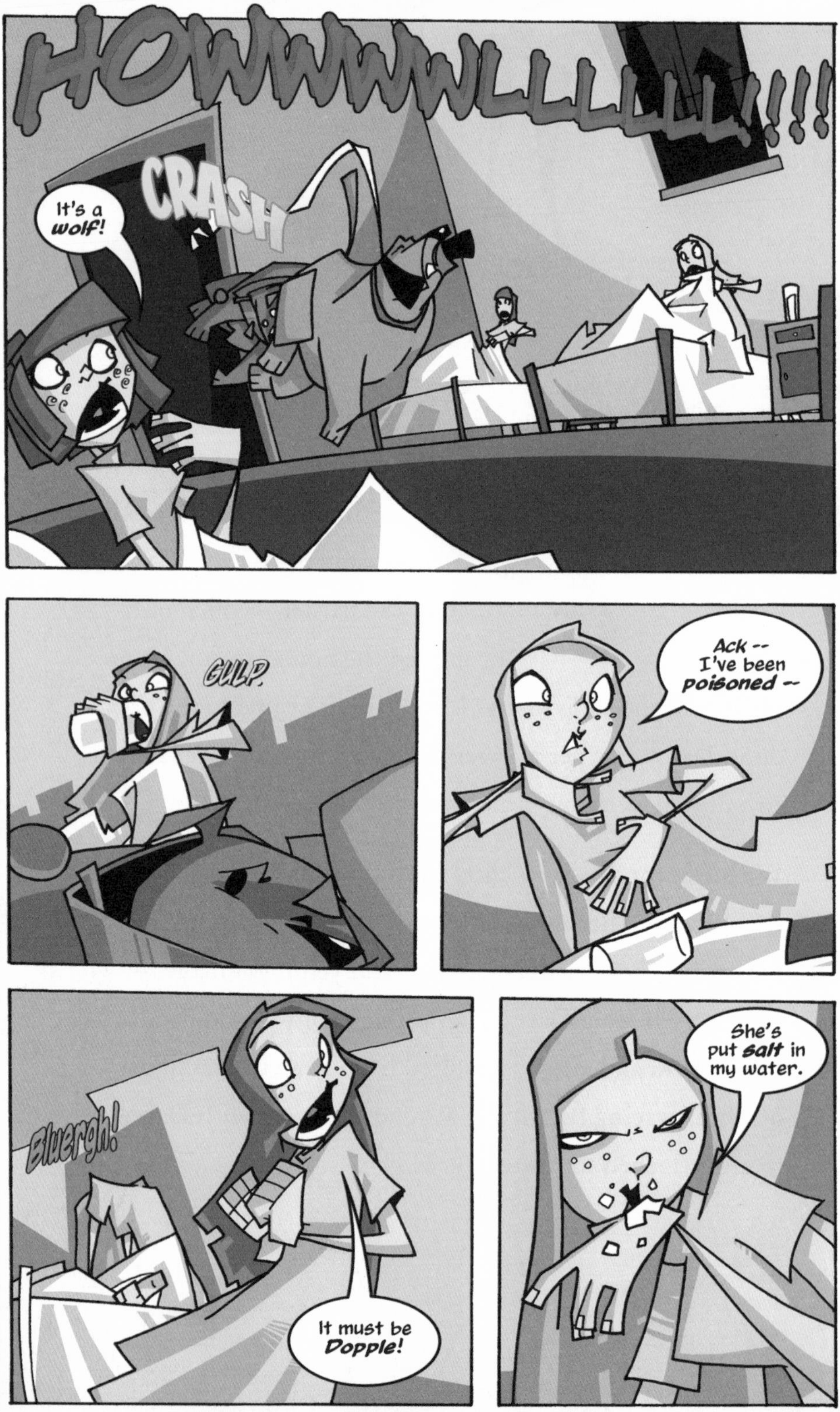
HOWWWWLLLLLLL!!!
CRASH
It's a wolf!
GULP.
Ack -- I've been poisoned --
Bluergh!
It must be Dopple!
She's put salt in my water.

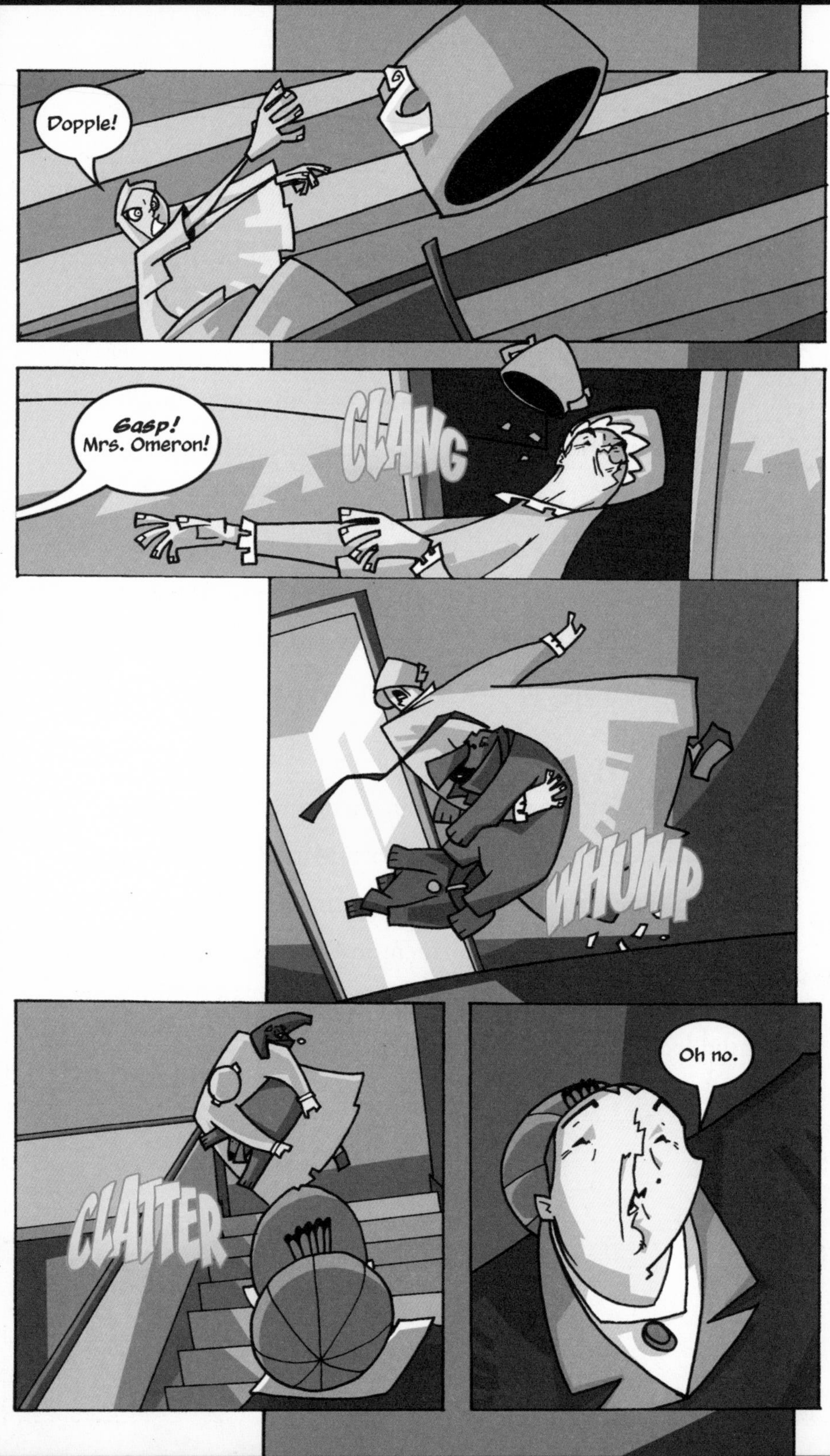
Dopple!
Gasp! Mrs. Omeron!
CLANG
WHUMP
CLATTER
Oh no.

Miss Rimmer stood in shock at the sight of beast, pet, and cook tumbling down the stairs toward her in a giant ball of flesh and fur. Before she could scream, Miss Rimmer was again knocked to the floor. Mrs. Omeron untangled herself from the hound and was flung upon the mistress with a thump. The two ladies grappled with each other to get free, which was all the more difficult since they kept tripping over Mrs. Omeron's nightdress. Screaming, fleeing children ran down the stairs and gathered around the two entwined bodies as urgent howls continued to fill the night air.

Gilbert had at last succeeded in throwing Darcy from his backside when he collided with Miss Rimmer for the second time. He continued to yelp in pain as he raced out the door away from his tormentor. Darcy stood by the open door and barked loudly, jumping up and down on her hind legs, fearful to go any farther.

Outside, Kobold grabbed the now-tattered leash and returned Gilbert to the back of the gray prison van. For the first time in his life, Gilbert was pleased to be caged. He was safe from the ravages of the fat, frenzied dog.

Martinet did not look pleased. He pounded his fist against the side of the van as he shouted at Kobold. "They're getting away. You said you had a beast that would find them. Look at what it's done!"

"My hound has done nothing," Kobold protested. "It was her fat animal that did the damage," he raged.

"My dog was protecting herself and these children!" screamed Miss Rimmer, who by now was standing on the top step surrounded by a posse of frightened girls. "Bring Erik and Dopple back tonight, Mr. Martinet, or you will not have a job in the morning."

Chapter Nine

Madame Petrusa

MADAME PETRUSA LAY facedown on the table. The strange words she was uttering stopped suddenly, and all was quiet. Then Brummagem mumbled something to Muzz Elliott, who glared at Crowley. In turn he yawned furiously.

"I take it we shan't be eating?" Crowley asked, realizing that the séance had already begun.

"Food or phantasms? What do you prefer?" Brummagem asked as he pulled the thick curtains across the door, turned off the electric chandelier, and lit two candles, placing them on the table. "Muzz Elliott would like to hear from Oscar, and it's better to listen to him than to your stomach."

"Do you have a word for us, madame?" Muzz Elliott asked Petrusa.

There was no reply. The woman just breathed heavily, drops of perspiration dribbling down her nose and onto the tablecloth.

Saskia held on to her chair with both hands. Next to her, Crowley fiddled with his monocle. "Get on with it, Petrusa," he moaned. "The sooner you wire yourself to the spirits, the sooner I can eat."

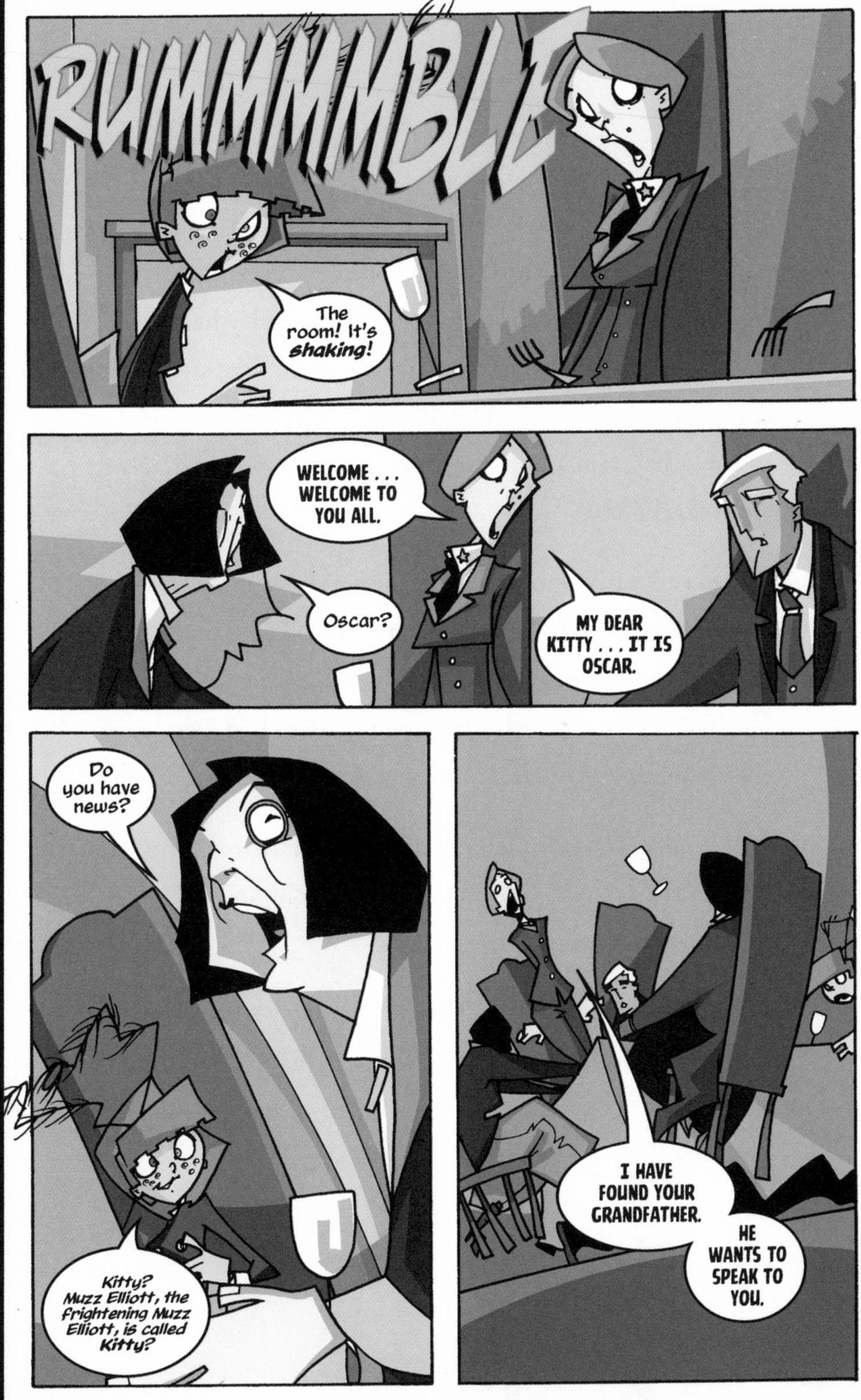
RUMMMMMBLE
The room! It's *shaking!*
WELCOME . . . WELCOME TO YOU ALL.
Oscar?
MY DEAR KITTY . . . IT IS OSCAR.
Do you have news?
Kitty? Muzz Elliott, the frightening Muzz Elliott, is called *Kitty?*
I HAVE FOUND YOUR GRANDFATHER.
HE WANTS TO SPEAK TO YOU.

Saskia couldn't believe what she was now seeing. The room was filling with strands of smoke that oozed from Madame Petrusa's ears, and it was as if gravity had been reversed—all around her, objects began to float in midair. A large potted plant wobbled from one side of the room to the other, and a portrait of Muzz Elliott's grandfather spun on the wall.

Saskia suddenly remembered a circus show she had seen with her mother and Sadie, where tables had danced through the air and even an elephant had appeared to fly. She had believed it to be magic—until she had overheard someone explaining how the trick had been done.

"All it takes is someone to manipulate the wires from behind the scenes," Saskia thought. "Hold on—where did Brummagem go?"

"What does Lord Trevellyn say?" Crowley's booming voice interrupted Saskia's thoughts, as his knife and fork took on a life of their own and slipped across the table onto the floor.

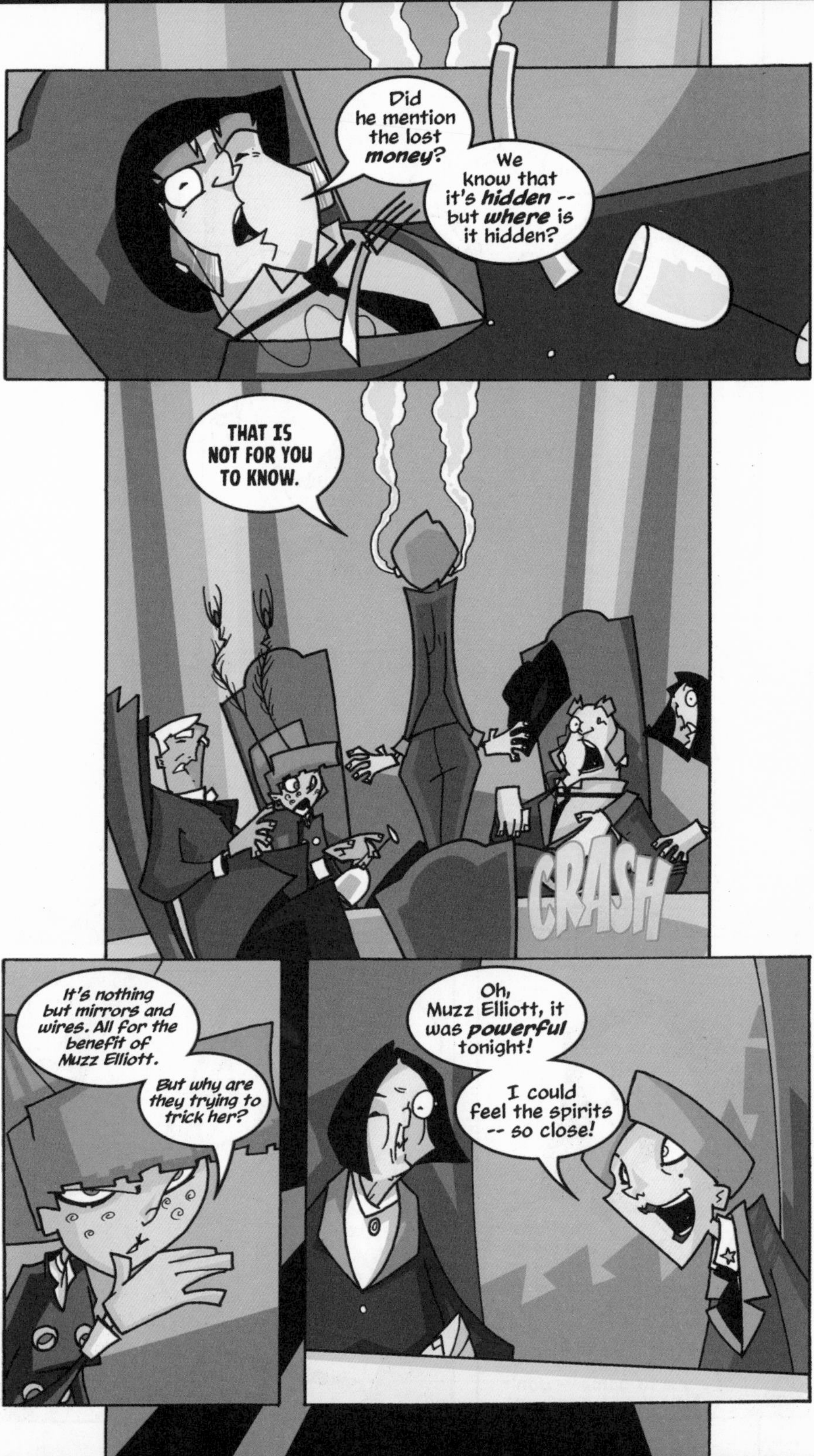
Did he mention the lost money?
We know that it's hidden -- but where is it hidden?
THAT IS NOT FOR YOU TO KNOW.
CRASH
It's nothing but mirrors and wires. All for the benefit of Muzz Elliott.
But why are they trying to trick her?
Oh, Muzz Elliott, it was powerful tonight!
I could feel the spirits -- so close!

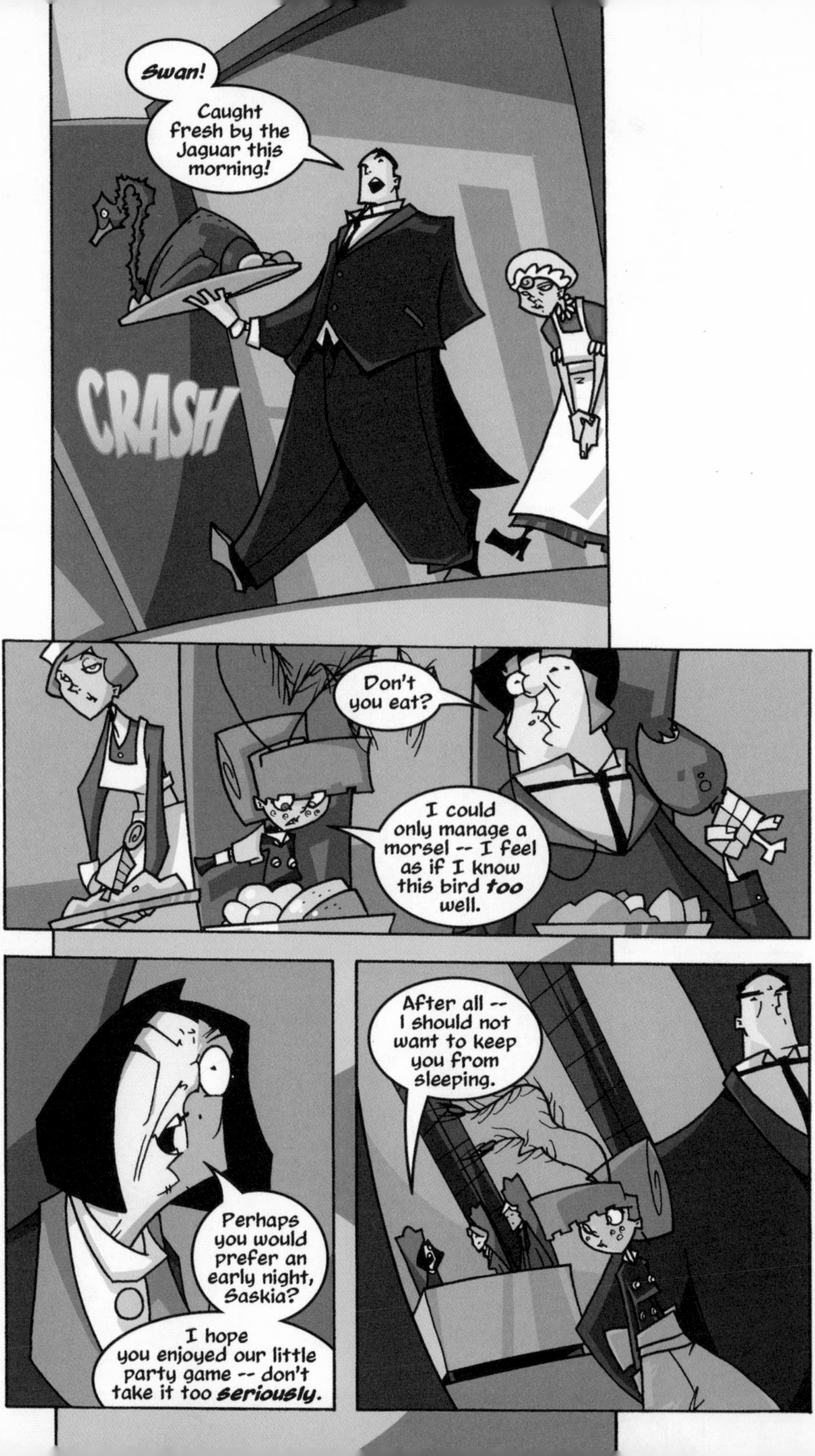
Swan!
Caught fresh by the Jaguar this morning!
CRASH
Don't you eat?
I could only manage a morsel -- I feel as if I know this bird too well.
Perhaps you would prefer an early night, Saskia?
I hope you enjoyed our little party game -- don't take it too seriously.
After all -- I should not want to keep you from sleeping.

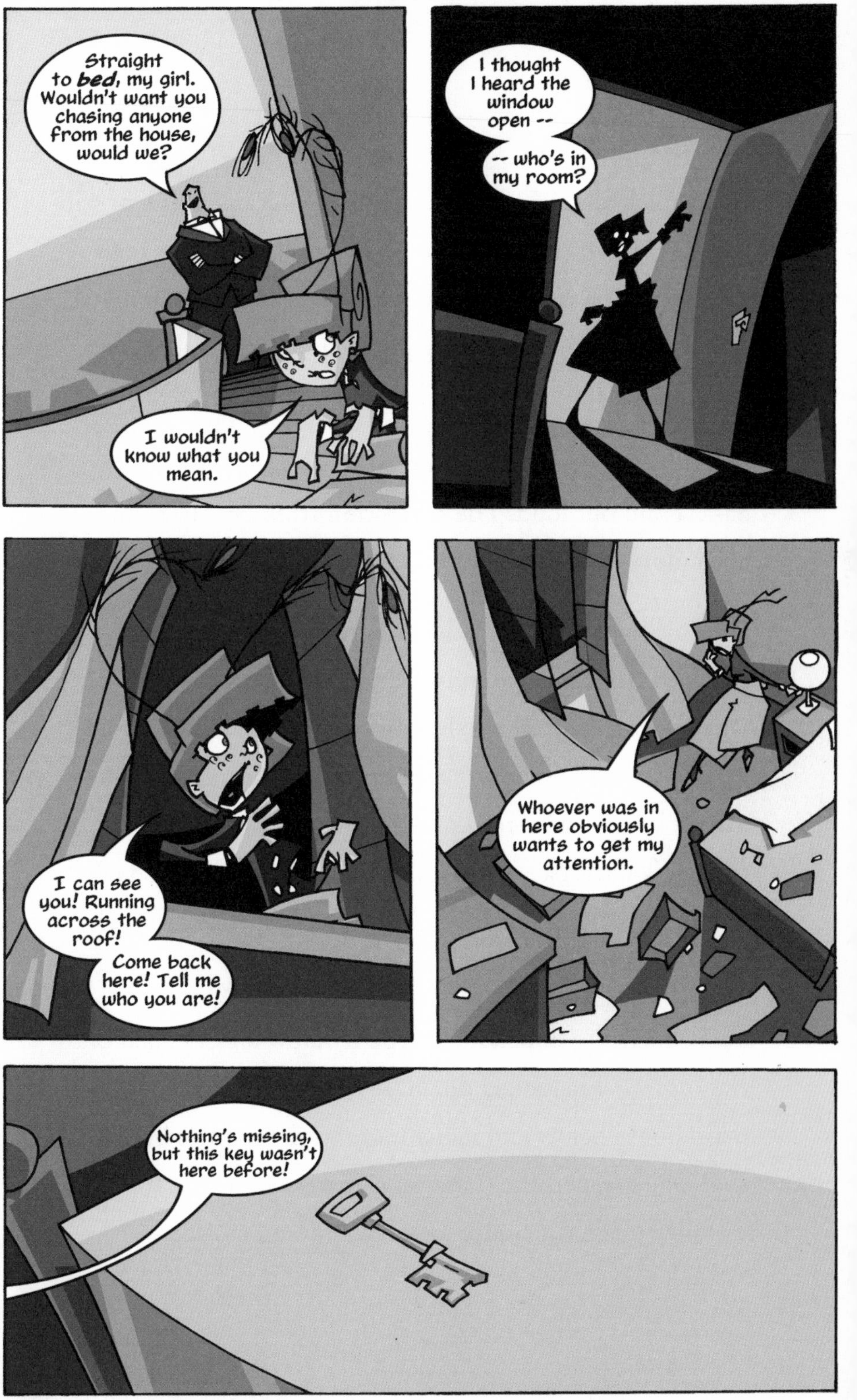
Straight to bed, my girl. Wouldn't want you chasing anyone from the house, would we?
I wouldn't know what you mean.
I thought I heard the window open --
-- who's in my room?
I can see you! Running across the roof!
Come back here! Tell me who you are!
Whoever was in here obviously wants to get my attention.
Nothing's missing, but this key wasn't here before!

Saskia picked up the key and held it in her hand. It was still warm, as if whoever had left it had clutched it close for a long time. She rubbed her fingers across the smooth metal. It was well worn and too big for the lock on her door. She thought for a moment and then knew what to do.

"If Sadie were here she'd go after the person who left this," Saskia said out loud. The separation from her sister hurt even more at the thought. "What do I have to lose?"

She quickly cleared away the mess on the floor. Then she searched the wardrobe and found an old coat, a hat, and a whalebone corset, which she stuffed under the sheets to make it look like she was sleeping. She put on a pair of boots, a thick jacket, and some leather gloves that were hanging together on the back of the door. She tied a belt around her waist and then slipped the key into her pocket and turned out the light.

Soon she had climbed out of the window and stepped onto the roof. Saskia looked down. It was two floors to the main house below and many more to the ground beneath that. She gripped the stone mock battlement that from a distance made the house look like a grand castle.

The ledge was the width of two spanned hands and was coated with lead. To Saskia's right was a drop to the gravel drive; to her left was the roof of the house. She felt giddy, cold, and completely on her own.

Saskia pulled the window closed behind her. To her horror, the latch slipped and locked the frame from the inside. She was stuck now—there was no going back. The wind blew, and the cold night air swirled about her. In the wood she could again see the lamplight that she had watched before dinner. It flashed like a beacon as though whoever carried it—was it Muzz Elliott?—was signaling to someone in the house.

"Sadie," she whispered, "where are you?"

For a moment she remembered the look on her sister's face when Saskia had been chosen and Sadie was to be left behind. The words Sadie had spoken came back to Saskia: "Imagine that, Saskia, a room of your own in a big house. . . . I'll come and find you."

"I'll find you, Sadie," she answered. "I'm not staying here, not without you." Her words were carried on the wind, out across the heath.

rain started to *fa*

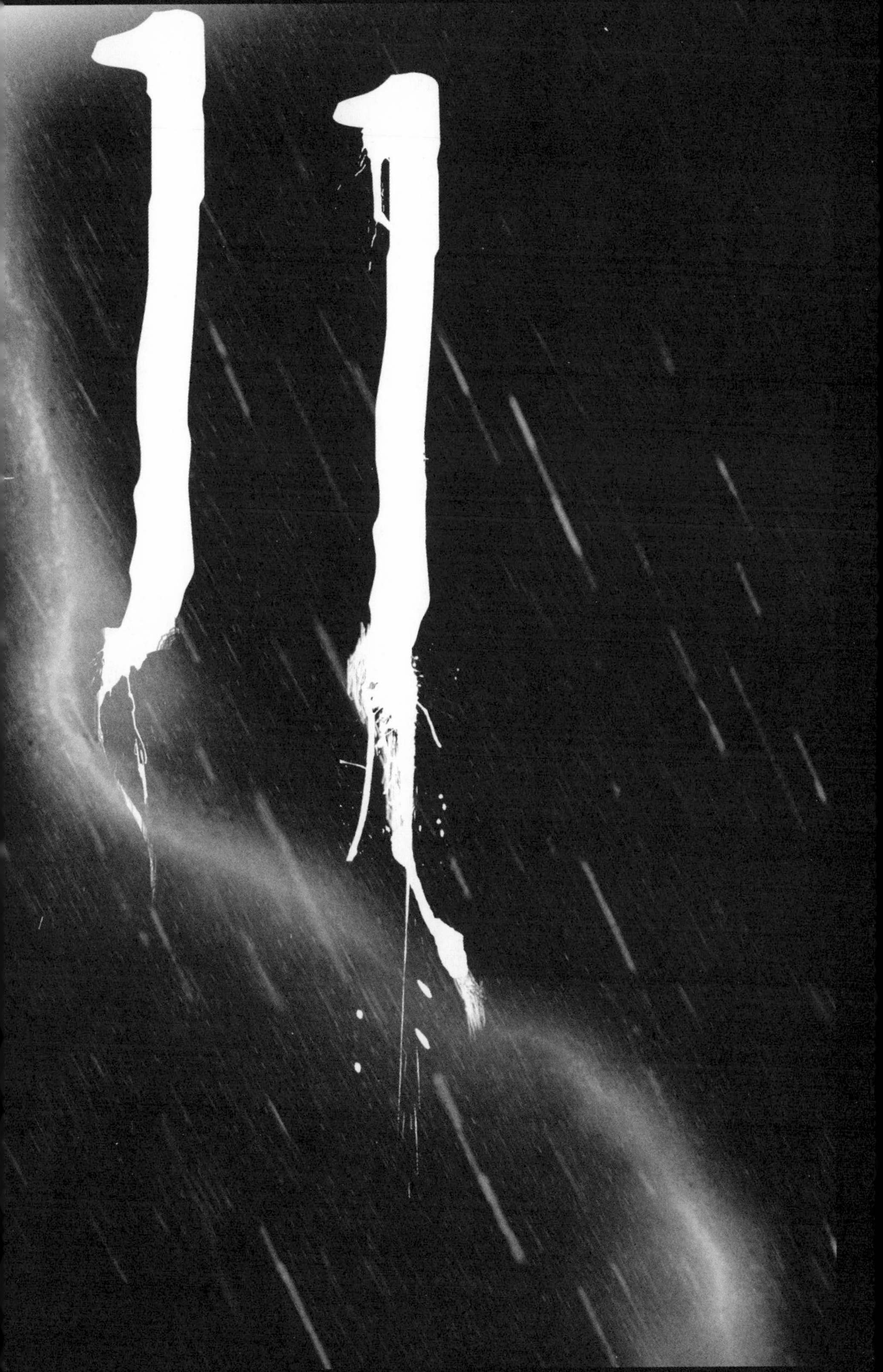
11

At first it dripped from the sky, splashing against the lead and dribbling down the stone. It beat faster, harder, as Saskia crept across the battlement toward the far tower. She kept her eyes on the lamplight in the wood. As before, it moved closer to the house, in and out of the trees.

All the time, the wind blew and the rain bit at her skin. Saskia looked down. Her head swirled with the height. The ground looked like it would reach up and pull her from the ramparts. She felt sick; she imagined the sliver of roasted swan beating its wings in her stomach and trying to jump from her mouth. Her heart thumped faster.

The ledge was covered in green, bubbling moss that squished underfoot like a thick, wet sponge cake. Saskia held on to each pinnacle of stone that formed the mock battlements and moved slowly across the slippery surface. Every time she looked down she felt dizzier. A sudden gust of wind whipped around her. She twisted, her foot slipped, and then she fell.

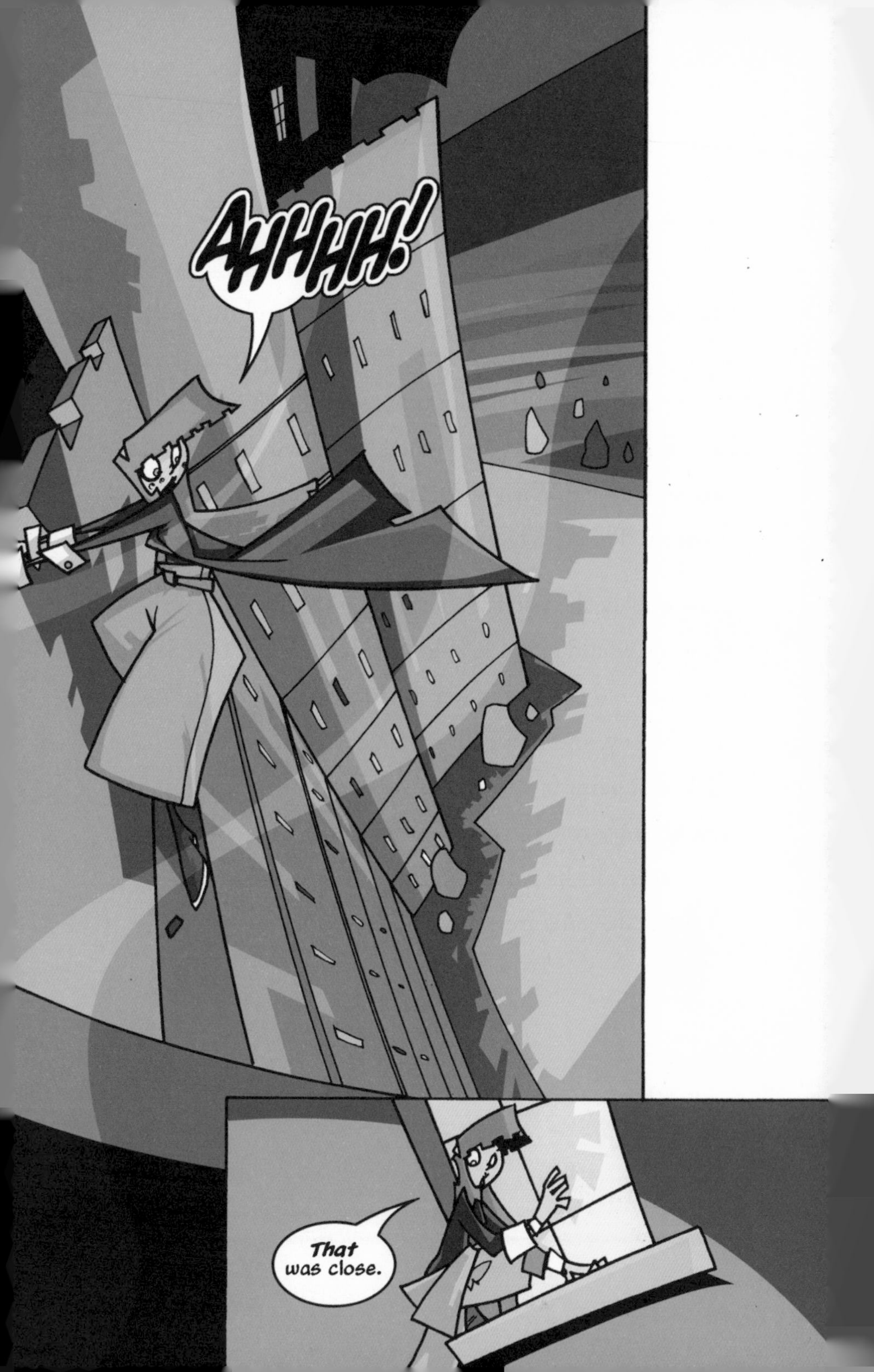
AHHHH!
That was close.

Her heart still beating fast, Saskia clung tightly to the narrow window ledge of the far tower. Her arms ached from pulling herself back up onto the battlements after her fall. She kept her eyes glued to the window and did not look down. With one hand, she pushed against the window. This one too was locked. Saskia was trapped.

Desperately she tried again, hoping that somehow the window would open. It held fast. It was then that Saskia remembered the key in her pocket. She reached in, took out the key, and tapped it in the corner of the glass pane. Flakes of paint fell away. Saskia chipped more and more until the bottom of the glass came into view. Soon she had taken all the paint and caulk from the glass and pushed two nails from the windowpane.

Saskia took a piece of glass from the window, slipped her hand inside, and opened the latch. She grinned in triumph. The Dopple twins had used this trick before to escape from their dormitory at Isambard Dunstan's in the dead of night. Once they had stolen a fat carp from the fish pond and left it in the water bowl of Miss Rimmer's private toilet. Even in the midst of her current danger, Saskia couldn't help smiling at the memory.

Her feet slipped on the wet moss as she scrambled to pull herself through the open window. She closed the window, stuffed the hole with the edge of the curtain, and looked around. The room was empty. It was identical to hers but had not one stick of furniture. She opened the door and peered into the thick blackness of the passageway.

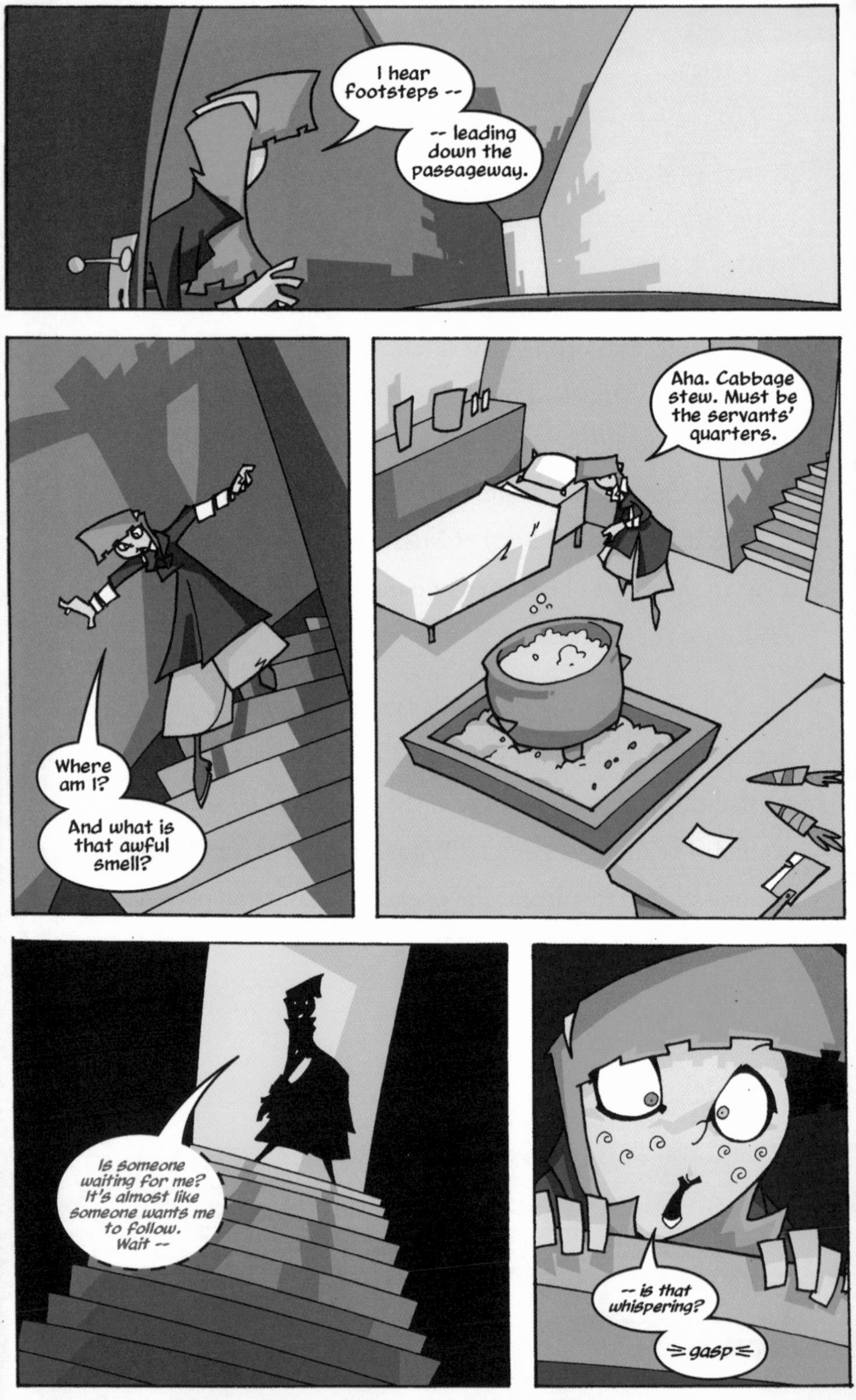
I hear footsteps --
-- leading down the passageway.
Where am I?
And what is that awful smell?
Aha. Cabbage stew. Must be the servants' quarters.
Is someone waiting for me? It's almost like someone wants me to follow. Wait --
-- is that whispering?
gasp

Crouching down like a mouse at the top of a flight of stairs, Saskia peered over the edge of the musty carpet. She could see a door that led to the outside at the back of the house.

There, at the bottom of the stairs, with his back to her, stood Brummagem. In his hand he held a torch. He was dressed in dark clothes and wrapped in a thick scarf. He was talking to a woman in a long coat with a hat pulled down to her eyes. At first Saskia couldn't make out his words, but as she listened, she caught snatches of what he was saying and realized who he was speaking to. As the woman turned, she looked up.

It was the woman Saskia had followed into the garden. The perfect image of Muzz Elliott but clothed like a London burglar.

Chapter Ten

The Magician of Hampstead

AS SADIE AND ERIK RAN through the woods they could hear the screams of rage coming from the school. Miss Rimmer howled and shrieked like an old owl.

"Get them . . .

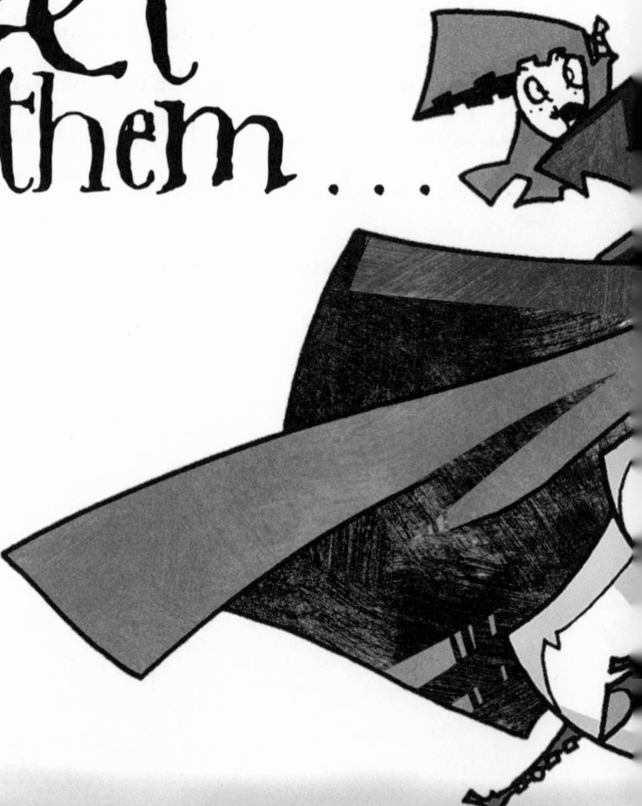

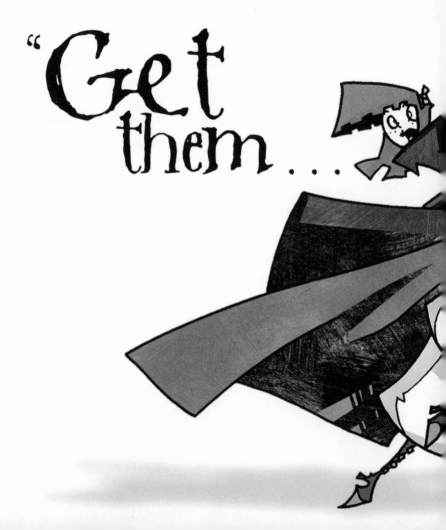

bring them back . . .

now!"

. . . she shouted at Kobold and Martinet.

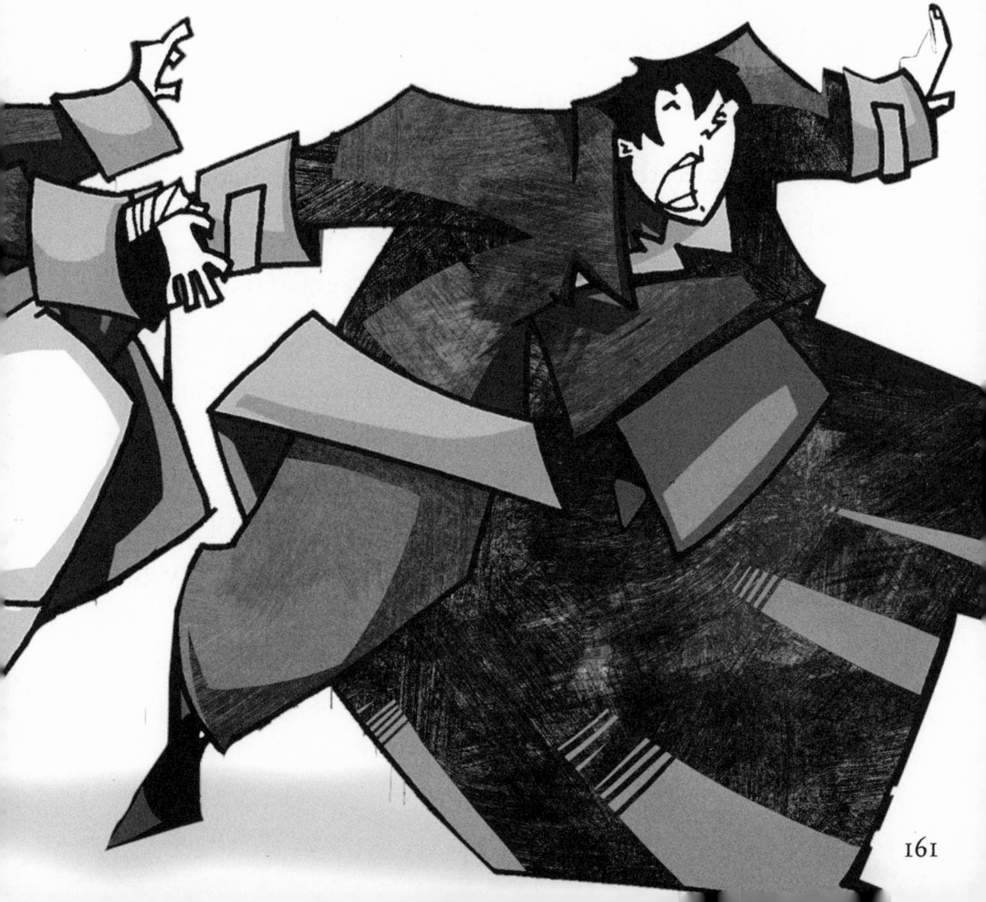

Erik pulled the coat around his shoulders and tried to keep hold of Sadie's hand.

"They're coming after us?" Sadie whispered as they paused under the branches of a large fir tree that dripped and drizzled beads of rain.

"As sure as eggs—" Erik said, unable to finish his words as the cry of the bloodhound echoed through the night. It seemed to come from all around them. Wherever the hound was, he was very near. "We have to run," Erik said, pulling on Sadie's arm. "Over here."

They scrambled through the trees and across the open heath toward the light of the large houses that edged Hampstead Way. Now they were in open grassland with nowhere to hide. As they bounded on, a shallow mist crept up Parliament Hill toward them. It swirled in dark patches like gray horsemen galloping through the night.

Suddenly there was a short, shrill scream as Erik tripped and plunged headlong over what appeared to be a low wall.

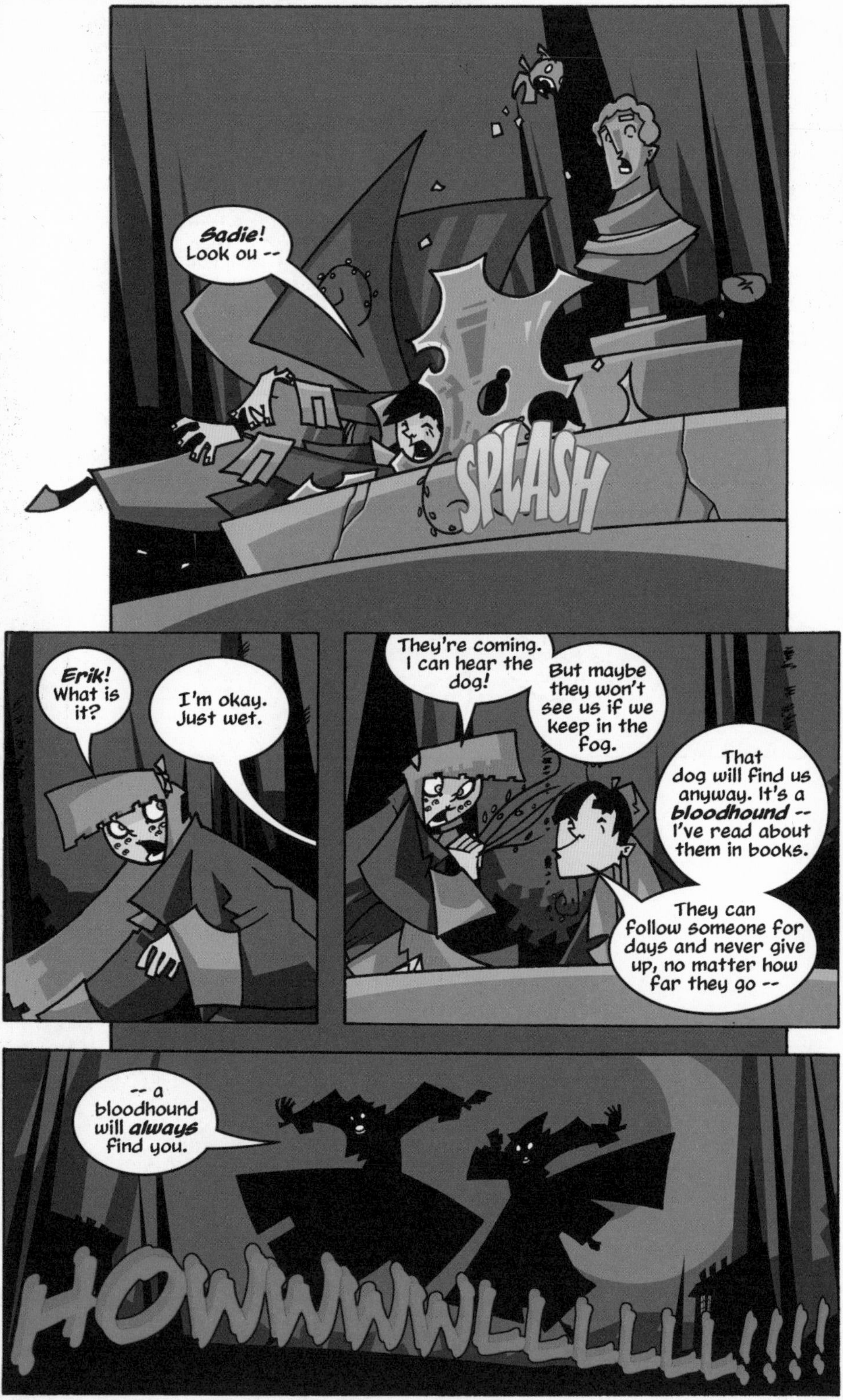

Sadie! Look ou --
SPLASH
Erik! What is it?
I'm okay. Just wet.
They're coming. I can hear the dog!
But maybe they won't see us if we keep in the fog.
That dog will find us anyway. It's a bloodhound -- I've read about them in books.
They can follow someone for days and never give up, no matter how far they go --
-- a bloodhound will always find you.
HOWWWWLLLLLLL!!!!

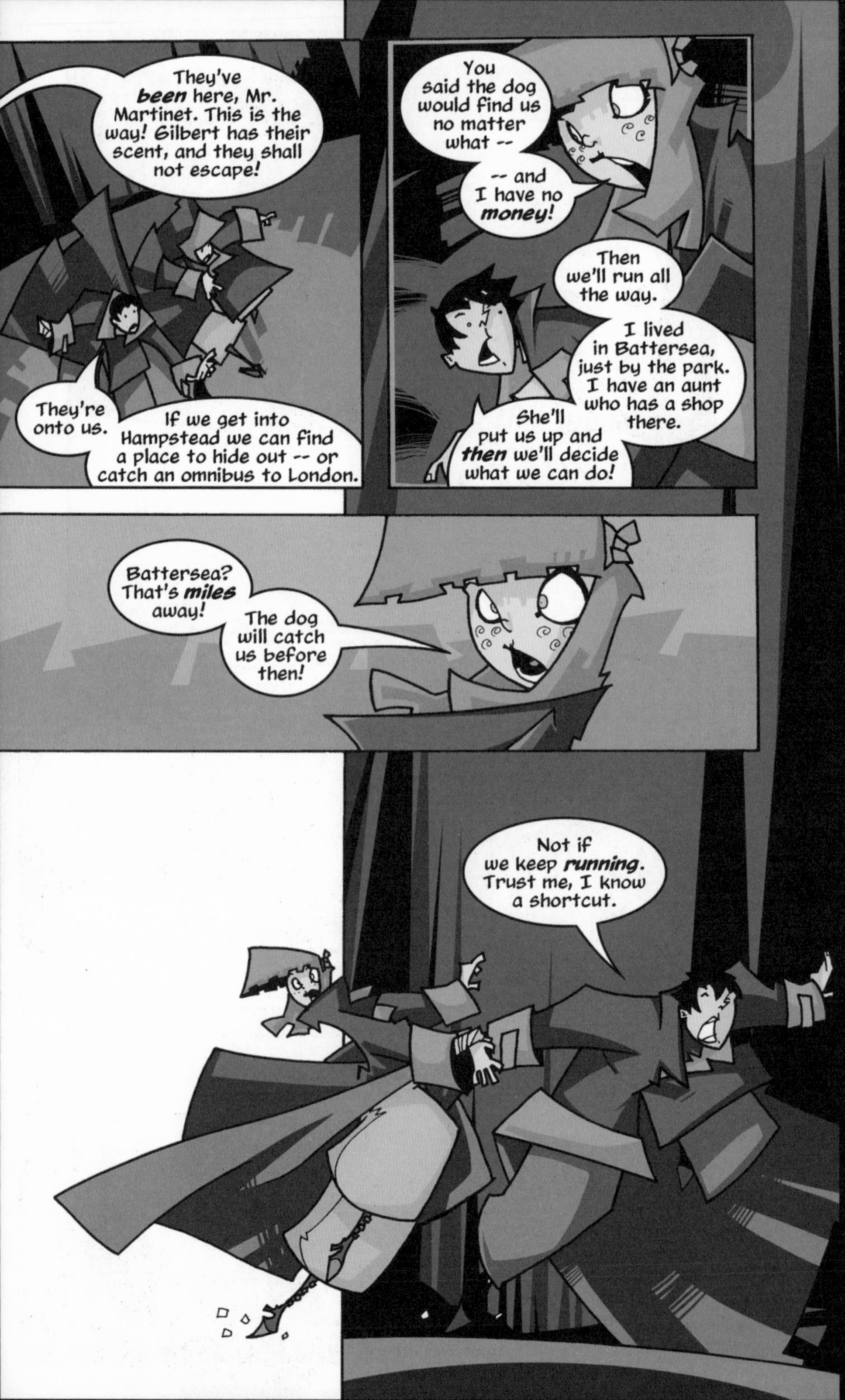
They've been here, Mr. Martinet. This is the way! Gilbert has their scent, and they shall not escape!
They're onto us.
If we get into Hampstead we can find a place to hide out -- or catch an omnibus to London.
You said the dog would find us no matter what --
-- and I have no money!
Then we'll run all the way.
I lived in Battersea, just by the park. I have an aunt who has a shop there.
She'll put us up and then we'll decide what we can do!
Battersea? That's miles away!
The dog will catch us before then!
Not if we keep running. Trust me, I know a shortcut.

In ten paces they had crossed the road and left the heath behind. Houses loomed out of the fog before them. The windows glinted like diamonds, lit by the line of gas lamps that ran along each street. Row upon row of metal railings guarded each fine house, and every door was lit with its own lamp to welcome the weary.

Sadie and Erik ran downhill. The big, stately houses changed quickly to small, neat buildings that were fronted by shop windows. Erik's boots squished as he ran, the water from the fountain oozing from them. He shivered with the cold as he and Sadie rushed through the empty streets.

On the corner of the road stood a policeman. Erik saw him first and dragged Sadie into the doorway of a shop. In the light of the gas lamp, they could see him preening his long mustache and rubbing his chin. He leaned against the wall and every few seconds took out a pocket watch and looked at the time.

"He's waiting the point," Erik whispered.

"What?" asked Sadie.

"Waiting for the sergeant to come along and sign his notebook. I've seen them do it tons of times. Know your enemy—that's what my dad said."

"Your dad was an enemy of the police?" Sadie asked.

"A burglar from a long line of burglars. And he taught me everything he knew."

"But he left you behind?"

"Went for some cigarettes and never came back. I expect he did a job along the way and got caught. I miss my old man, but I don't miss the stealing," Erik said, still spying on the copper.

From up the hill came the sound of the barking hound and the tramping of footsteps. Kobold and Martinet were in hot pursuit. The bloodhound had found its way across the heath and now easily followed the runaways' trail through the streets. It sniffed and snorted as it pulled Kobold on the long leash, following the intriguing scent of Erik and Sadie.

"This way." Kobold's voice rattled from building to building and down the empty street.

Erik pulled Sadie deeper into the shadows of the shop doorway.

"We'll have to run for it. The copper can't catch both of us," he whispered. "I'll run at him and you keep going. Take the first alleyway you come to, and we'll meet up there."

Now run, Sadie—

run as if your life depended on it.

"I don't want to go back." With that Erik dashed from the doorway and ran breakneck toward the surprised policeman. Sadie chased behind.

"Coming to kill us—two men," Erik shouted at the cop as they ran toward him, "and a mad dog!"

Gilbert's distant howling and Kobold's manic screaming added to what Erik had said. The constable looked at the drenched boy and believed every word. He pulled a silver whistle from his pocket and blew it.

Sadie ran on and Erik followed.

"What made you say that?" she asked as he got to the alleyway seconds after her and ran into the darkness.

"First thing that came into my head. Had to think of something. Maybe he'll arrest them."

"Do you know where you're going?" she asked as the alleyway narrowed and the walls hemmed them in.

"Sort of . . . think so . . . not really," Erik admitted as the passage became too narrow to run any farther.

"It's a dead end," Sadie whispered, looking up at a blank wall that reached to the black night sky. "What'll we do?"

There was no time for Erik to reply. From the far end of the alleyway, where it joined the street, came the tap, tap, tap of steel-tipped shoes. In the darkness they could see no one, just the faint red light of a burning cigar.

Erik pushed Sadie behind two large trash cans that stood side by side. They hid close to each other and waited to be discovered.

"Oh well," Erik whispered faintly. "It's the farthest anybody has escaped."

"So . . . they're looking for you?" said a voice from above them.

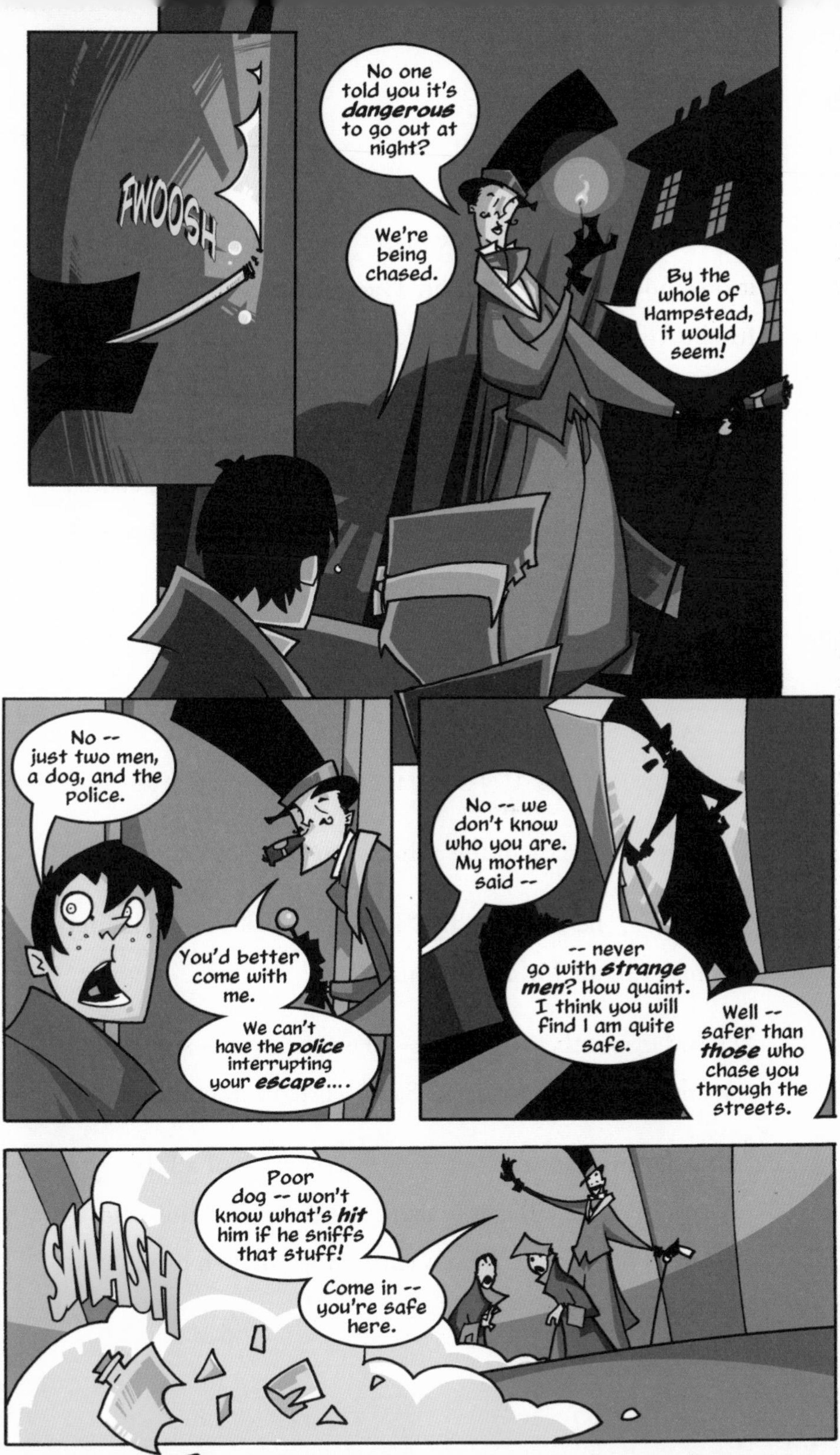
FWOOSH
No one told you it's *dangerous* to go out at night?
We're being chased.
By the whole of Hampstead, it would seem!
No -- just two men, a dog, and the police.
You'd better come with me.
We can't have the *police* interrupting your *escape*....
No -- we don't know who you are. My mother said --
-- never go with *strange men*? How quaint. I think you will find I am quite safe.
Well -- safer than *those* who chase you through the streets.
SMASH
Poor dog -- won't know what's *hit* him if he sniffs that stuff!
Come in -- you're safe here.

Once they were inside, the man took off his hat and placed it on a hook beside the door. The room was lit by a large fire burning in the grate. Erik looked around. Hanging from the ceiling was the most bizarre collection of devices he had ever seen. There was a replica of a gallows and a guillotine. Next to that was a large hoop, coated in twine, and by its side the front end of a horse costume. Above the fireplace was an old poster that read:

PARIS, 1908

THE GREAT POTEMKIN—ILLUSIONIST
AND STORYTELLER EXTRAORDINAIRE

AND THE UNDOUBTABLE MR. WOSS

The man saw Erik looking at his worn-out picture.

"That's me," he said proudly. "I am the Great Potemkin, but you may call me Mr. Potemkin."

"I heard my mother talk of you—she's an actress—she said something about an accident," Sadie blurted without thinking.

"A minor mishap, and yet my greatest trick of all. In my time I made villages disappear before the kings and emperors of Europe. But an exploding chicken brought an end to everything."

“Exploding chicken?” Erik asked as he dried himself by the fire.

“It was a great illusion that would have spellbound the world. My assistant, Mr. Woss, was to climb a long pole and balance at the top. I, in turn, would fire exploding chickens into the air. Then at the height of the conflagration, Mr. Woss would disappear in a shower of feathers before everyone’s eyes. Never before had the trick been done.

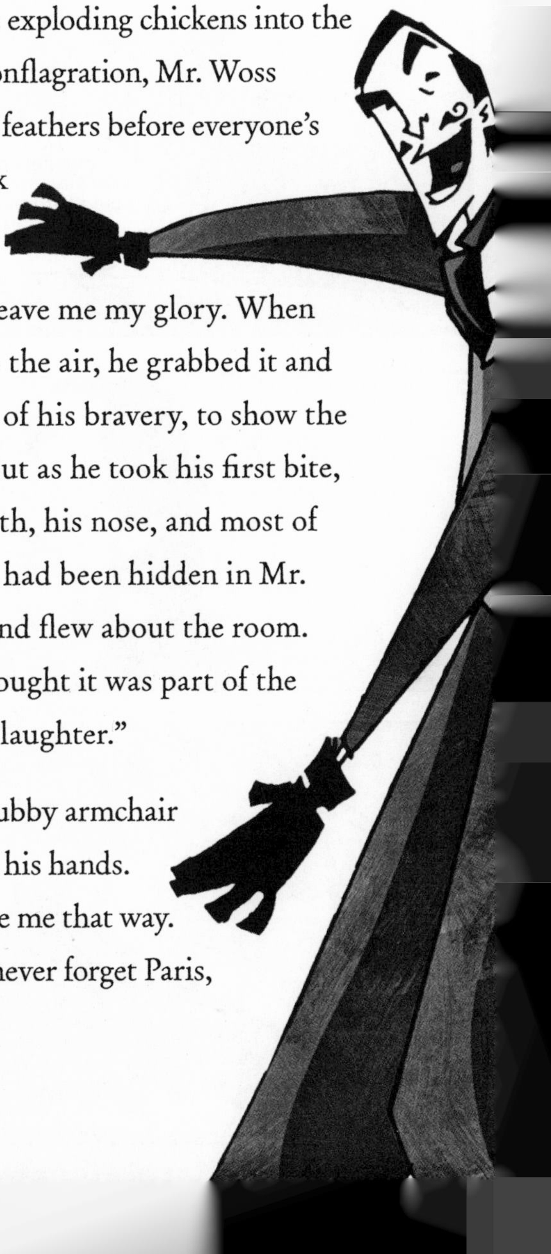

“But Mr. Woss couldn’t just leave me my glory. When the last chicken was fired into the air, he grabbed it and took a bite. He did it to boast of his bravery, to show the world he was greater than I. But as he took his first bite, the explosion blew out his teeth, his nose, and most of his head. Several pigeons that had been hidden in Mr. Woss’s vest burst into flame and flew about the room. The archduke of Germany thought it was part of the performance and roared with laughter.”

Mr. Potemkin sank into the grubby armchair by the fire and held his head in his hands. “I never thought he would leave me that way. Everything was ruined. I will never forget Paris, November 1908 . . .”

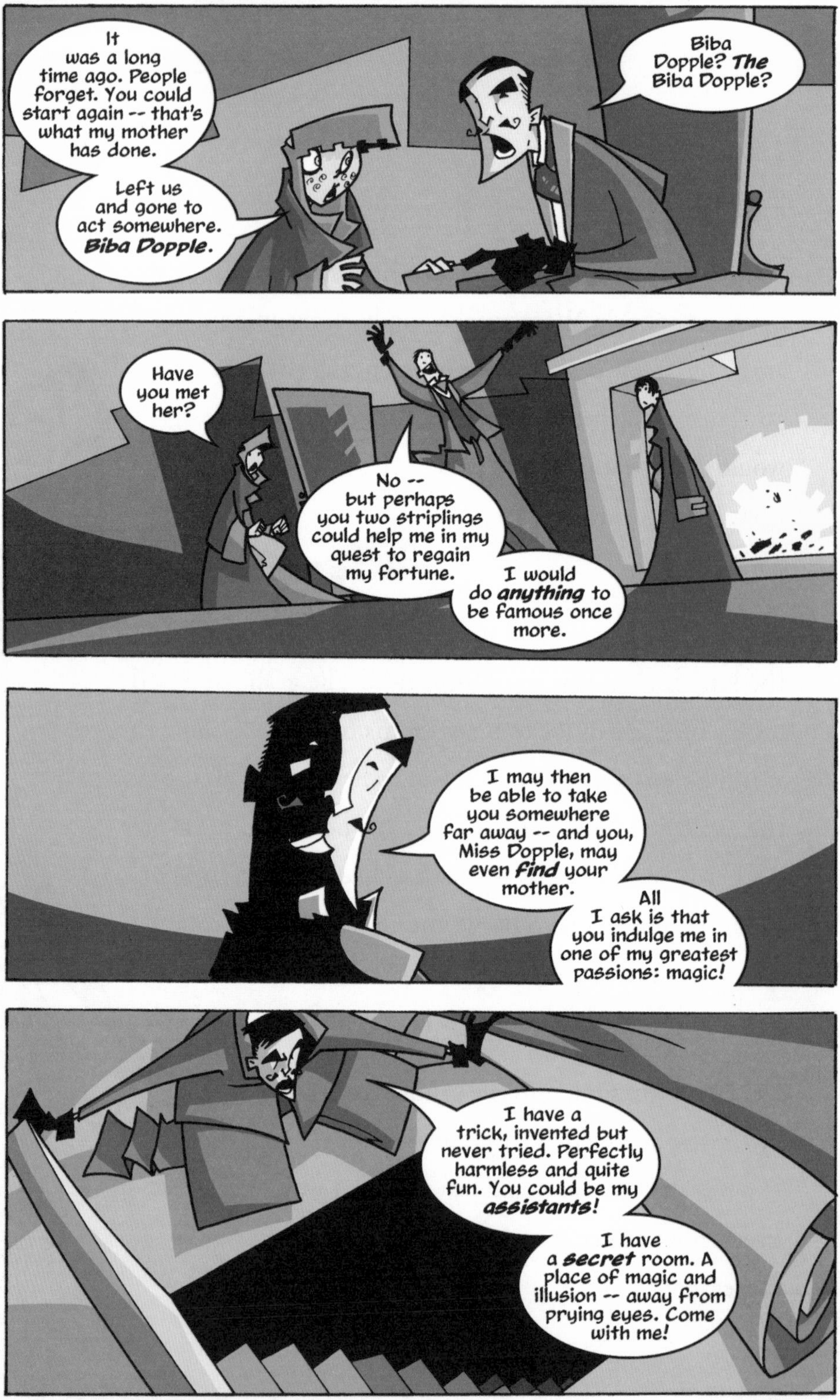
It was a long time ago. People forget. You could start again -- that's what my mother has done.
Left us and gone to act somewhere. Biba Dopple.
Biba Dopple? The Biba Dopple?
Have you met her?
No -- but perhaps you two striplings could help me in my quest to regain my fortune.
I would do anything to be famous once more.
I may then be able to take you somewhere far away -- and you, Miss Dopple, may even find your mother.
All I ask is that you indulge me in one of my greatest passions: magic!
I have a trick, invented but never tried. Perfectly harmless and quite fun. You could be my assistants!
I have a secret room. A place of magic and illusion -- away from prying eyes. Come with me!

Jumping through the trapdoor, Potemkin nimbly danced down each step, beckoning for Sadie and Erik to follow. In no time, all three stood in a dimly lit cellar with a stone floor and damp walls.

In the center of the room was a large metal contraption with several wires coming from each handle and a small wheel on the top like a carnival ride. Dangling from the wheel were two brass helmets, each one containing several small lightbulbs.

"It is a Matter Illuminator," Potemkin said as he placed the helmets on Sadie and Erik without asking. "The illusion is to make people believe that lightning can be conducted through the body to illuminate the lamps. Imagine: Are our friends electric? That will be the question they ask."

"But it's not lightning out," Erik said.

"That's why the machine is connected to the generator. Wherever the illusion is performed I will take with me my very own thunderstorm. All you have to do is take hold of the grips, and everything else is pure trickery." Potemkin was so excited that he jumped up and down and jigged from one foot to the other.

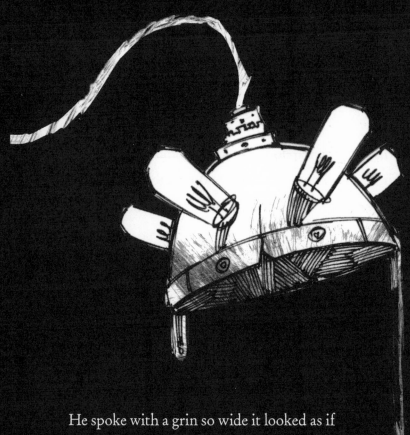

He spoke with a grin so wide it looked as if
it would cut his head in two. "On the count
of three, grab the handles. One . . . two . . .
three . . ."

Without thinking, Sadie and Erik took hold
of the handles. Their hands suddenly stuck
to the leather straps. Erik pulled, unable to
free himself.

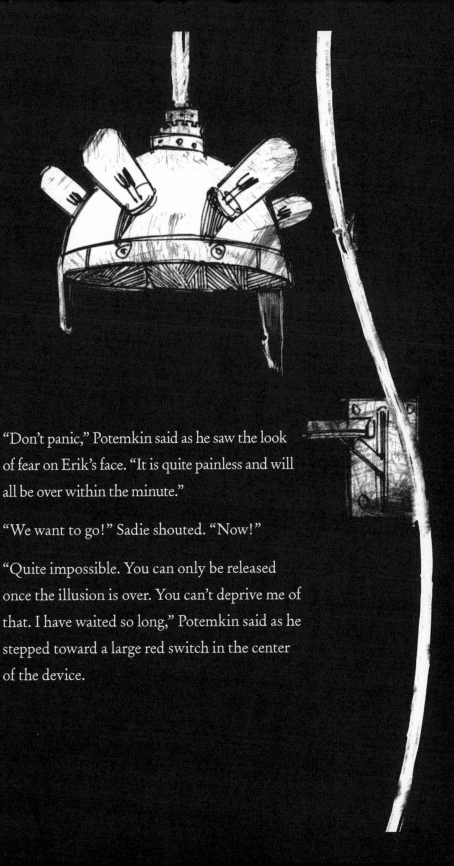

"Don't panic," Potemkin said as he saw the look of fear on Erik's face. "It is quite painless and will all be over within the minute."

"We want to go!" Sadie shouted. "Now!"

"Quite impossible. You can only be released once the illusion is over. You can't deprive me of that. I have waited so long," Potemkin said as he stepped toward a large red switch in the center of the device.

Chapter Eleven

The Insignificant Other

SASKIA SLID ALONG THE carpet until she was out
of sight. Then, when Brummagem's words had died down
to just a whisper, she got to her feet and crept along the
landing. The back door slammed, and the wind whistled
through the house. For a moment all was still. Then Saskia
heard Brummagem stomp through the kitchen and along
the corridor. Listening closely, she was sure someone was
walking with him. She followed carefully, keeping to
the wall. At the bottom of the stairs she turned into the
kitchen and quickly poured a small glass of milk from
a jug on the table.

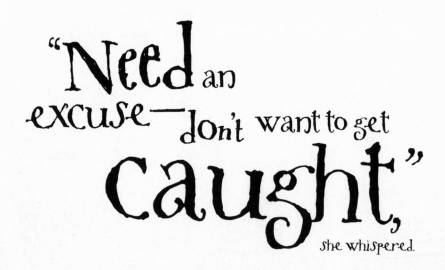

"Need an excuse—don't want to get caught," she whispered.

"I'll tell him I couldn't sleep and went to find a drink."

She sipped the milk as she walked. It tasted warm and frothy, with a hint of vanilla. Saskia followed Brummagem down the long corridor that led from the kitchen to the main hall. She kept her distance but could see two shadows cast against the wall and could hear two voices muttering to each other.

Saskia turned a corner and saw Brummagem with Muzz Elliott's double in the hallway by the stairs. The woman had taken off the hat and coat she had been wearing and now looked more like Muzz Elliott than ever. Saskia watched curiously as the two searched behind every picture that hung from the wall. There was a sudden jangling of the servant's bell.

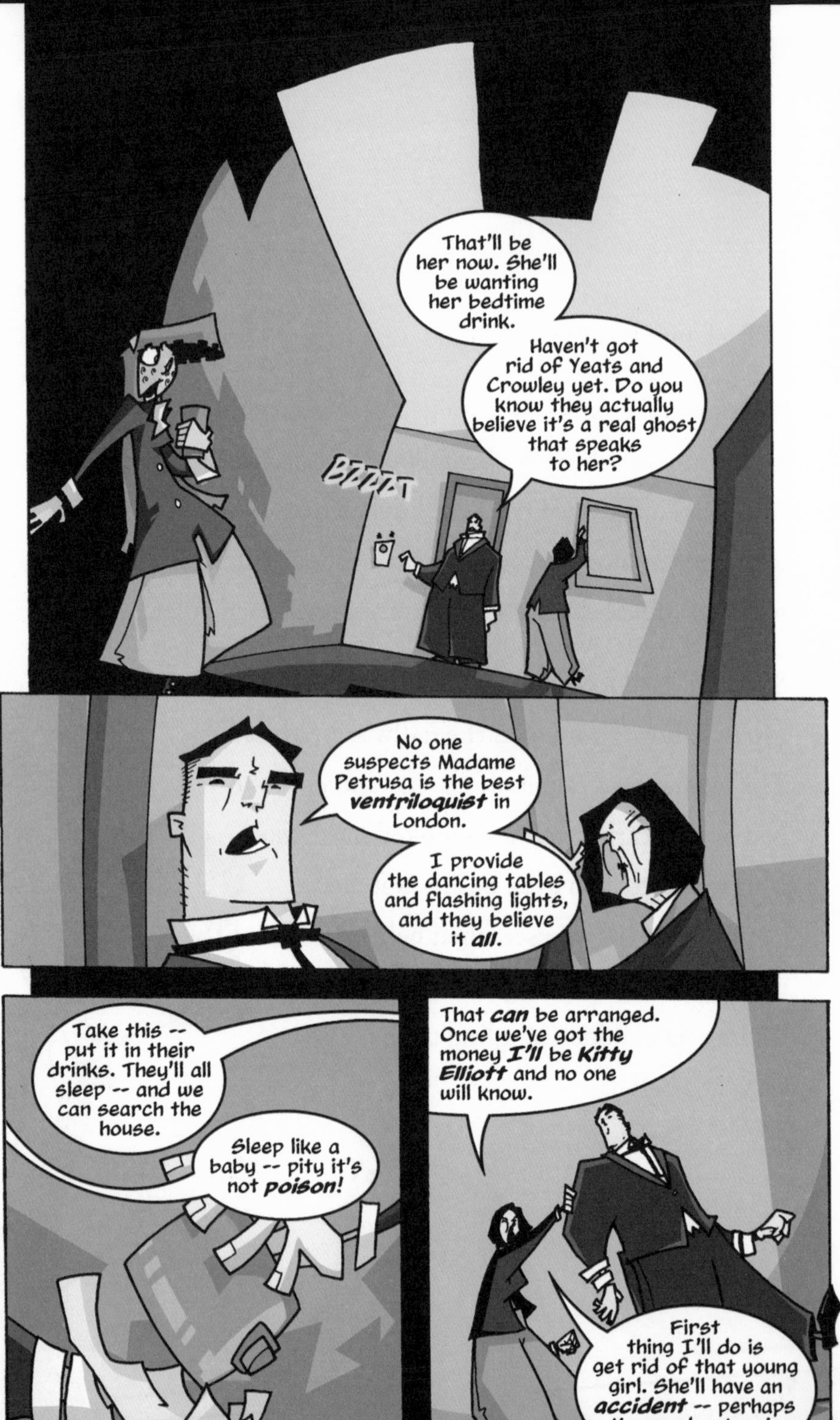

BZZZT
That'll be her now. She'll be wanting her bedtime drink.
Haven't got rid of Yeats and Crowley yet. Do you know they actually believe it's a real ghost that speaks to her?
No one suspects Madame Petrusa is the best *ventriloquist* in London.
I provide the dancing tables and flashing lights, and they believe it *all*.
Take this -- put it in their drinks. They'll all sleep -- and we can search the house.
Sleep like a baby -- pity it's not *poison*!
That *can* be arranged. Once we've got the money *I'll* be *Kitty Elliott* and no one will know.
First thing I'll do is get rid of that young girl. She'll have an *accident* -- perhaps the pond, a tragic drowning?

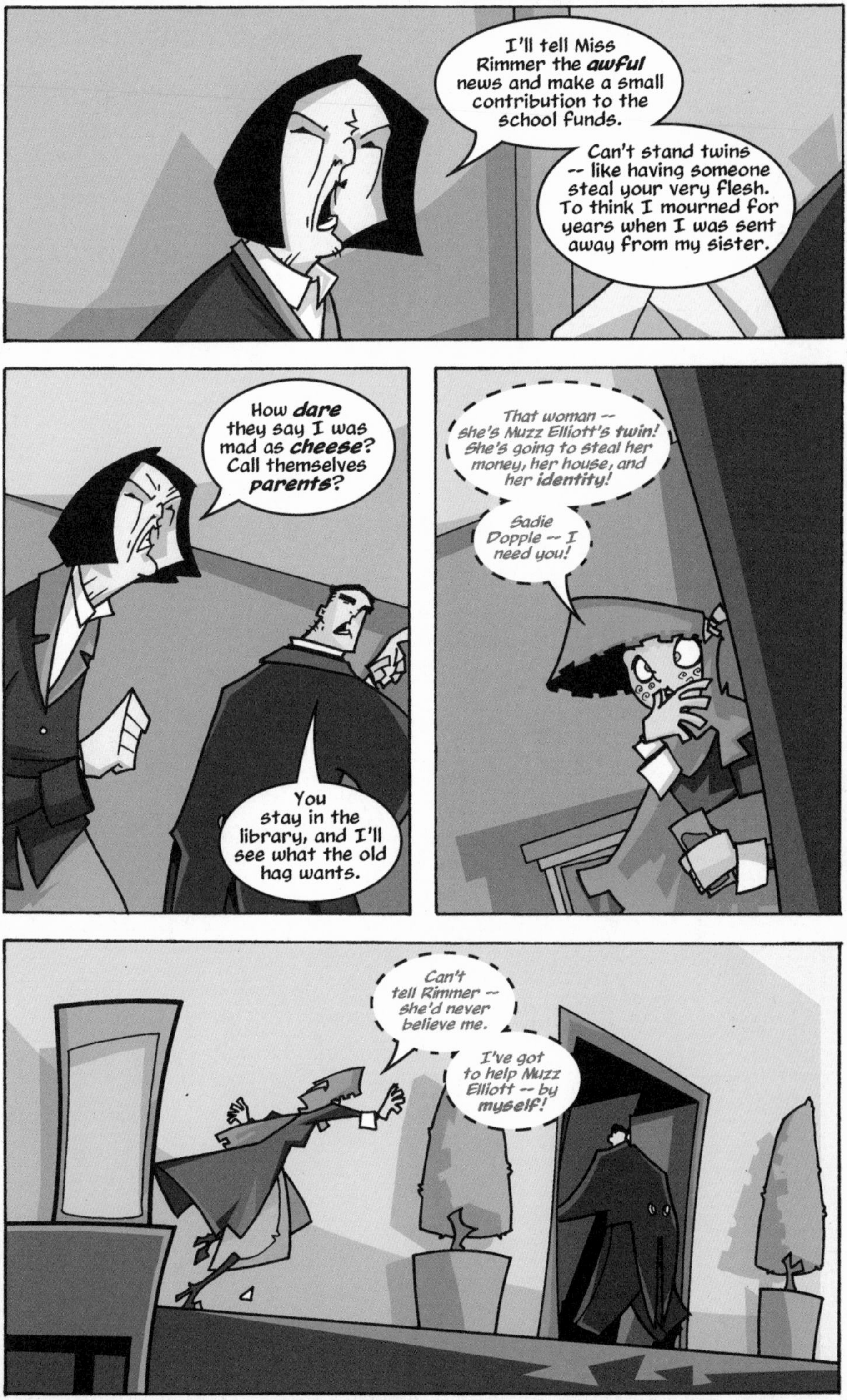

I'll tell Miss Rimmer the *awful* news and make a small contribution to the school funds.
Can't stand twins -- like having someone steal your very flesh. To think I mourned for years when I was sent away from my sister.
How *dare* they say I was mad as *cheese*? Call themselves *parents*?
You stay in the library, and I'll see what the old hag wants.
That woman -- she's Muzz Elliott's **twin!** *She's going to steal her money, her house, and her* **identity!**
Sadie Dopple -- I need you!
Can't tell Rimmer -- she'd never believe me.
I've got to help Muzz Elliott -- by **myself!**

Saskia tiptoed along the passageway behind Brummagem, pausing for a moment in the shadows as he ducked into the kitchen and returned with a tray of drinks. He proceeded toward a parlor door, from behind which Saskia could hear muffled conversation and polite laughter. Brummagem tapped on the door and entered.

Sneaking quietly along the corridor, Saskia got to the door and put her eye to the keyhole.

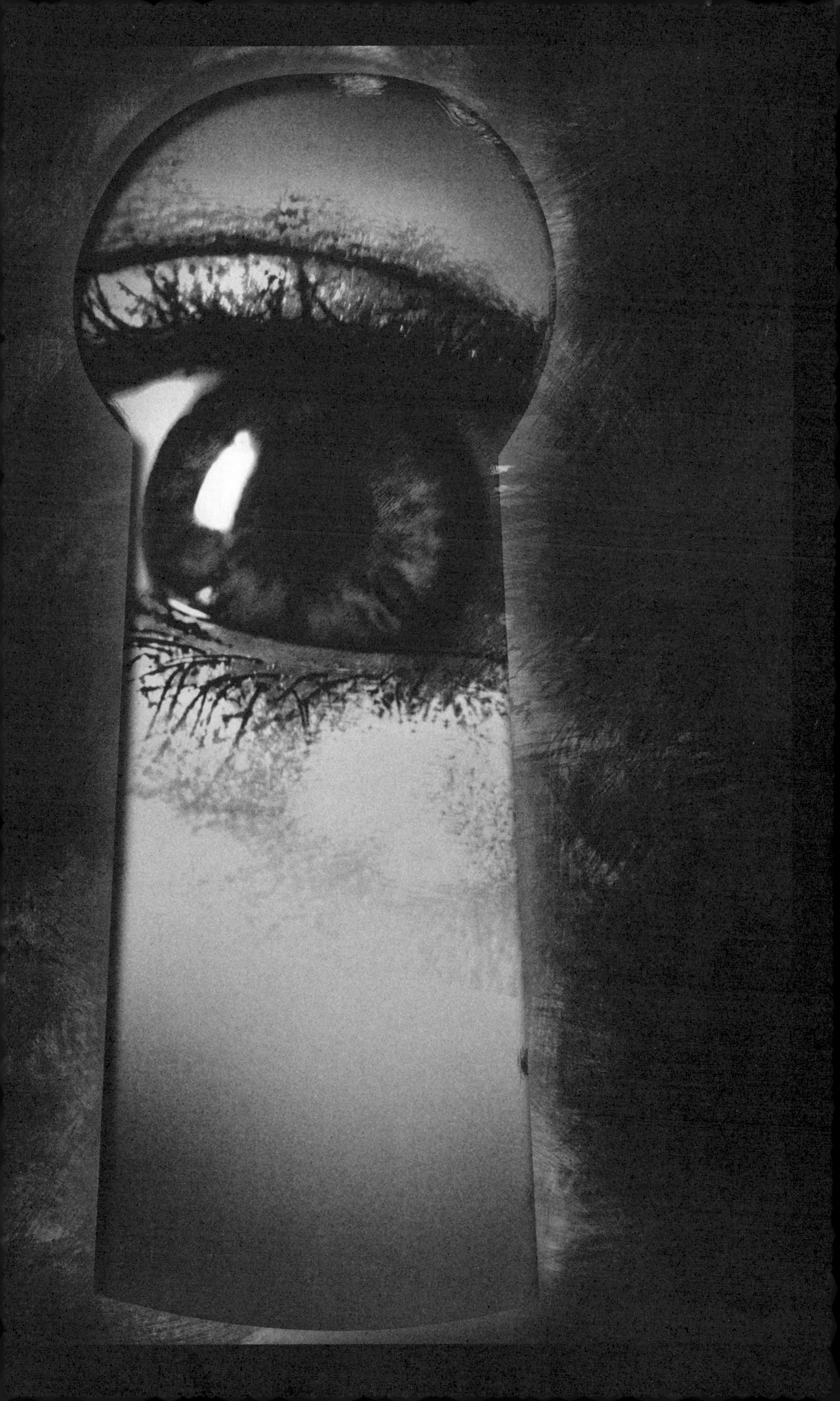

Muzz Elliott sat regally in an armchair, and Madame Petrusa was curled up on a cushion near the fire. Yeats and Crowley stood nearby. "Brummagem," said Muzz Elliott impatiently, "I thought I would die of thirst. Where have you been, and why was the back door open?"

"A caller, madam. A tramp of the road. . . . I sent him packing."

"Good man, Brummagem. Can't have them coming here and spoiling our evenings."

"I agree, Muzz Elliott, I agree," said Crowley.

"Coffee, madam?" Brummagem asked. He nudged Crowley out of the way and placed the tray on the table. "I apologize, Madame Petrusa—I forgot your tea. I will bring it now."

Saskia jumped back from the keyhole and scurried into the shadow of a potted tree beside the door. She heard the door creak open and saw Brummagem step outside. He paused for a moment and slowly looked up and down the passageway, as if he suspected Saskia's presence. She bit her lip, hardly daring to breathe.

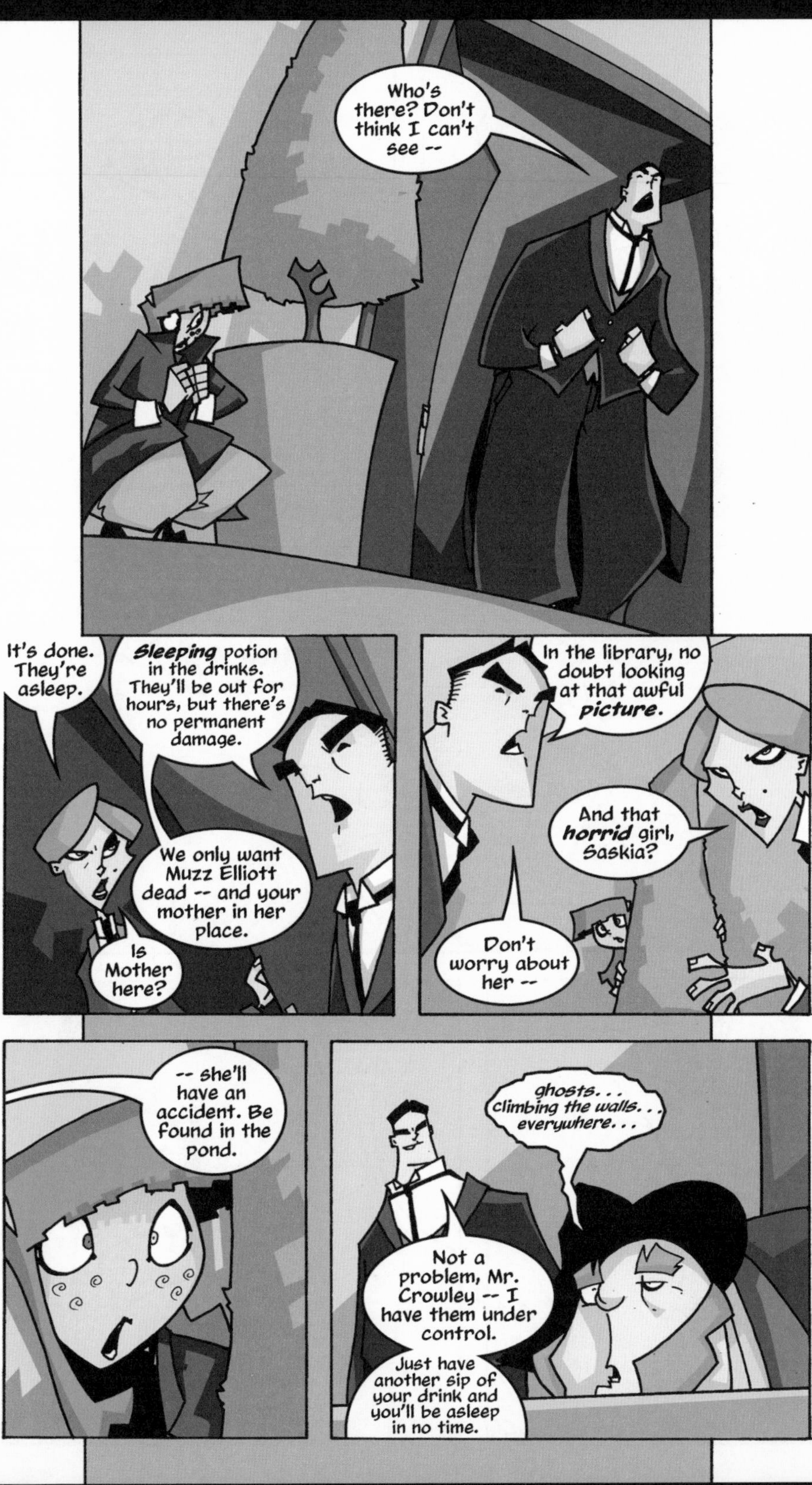
Who's there? Don't think I can't see --
It's done. They're asleep.
Sleeping potion in the drinks. They'll be out for hours, but there's no permanent damage.
We only want Muzz Elliott dead -- and your mother in her place.
Is Mother here?
In the library, no doubt looking at that awful picture.
And that horrid girl, Saskia?
Don't worry about her --
-- she'll have an accident. Be found in the pond.
ghosts. . . climbing the walls. . . everywhere. . .
Not a problem, Mr. Crowley -- I have them under control.
Just have another sip of your drink and you'll be asleep in no time.

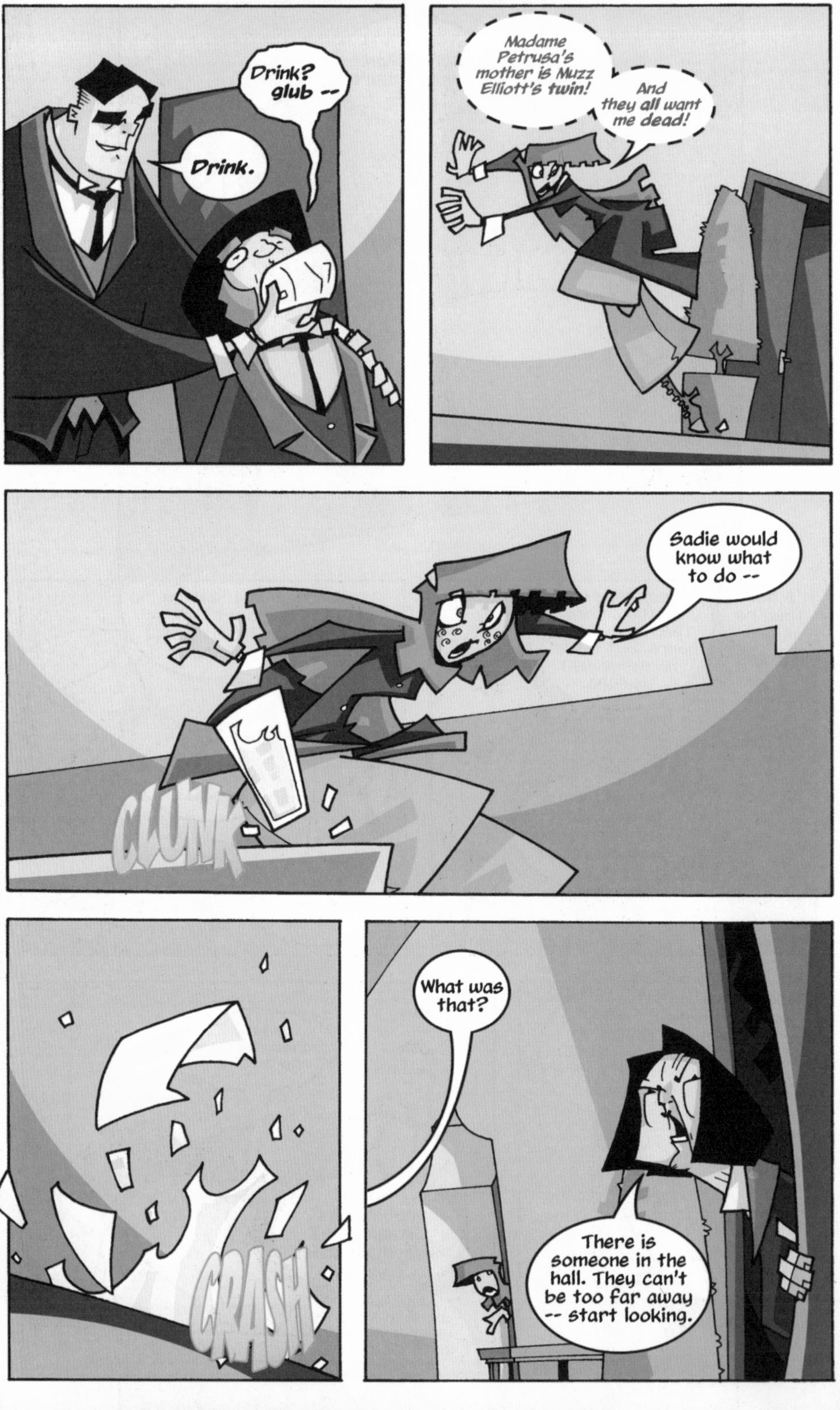
Drink? glub --
Drink.
Madame Petrusa's mother is Muzz Elliott's twin!
And they all want me dead!
Sadie would know what to do --
CLUNK
CRASH
What was that?
There is someone in the hall. They can't be too far away -- start looking.

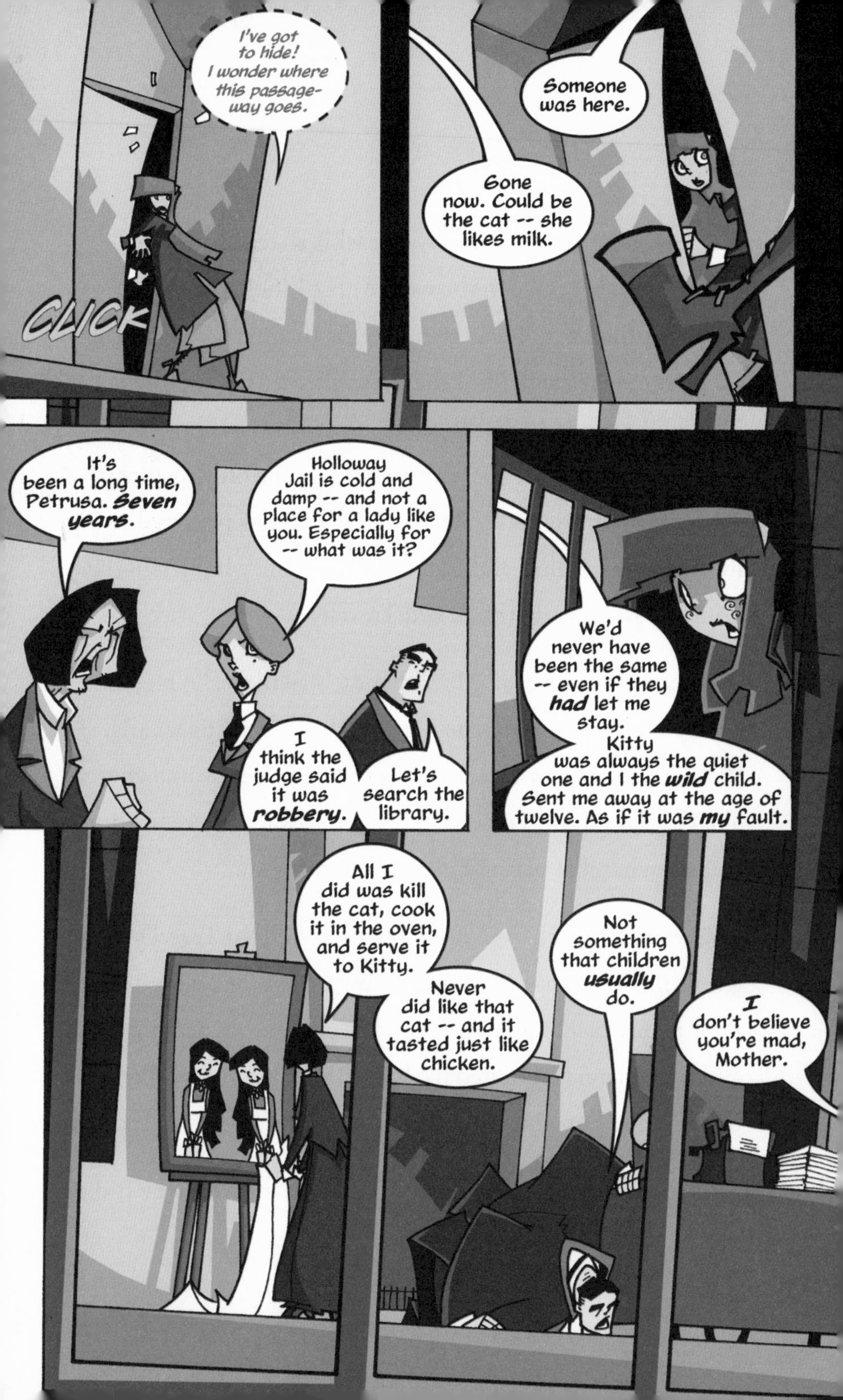

I've got to hide! I wonder where this passage-way goes.
CLICK
Someone was here.
Gone now. Could be the cat -- she likes milk.
It's been a long time, Petrusa. Seven years.
Holloway Jail is cold and damp -- and not a place for a lady like you. Especially for -- what was it?
I think the judge said it was robbery.
Let's search the library.
We'd never have been the same -- even if they had let me stay.
Kitty was always the quiet one and I the wild child. Sent me away at the age of twelve. As if it was my fault.
All I did was kill the cat, cook it in the oven, and serve it to Kitty.
Never did like that cat -- and it tasted just like chicken.
Not something that children usually do.
I don't believe you're mad, Mother.

Hidden in the secret passageway, Saskia watched the whole scene through a grille in the wall. Muzz Elliott's sister was staring at the picture on a stand beside the fireplace. The gilt frame shone in the light of the chandelier that hung above Muzz Elliott's desk. Saskia realized why Muzz Elliott never wanted anyone to see the painting. It was the only memory she had of her lost sister. A sister who was now prepared to murder Kitty Elliott and Saskia for the money hidden in the house by her grandfather, Lord Trevellyn.

"My house," muttered Muzz Elliott's twin as she pierced the eyes of her twin in the painting with her fingernails. "My house and my money. It has to be in here somewhere. That's what Grandfather always said—somewhere in the library where he never thought to look again."

The woman looked over at the painting of Lord Trevellyn on the wall. Her grandfather stared down from the picture, his boot firmly planted on what was left of the exploded donkey. With one hand he pointed to the stuffed hind end of the donkey that hung on the wall next to him.

"The donkey," she gasped out loud. "That's where he hid the money."

"The beast!'" cried Madame Petrusa.

"The beastly beast!" cried Brummagem.

"Silence!" cried Muzz Elliott's twin sister.

Ignoring the command, Brummagem exclaimed, "It's the only place no one has ever thought of looking!" He darted about the room, looking for something to impale the animal with.

Greedily Brummagem leaped to the desk and from there jumped over to the wall and grabbed at the hind legs of the donkey. He dangled momentarily, glancing from Madame Petrusa to her mother and back again like he was waiting to be told what to do next.

As he held fast, his fingers straining on the beast's hooves, plumes of dust and dead mites billowed in a thick cloud around him. Brummagem held tight—knuckles white, teeth clenched, and eyes wide. He didn't wait long. Within seconds, the body of the donkey began to creak and groan. There was a sudden jolt, and the legs began to stretch longer and longer, as if the beast were growing before their eyes.

The dried, starched carcass began to tear from the wooden shield that held it to the wall. With an undignified crash, Brummagem fell to the floor, followed by the donkey's remains. Brummagem's head was firmly submerged deep within the nether regions of the animal. All that the women could see were the Irishman's flailing legs.

"I've found it," he muttered, and sneezed. Gold and silver clanked within the creature with every movement he made. "It's not banknotes that he hid . . . but gold."

Without speaking, Muzz Elliott's twin sister grabbed the sword from the wall, spun like a wild gypsy, and raised the weapon above her head to strike the stuffed beast.

"Mother!"
screamed Petrusa.

"You'll kill
him."

"He's already dead, shot by my grandfather."

"Not the donkey—Brummagem."

It was too late. The sword fell quickly and mercilessly. It sliced easily through the tanned hide and the copious stuffing, narrowly missing Brummagem's nose.

The donkey opened right down the center, and out poured a thousand gold sovereigns and countless gold and silver crowns the size of bottle tops. It was a treasure beyond treasure. Brummagem's dirty face stared up from inside the donkey's remains.

"I think I'm stuck," he said feebly as he struggled to free himself from the grip of the animal's innards. "It's . . . it's choking me," he continued, spitting a dried beetle from his mouth.

Brummagem wobbled back and forth as he tried to stand. Gold and silver spilled across the floor. Madame Petrusa grabbed the coins and began filling her pockets. Her mother pushed her out of the way, grasped what was left of the donkey's carcass, and pulled. Brummagem screamed as his ears were folded forward against the side of his head. The treasure emptied from the beast onto the carpet. Muzz Elliott's twin sister smiled.

"Now we can have my Kitty poisoned—and that Saskia girl thrown in the lake."

Chapter Twelve
The Black Maria

IN THE CELLAR OF the magician's hovel, Sadie and Erik looked on in fear. A frenzy had taken hold of the Great Potemkin. In an instant he had changed completely. Gone was the smile, gone the twinkle in his eyes, and gone the snickering that had accompanied every word. His demeanor had transformed to that of a sniveling madman who frantically flicked the switch on his storm-making carousel back and forth. He grew even more distressed every time the Matter Illuminator failed to electrocute his two new assistants and light up the lamps placed in the tight helmets on their heads.

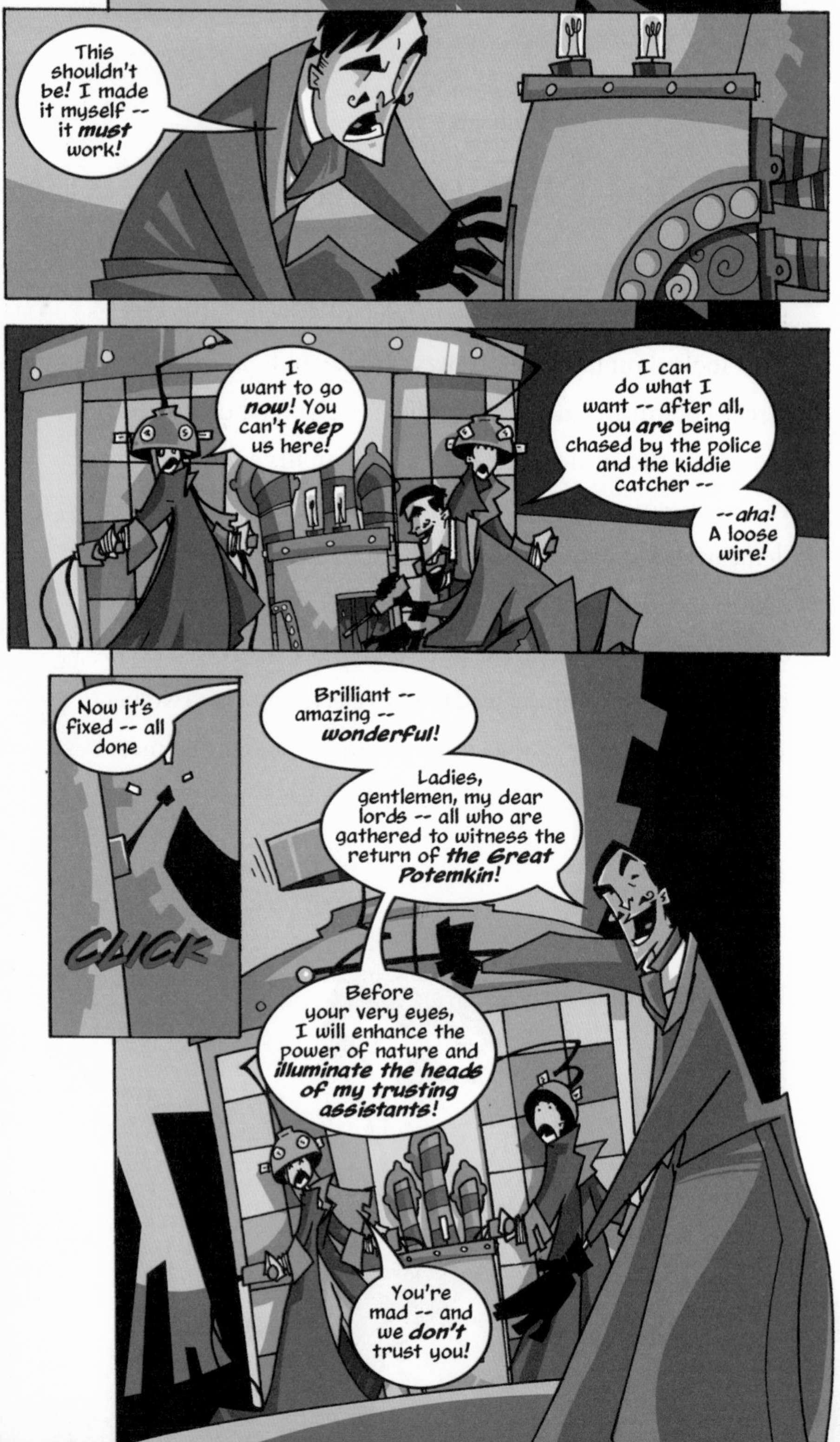
This shouldn't be! I made it myself -- it *must* work!
I want to go *now*! You can't *keep* us here!
I can do what I want -- after all, you *are* being chased by the police and the kiddie catcher --
-- *aha*! A loose wire!
Now it's fixed -- all done
CLICK
Brilliant -- amazing -- *wonderful*!
Ladies, gentlemen, my dear lords -- all who are gathered to witness the return of *the Great Potemkin*!
Before your very eyes, I will enhance the power of nature and *illuminate the heads of my trusting assistants*!
You're mad -- and we *don't* trust you!

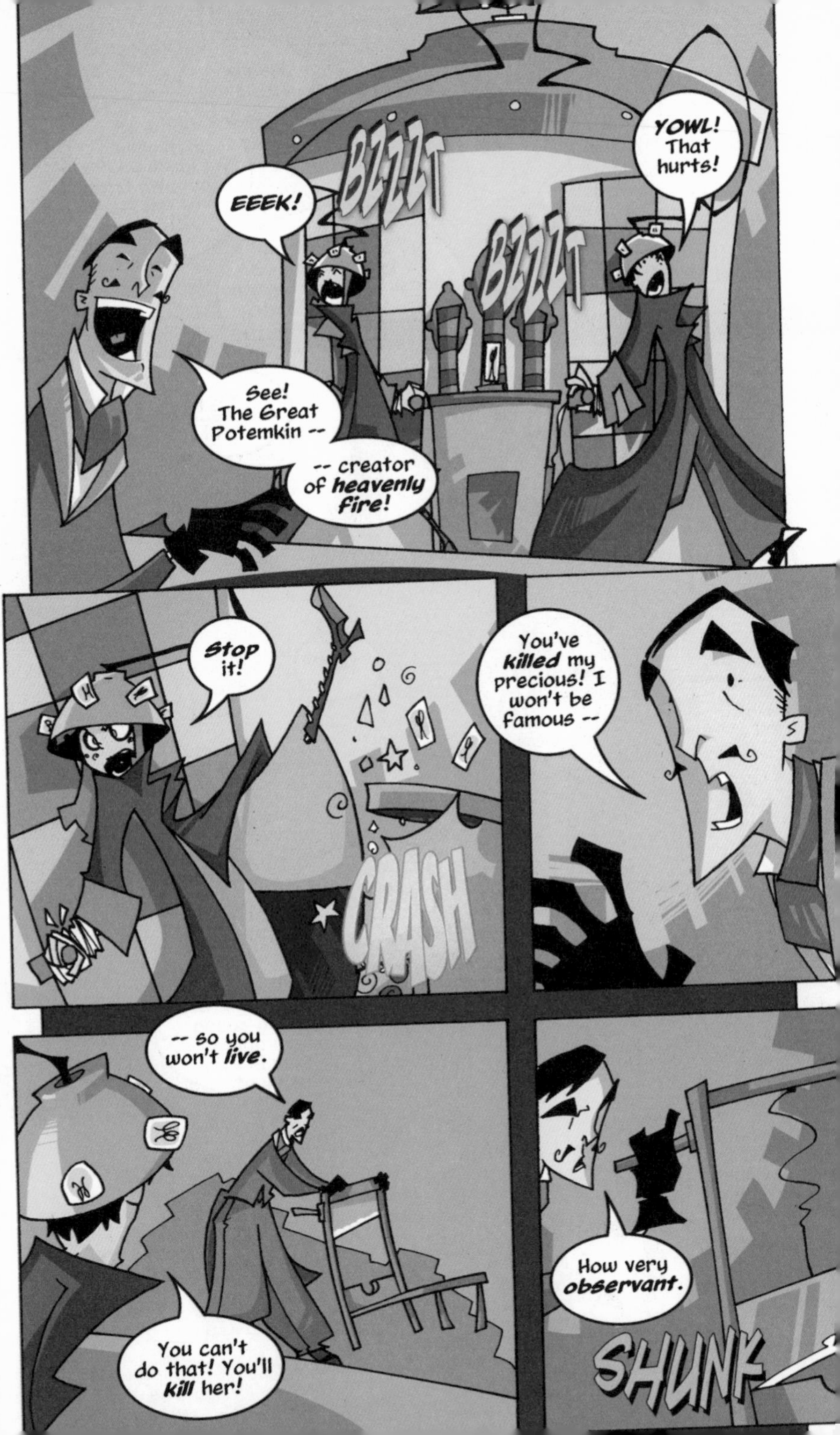
EEEK!
BZZZT
BZZZT
YOWL! That hurts!
See! The Great Potemkin --
-- creator of heavenly fire!
Stop it!
CRASH
You've killed my precious! I won't be famous --
-- so you won't live.
You can't do that! You'll kill her!
How very observant.
SHUNK

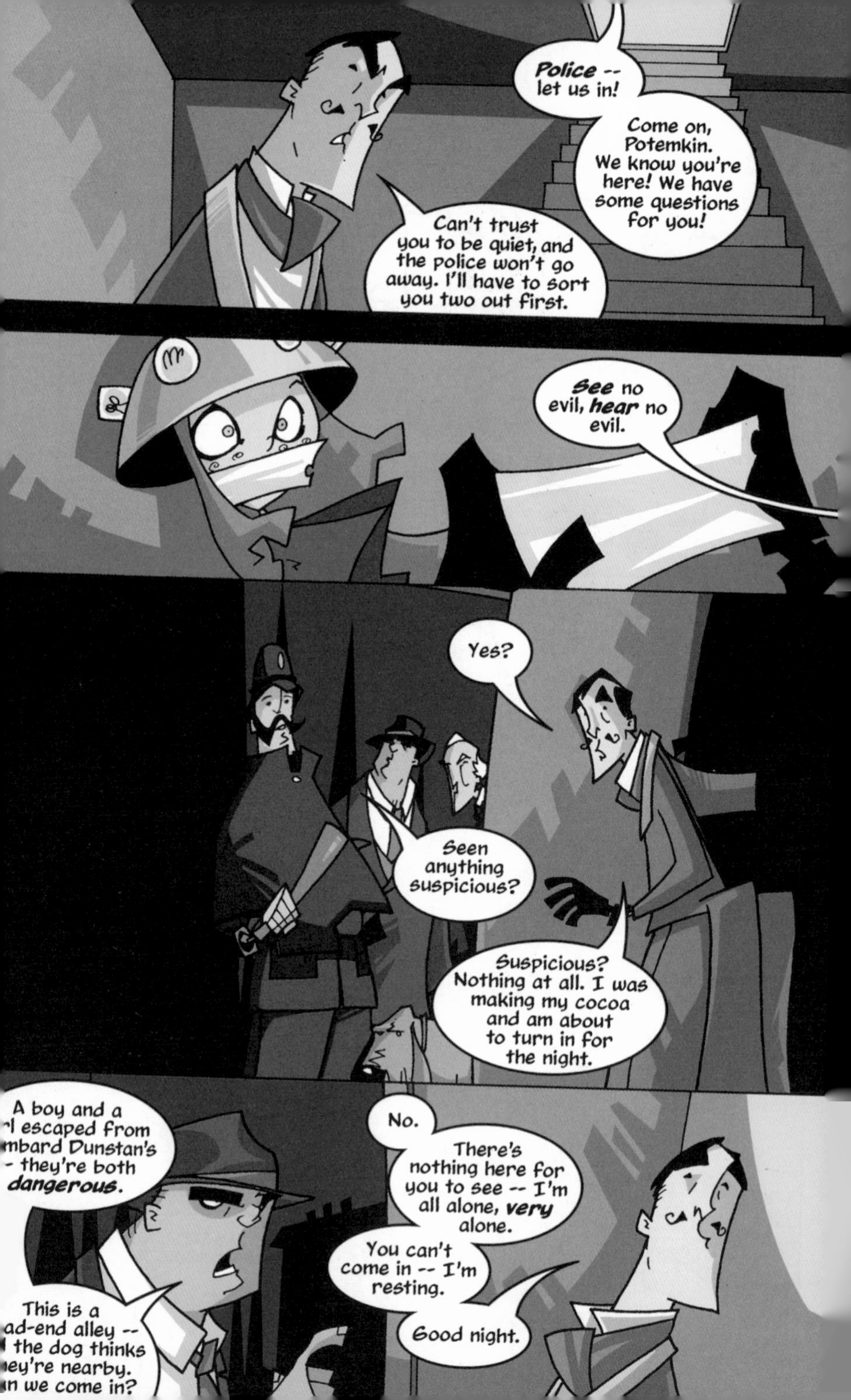
Police -- let us in!
Come on, Potemkin. We know you're here! We have some questions for you!
Can't trust you to be quiet, and the police won't go away. I'll have to sort you two out first.
See no evil, hear no evil.
Yes?
Seen anything suspicious?
Suspicious? Nothing at all. I was making my cocoa and am about to turn in for the night.
A boy and a
escaped from
Dunstan's
they're both dangerous.
No.
There's nothing here for you to see -- I'm all alone, very alone.
You can't come in -- I'm resting.
Good night.
This is a
alley --
the dog thinks
nearby.
we come in?

Potemkin's words were completely ignored by Kobold, Martinet, and the constable. Together they hurled themselves against the door—just as Potemkin was attempting to slide the fragile bolt into place. He was blasted across the room, catapulting over the table and across the tattered armchair before ending up slumped in the fireplace.

The three men were followed closely by Kobold's hound. Gilbert swayed slightly, suffering from the effects of the green liquid Potemkin had poured on the ground. But he was a bloodhound from a line of legendary beasts; his mother was a bloodhound once used by a great Victorian detective and his father a bullmastiff that had haunted Dartmoor, and Gilbert could not be thrown off a scent as easily as Potemkin had guessed.

The hound bounded onto Potemkin. He pushed the magician's raglike body this way and that as he slobbered on the floorboards and wrinkled the rug beneath the man. He glared at Potemkin eye to eye and curled his lip in a snarl.

Martinet stepped forward. . . .

"Where are they?"
he demanded.

"Who?" asked Potemkin in an oddly high-pitched voice.

"Dopple and Ganger—they're very dangerous," said Kobold. "The hound says they're here, and here they are."

"I don't know what you're talking about," moaned the magician as he tried to spread himself across the floor like a worn-out carpet in an attempt to hide the cellar door. "I don't know anyone by that name. . . ."

"Find them, Gilbert—scent them out," Kobold said.

The dog needed no encouragement. He dug at the floorboards and pressed his nose against the fireplace. He scratched against the slats and gnawed the wood. All the while, Potemkin attempted to confuse the creature by squawking like an owl, and he covered the looped handle to the cellar below.

Ever obedient, Gilbert pressed on in his task. Potemkin pushed the dog away with his feet, kicking the bandages that were wrapped around the beast like a diaper as a souvenir of his previous encounter with Darcy.

In the cellar below, Sadie and Erik heard the ear-piercing screams as the hound bit through the seat of Mr. Potemkin's pants. The shrieks lasted for several seconds and were accompanied by a frantic banging on the floor as he attempted to wrestle the dog free from what Gilbert now thought to be a bedtime snack. Then there came a scuffling while the once proud magician rolled around the room in much distress.

Then there was the creak of a hinge as someone above discovered the trapdoor, which Potemkin was no longer able to hide, and pulled it open. Martinet jumped into the cellar.

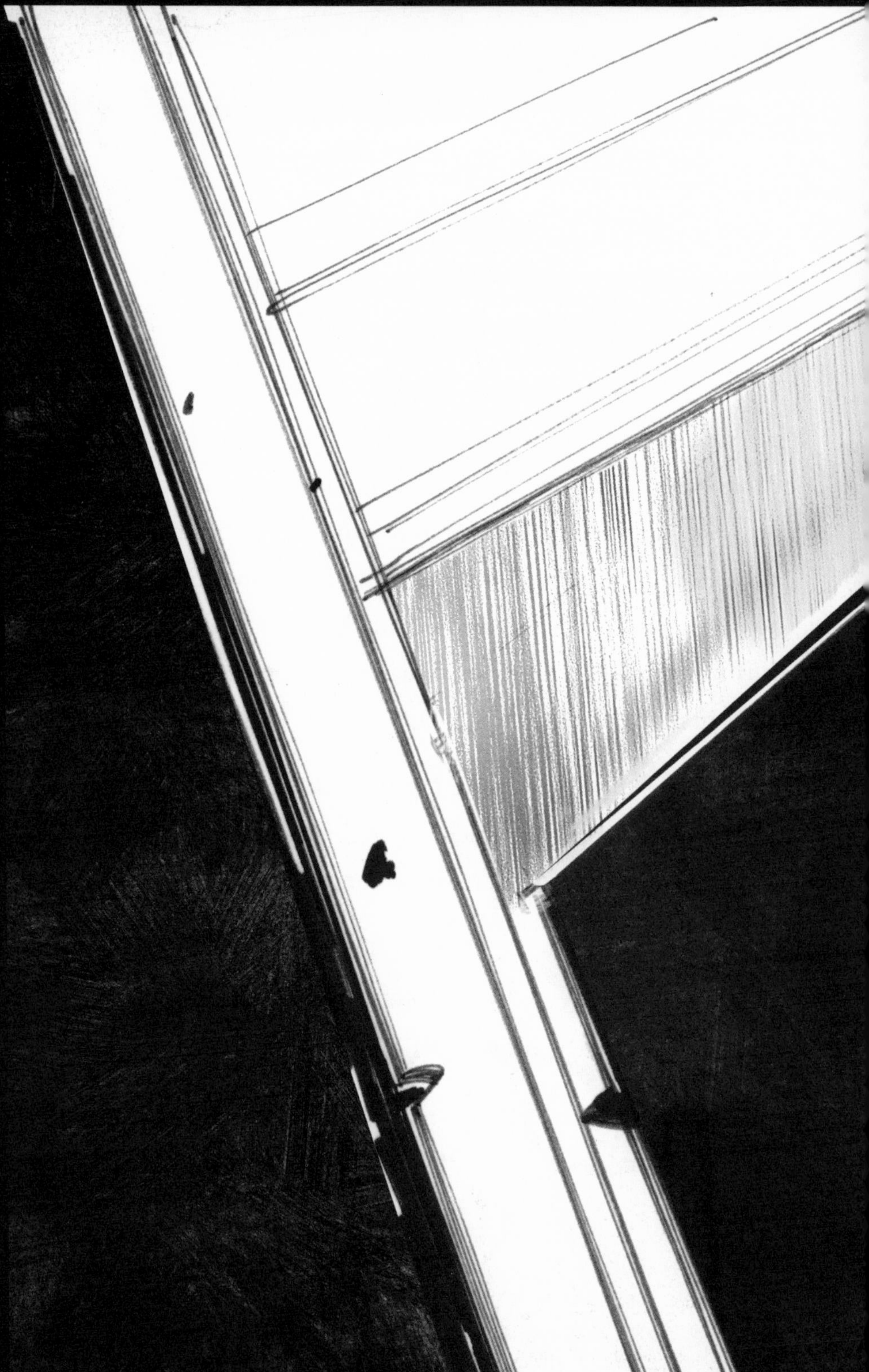

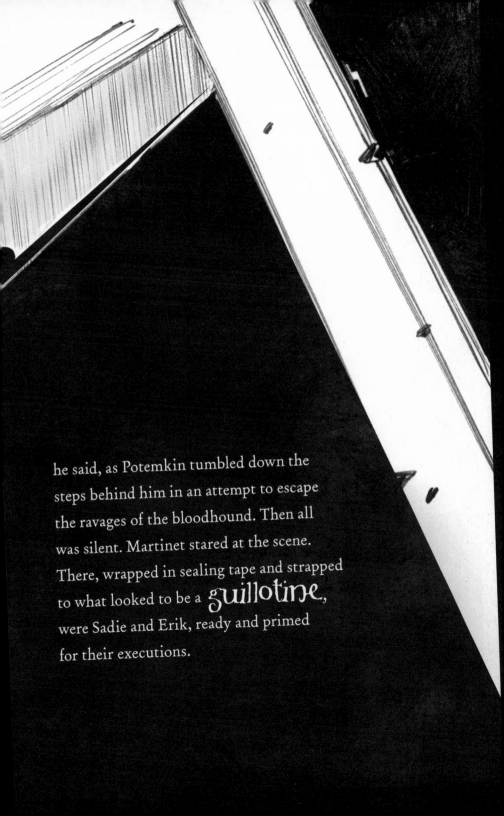

he said, as Potemkin tumbled down the steps behind him in an attempt to escape the ravages of the bloodhound. Then all was silent. Martinet stared at the scene. There, wrapped in sealing tape and strapped to what looked to be a guillotine, were Sadie and Erik, ready and primed for their executions.

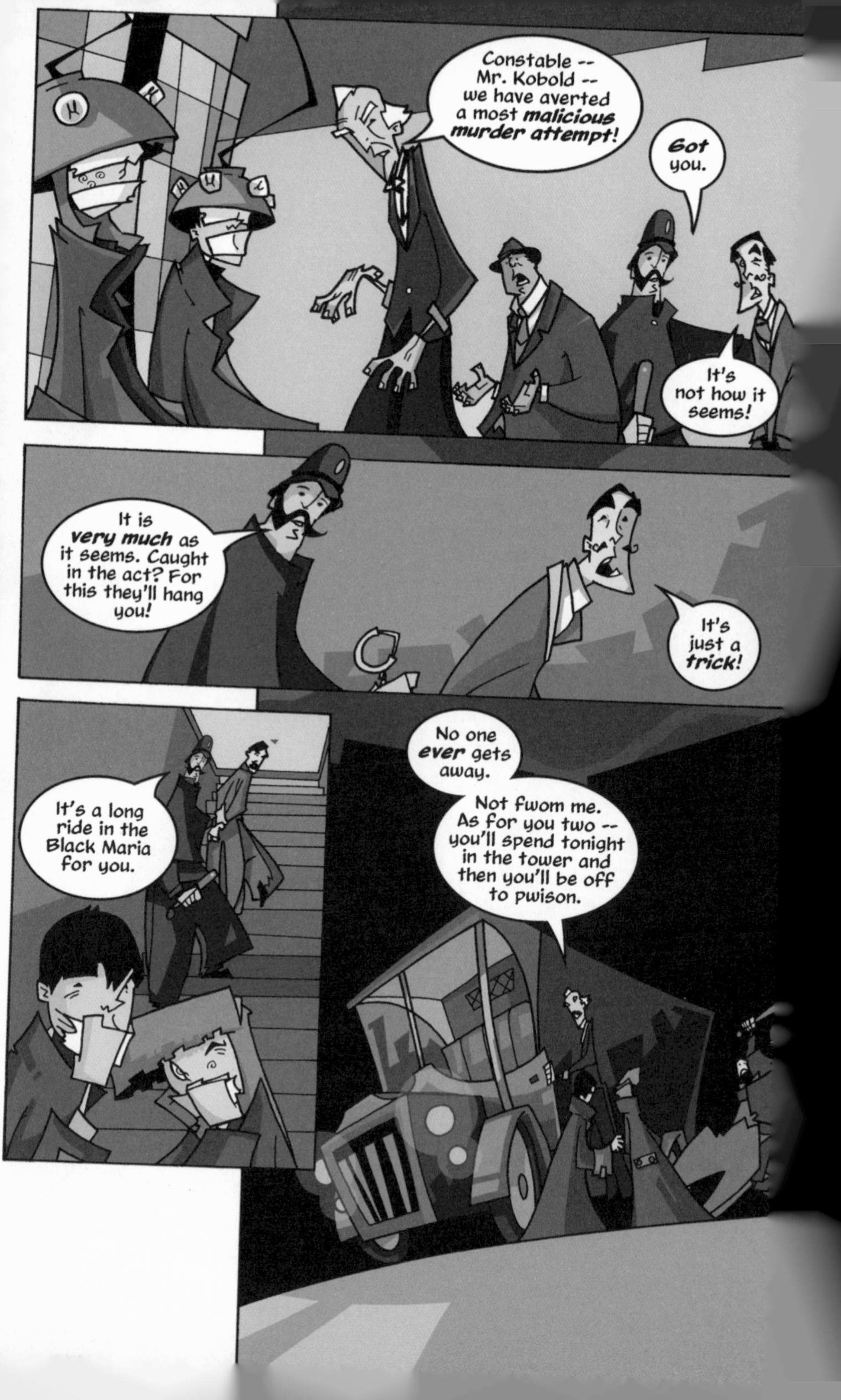
Constable -- Mr. Kobold -- we have averted a most malicious murder attempt!
Got you.
It's not how it seems!
It is very much as it seems. Caught in the act? For this they'll hang you!
It's just a trick!
It's a long ride in the Black Maria for you.
No one ever gets away.
Not fwom me. As for you two -- you'll spend tonight in the tower and then you'll be off to pwison.

"What have we done?" Erik asked as the police van set off shakily up Hampstead High Street.

"I'll think of something by the morning," Martinet babbled. "Mr. Kobold and I will fit the cwime to the circumstances and swear on oath that it was all twue. After all, we've just stopped a murder. Could be something very special in it for the both of us." He sounded extremely pleased with himself.

Potemkin rattled the black steel grille that separated the Black Maria's prison cage from its driver's seat. He sneered at Sadie and Erik and snarled as he spoke.

"Don't think these bars will keep me in. Handcuffs and locks mean nothing to the Great Potemkin."

"Tell it to the judge, Mr. Potemkin. See if your fame will get you off child kidnapping and attempted murder," Kobold said as he stroked his faithful but much-bruised hound.

The Black Maria trundled slowly up the hill, past the rows of shops, and out onto Hampstead Way. Sadie counted the number of the houses as they drove shakily by. The noise from the engine and the rattling of the van now made it impossible to speak. Once or twice she looked at Erik.

She could see that his taste for adventure had now been filled and knew that he was thinking of Miss Rimmer and his future.

"Sometimes you do things and don't think what could happen, Sadie," he tried to say above the noise of the rattling engine. "Sometimes you do things and never think of the consequences. . . ."

From the back of the van came a loud explosion. Plumes of dense, black smoke were blown through the grille and into the cab. The Black Maria unexpectedly lurched as the cage

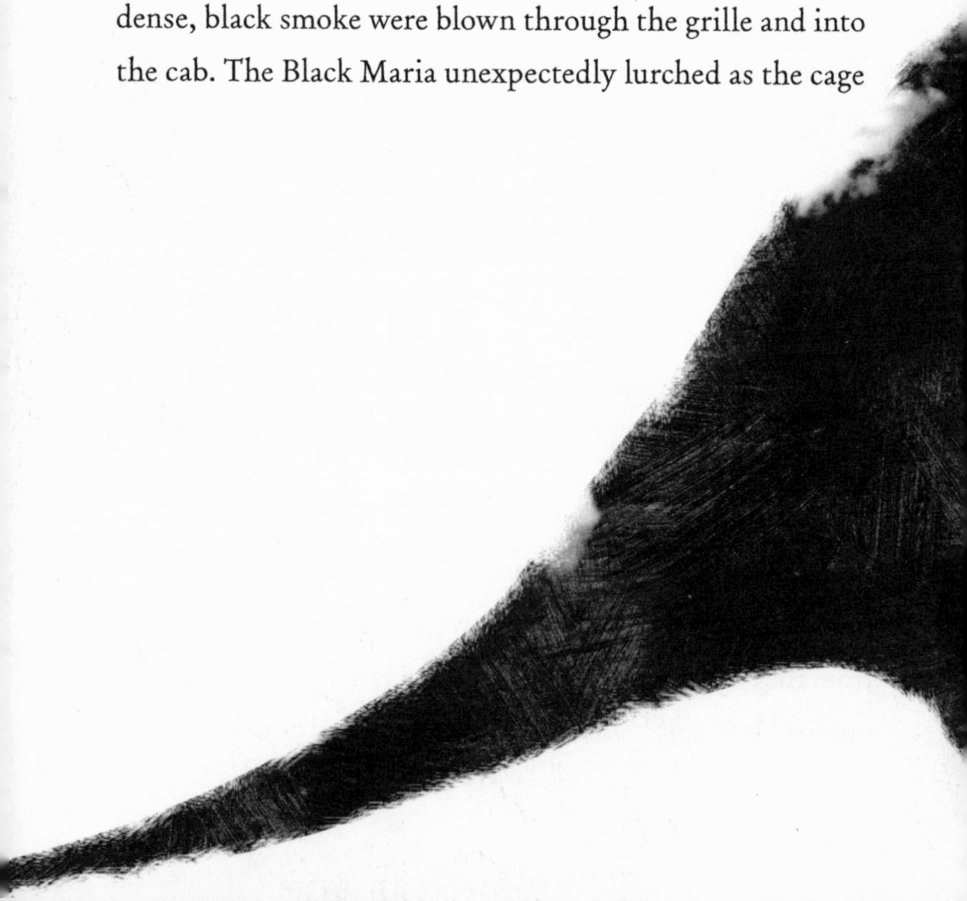

door opened and then slammed shut. Sadie turned and peered through the hatch. The bloodhound growled. Sadie got to her feet and stared into what was now an empty cell.

"He's gone!" she shouted.

"The Great Potemkin has Vanished!"

The van skidded to a halt. Smoke billowed from every window as if the vehicle were on fire. Kobold leaped from the passenger seat, quickly followed by the hound and Martinet. The driver paused for a moment and then slid open his door and stepped outside.

Sadie and Erik could hear Kobold shouting as the bloodhound gave chase to the Great Potemkin. Erik looked at Sadie and then at the driver and smiled, the eagerness for adventure slowly returning to his face.

"But you can't drive," she whispered.

"Wait and see," Erik replied as he slowly slid from the backseat. "NOW!" he shouted. He jumped in the driver's seat, slammed the door, and slipped the lock at the same time. The constable beat wildly against the window and screamed furiously. Erik grinned. "Come on, Dopple. Where to?"

"Spaniards House—that's where they took Saskia. I think it's just across the heath."

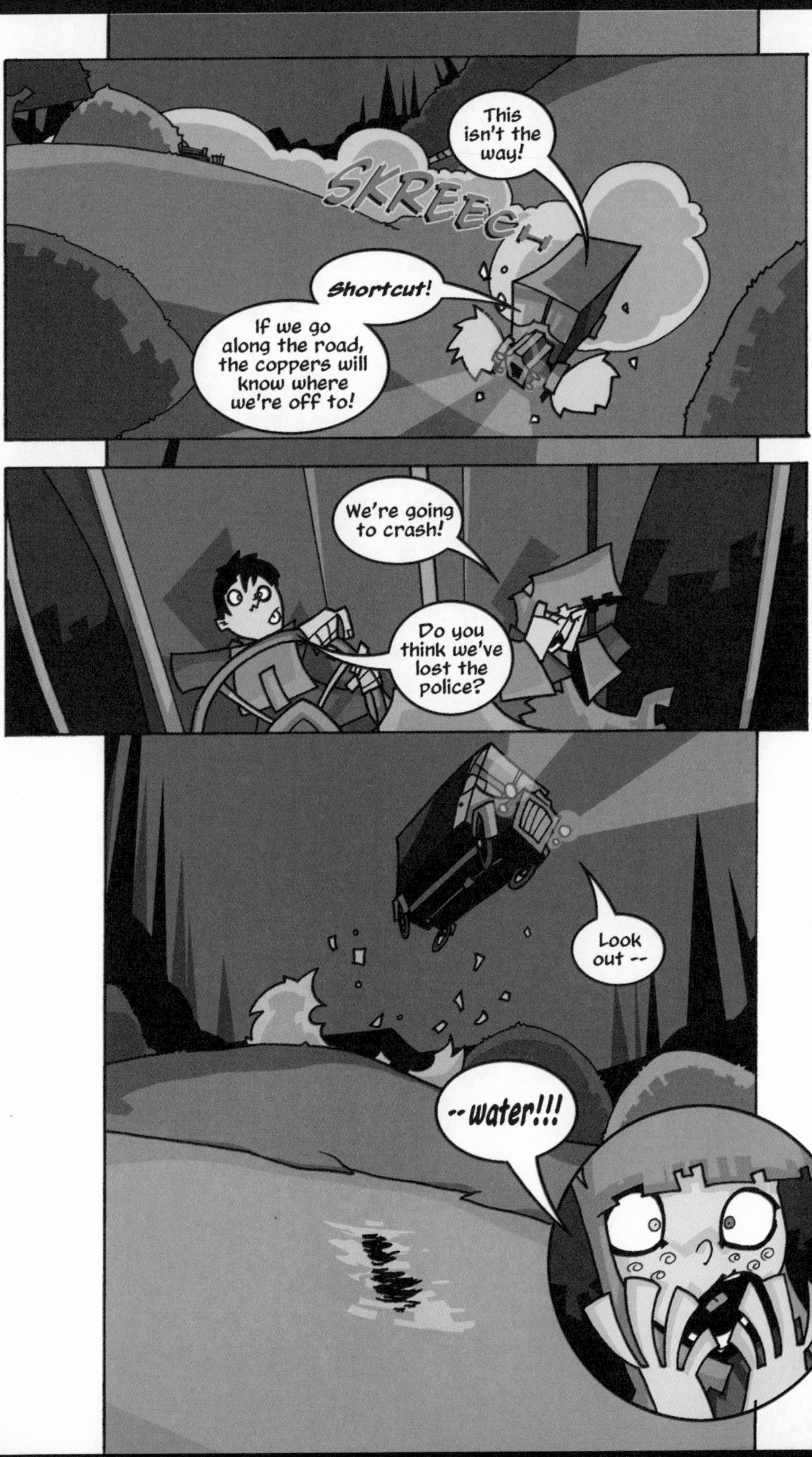
This isn't the way!
SKREEECH
Shortcut!
If we go along the road, the coppers will know where we're off to!
We're going to crash!
Do you think we've lost the police?
Look out --
-- water!!!

Time seemed to stop, just for a moment. Sadie looked at Erik and took hold of his hand. Then there was a tremendous splash. Water came in from everywhere. It was thick and black. Sadie couldn't see.

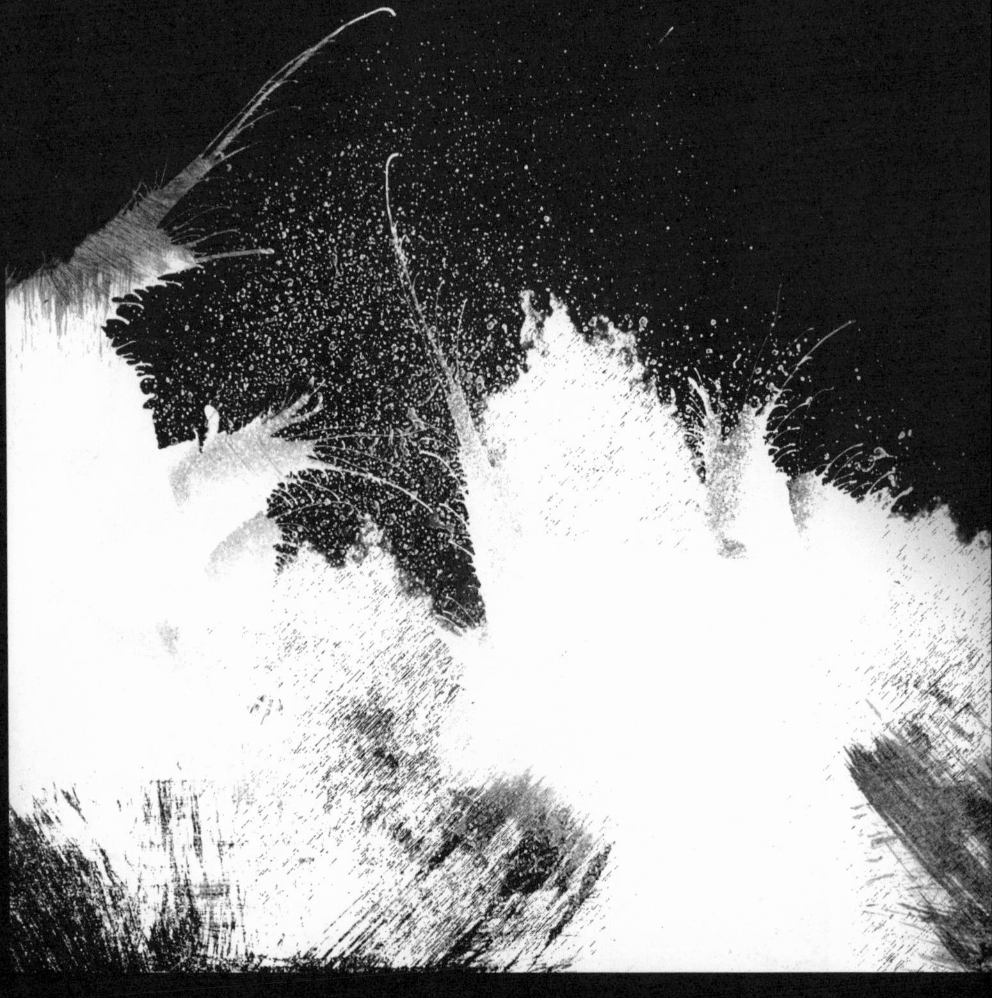

The door was jammed. The Black Maria was filling with water and slowly beginning to sink. Sadie turned to look at Erik, but he was gone.

"Erik! Erik!" she shouted as the water rose higher and higher.

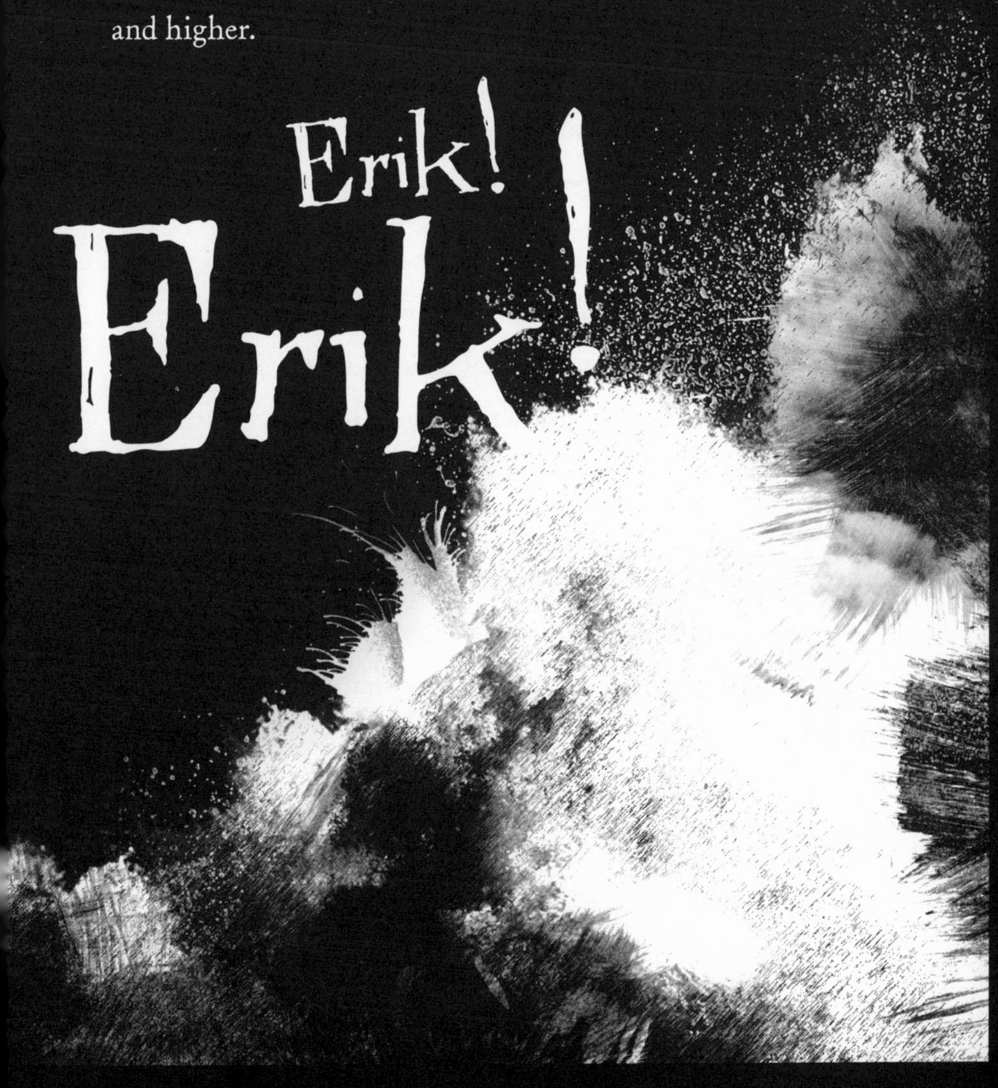
Erik!
Erik!

Chapter Thirteen
Toil AND Trouble

SASKIA CROUCHED in the secret passageway and looked into the library. Brummagem and Madame Petrusa were greedily scooping up handfuls of the gold coins that lay scattered across the room. Muzz Elliott's sister was standing by the fireplace, staring at the painting of herself and her twin. Saskia turned her head to watch Brummagem dive for a large pile of coins—and out of the corner of her eye caught sight of something in the passage.

A small device was hanging from the ceiling by two wires. It was narrow at one end but grew wider at the other end, like a funnel. She stepped closer to it and recognized what it was. A megaphone! Saskia followed the wires upward with her eyes and saw that they joined several other wires leading off in various directions along the wall. One of the wires ran across the low ceiling and down the opposite wall, where a beam of wood hung between two panels on each side. In an instant, Saskia knew that when the puppet had spoken and objects in the room had chattered away, someone had been watching her from this very place. "Madame Raphael?" she breathed.

In the library, Brummagem was speaking. Saskia looked back through the grille. "Who would have thought Cicely Elliott would return and take what was hers? Bet you never would have believed that when I met you at King's Cross," Brummagem said to Muzz Elliott's twin as he picked up a coin that was lodged between two wooden boards and slipped it into his pocket. "There I was, wandering by the station, and there you were, hanging about for a pocket to pick. Recognized you right away. I'd seen your face in the picture. Knew who you were, and now you're here, Cicely Elliott."

"It's not Elliott. I'm Cicely Windylove. I stopped being an Elliott the day I left this place. Now that I'm back, I could get used to it again," she replied as she poked the fire with the tip of the sword she was still holding. "The first thing I'll do is have this painting burned. Never did like it."

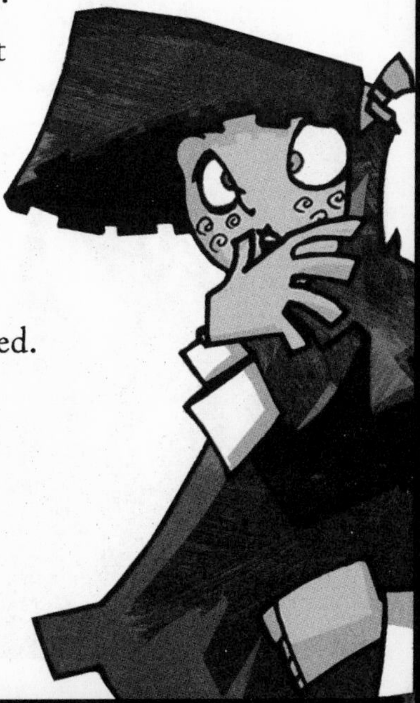

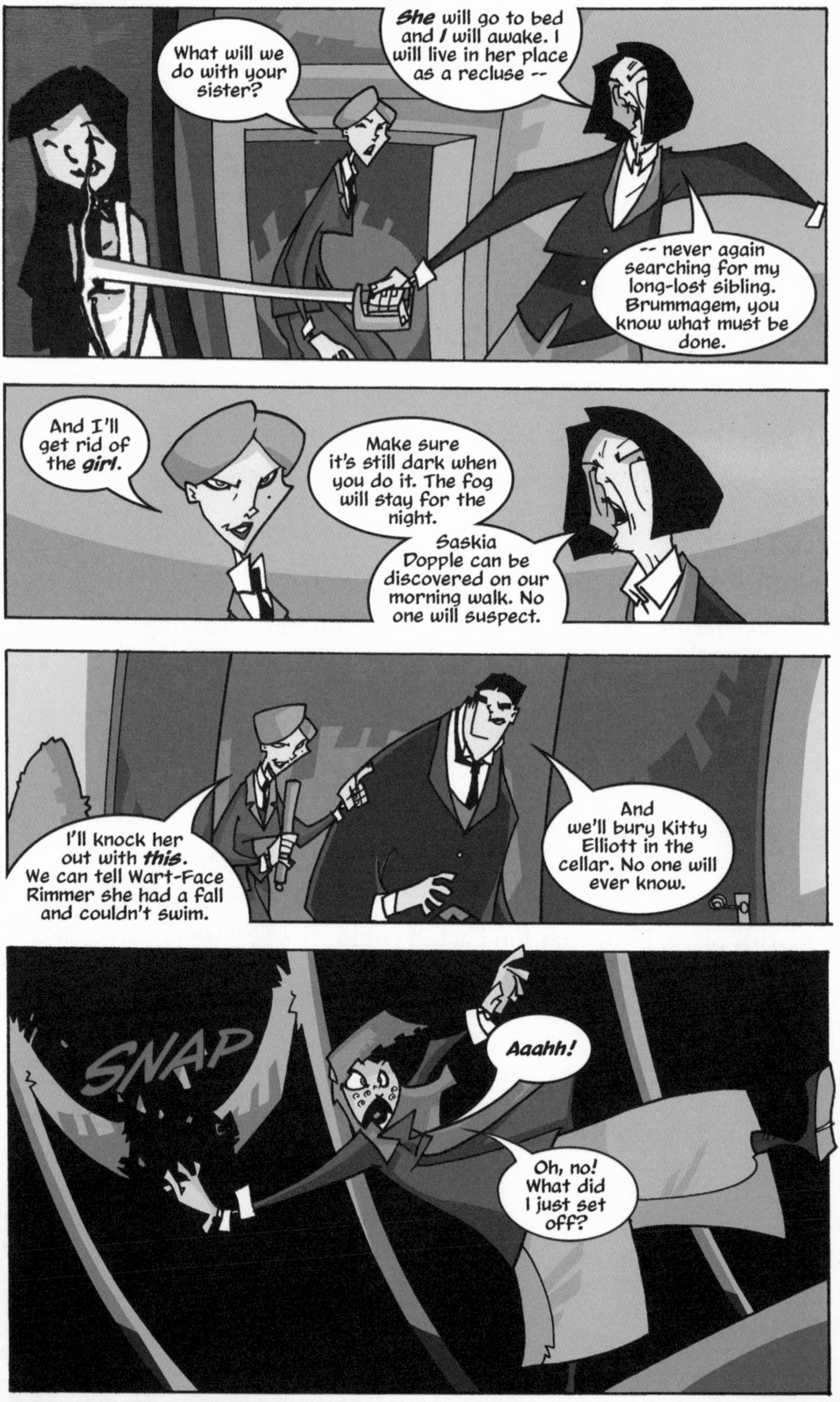
What will we do with your sister?
She will go to bed and I will awake. I will live in her place as a recluse --
-- never again searching for my long-lost sibling. Brummagem, you know what must be done.
And I'll get rid of the girl.
Make sure it's still dark when you do it. The fog will stay for the night.
Saskia Dopple can be discovered on our morning walk. No one will suspect.
I'll knock her out with this. We can tell Wart-Face Rimmer she had a fall and couldn't swim.
And we'll bury Kitty Elliott in the cellar. No one will ever know.
SNAP
Aaahh!
Oh, no! What did I just set off?

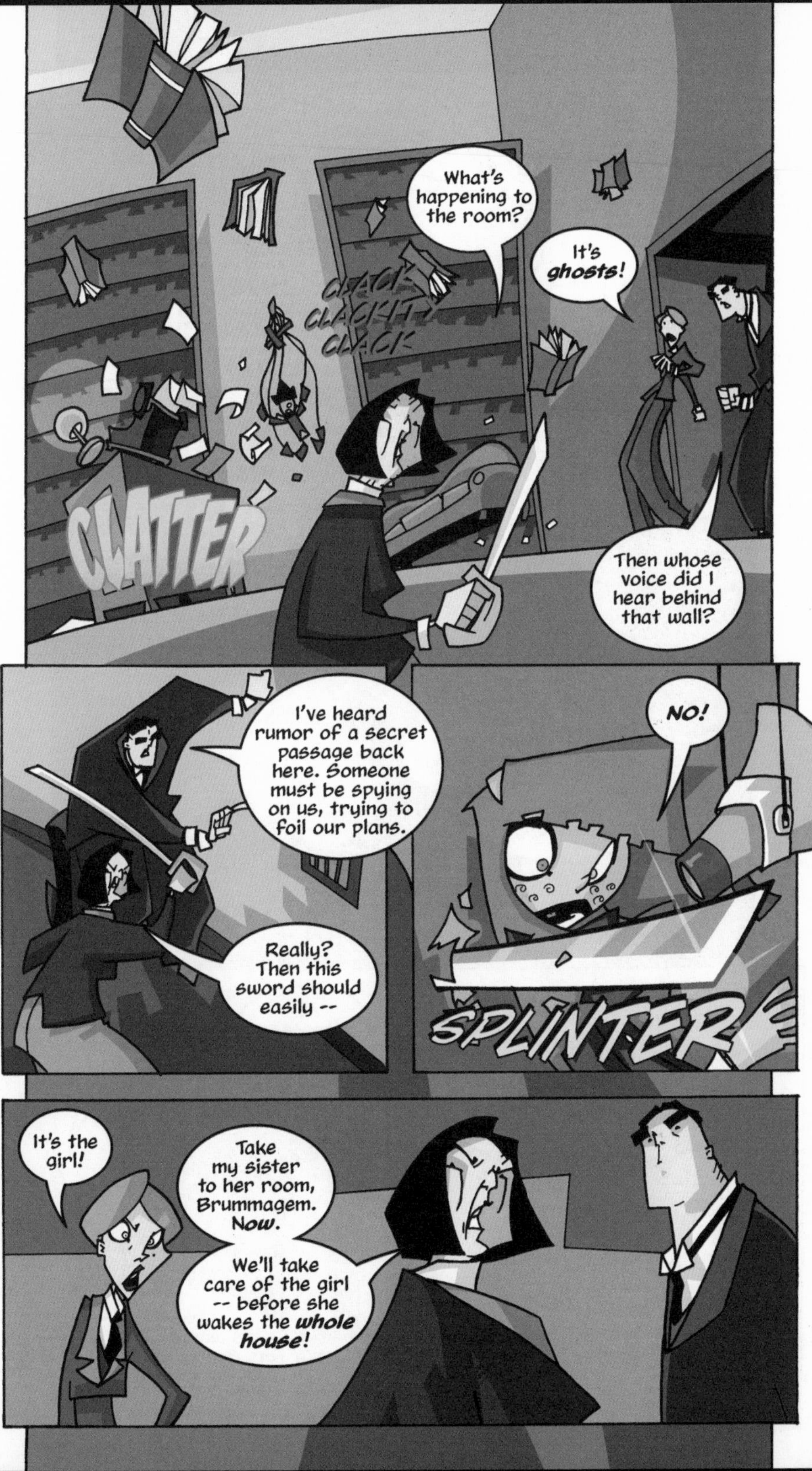

What's happening to the room?
It's *ghosts!*
CLACK CLACKITY CLACK
CLATTER
Then whose voice did I hear behind that wall?
I've heard rumor of a secret passage back here. Someone must be spying on us, trying to foil our plans.
Really? Then this sword should easily --
NO!
SPLINTER
It's the girl!
Take my sister to her room, Brummagem. *Now.*
We'll take care of the girl -- before she wakes the *whole house!*

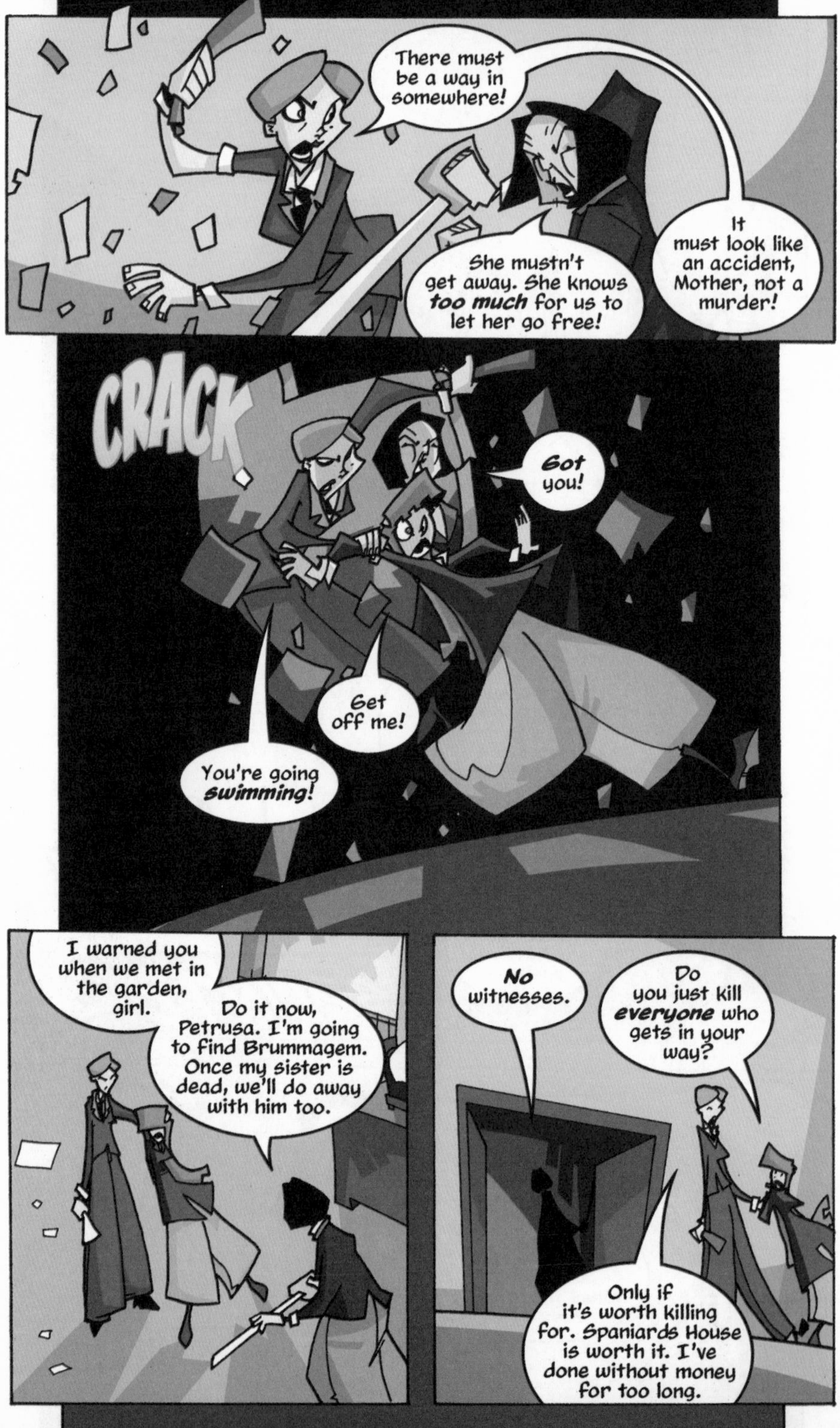
There must be a way in somewhere!
She mustn't get away. She knows **too much** for us to let her go free!
It must look like an accident, Mother, not a murder!
CRACK
Got you!
Get off me!
You're going *swimming*!
I warned you when we met in the garden, girl.
Do it now, Petrusa. I'm going to find Brummagem. Once my sister is dead, we'll do away with him too.
No witnesses.
Do you just kill *everyone* who gets in your way?
Only if it's worth killing for. Spaniards House is worth it. I've done without money for too long.

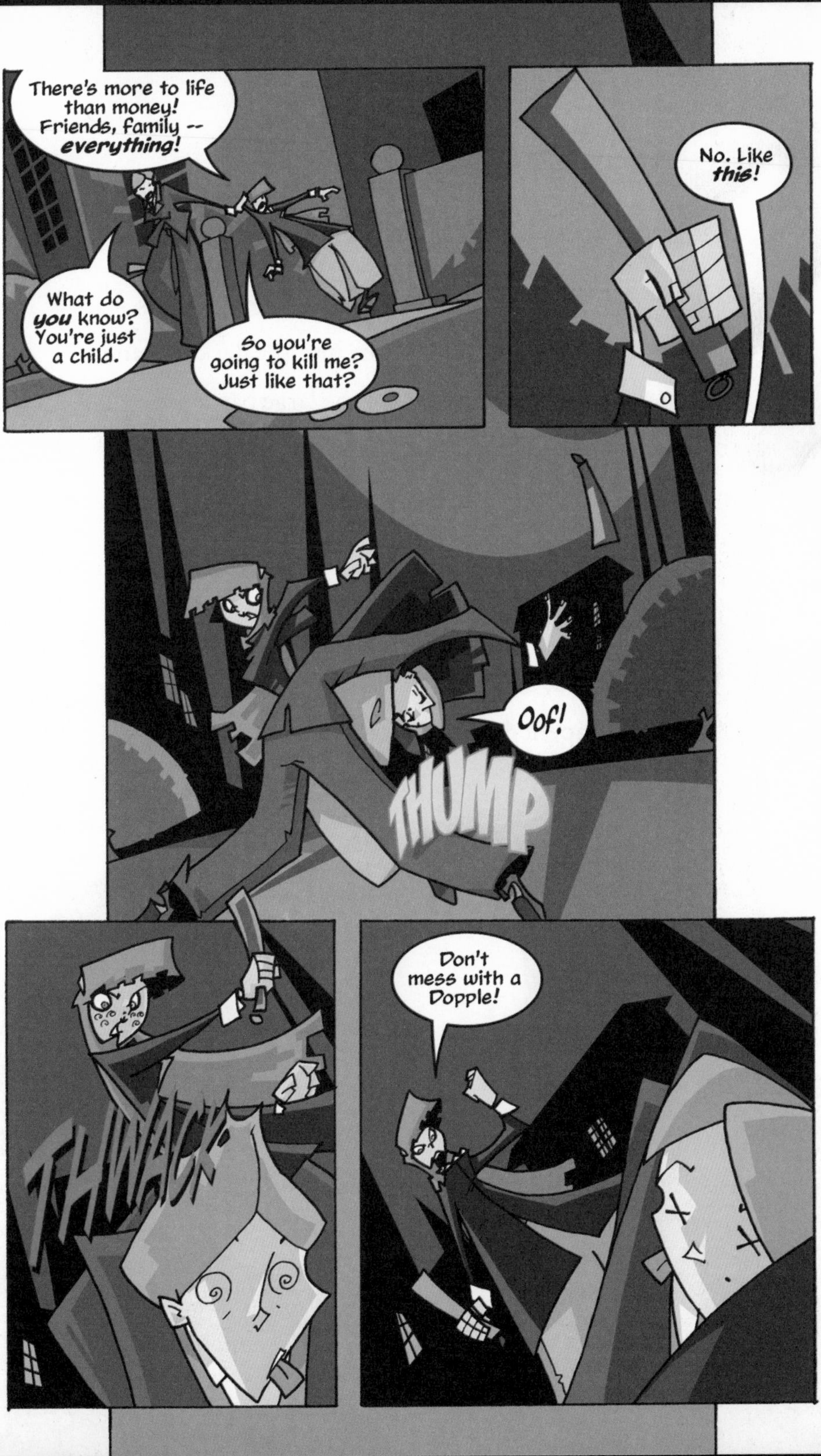

There's more to life than money! Friends, family -- *everything*!
What do *you* know? You're just a child.
So you're going to kill me? Just like that?
No. Like *this*!
Oof!
THUMP
THWACK!
Don't mess with a Dopple!

Madame Petrusa lay unconscious in the wet grass.

Saskia looked back at Spaniards House. The door was
open. A shaft of yellow light broke into the darkness and
shimmered in the fading mist. In the large bay window on
the second floor that overlooked the garden, Saskia could
see two dark figures silhouetted against the glass.

It was Muzz Elliott's room. Saskia knew that the shadows
must belong to Brummagem and Cicely Windylove.

"Where are you, Sadie?" she asked out loud. She felt
strangely compelled to run back to the house.

From far out on the heath, Saskia could hear the sounds of people shouting and a dog barking. She looked toward the commotion but in the mist could see nothing. All she knew was that she had to help Muzz Elliott. If she waited a minute longer, the staff wouldn't believe her when they returned in the morning; all they would see was Cicely Windylove, identical in every way to Muzz Elliott, but unbeknownst to them, far more dangerous. They would never know that the real Muzz Elliott was buried in the cellar. They would never know that the treasure had been found and that the mistress of the house was the missing twin sister.

As Saskia ran up the steps of the house and through the open door, all was silent. She immediately peered into the library. It was a scene of devastation. The severed donkey was strewn across the rug by the fire. The once neat panels that lined the room were smashed to pieces. Saskia looked through the hole in the wall and spied the megaphone, still hanging by its wires in the passageway beyond.

A single gold sovereign lay in the doorway. Saskia snatched it from the floor and slipped it quickly into her pocket. "Evidence," she said, running along the corridor to the room where Yeats and Crowley had been sedated.

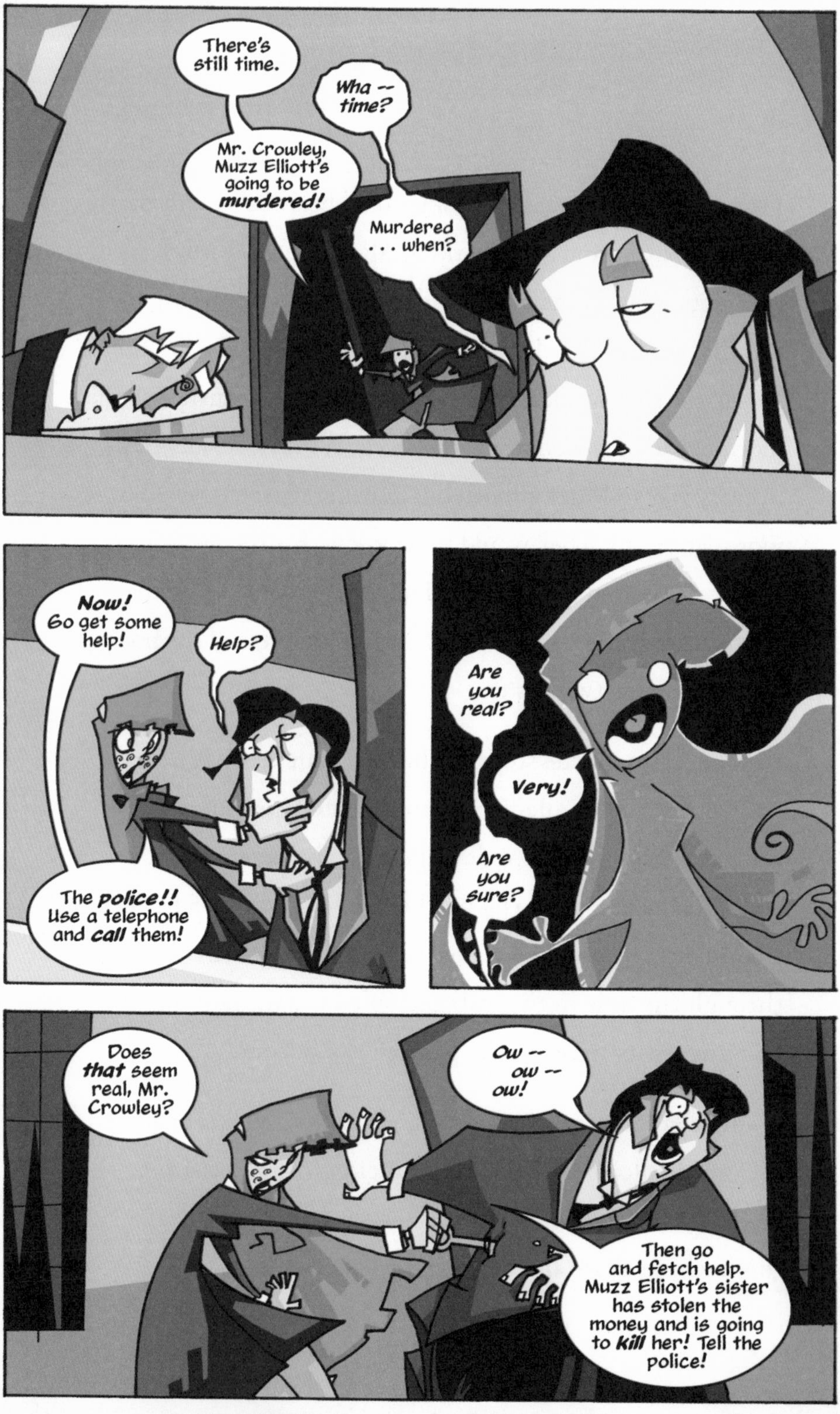

There's still time.
Wha -- time?
Mr. Crowley, Muzz Elliott's going to be *murdered!*
Murdered . . . when?
Now! Go get some help!
Help?
The *police!!* Use a telephone and *call* them!
Are you real?
Very!
Are you sure?
Does *that* seem real, Mr. Crowley?
Ow -- ow -- ow!
Then go and fetch help. Muzz Elliott's sister has stolen the money and is going to *kill* her! Tell the police!

From upstairs came the sound of something or someone being dragged across the floorboards and along the corridor.

"Do it," Saskia said to Crowley as she ran from the room into the hallway.

The large front door was now shut tight. A long brass bolt had been slipped into its keeper and locked securely.

"They know," she said to herself, walking silently up each stair. Above her head, the portrait of Lord Trevellyn stared down. He looked even more afraid to smile than he had before. It was as if the shadowy figure in the background of the picture were growing larger and more intimidating. Saskia heard the ringing of the servant's bell in the hallway downstairs. It clattered and chimed, frantically calling for someone to come.

"Muzz Elliott," she said, skirting the walls and creeping along the corridor. The sound of the bell came again. Saskia listened. Far ahead she could hear moaning.

"Help me... please... someone... help me."

It was a frail voice, strained and half asleep.

"It's her," Saskia thought as the urgent call came again.

Turning the corner, Saskia came to the door of the room. It was half open. The servant's bell had stopped ringing, and she could hear no one. She looked inside. A small table lamp lit the room. There on the large iron-framed bed was Muzz Elliott. She was dressed in a nightgown, and her hands were tied behind her back.

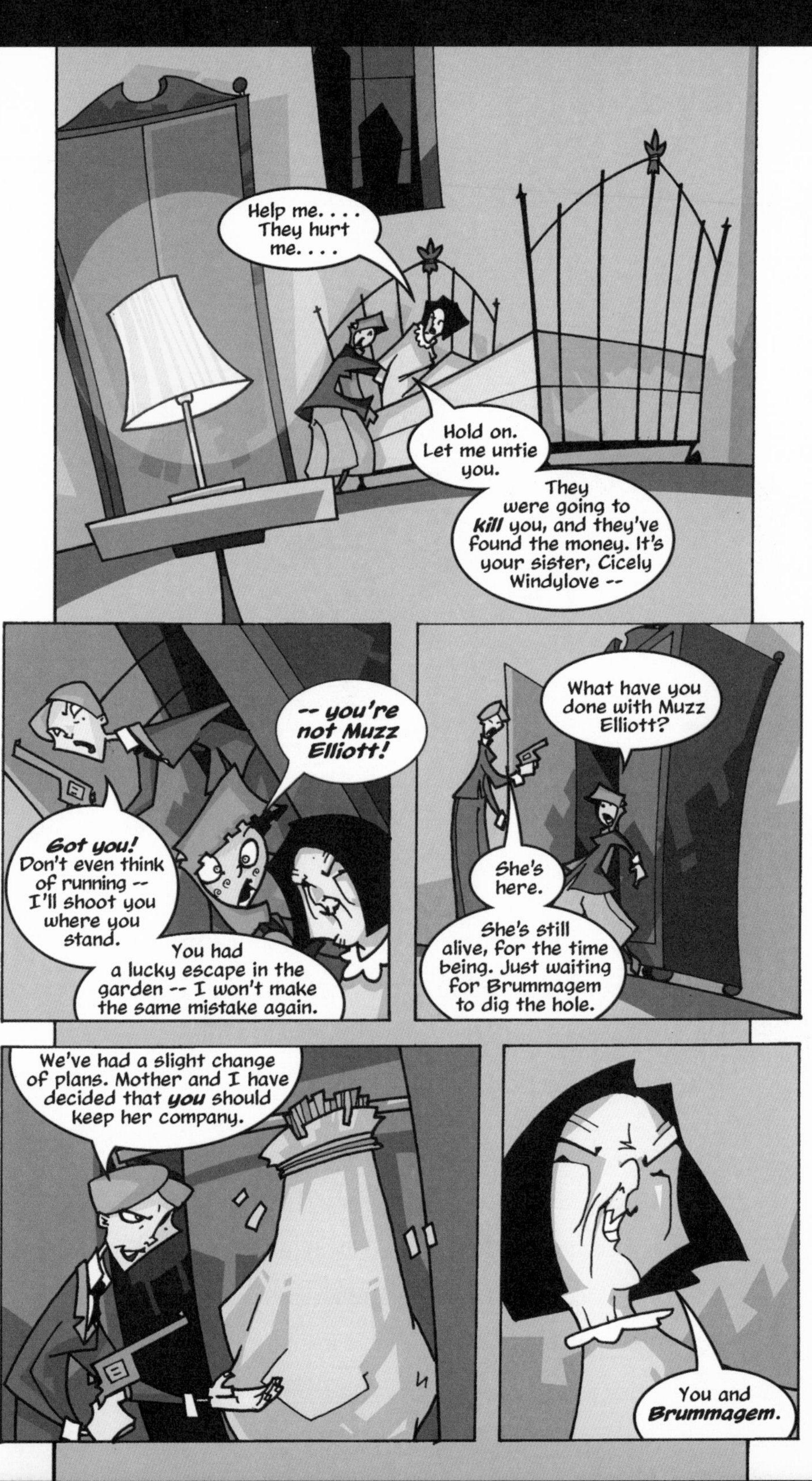
Help me. . . . They hurt me. . . .
Hold on. Let me untie you.
They were going to *kill* you, and they've found the money. It's your sister, Cicely Windylove --
-- *you're not Muzz Elliott!*
Got you! Don't even think of running -- I'll shoot you where you stand.
You had a lucky escape in the garden -- I won't make the same mistake again.
What have you done with Muzz Elliott?
She's here.
She's still alive, for the time being. Just waiting for Brummagem to dig the hole.
We've had a slight change of plans. Mother and I have decided that *you* should keep her company.
You and *Brummagem.*

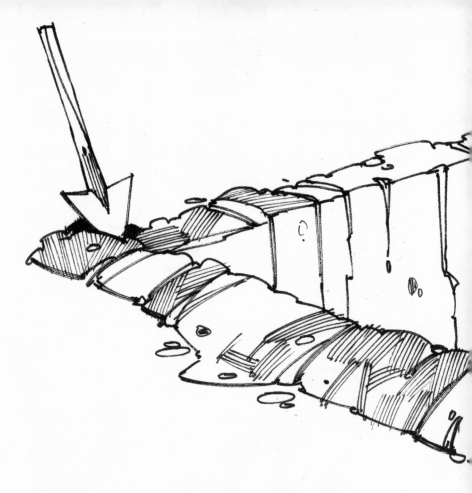

In a matter of moments, Saskia was wrapped in a linen sack and hung next to Muzz Elliott. She dangled helplessly above the metal laundry chute. The sound of digging echoed from far below.

She heard the door to the bedroom close and footsteps pound along the landing and down the stairs. Madame Petrusa and her mother walked away quickly, laughing. Saskia twisted and turned as she wrestled to get the key out of her pocket.

Deep enough?

Far below she could hear voices.

"Can you dig faster?" asked Cicely Windylove over the clattering of a shovel slicing through dirt.

"Deep enough?" rumbled Brummagem's voice.

"Petrusa and I have decided it needs to be deeper—and wider. We have another guest who requires a bed for eternity." Cicely Windylove's voice echoed up into the chute.

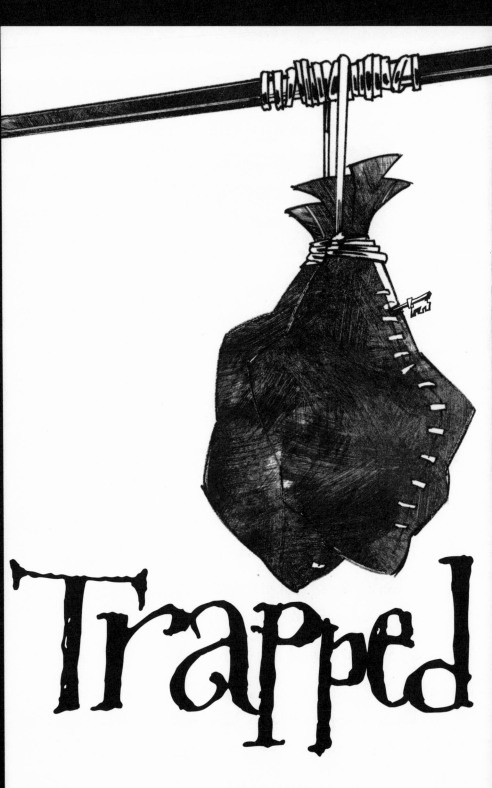

Trapped

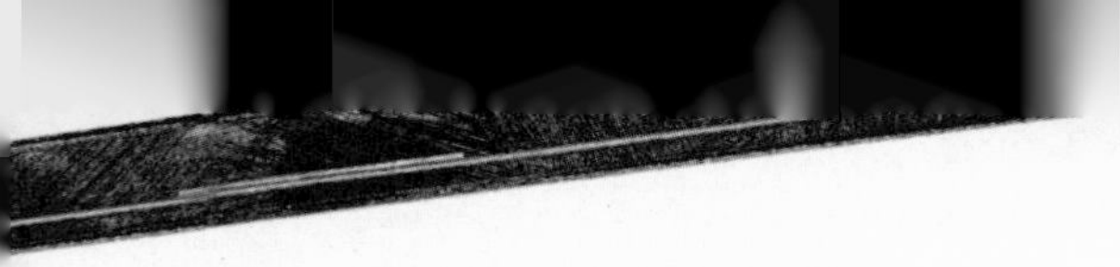

Saskia pushed against the side of the sack, which held her tightly. Twisting her wrist, she managed to free her hand. She slipped the key from her pocket and gripped it in her fingers. Pressing the edge against the tight linen, Saskia began to rub, hoping the key would pierce the fabric. She listened as Brummagem continued to dig. The sound of each slice of the shovel against the hard ground rattled through the chute. Next to her, Muzz Elliott began to wake from her sleep. Saskia knew they had to escape.

"Don't say anything, Muzz Elliott," Saskia whispered. "There are thieves in the house, and we've been seized."

"Where are we?" her guardian asked quietly.

"Trapped over the laundry chute," Saskia answered. "I'll soon be free, and I'll get help."

"Find Brummagem—he'll know what to do," Muzz Elliott said as she struggled in her linen bag.

"No," replied Saskia. "He's one of them."

Chapter Fourteen
Breathe

IT TOOK NO TIME at all for the Black Maria to begin sinking down into the muddy lake. The still, dark water oozed through the doors like black soup. It stank of dead leaves and rotting grass.

Sadie listened to the glug, glug, glug as the van sank deeper and deeper. The rising water trapped her inside the cab as it slowly crept up the windshield and swirled around her chest. From everywhere it poured in, faster and faster. She kicked against the handle of the door, which was jammed shut by the weight of the torrent.

As the water got higher, Sadie stood on the passenger seat. Her head was pressed against the roof. She gulped the waning pocket of air.

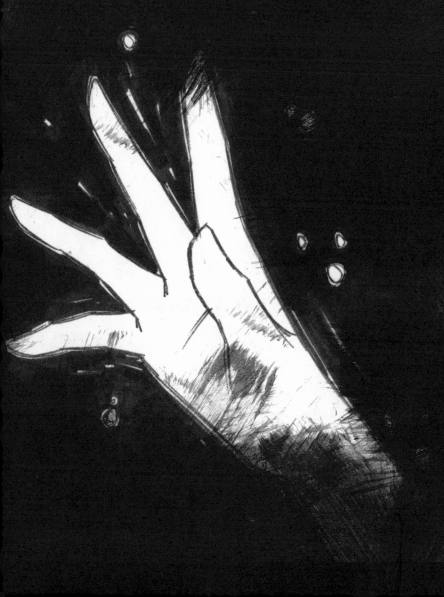

"Erik!" she cried out helplessly in the pitch black. "I'm trapped." The words seemed dulled by the sound of the water. Sadie shouted again. "Erik, I'm trapped!"

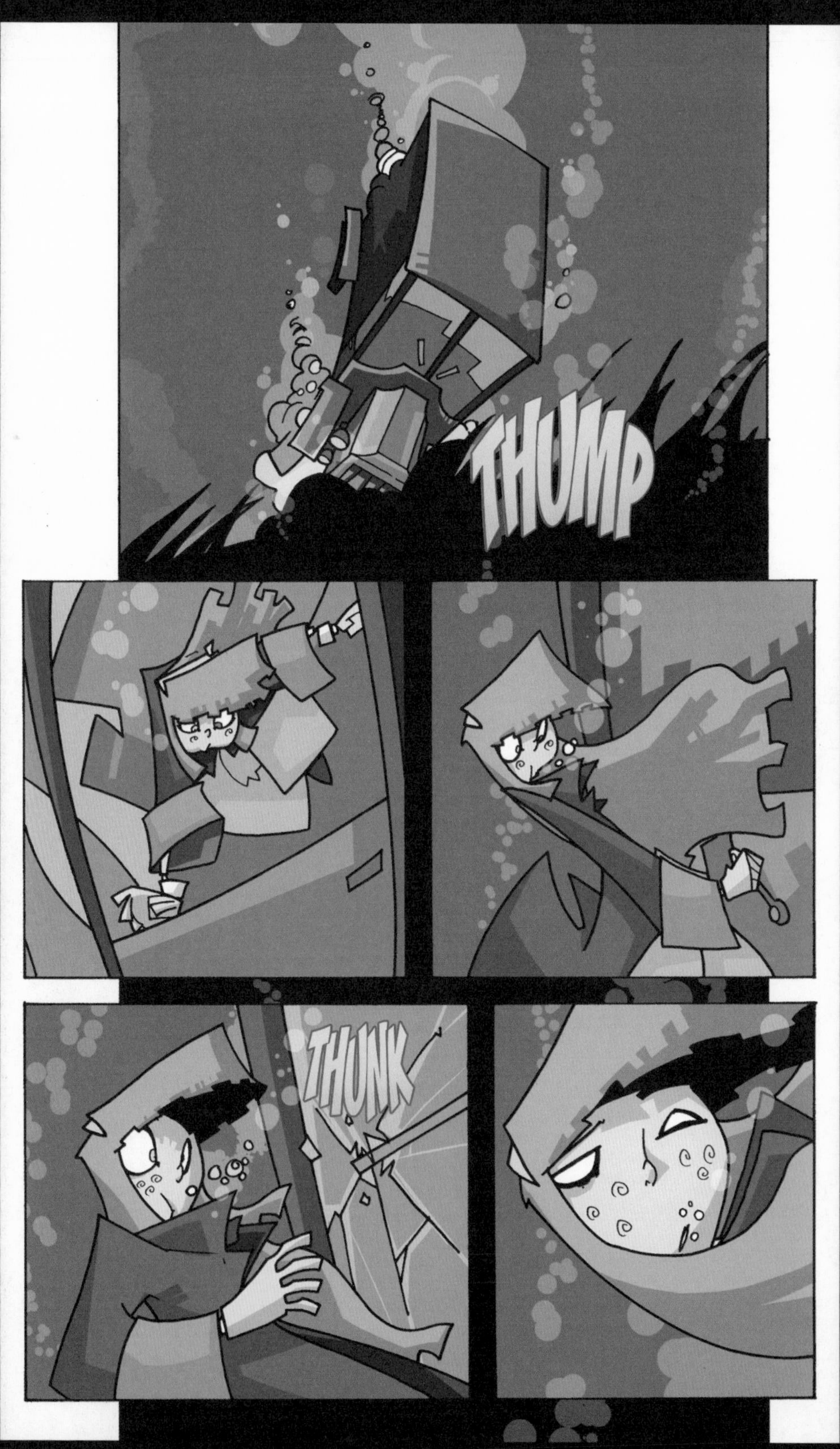
THUMP
THUNK

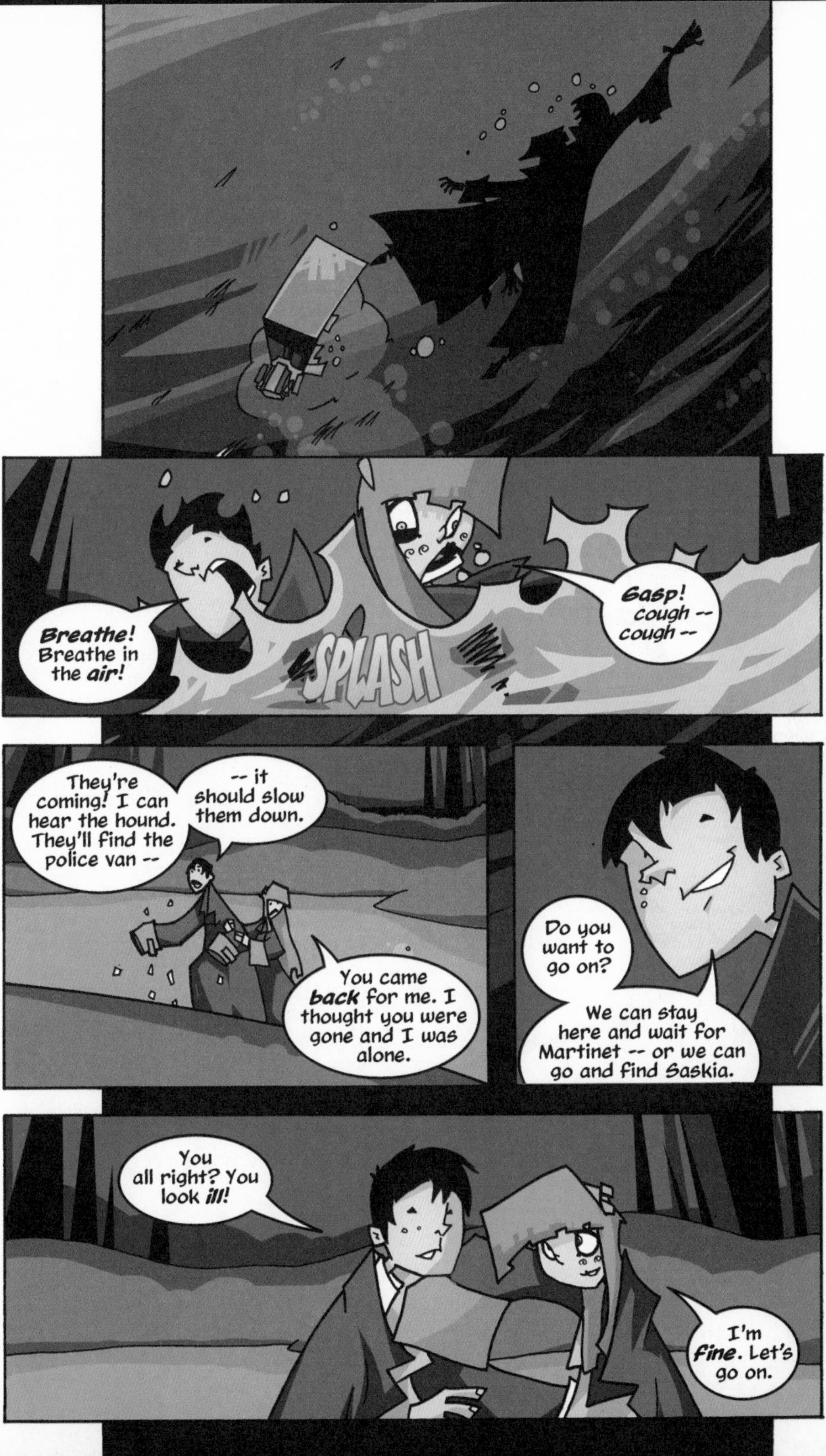

Breathe! Breathe in the air!
SPLASH
Gasp! cough -- cough --
They're coming! I can hear the hound. They'll find the police van --
-- it should slow them down.
You came back for me. I thought you were gone and I was alone.
Do you want to go on?
We can stay here and wait for Martinet -- or we can go and find Saskia.
You all right? You look ill!
I'm fine. Let's go on.

Erik turned and began to run through the wet grass.
Sadie followed close behind. Her heart still pounded, and
every breath burned her lungs. But the smile that beamed
across her face spoke of the hope within her heart.
She had been saved from drowning, and a new
courage was forming inside of her. From the top
of the heath she could hear the
barking of Kobold's hound
and the blast of police
whistles. She didn't care,
even though she
thought that she
and Erik would
most likely end
up in jail because
of what they had
done. She also knew she would never see
her sister again unless she got to
Muzz Elliott's house.

For the next mile, neither of them
spoke. Sadie dripped grubby pond water with every step.
The cold stuck to her flesh as she ran.

As they entered the woods, the mist began to clear. By an old swimming hole a lofty, green gas lamp gave out a ghostly glow. It lit the tall, bare trees and roosting gray doves that huddled together against the night.

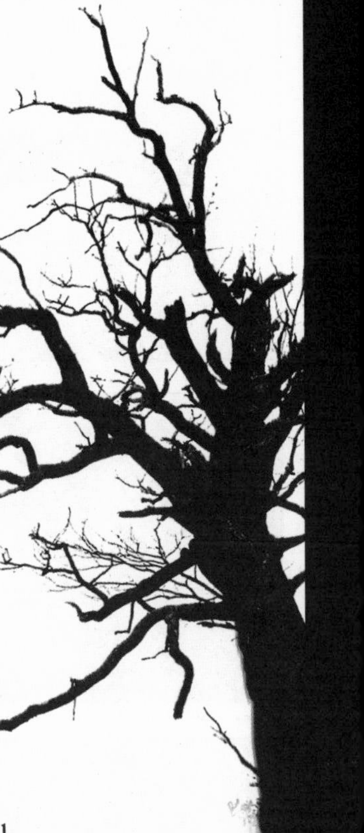

By a small wooden shack near the swimming hole, Sadie could see the tip of a smoldering cigar. It burned brightly in the darkness, a wisp of thick smoke spiraling into the night.

"Erik," she said softly as they slowed to a walk, "we're being watched."

"I know," he said in a calm voice. "We've been followed since we got out of the pond."

"Is it Kobold or Martinet?" she asked.

"I don't think so," he said. He took her hand and led her through a small grove of trees that rattled in the breeze. Slowly, the mist began to clear from Parliament Hill.

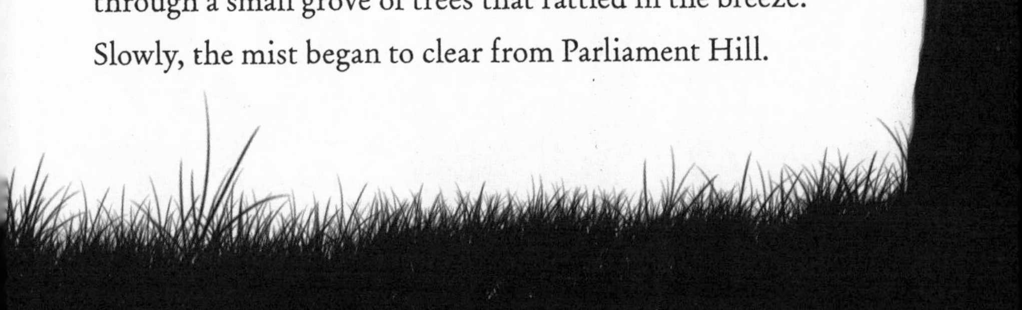

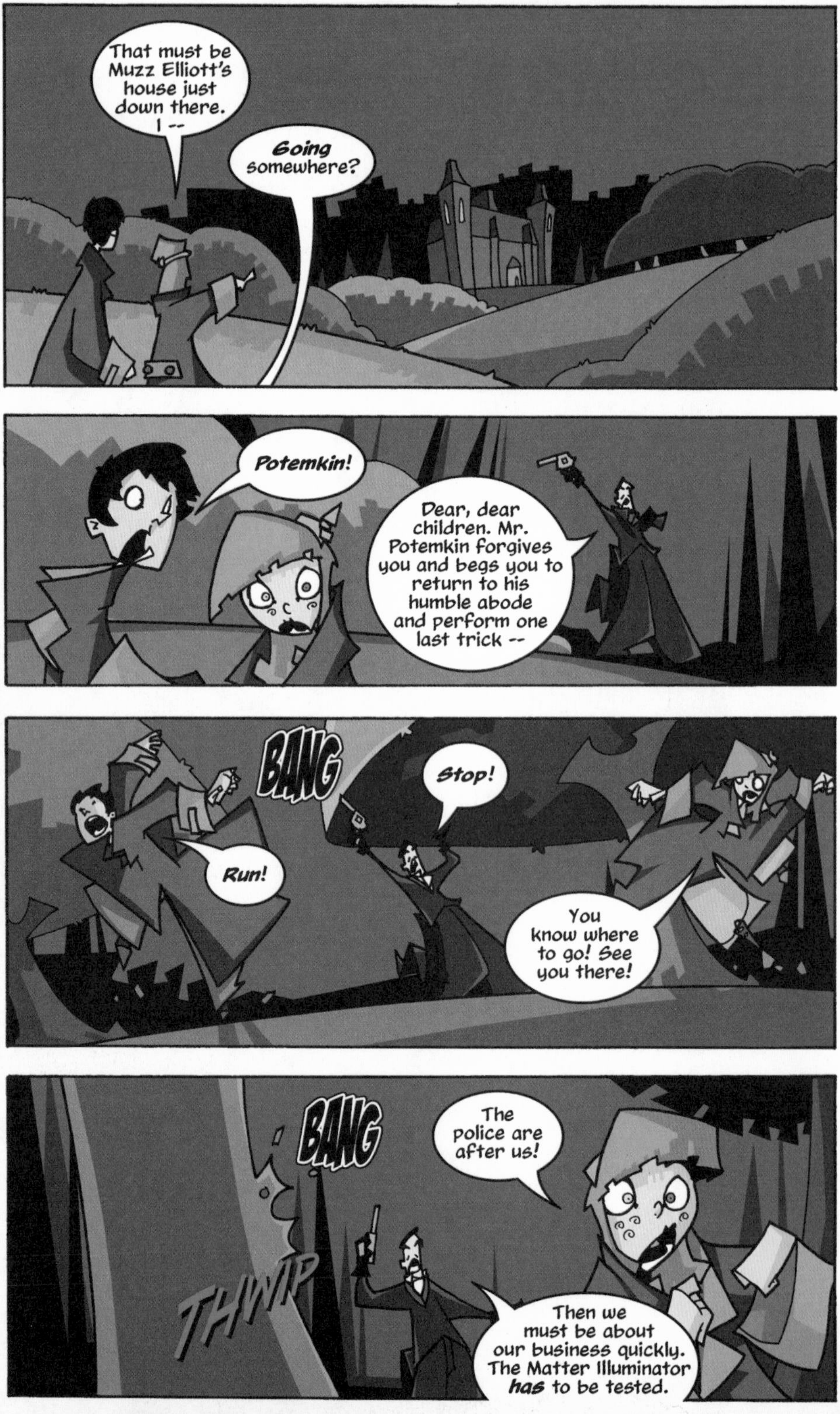
That must be Muzz Elliott's house just down there. I --
Going somewhere?
Potemkin!
Dear, dear children. Mr. Potemkin forgives you and begs you to return to his humble abode and perform one last trick --
BANG
Stop!
Run!
You know where to go! See you there!
BANG
The police are after us!
THWIP
Then we must be about our business quickly. The Matter Illuminator *has* to be tested.

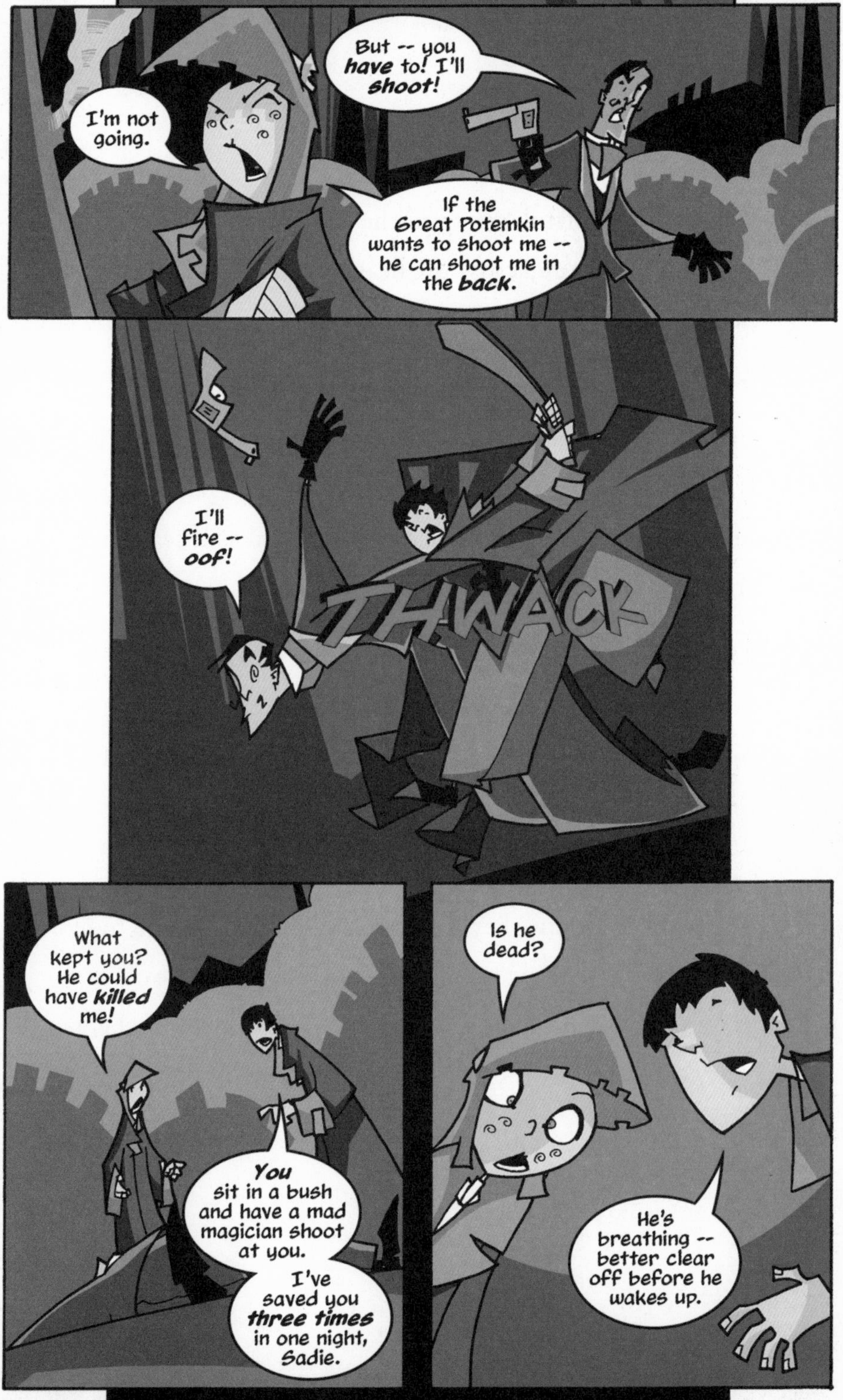
I'm not going.
But -- you have to! I'll shoot!
If the Great Potemkin wants to shoot me -- he can shoot me in the back.
I'll fire -- oof!
THWACK
What kept you? He could have killed me!
You sit in a bush and have a mad magician shoot at you.
I've saved you three times in one night, Sadie.
Is he dead?
He's breathing -- better clear off before he wakes up.

Erik took the pistol, removed the last remaining bullet, and threw the gun across the heath. "Let's go," he said and headed into the trees.

Ahead Erik and Sadie could see the string of gas lamps that ran along the road to Spaniards House. Far to the left was the dark silhouette of Jack Straw's Inn. The headlights of a car went back and forth along the road as if searching the trees for someone hiding within.

"They know we're on the heath," Sadie said mournfully as she realized that now Kobold and Martinet were not the only ones chasing them. "All I want is to see Saskia again before I get caught and taken to whichever prison they send people like me to."

"How do you know they'll catch us? We're old enough to live our own lives. I could get a job and so could you. We could search for your mother—go to France, Germany, anywhere. They'd give up in the end. After all, what have we done?"

"Run away from Isambard Dunstan's School, electrocuted a teacher, stolen a police van, crashed it into a pond, and assaulted a magician with a fence post. Nothing, really," Sadie replied as the sudden weight of one night pressed down on her.

"Forget all that, Sadie Dopple. We'll find your sister and be off. London is a sea of people, and they'll never find us. Or we could get a ship from the docks and be in France by Friday. What do you think?" Erik asked as they reached the tall fence that surrounded Spaniards House.

"I think we should ask Saskia."

"How will you do that? It's the middle of the night, and she doesn't know we're here," Erik said. They climbed the fence and hid in the bushes opposite the front door of the house.

Sadie didn't have time to speak. A car sped down the driveway and pulled up outside the house. Two men in plain clothes got out and, without looking around, went straight to the door and hammered urgently.

"Who are they?"

Erik whispered, pushing the twigs of a
sharp branch away from his face.

The door to the house opened. Sadie saw a man in a
dark suit step outside and close it behind him. He was
tall with thick, muscular arms.

"We've lost two children from Isambard Dunstan's
School," she heard one of the men say. "We were told the
sister of one of them lives here. They could be on their
way. Can we see the girl?"

"The house is shut up for the night," the man replied in a
thick Irish accent. "I'll tell the child in the morning and keep
an eye out myself." The man yawned. In the light from the
house, Sadie could see his face wrinkle as he shook the hand
of the man who had spoken and watched the two detectives
get back in the car and drive off.

"Stupid fools," the Irishman said as the
car roared back up the road. "When they get
back, she'll be dead." He was speaking to someone
listening behind the door. As he stepped inside,
Sadie and Erik could see a dark outline standing in the
shadows of a great hall.

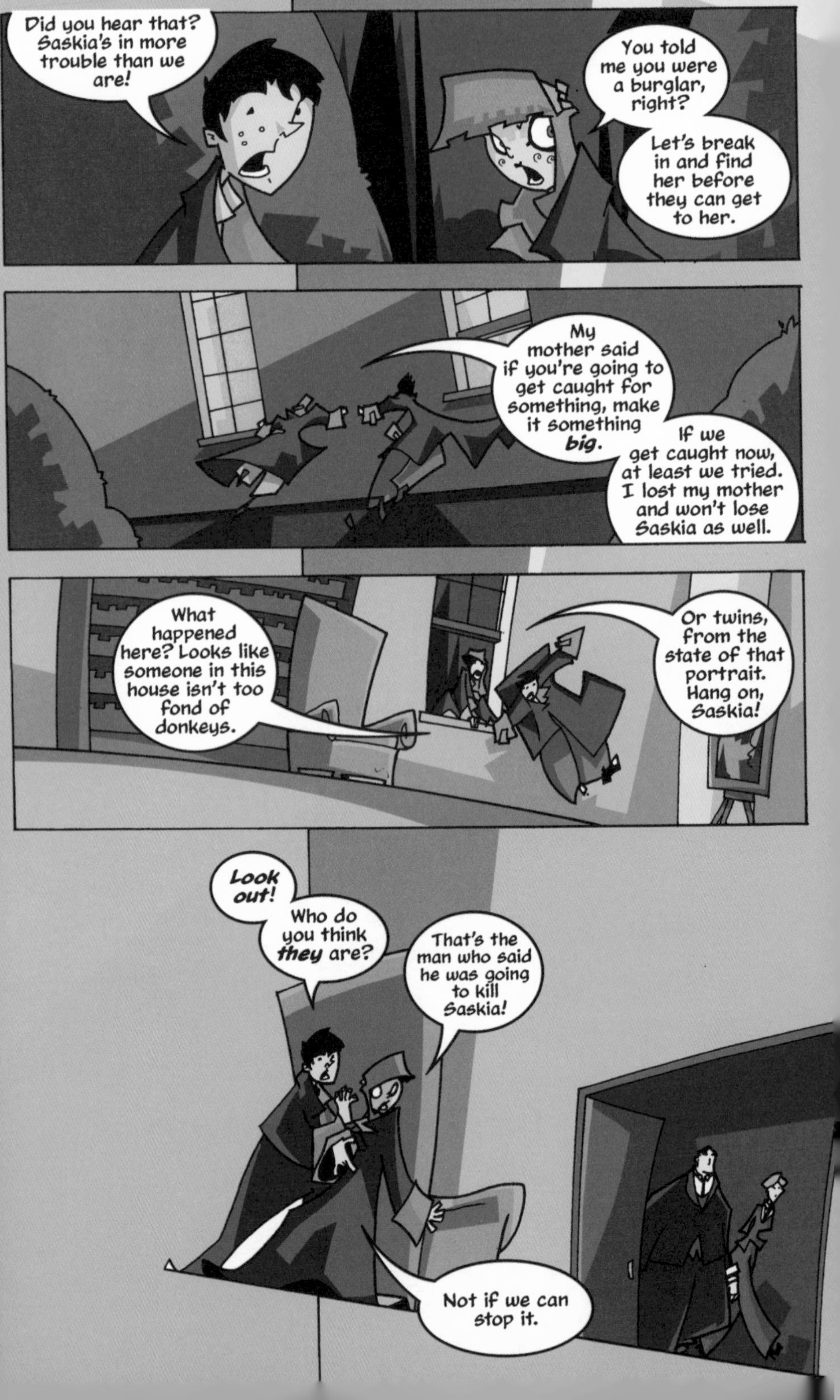
Did you hear that? Saskia's in more trouble than we are!
You told me you were a burglar, right?
Let's break in and find her before they can get to her.
My mother said if you're going to get caught for something, make it something *big*.
If we get caught now, at least we tried. I lost my mother and won't lose Saskia as well.
What happened here? Looks like someone in this house isn't too fond of donkeys.
Or twins, from the state of that portrait. Hang on, Saskia!
Look out!
Who do you think *they* are?
That's the man who said he was going to kill Saskia!
Not if we can stop it.

As the two strangers passed by the open doorway, Sadie overheard the woman speaking. Her words sounded angry and bitter. "You have to do it now, Brummagem," she said urgently. "If the police want to speak to that girl, then she'll have to be gone and gone fast. Go get her from upstairs and bring her here. We'll hide them both in the cellar and bury them later."

Erik and Sadie waited behind the armchair until the woman's voice began to grow distant. Then Sadie pulled Erik into the dark corridor and closed the door behind her. In the hallway they could hear the two arguing ahead of them. The Irishman proclaimed in a voice they could hear quite clearly from the other end of the corridor that he didn't know why he had to do everything while everyone else just watched. He made it clear he knew that he would have to be the one to do "the business," as he kept calling it, and that they would walk scot-free should the police find them out. "Not fair, never is, never is," he said over and over.

Sadie and Erik sneaked up the passageway, and soon they were on the floor above. There was another long corridor with four doors that all looked the same.

The one farthest away was slightly open. A chink of light burst into the passageway. They crept closer, all the while listening for footsteps. Sadie felt sick; her stomach kept turning. Erik held her shaking hand.

"Frightened?" she asked in the quietest of voices, just above a breath.

"Done it many times. This is the best bit," he replied, smiling.

Sadie peered into the room. A woman in a suit was struggling with a linen bag. The bag was muttering angrily. Sadie knew it was her sister.

Chapter Fifteen

AND Then There Were Three

MADAME PETRUSA DIDN'T have time to turn before two dark shapes ran into the room and pushed her to the floor. She attempted a forlorn scream as a pair of hands stuffed a cloth in her mouth. She was gagged speechless; all that came out of her mouth was a feeble squeak. A crisp white pillowcase was forced over her head, and her hands were squeezed behind her back and thumbs tied together with string.

"Stay where you are," Sadie said.

"Sadie?" moaned the voice from the linen bag. "Sadie, is it you?"

"It's me and Erik," Sadie replied as Erik finished tying up Madame Petrusa until she looked like an overstuffed rag doll.

"They're going to kill Muzz Elliott and bury her in the cellar!" said Saskia. "They've stolen her money—money hidden in the house. She has a twin sister, and when she's dead her sister will pretend to be her." Saskia pulled on the thick cord that was twisted inside the linen bag.

"We heard them say they would kill you," Erik butted in.

"Why do you think I'm in this sack, Erik? Get me out!"

Sadie pulled at the sack, and in an instant her sister's head popped through the hole.

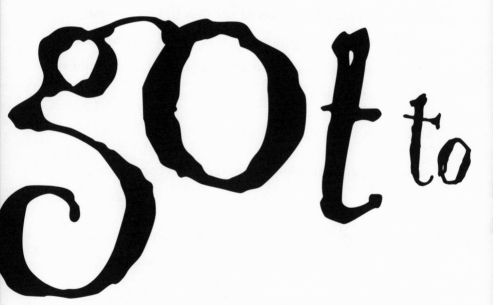

got to

"Always late, couldn't even be born on time," Sadie said with a smile. For a moment, in the dim lamplight, she thought of her mother. It lasted only an instant, but that flash of time was enough to bring to mind every speck of anger she had ever experienced. "We've got to stop her, got to stop her now!"

Stop her!

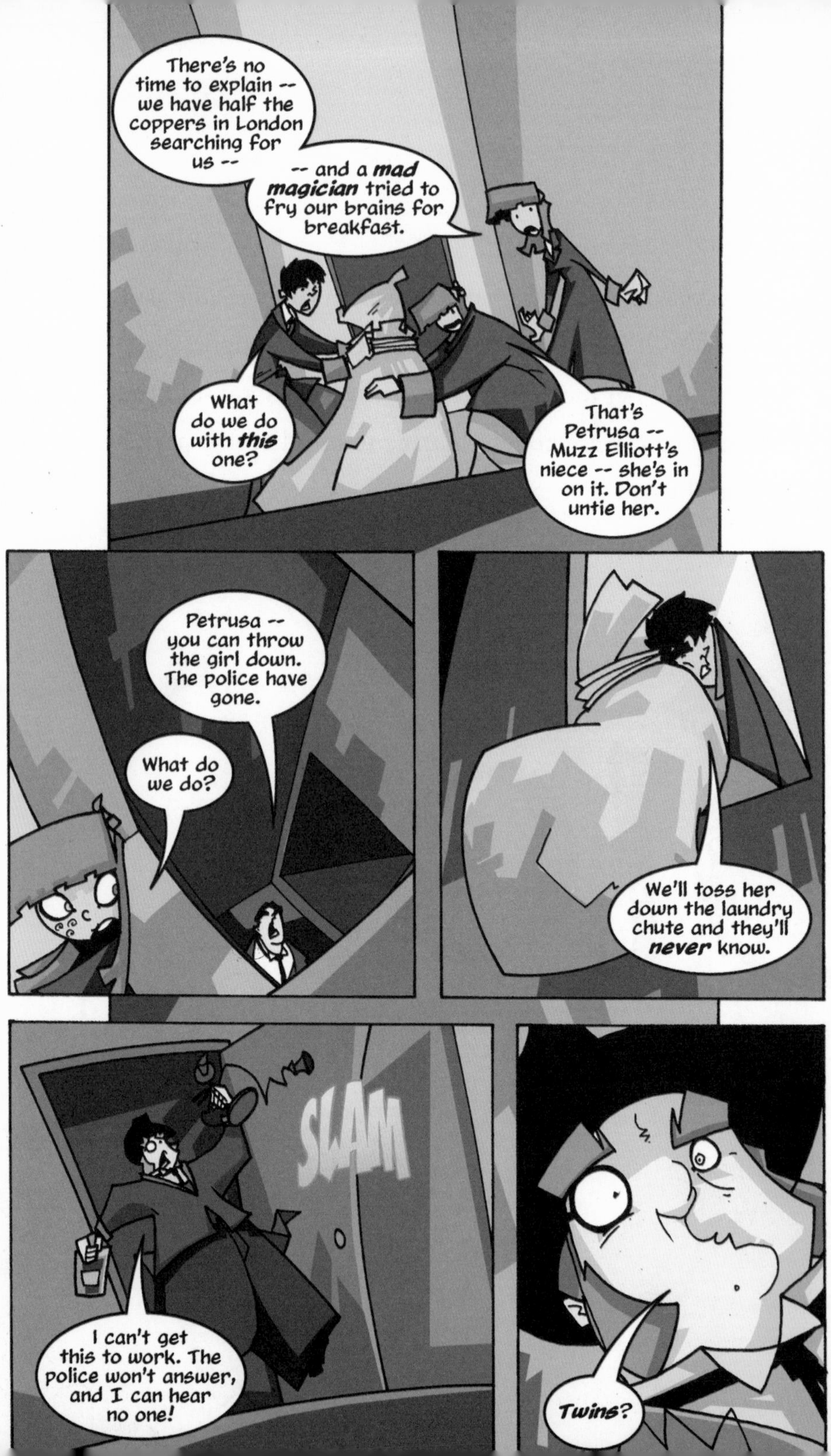
There's no time to explain -- we have half the coppers in London searching for us --
-- and a *mad magician* tried to fry our brains for breakfast.
What do we do with *this* one?
That's Petrusa -- Muzz Elliott's niece -- she's in on it. Don't untie her.
Petrusa -- you can throw the girl down. The police have gone.
What do we do?
We'll toss her down the laundry chute and they'll *never* know.
SLAM
I can't get this to work. The police won't answer, and I can hear no one!
Twins?

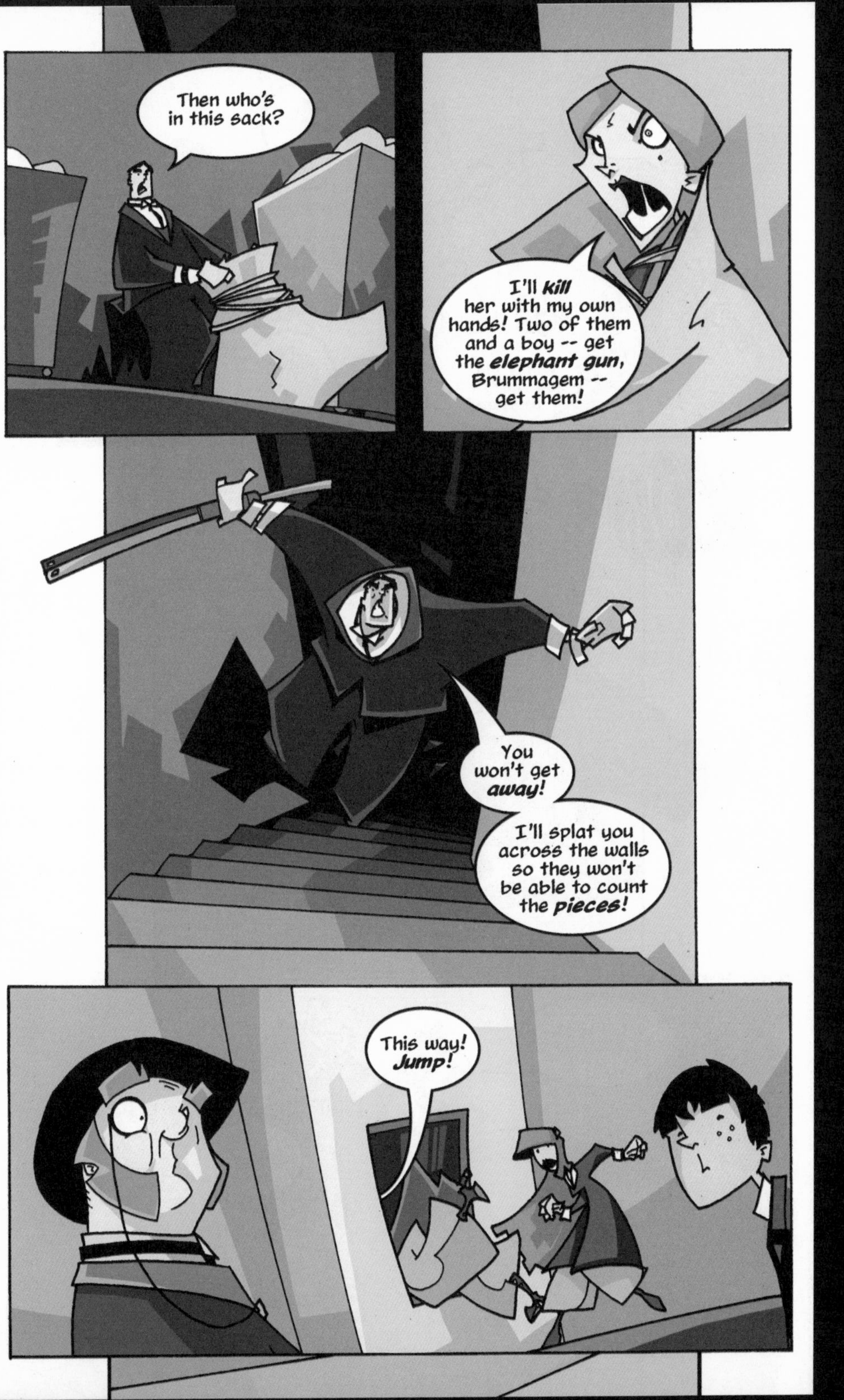
Then who's in this sack?
I'll kill her with my own hands! Two of them and a boy -- get the elephant gun, Brummagem -- get them!
You won't get away!
I'll splat you across the walls so they won't be able to count the pieces!
This way! Jump!

Stay where you are!
I won't run -- you don't have to shoot!
Oh, but I do --
BOOM
CRASH
No!
Stay back, monster!
Get off me!

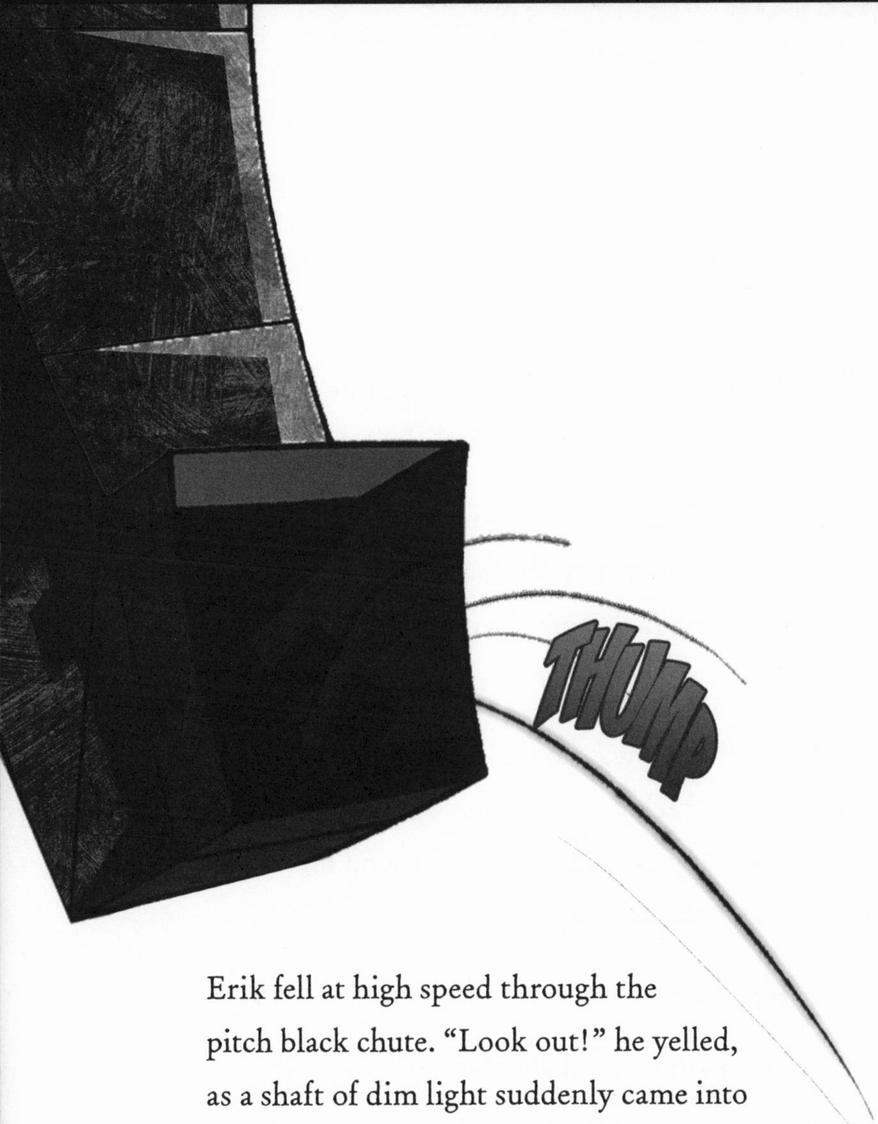
THUMP

Erik fell at high speed through the pitch black chute. "Look out!" he yelled, as a shaft of dim light suddenly came into view. He landed with a distinct bump and was then sent spinning across a polished tile floor and in front of a large, black coal heater. Above his head was a flickering lightbulb that could barely hold its glow. To his right was a large wicker basket wedged against a door.

"Sadie, Saskia," he whispered in the half-light, "the mad Irishman tried to shoot me."

There was no reply. Erik was alone, but he knew that the Irishman would soon be after him. Erik didn't wait.

He jumped up, opened the door, and went into the next cellar. It was colder than the laundry room, but it too was lit by a solitary, flickering electric light.

"Sadie? Saskia?" he asked again, hoping they were hiding nearby. Still there was no reply. He could feel the hairs bristle on his neck as if someone were standing behind him. Erik stopped, afraid to turn around but sure he could hear someone breathing close by.

"And then there were three," said a voice from the shadows.

Erik turned—but could see no one.

"Three children, and all will have to be gotten rid of." The voice came again from the other side of the cellar.

Erik turned toward it. Still no one was there.

"So which one is which?" the voice, now in front of him, asked begrudgingly.

"I'm Sadie, and she's Saskia," Sadie said from somewhere very close by.

Erik could see no one. He looked around the room, and there in the shadows, halfway up the wall, was a small grille that blew a stream of cold air into the cellar.

"Then you'd better say good-bye, for this is the last glimpse you two will ever have of each other." The voice rattled on, gruff and gravelly. "If the police are on their way, I suggest we throw them in the pond. If we bury them here, that bloodhound will sniff them out, and we'll be hanged."

"It'll have to be done quickly," another voice said.

Erik recognized the voice of Madame Petrusa. He tried to think of what to do.

"Take them to the pond . . . NOW!" the first voice said. Erik heard a door open and then quickly slam shut.

"He got away and is somewhere in the cellars," a man's voice panted.

"Leave him, Brummagem." The gruff voice came through the air vent. "We'll lock him in, and he won't go far. You deal with my sister, and we'll get rid of these two. The boy can wait. Who'll miss another runaway?"

Brummagem and Madame Petrusa laughed. Their cackling voices echoed through the vent in the chilled air. Erik shivered yet again.

"Better be quick," he said to himself as he got to the far door and, opening it slightly, sneaked a peek into the next room.

To his surprise, there was yet another cellar with a vaulted stone roof. At the far end, lit by amber twilight, was Brummagem. He beat at the ground with an old shovel. Next to him was a squirming and moaning linen sack. Erik thought it must be Muzz Elliott, gagged and waiting to be put in the hole that Brummagem was now digging furiously. "Got to do something—quick," Erik thought, noticing a laundry cart on four caster wheels by the door. "If I just . . ."

He didn't finish the thought. Grabbing the handle of the cart, he ran at full speed across the room. The cart rattled, its casters crunching against the tiled floor.

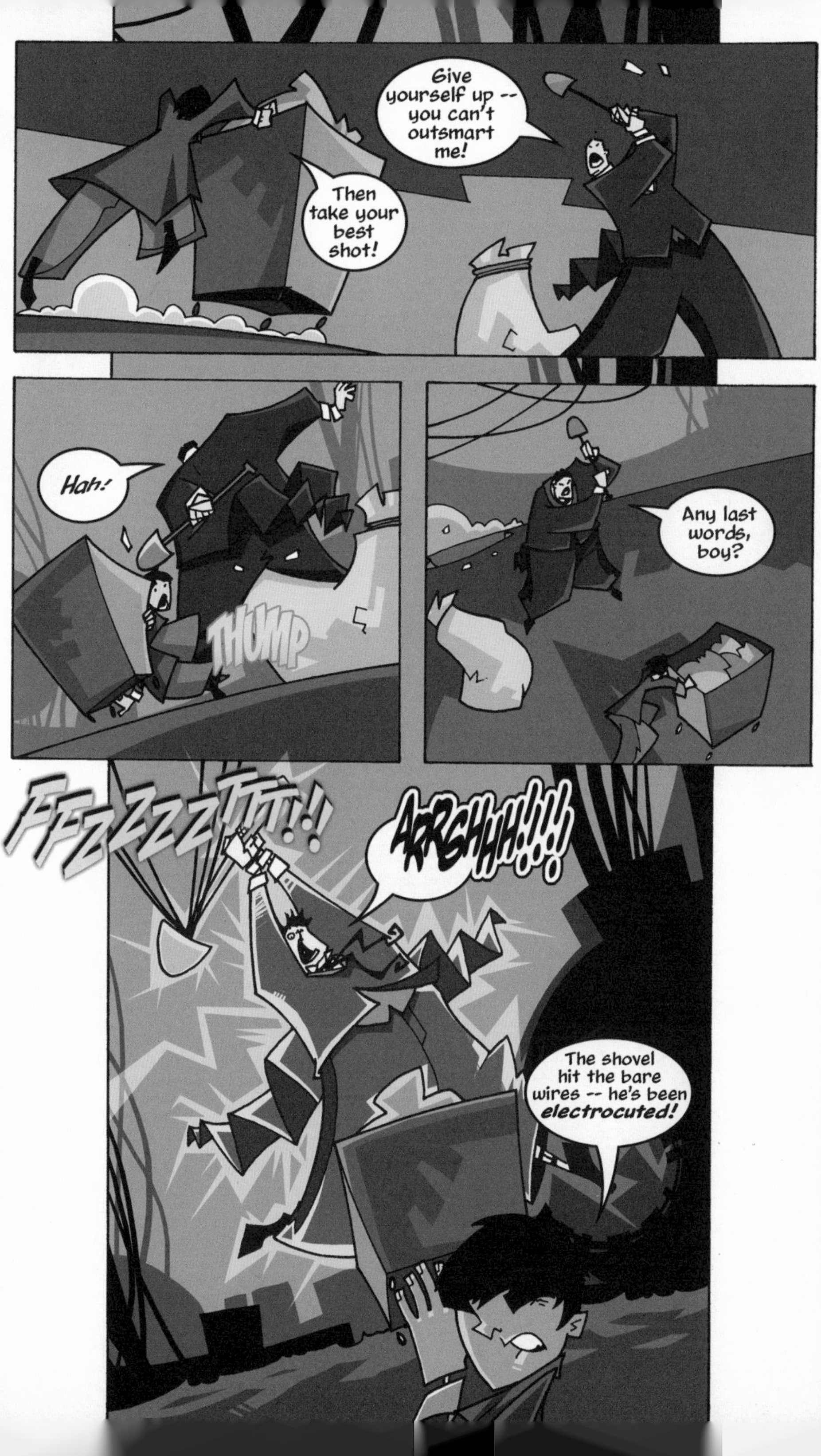
Give yourself up -- you can't outsmart me!
Then take your best shot!
Hah!
THUMP
Any last words, boy?
FFZZZZZTTT!!
ARRGHHH!!!!
The shovel hit the bare wires -- he's been *electrocuted!*

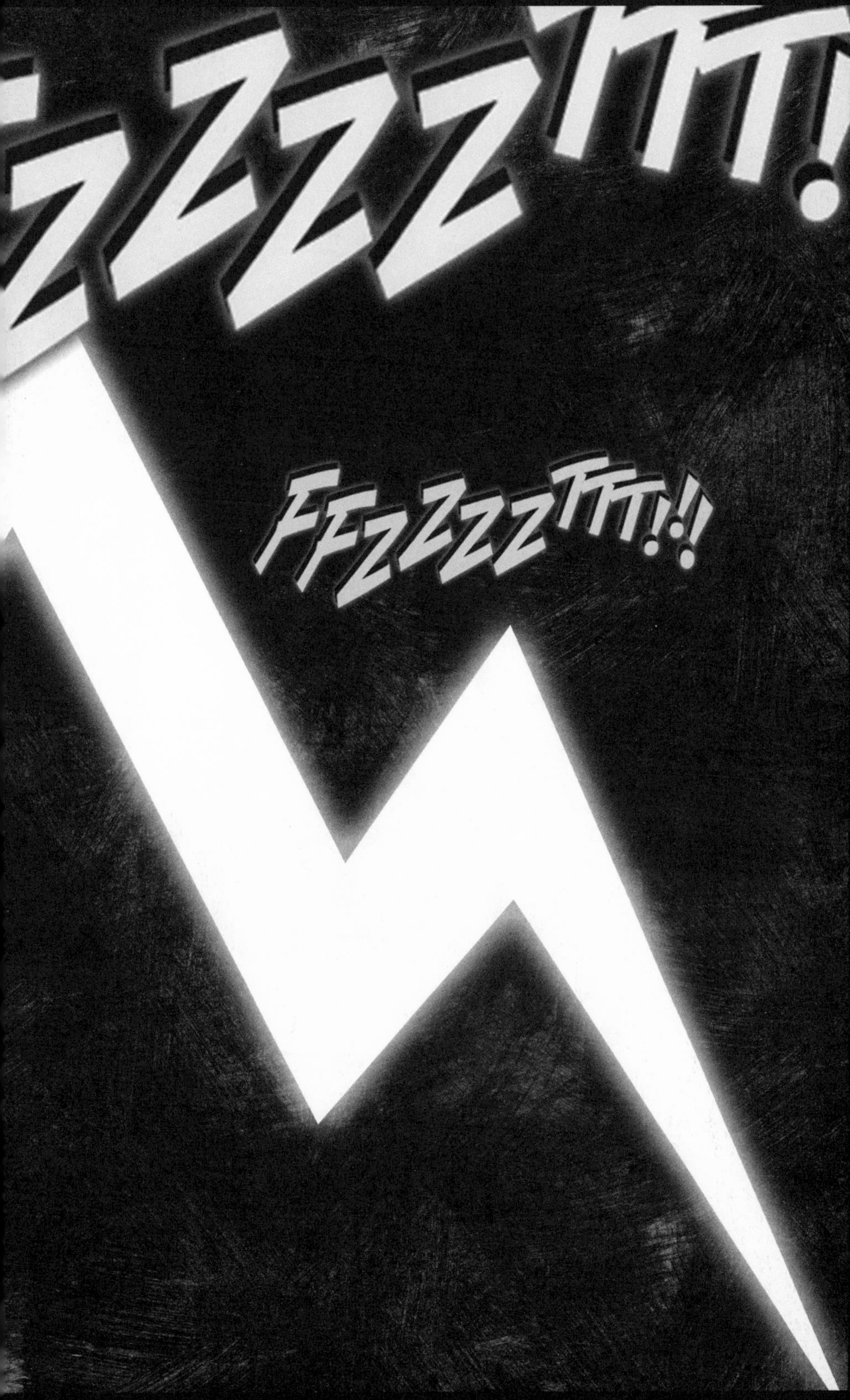
FFZZZZTTT!!

Erik kicked the laundry cart, and like an old puppet with no strings, Brummagem fell in. The shovel crashed into the hole that Brummagem had been digging. He twitched and moaned as Erik slammed the lid shut. Erik tied the two leather straps and slipped the metal catch.

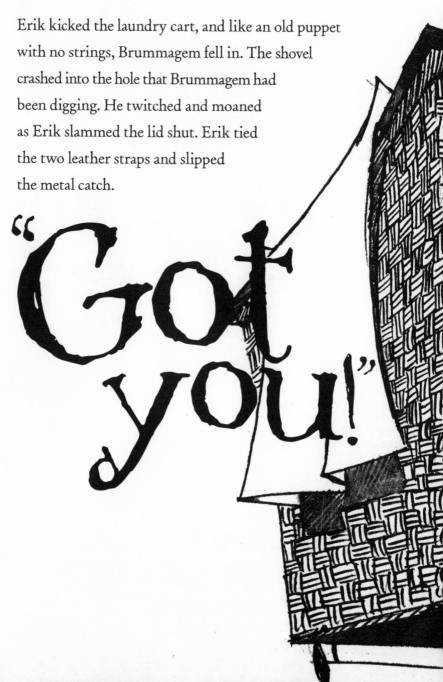

"Got you!"

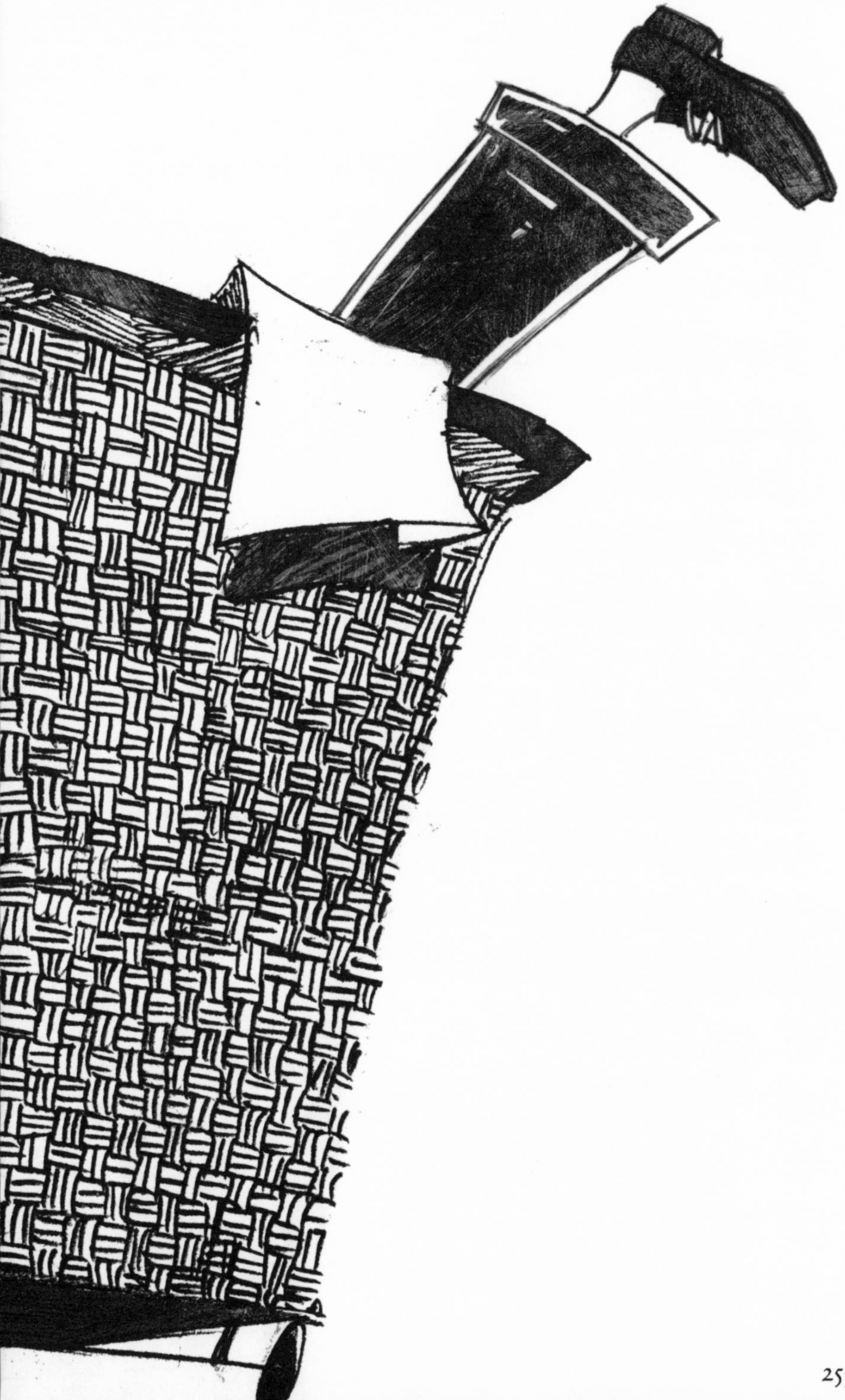

he said out loud, then turned to the linen sack wriggling on the floor. "Muzz Elliott?" Erik asked the sack.

There was a muffled reply and more fidgeting from inside.

In a minute, with Erik's help, Muzz Elliott was free.

"Who are you?" she demanded as Erik untied the final rope from around her feet.

"Erik, from Isambard Dunstan's. We came to save you."

"Me? You came to save me?" Muzz Elliott asked.

"You're worth saving, just like everyone," he said with the smile that had sometimes worked on Miss Rimmer.

"Then we'd better save Saskia and her sister. I can't be paying good money for a child and have her killed on her first day. That would not look good at all," Muzz Elliott said matter-of-factly.

"He's in the laundry cart."

"Dare I ask how?"

"Better not."

"He is a man in whom I am deeply disappointed. I hope whatever you did to him he will never forget. Look at that shoddy hole. To think they would have buried me in that. It's not even square, and the sides are uneven."

Erik looked at the shaking cart and knew that indeed, Brummagem would never forget this experience. Inside the cart, the chauffeur and handyman vibrated as the final pulses of electricity traveled through the wheels onto the cold floor. After checking the straps once more, Erik followed Muzz Elliott up the small flight of steps and into the hallway.

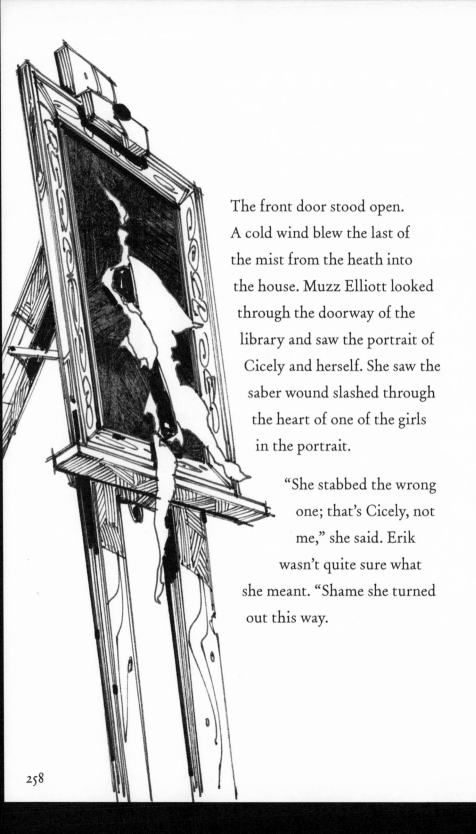

The front door stood open.
A cold wind blew the last of
the mist from the heath into
the house. Muzz Elliott looked
through the doorway of the
library and saw the portrait of
Cicely and herself. She saw the
saber wound slashed through
the heart of one of the girls
in the portrait.

"She stabbed the wrong
one; that's Cicely, not
me," she said. Erik
wasn't quite sure what
she meant. "Shame she turned
out this way.

"My sister was my best friend and the only person I ever wanted to be with—until she started losing her mind. She began hearing voices in her head. They would tell her to do things, and she couldn't refuse."

"My dad said that—especially when he was on his way home from the pub," said Erik.

Muzz Elliott grunted and raised an eyebrow. She stepped toward the door and then stopped. "I have something in the desk that will be useful," she said. She disappeared momentarily and then came back clutching a black army pistol. "It was my grandfather's. Here, boy . . . Erik . . . take it. It is not seemly for a lady to carry such a thing."

Erik took the pistol and slipped it in his belt, under his damp coat. He trudged behind Muzz Elliott into the night that by now was at its darkest.

Chapter Sixteen

The Second Warning

IN THE FAR GARDEN, beyond the rhododendrons, Saskia and Sadie stood on the small stone terrace by the pond and waited. Their hands had been bound and their mouths gagged. Madame Petrusa stood close by as her mother made the final preparations. Cicely Windylove had changed out of her nightgown and, except for the absence of a monocle over her left eye, was the exact image of her sister.

"It has to look as if they drowned," she said as she prepared a large glass syringe. "This will make them sleep, and is untraceable in their bloodstreams."

From the direction of the road, a bloodhound bayed in pursuit.

"We have to hurry, Mother—they'll be here soon," Madame Petrusa said as they heard a police whistle calling the searchers onward.

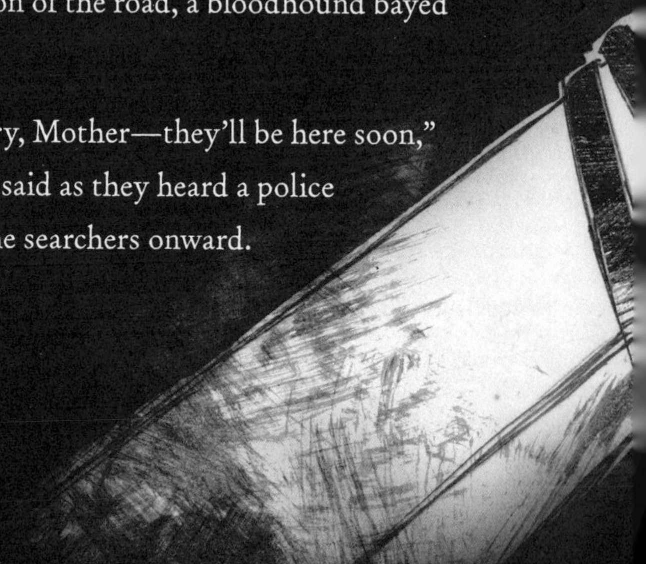

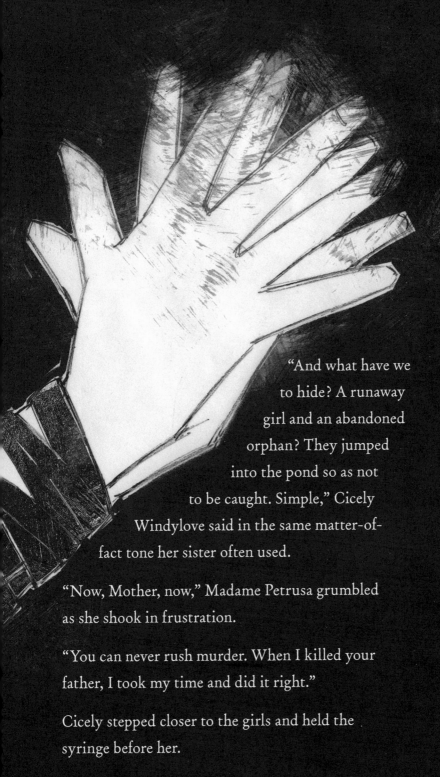

"And what have we
to hide? A runaway
girl and an abandoned
orphan? They jumped
into the pond so as not
to be caught. Simple," Cicely
Windylove said in the same matter-of-
fact tone her sister often used.

"Now, Mother, now," Madame Petrusa grumbled
as she shook in frustration.

"You can never rush murder. When I killed your
father, I took my time and did it right."

Cicely stepped closer to the girls and held the
syringe before her.

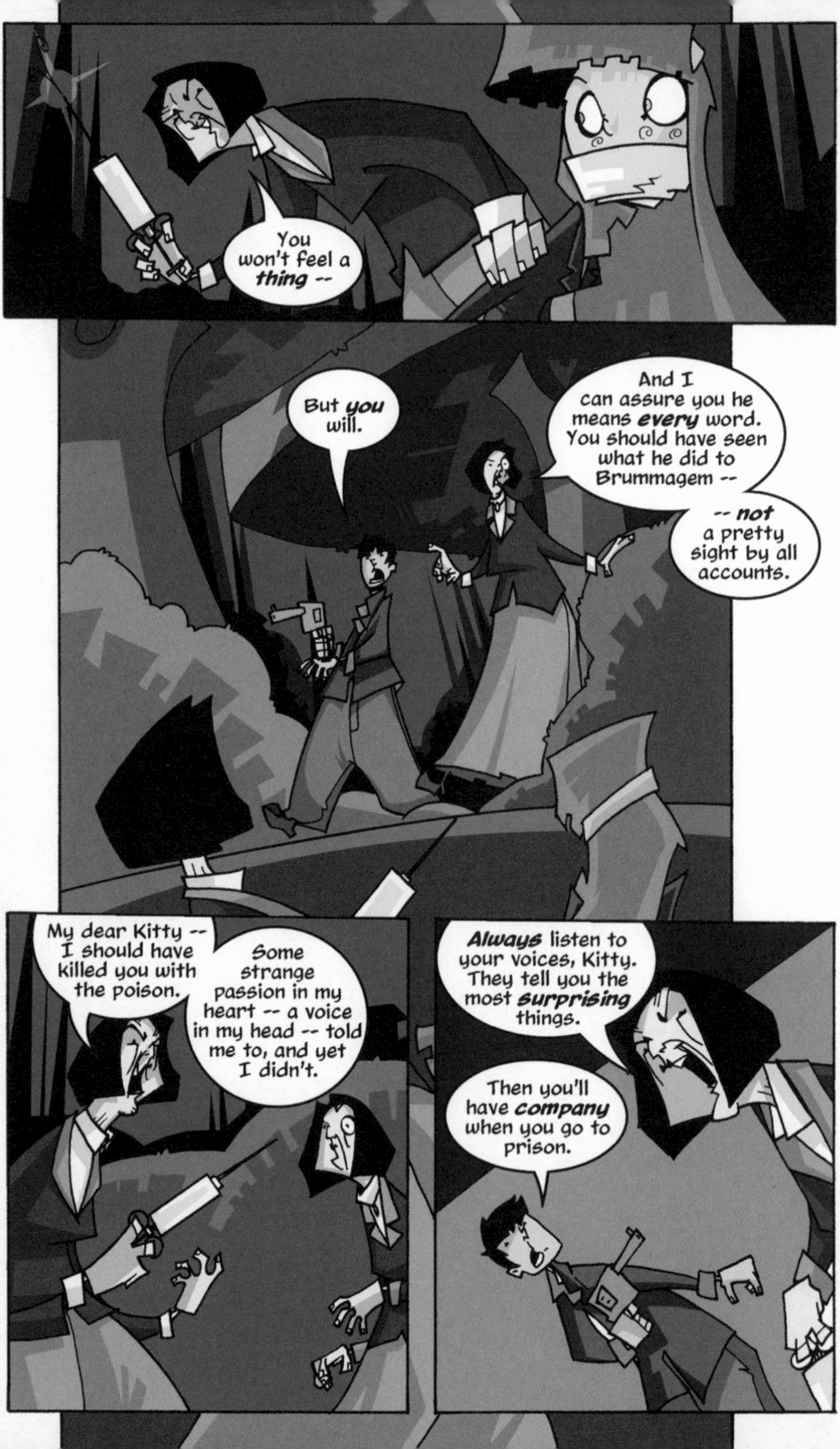

You won't feel a *thing* --
But *you* will.
And I can assure you he means *every* word. You should have seen what he did to Brummagem --
-- *not* a pretty sight by all accounts.
My dear Kitty -- I should have killed you with the poison.
Some strange passion in my heart -- a voice in my head -- told me to, and yet I didn't.
Always listen to your voices, Kitty. They tell you the most *surprising* things.
Then you'll have *company* when you go to prison.

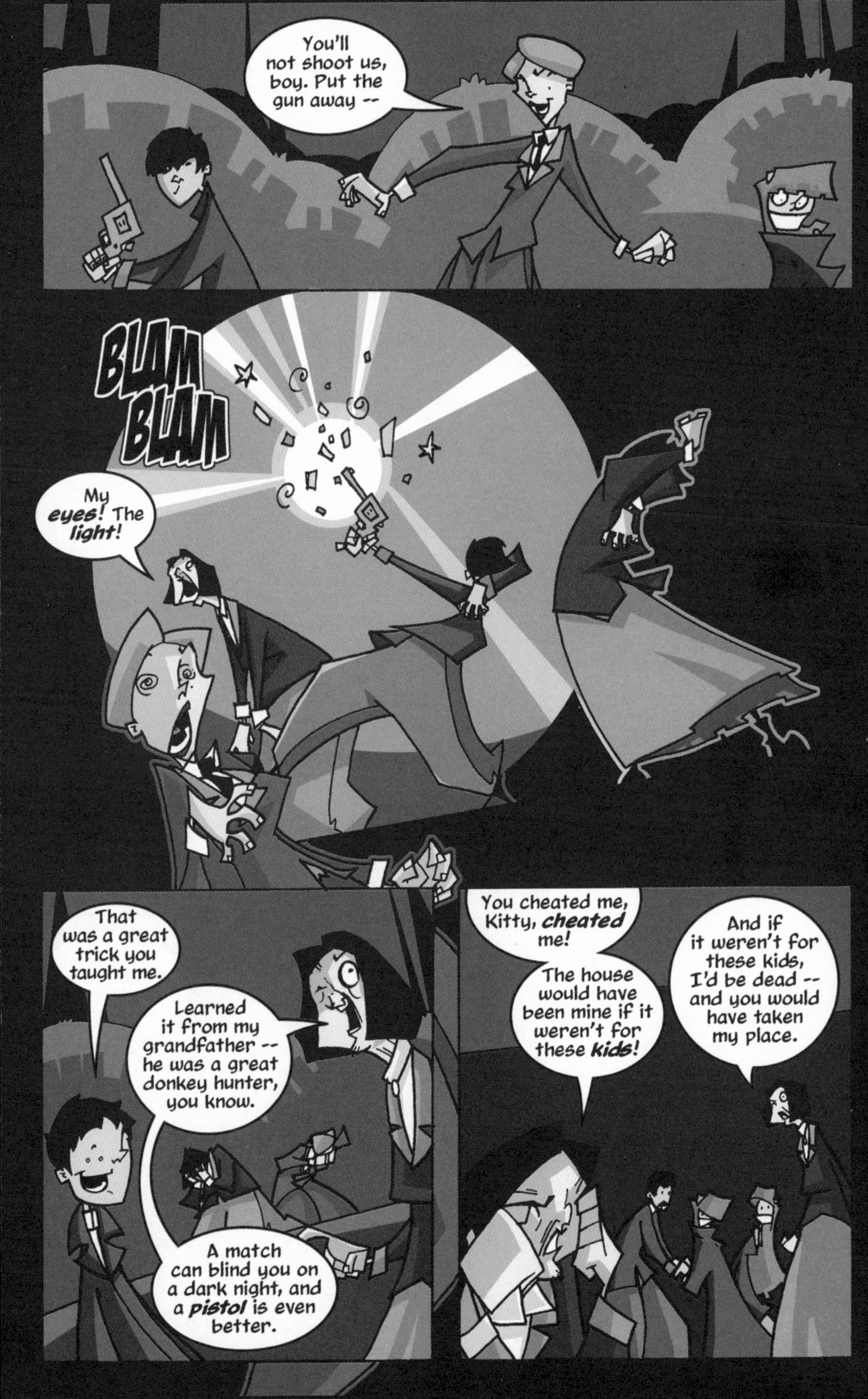
You'll not shoot us, boy. Put the gun away --
BLAM BLAM
My *eyes*! The *light*!
That was a great trick you taught me.
Learned it from my grandfather -- he was a great donkey hunter, you know.
A match can blind you on a dark night, and a *pistol* is even better.
You cheated me, Kitty, *cheated* me!
The house would have been mine if it weren't for these *kids*!
And if it weren't for these kids, I'd be dead -- and you would have taken my place.

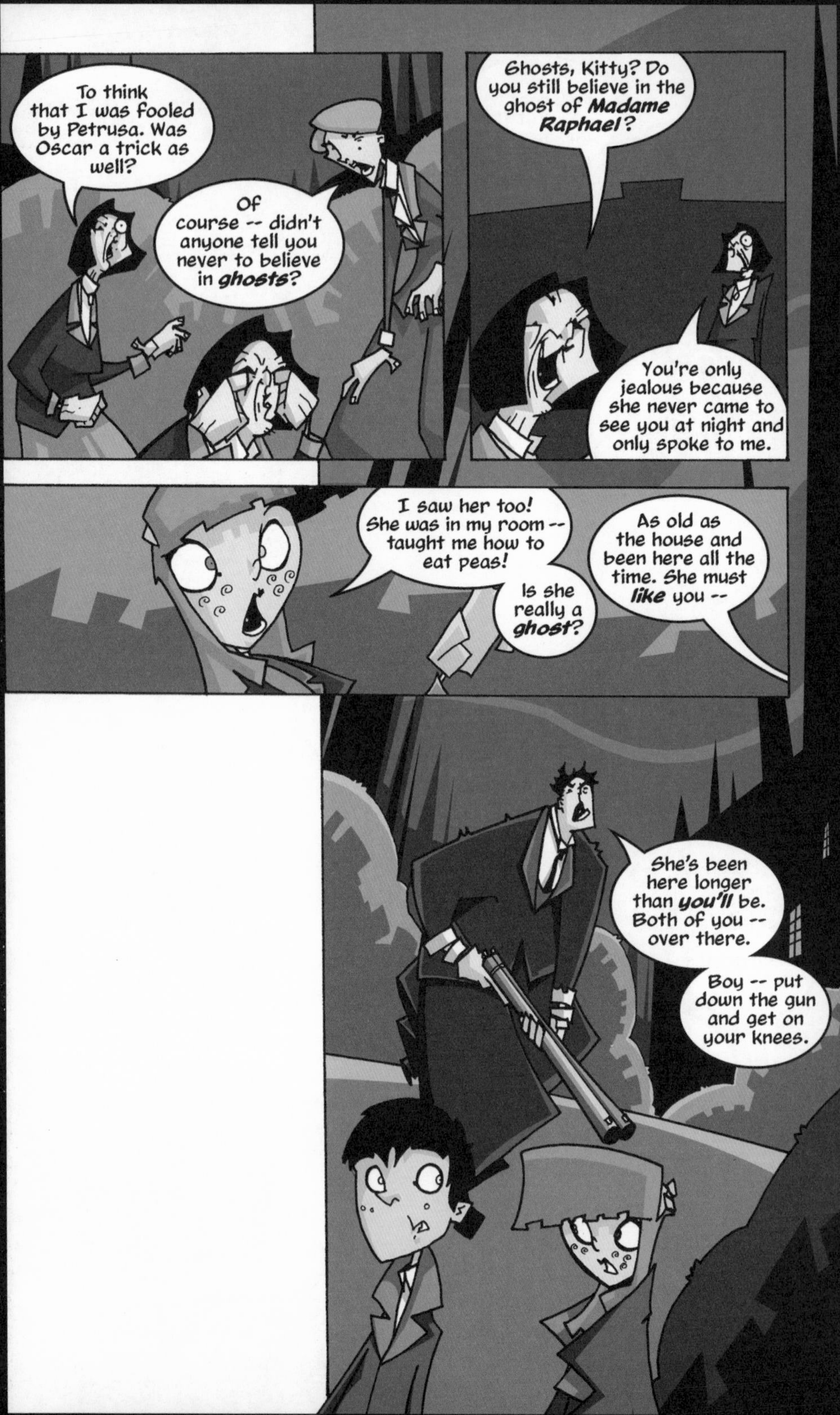
To think that I was fooled by Petrusa. Was Oscar a trick as well?
Of course -- didn't anyone tell you never to believe in *ghosts*?
Ghosts, Kitty? Do you still believe in the ghost of ***Madame Raphael***?
You're only jealous because she never came to see you at night and only spoke to me.
I saw her too! She was in my room -- taught me how to eat peas!
Is she really a ***ghost***?
As old as the house and been here all the time. She must ***like*** you --
She's been here longer than ***you'll*** be. Both of you -- over there.
Boy -- put down the gun and get on your knees.

"You cheated me, Brummagem," Muzz Elliott said.

"Had to be done. A chance meeting with your sister at King's Cross and all became clear. Every man has his price."

"And some come quite cheap," Saskia said. "Do you know that they were going to kill you, Mr. Brummagem? You ask Petrusa. I heard her mother say they wanted no witnesses, and that included you."

"Not true!" shouted Petrusa. "She's lying."

"Didn't think I'd fall for that one, did you?" he asked Saskia as he aimed the gun at Muzz Elliott. "I should have done this years ago."

"If it was good enough for Grandfather's donkey, then it's good enough for me," she said proudly, folding her arms in defiance. "If there's one thing the British know how to do, it is to die well."

"Then we shall see,"

Brummagem muttered,

as he aimed the gun at her.

"I wouldn't **Shoot** it again so soon after it has **been fired;** my grandfather always said—"

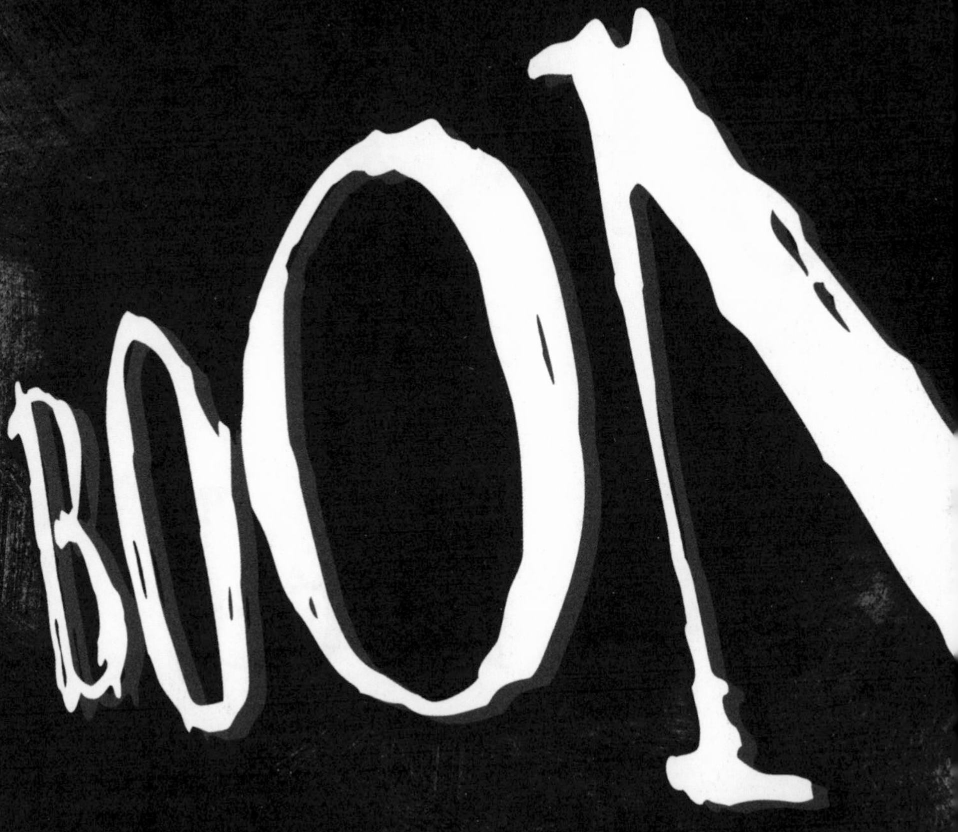
BOO

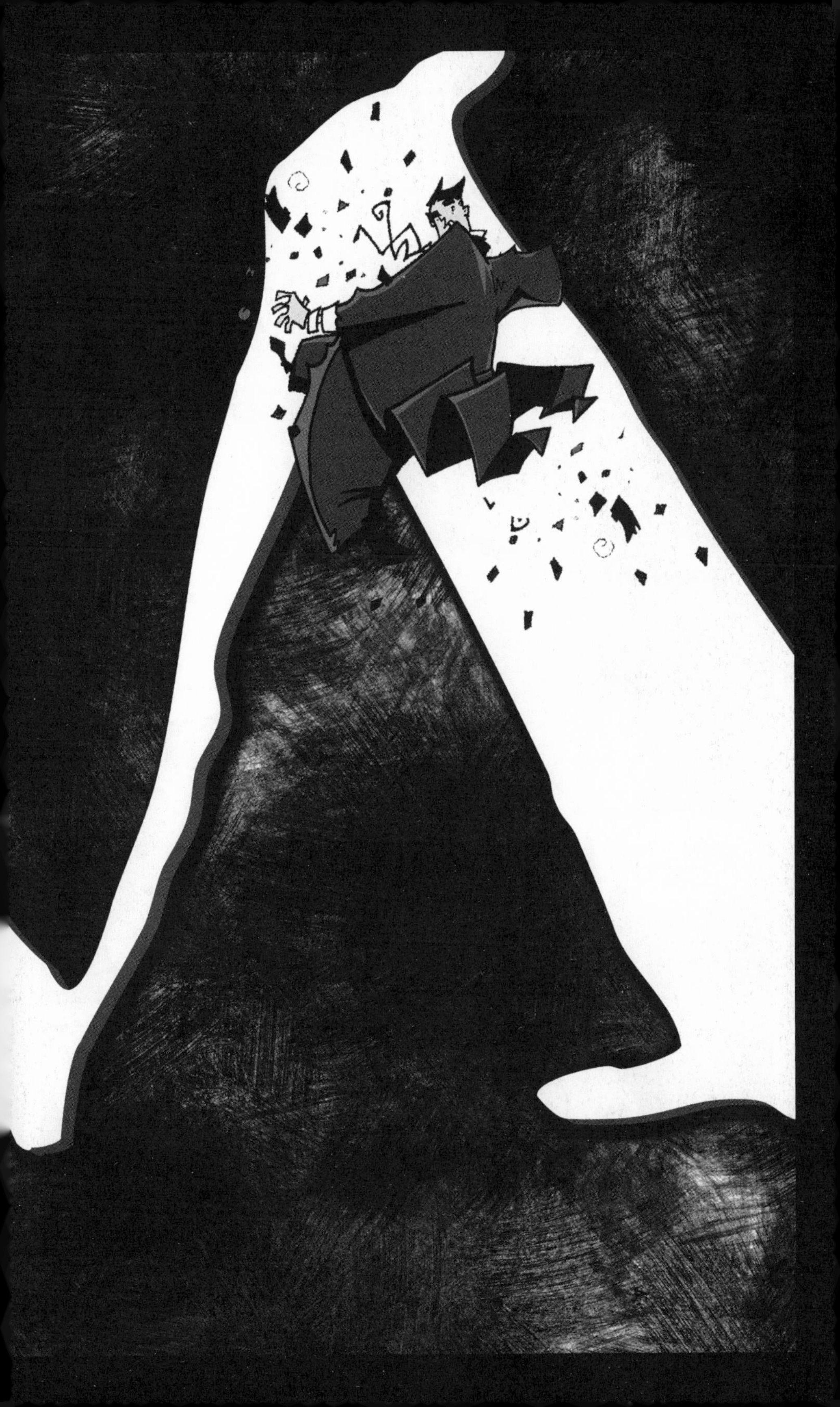

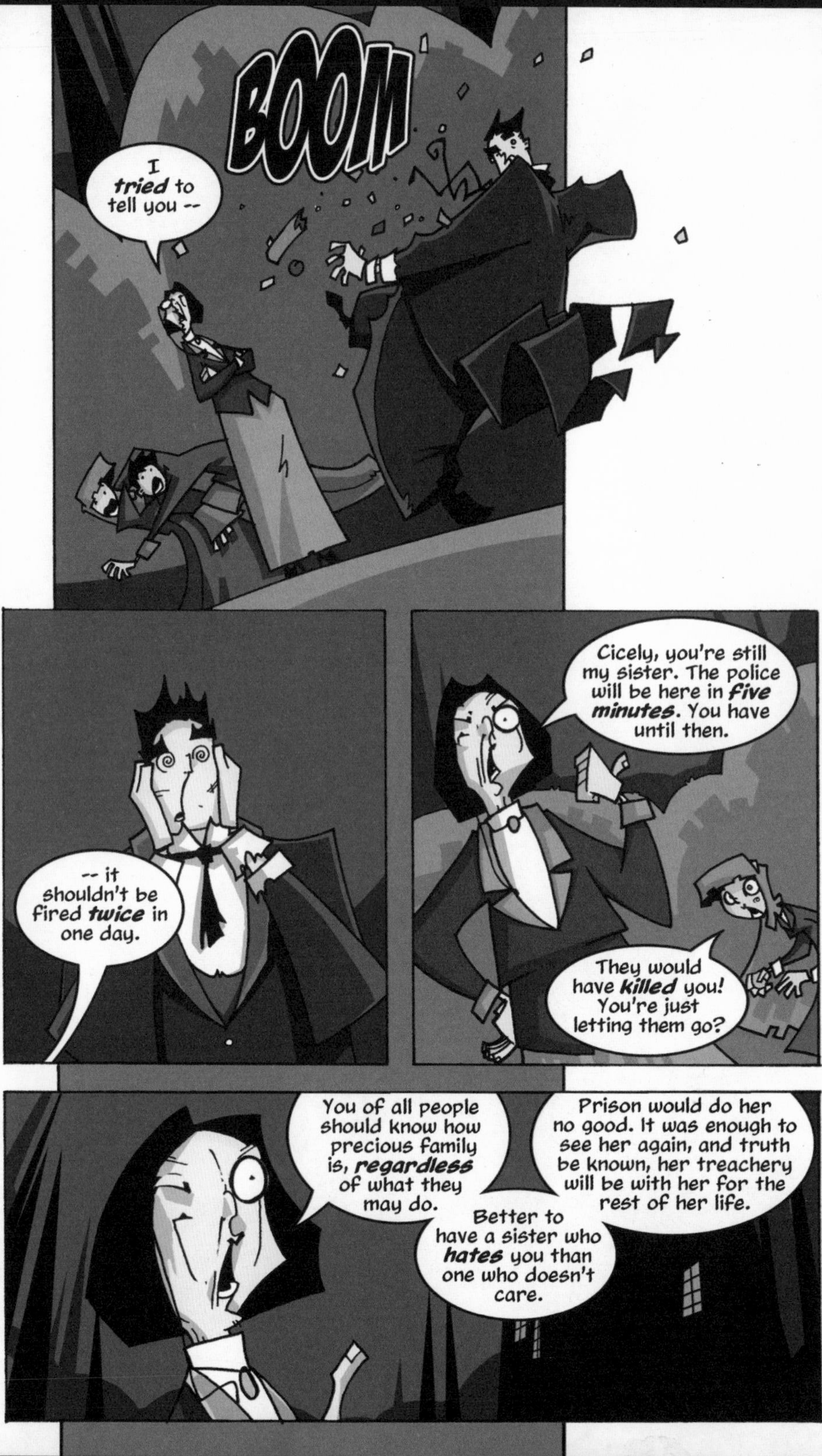
BOOM
I tried to tell you --
-- it shouldn't be fired twice in one day.
Cicely, you're still my sister. The police will be here in five minutes. You have until then.
They would have killed you! You're just letting them go?
You of all people should know how precious family is, regardless of what they may do.
Better to have a sister who hates you than one who doesn't care.
Prison would do her no good. It was enough to see her again, and truth be known, her treachery will be with her for the rest of her life.

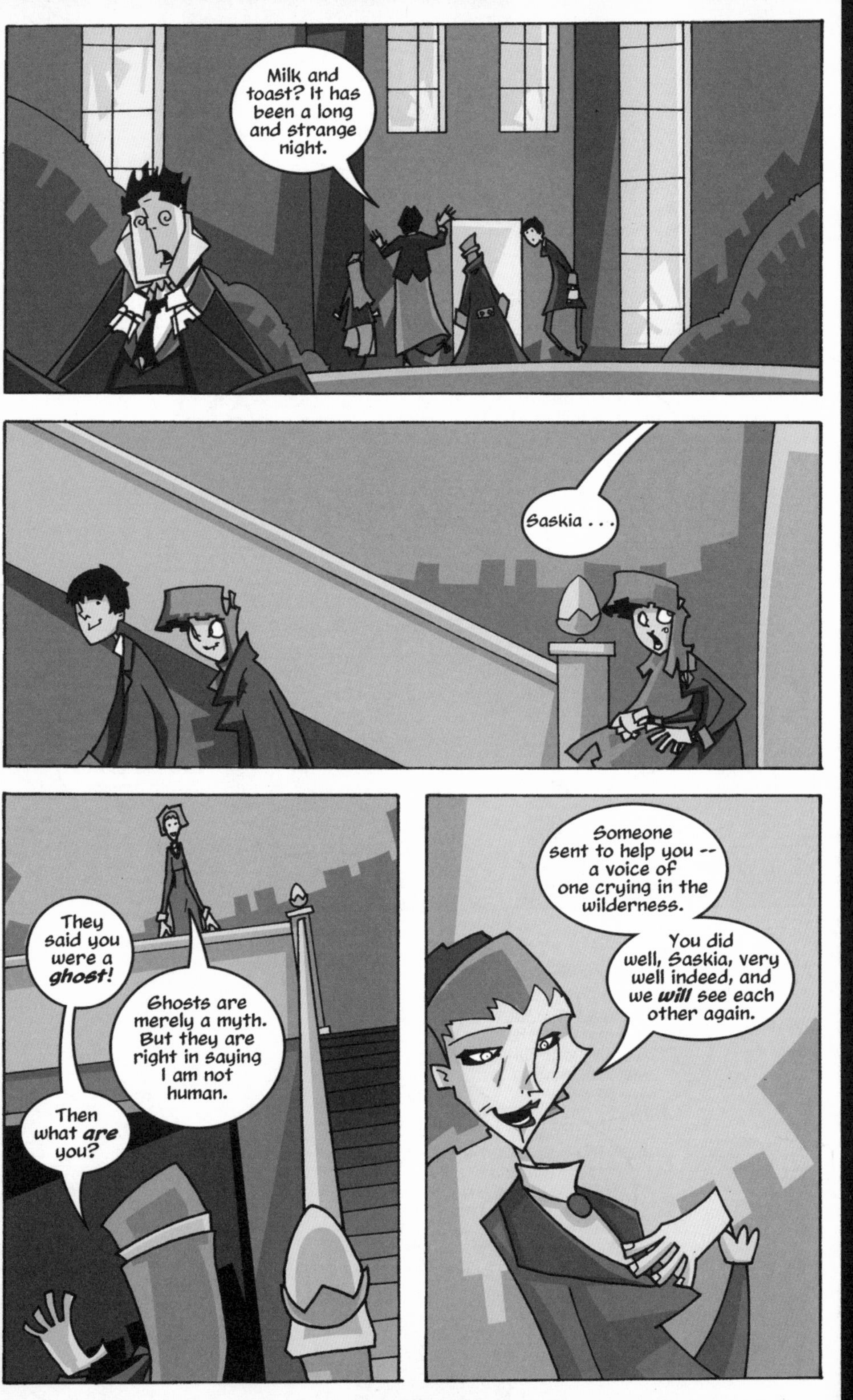
Milk and toast? It has been a long and strange night.
Saskia . . .
They said you were a *ghost*!
Ghosts are merely a myth. But they are right in saying I am not human.
Then what *are* you?
Someone sent to help you -- a voice of one crying in the wilderness.
You did well, Saskia, very well indeed, and we *will* see each other again.

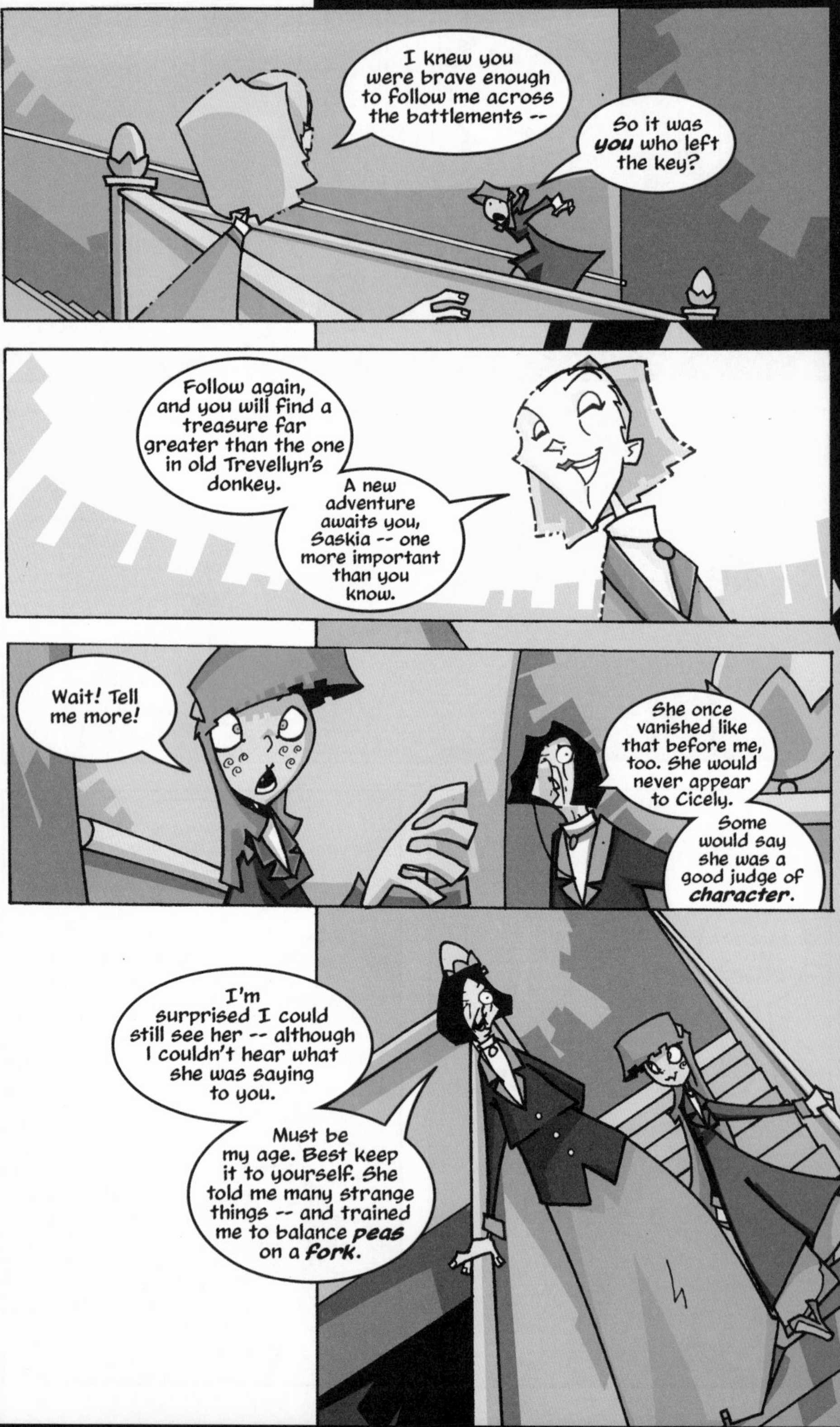

I knew you were brave enough to follow me across the battlements --
So it was *you* who left the key?
Follow again, and you will find a treasure far greater than the one in old Trevellyn's donkey.
A new adventure awaits you, Saskia -- one more important than you know.
Wait! Tell me more!
She once vanished like that before me, too. She would never appear to Cicely.
Some would say she was a good judge of *character*.
I'm surprised I could still see her -- although I couldn't hear what she was saying to you.
Must be my age. Best keep it to yourself. She told me many strange things -- and trained me to balance *peas* on a *fork*.

Muzz Elliott and Saskia laughed together as they reached the bottom stair, where Erik and Sadie were waiting for them. "Saskia, what—" Sadie began but was cut off as the front door opened suddenly. The constable led three men inside: Kobold and Martinet, followed by a handcuffed Brummagem.

"We found him in the garden, Muzz Elliott," the constable announced. "Pockets full of gold and babbling like a madman about the Dopple sisters. I see they are both here."

"And they shall stay," said Muzz Elliott. "At least for the night—and Erik as well. He saved my life. Besides, he needs a bath. Tell Miss Rimmer that she must come and see me in the morning."

Sadie and Saskia turned to face each other, then looked at Erik. Muzz Elliott smiled.

"I was right to bring you here, Saskia. Shame I had not the foresight to bring Sadie—and Erik. Old age often stops us from doing what is right," she said softly. Her eyes twinkled warmly and wrinkled with happiness at the creases.

That night they ate their fill of milk and toast. Cozy and dry in the warm kitchen, they talked of all that had gone on. An hour later, Sadie, Saskia, and Erik left the kitchen. The girls linked arms and climbed the winding stairs in happy silence, heading up to the tower that now seemed strangely welcome, knowing that they would have the chance to talk long into the night. Together again . . .

"It's a great thing, being a detective," Erik said thoughtfully as they headed up the final staircase. "I wonder if we will ever do this again?"

"How should I know?" protested Sadie. She stopped short on the top step and turned to Saskia, who looked worried. "Let's not think about it; at least we have a place to stay tonight. Where no one's trying to electrocute us."

"Or stuff us into sacks," agreed Saskia.

"Or send their wild dogs to eat us alive," added Erik. They laughed as Saskia pushed open the door to the tower room.

"All this is yours?" Sadie asked in wonder.

"Ours—at least for now," Saskia answered. "Erik can have a room too; there are a dozen more down the hall at the bottom of the tower."

Sadie and Erik wandered around the tower room, wide eyed at its luxury. "Look, Erik! A telephone!" Sadie exclaimed.

Saskia threw herself on top of the bed and heard a rustling sound. Moving to the side, she pulled a crumpled piece of paper out from underneath her.

"What's that?" asked Sadie.

"A note, just like the one I found when I first got here, warning me . . ."

Although the writing was the same, this message was very different. Saskia hesitated. Muzz Elliott had warned her to keep these things to herself . . . but Muzz Elliott had been alone and friendless for many years. Saskia wasn't, and she knew there was no way she could help sharing this secret with the two people she trusted most. She read aloud:

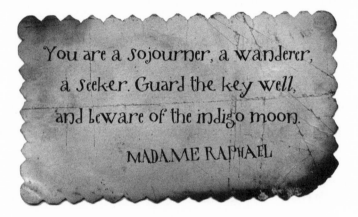

You are a sojourner, a wanderer, a seeker. Guard the key well, and beware of the indigo moon.

MADAME RAPHAEL

"The indigo moon," echoed Erik, grabbing the note to study it. "What on earth is that?"

Saskia slipped her hand into her pocket and touched cold metal. The key was still there.

"So where do we find this Madame Raphael?" Sadie asked.

"I don't know. She just appeared," replied Saskia, knowing they wouldn't understand her.

"Like a ghost?" asked Erik.

"More than that," Saskia said. "I think she is an angel."

"Angel? Here?" asked Sadie in disbelief.

"I'll see her again. I know it," Saskia answered curtly.

"An angel that leaves you notes under the pillow?" Erik questioned, as he looked out the window.

Saskia didn't reply. She had all that she needed to believe, impressed upon her heart with word and key.

She looked at Sadie and locked gazes with her twin, knowing that Sadie sensed what she was feeling, even if she didn't yet know the whole story.

"Whatever it is, you won't be looking alone, you know," said Sadie firmly. "Will she, Erik?"

Erik glanced away from the window and saw identical grins slowly form on the twins' faces—the familiar smiles that he knew meant mischief.

"Of course she won't,'" he said aloud, knowing the night's adventure had bound them together.

Clasping hands with her sister, Saskia turned and caught Erik's eye as she asked a question to which she already knew the answer.

"Who's ready to find the indigo moon?"

About the Artists

DANIEL BOULTWOOD was born in London. He studied illustration at Richmond College and went on to work in computer game concept design. From there he moved into flash animation, creating games for DreamWorks and Warner Bros. It was here that he refined his style to the animation-inspired work it is today. He lives in London in a shed with two cats.

JOSEPH SAPULICH is an award-winning artist who has worked in the film industry for over fifteen years. He has been an art director on several projects for Disney, and he has also served as an art director and visual development artist for feature films and television. He recently illustrated a children's Bible and is busy working on several film and book projects. Joseph lives in Chicago with his wife and two children.

TONY LEE (adapter) began his career in games journalism and magazine features, moving into radio in the early nineties. He spent over ten years working for television, radio, and magazines as a feature and script writer, winning several awards. In 2005 he adapted G. P. Taylor's SHADOWMANCER novel into a graphic novel for Markosia.

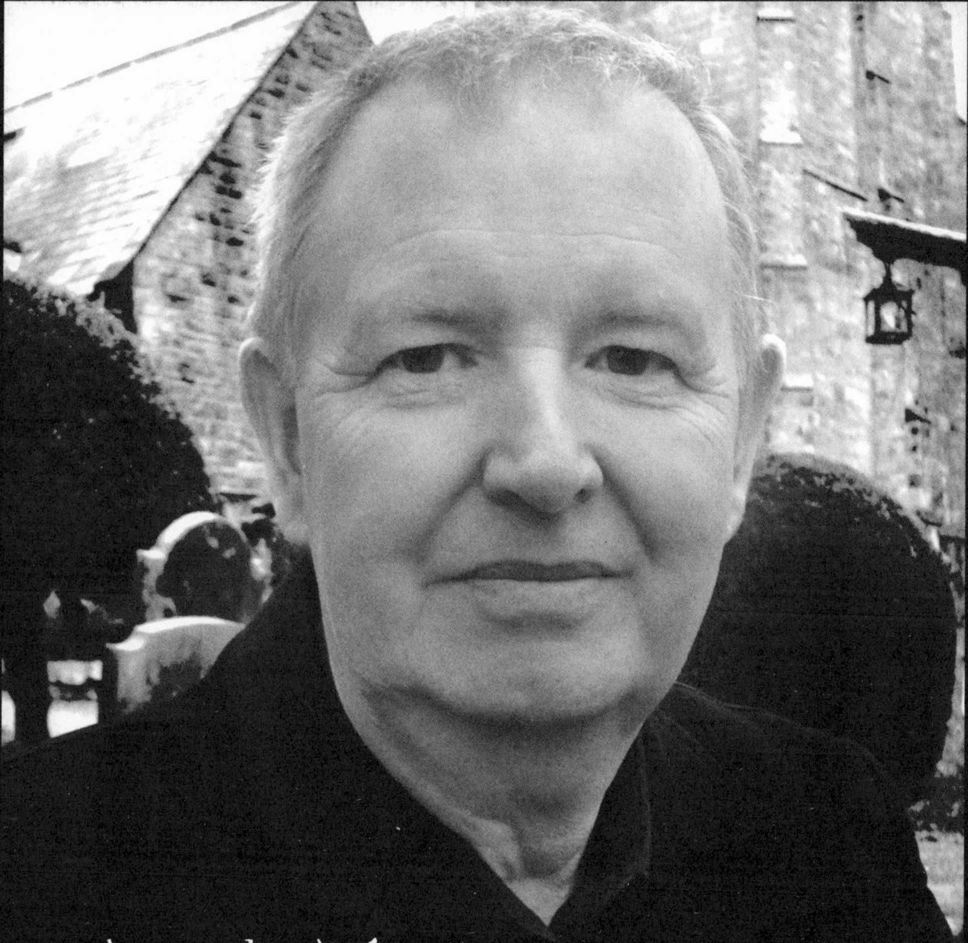

About the Author

A motorcyclist and former rock band roadie turned Anglican minister, G. P. Taylor has been hailed as "hotter than Potter" and "the new C. S. Lewis" in the United Kingdom. His first novel, SHADOWMANCER, reached #1 on the NEW YORK TIMES bestseller list in 2004 and has been translated into forty-eight languages. His other novels include WORMWOOD (another NEW YORK TIMES bestseller, which was nominated for a Quill book award), THE SHADOWMANCER RETURNS: THE CURSE OF SALAMANDER STREET, TERSIAS THE ORACLE, and MARIAH MUNDI: THE MIDAS BOX. Worldwide sales for Taylor's books now total more than 3 million copies.

G. P. Taylor currently resides in North Yorkshire with his wife and three children.

Continue the
adventure

with Erik, Sadie, and Saskia....

ViSiT